BETH
SAULNIER

AUTHOR OF *RELIABLE SOURCES*

AN ALEX BERNIER MYSTERY

DISTEMPER

"A complex and engaging mystery." —Thomas Perry,
author of *The Butcher's Boy*, on *Reliable Sources*

"THE FIRST THING I SAW WAS HER SHOES, laid atop a stack of clothing. There was something plaid under them, but that's all I remember, because the next thing I saw was the girl herself.

"I screamed my head off, before something made me clamp my hand over my mouth. The scene was so obviously fresh. Some instinct told me that she'd been put there in the past few hours—minutes even—and that meant that whoever did it could still be there. A noise shook the trees and a branch snapped. It sent me running, snagging my tights on the undergrowth, and sprawling over a log. As I scrambled back up I could hear something behind me, but I was afraid to look back. Five seconds later I was on my bike, coasting faster and faster, the trees whipping by in a blur. I must have hit a rock, because the next thing I knew I was somersaulting over the handlebars. I landed with a thud, and then I was no use to anybody. . . ."

Novels by Beth Saulnier

Reliable Sources
Distemper

DISTEMPER

BETH SAULNIER

WARNER BOOKS

A Time Warner Company

WARNER BOOKS EDITION

Cover design by Robert Santori
Cover art by Franco Accornero

Warner Books, Inc.
1271 Avenue of the Americas
New York, NY 10020

Visit our Web site at
www.twbookmark.com

 A Time Warner Company

Printed in the United States of America

First Mysterious Press Paperback Printing: June 2000

10 9 8 7 6 5 4 3 2 1

Dedicated to:

the people and animals of the Tompkins County SPCA

and to the memory of Duncan
a noble canine

With many thanks to:

Brian Collins, DVM
for helping me tell my tail from my snout

Jimmy Vines
for still being the best agent a girl could have

Bill Malloy
for being a great editor and an all-round *ubermensch*

David Gibson
for the gift of time

Paul Cody
for getting me started

and Nikita, Elizabeth, Shardik, Magritte, Austen,
and the *real* Shakespeare
for being such good dogs (most of the time)

DISTEMPER

1

THEY FOUND THE FIRST BODY IN APRIL, WHICH IS WHEN things tend to turn up around here. The sun came out for the first time in six months, the top crust started to melt, and some poor bastard cross-country skiing in his shirt-sleeves saw her foot sticking out of the snow. He'd practically skied right over her, he told the newspaper later, and that seemed to upset him most of all—the thought that if he'd looked away for a second, he might have run her down, and desecrated her more than she'd been already.

But he didn't. He caught sight of her two yards in front of him, and he said that he never thought it was anything other than a corpse. He didn't think it was a doll, or an animal—whatever it is people usually say. He was just skiing along, minding his own business and thinking it was a great day to be alive, and the next thing he knew he had to make himself fall over sideways to avoid running over a dead girl.

The man was a scientist, an associate professor of

chemistry with a cool head and a woolly beard, and he had the presence of mind not to touch anything. He just picked himself up out of the snow, hustled back to his Volvo, and called the cops on his cell phone. He waited for them, because he knew he'd have to show them where the body was, and by the time the police got through interviewing him six hours later he was wishing to holy hell he'd gone rock climbing instead.

But for that first few minutes, as he was watching the police stretch yellow tape for fifty feet in each direction, he felt like he ought to stay, as though he owed her that much. He'd found her, and finders were keepers, and although his wet socks were telling him to get into the squad car, something else made him stand there in the trampled slush until he saw her face.

He never did see it, in the end. First the cops had to wait for the ambulance, then the detectives, then the medical examiner. At some point a sergeant noticed him standing around and told him he'd better go downtown and make a statement. By the time the skewing sunlight hit the body, the chemistry professor was down at the police station, and the cops were impounding his skis.

It was just as well, he'd say whenever someone asked, because he wouldn't have wanted to see her after all. There was a reason he hadn't gone to medical school, had gone into academia instead, and it had a lot to do with not having to look at women left under the snow for three months, naked and nearly frozen solid. It had been a bad winter, nasty even for upstate New York, and judging from how much snow was under her and how much was on top they figured she'd been there at least since February. They found her clothes folded nearby: blue jeans lined with polar fleece, dark green turtleneck, wool sweater with pewter buttons, homemade mittens, red rag socks, calf-high work boots, panties, underwire bra sized 32-B. It was all there, nothing missing, nothing even torn.

The first thing they noticed about the body itself was that the knees were scraped and bloody, as though she'd been praying on cement. Then they saw that the palms of her hands were the same, bruised and raw, and they wondered if maybe she'd tried to crawl for her life. There was no purse, no jewelry, no identification at all. She was a girl in her late teens or early twenties, with straight teeth and good skin. She was apparently healthy, until someone intervened. She was naked, and she was dead, and she was found outside a town where there are fifteen thousand others just like her.

She didn't belong here, though, at least not officially. Benson University likes to keep track of its undergraduates, since having them drop dead is bad for business, and nobody anywhere near her description had gone missing. A sophomore had wigged out in the middle of a chemical engineering exam—just started screaming and bolted—but he was male, and anyway they found him living in a yurt outside Buffalo a couple of weeks before the girl's body turned up. There was a junior whose sorority sisters called the police when she didn't come back after winter break—but she was black, and the dead girl was white. No one from the town had been reported missing. So the conventional wisdom around here (or at least the gossip) was that she must have come from somewhere else, willingly or otherwise.

It's hard to describe what happens to a place when a dead girl is found. You know somebody had to put her there, and to do it that somebody must have been among us, if only briefly, and for that space of time no one was safe. You start to wonder if maybe you had passed this person in the hardware store while he was buying duct tape; if you were behind his Chevy while she was tied up in the trunk. You go to the supermarket and the contents of every man's shopping cart feels like physical evidence. (Is that Diet Pepsi for him or his prisoner? Is buying eight dozen Ring-Dings legal proof of insanity in New York State?)

If you're a woman, you realize that but for a bit of blind luck it could have been you. It could have been one of your friends, or your mother, or the lady who does your manicure, or the girl in your class you can't stand but wouldn't want that to happen to; you realize you really *wouldn't* wish it on your worst enemy. You wonder what you would've done if it had been you, whether you would have been able to use your brains or your muscles or some other edge to save yourself, and in the end you figure that you would, since anything else is unthinkable. You fantasize about interceding when the dead girl was dying, imagine yourself saving her and killing him, and going on the TV news to say you're no hero, you're just glad you got there in time. You think about buying a gun.

When they found that first body up on Connecticut Hill, the town didn't actually panic, not yet. People tend to believe just what they want to, and we wanted to believe it was a one-shot deal. Back then it was easy to think that maybe the girl had a fight with her boyfriend that turned ugly, and he'd panicked and left her body in the middle of nowhere. Or maybe she'd been responsible for her own death—had crossed the wrong person, or threatened to tell some guy's wife that they were having an affair, and he killed her to shut her up.

That's what we said when we talked about it, which was just about constantly. No one really bought the stories, though; they were all too easy, and not nearly horrible enough to fit the evidence. The police didn't say a whole lot, but the rumors started soon enough, and within a few days everyone in town knew what clothes she'd been wearing, and how they'd been folded neatly beside her, and how her hands and knees were all scraped up, and that there were strange marks on her neck shaped like diamonds. It was hard to think that could have been done to her by a boyfriend, or anyone who'd ever cared about her at all.

If we'd been in a different sort of place, one that didn't have social consciousness hemorrhaging from every crack in the pavement, everyone might have been satisfied with gossip and low-grade fear. But folks around here believe in action, because it's the only thing that keeps us warm in the winter, and sure enough someone up on campus organized a meeting. As is the tradition here, they advertised it by chalking RALLY FOR WOMEN'S LIVES on various spots on the sidewalk, and before you could blink someone else went around and turned all the Es in WOMEN into Ys.

"Do you think they'll ever catch him?" my roommate Emma asked in her Masterpiece Theatre accent. "Or will it remain *un crime insoluble*?"

We were stretched out in the living room of our house on the outskirts of downtown, a Victorian of the dubious structural quality that landlords are willing to rent to three veterinary students, one ornithologist, and an underpaid reporter. There were twelve of us altogether, if you count the three dogs and four cats. Marci is from San Diego and all of four-foot-eleven in her Keds; C.A. is an army brat who has, on more than one occasion, made good on her threat to bench-press Marci. They're both third-year vet students and the workload means they're hardly ever home. Emma, who comes from London and never lets anyone forget it, did vet school in the U.K. and is here for a fellowship in radiology. Steve, our token guy, is an ornithologist who studies night migration. I'm still not clear on what this is, but it seems to involve lots of time in the woods, freezing his butt off and wearing headphones.

I'd only lived with them since January, when their fifth roommate took off for a research job down South. I'd been looking for a place since my housemate Dirk and his boyfriend Helmut had their commitment ceremony and moved in together. I know they felt guilty about kicking me out, but it was really Dirk's place, and besides it's bad karma to get in the way of true love. (I even let him have custody of our cats.) They found me my new spot through Steve, who's Helmut's ex, so it's all very symmetrical. I didn't even have to carry a box. I just threw my dog Shakespeare in the car, and three hunky guys moved all my stuff. Life could be worse.

"Of course they'll catch him," C.A. said. "What else have the cops got to do all day? They'll solve it, they'll convict him, and ten years from now after he's been living like Bill Gates on the taxpayers' dime, they'll finally get around to frying the son of a bitch."

"Do you kiss your mother with that mouth?" Marci said. "And you know they don't fry them anymore. They give them the needle, like a schnauzer. It's veterinary science's contribution to the justice system."

"You Yanks do cherish your capital punishment," Emma said from my BarcaLounger, where she was letting her dog Tipsy lick gin and tonic off her fingers. He's a standard poodle she got from the animal shelter when she moved here, and named him in honor of her lush of an ex-husband.

"You know, Ems, I seem to recall that at the end of all those Agatha Christie mysteries, they took the killer out and hanged him by the neck 'til he was dead, so there's no need to go all civilized," Steve said.

Emma tossed back the rest of her drink. The dog looked depressed.

"So has anybody heard anything else about the murder?" C.A. asked, sounding like she was enjoying it more than decency allowed. "How about you, Alex? You read the newspaper. Come on, you *are* the newspaper. What's the scoop?"

"Nothing new," I said. "Just a rehash. City editor's going nuts. They still haven't ID'ed her. They're checking missing persons for the whole Northeast. Ontario too."

"I can't believe they don't even know who she is," C.A. said. "Wouldn't you think they'd at least have figured out that much by now? She was out there for months. Someone must have missed her."

"You'd think," I said. "But maybe she wasn't from anywhere around here. The cops said they have to keep widening their investigation, which means exactly nothing."

Emma plucked the newspaper from the coffee table.

"She was rather pretty too. Pity." After the body was found, a police artist did a color sketch of the girl. She stared out from beneath the *Gabriel Monitor*'s masthead like something not quite dead but not really alive either, as though whoever drew her didn't dare add any sort of expression that might have confused someone who could identify her. She had long, straight brown hair with bangs just above her eyebrows, a smallish mouth over a pointy jaw, indistinct cheekbones, very large brown eyes. None of the features were particularly remarkable, but they added up to a kind of sweetness. The description said she was five feet tall and 105 pounds. When she was alive, people probably called her "perky."

"She remind you guys of anybody?" C.A. asked.

"You think you know her?" I asked.

"Damn straight."

"For real?" I was halfway out of my chair to call my editor. If we broke the ID of the girl, Bill would give me his firstborn.

"Look at those eyes. The totally vacant expression. Dye the hair blond, add a couple of pounds, age her a little, and who've you got?" C.A. jumped off the couch with her brassy brown curls waving around like garter snakes and snatched the paper from Emma. We stared back at her. "Hello. *Hell-o,* guys. Are you guys out to lunch or what? Take a look at her. It's our very own girlie girl. It's Marci all over again."

Marci opened her mouth, let it stay like that for a minute, then shut it again.

"Christ, C.," Steve said. "One of these days you're gonna make me forget I'm a fuckin' gentleman."

"What? What'd I say?"

"Really, Cathy Ann," Emma said. "That was quite un-called for. Particularly the crack about the weight."

"But just look at the . . ."

"Quit it," Steve said. "I'm serious. She's about to bawl."

"OK, kids," I said. "Can we calm down? She didn't mean it. She's just being a smart-ass. Come on, let's have another drink and . . ."

"She's right." The four of us stopped and stared at Marci, who was nose to nose with the newspaper.

"Who's right?" Steve said. "Not C.A. C.A.'s *never* right. Trust me on this. I've done studies."

Marci shook her head hard. "No, she's right. Look at the drawing. *Look* at it . . ."

"Nonsense," Emma said, taking back the paper. "It doesn't look a thing like . . . Oh, dear."

"Well, so what?" I said, plopping down on the couch next to Marci. "So you look like her. So what? I mean, clearly it's creepy and all . . ."

"Don't you get it?" Marci said with a little croaking sound. "These people, they have types. What if whoever killed her is still around here? What if he likes girls who look like . . . like us?"

"Whoever did it is long gone by now," I said. "And besides, maybe that drawing doesn't really look like her. It could be a bad likeness, right?"

"You know, maybe you're . . ." Marci started just as the phone rang and sent us hunting for the cordless. Emma found it first.

"Ahoy-hoy," she said, and listened for a minute. "I beg your pardon? Oh, no. Certainly not . . . Yes, I see. But I assure you . . . But really, there's no need. She's very much safe and sound. She's right here in this room, so you see . . . Really, sir, there's no need to take that sort of tone . . . Oh, very well." She put her thin white hand over the receiver. "Marci, it's, um, it's for you."

"Who is it?"

"It's, well, it's . . . the police."

She shot up off the couch but didn't take a step forward. "What do they want?"

"Hmm . . . How to put this? Well, darling, the fact is they want to make sure you're alive."

"Oh, my."

"Just as you say. Apparently, they have received eight phone calls in the past three hours identifying you as the body in the woods based on that dreadful sketch. I told them you still have a pulse, but they remain unconvinced. So you tell them." She crossed the room and delivered the phone.

"Uh, hello? Yes, this is Marci Simmons. Detective who . . . ?" She walked off to the kitchen with her finger in one ear and the phone in the other.

"So what did I tell you?" C.A. said. "If I'm lyin', I'm dyin'."

"Do you think there's any way she might be right?" Steve asked. "Do you think there's some guy out there who likes . . ."

"Look," I said. "If I were Marci, I'd be creeped out too, and so would anybody else. But I'm sure the truth is a hell of a lot less interesting."

"Don't you wonder what she went through?" C.A. said, apropos of nothing. "I mean, don't you think about it? What exactly happened to her?"

"I try not to," Emma said.

"Well I've been thinking about it a lot, wondering how he grabbed her or whatever, you know."

"How very morbid."

"No, I know what she means," I said. "I've been thinking about it too—trying to decide whether she did something stupid, drove around with her car doors unlocked maybe."

"Or hitchhiked," C.A. said. "Or let the wrong guy into her apartment to read the meter."

"Or parked next to a van," I said.

"Good God," Emma said. "Do they teach this sort of thing in high school?"

"Try sixth grade," C.A. said.

"Dreadful country."

"So you've remarked," I said as Marci came back in. "What'd the cops say?"

"Half my first-year anatomy class called to ID me. A couple of people from tap class too. Which is pretty stupid since they know I was alive and well as of last Sunday."

"Are you okay?"

"No." She sat back down on the couch and one of her three cats jumped heavily from the arm onto her lap. Marci didn't even notice, which is quite an accomplishment since Frank—a black-and-white tuxedo cat named after Sinatra—is fifteen pounds if he's an ounce.

"Come on, what did the cops say?" Steve prodded.

"That there's nothing to worry about."

"So there you go."

"They said there was no reason to believe it wasn't . . . what did they call it? 'An isolated incident.' And her looking like me was just a coincidence, and I'm not in any danger, and anyway I wasn't the only girl on campus who got misidentified."

"That should make you feel better," I said.

"Yeah, but it doesn't. I guess I . . . I don't know. Sympathize with her more."

"Perfectly natural. You'd be crazy if you didn't. But you know what? Pretty soon they're going to catch the guy and send him someplace where he's dating guys named Spike. You'll see. It'll all be over in a couple of days."

I was trying—and let's face it, failing—to sound tough. But the truth was that the whole situation got to me, like it got to all of us. I'd seen death before, up close and personal, but it didn't make it any less frightening. The dead girl in the snow was about our age, could have fit right there in our living room. The thought of her made us feel both stronger and more fragile. More than anything, she made us think about how lucky we were just not to *be* her.

We stayed up absurdly late that night talking about it, maybe a little bit scared to go to sleep because of what we might dream. And we might have stayed just a little bit scared if there hadn't been another dead girl, then another and another. And we might have had more midnight talks, thinking of the whole business in the third person, if I hadn't found the second body myself.

2

It was a Saturday near the end of May, just over six weeks after the chemistry professor's ski trip from hell. I'd picked up my mountain bike from its spring tune-up the night before and gotten out the door at nine; my housemates were all still unconscious or snuggled up with whoever they'd gone to bed with. In upstate New York, May is not to be confused with summer (sometimes it can't even be confused with spring), and I was wearing my heavy Vassar sweatshirt and a pair of biking tights. I'd only recently traded halfhearted jogging for halfhearted mountain biking, and it was the first ride of the season. My muscles were flaccid from not enough time on the Lifecycle over the winter, so even though I'd promised myself twenty miles I knew within two minutes that I'd be lucky to do ten. Since we live downtown in the flats between three hills, I had exactly one choice of where I could head without doing some serious uphill. I wound my way on back roads until I got to Route 13, the kind of fast-food and chain-store strip that hulks at the edge of every American town, and headed south.

I kept on the main drag for a while and turned off onto a country road that degenerated to dirt after a couple of miles. When I say mountain biking, I really mean road biking with fat tires and eighteen gears, but I usually try to go off into the woods a little just so I can say I did. There's a nice gentle trail about fifteen minutes away, wide without too many rocks and roots to send a girl to her doom, and it's just about my limit. Before I swung onto the path, I remember thinking that I was probably going to regret it. This turned out to be one mother of an understatement.

It was a sunny morning, which is unusual for Gabriel (affectionately known as the place clouds go to die). There was bright light coming through the trees, dappling the ground and making it hard to distinguish the hazards from the dirt. Even though it was chilly enough to make me comfy in my sweats, there was a hint of afternoon heat; every soccer mom in town would be poised for a flower-planting frenzy.

The path rose gently at first, with occasional muddy ruts and crisscrossing tracks that showed I wasn't the first biker out there that season. I had my Walkman on, which the traffic law says you're not supposed to do but I couldn't possibly exercise without, and as the grade got sharper I was listening to Ben Folds Five and sweating hard.

Ever since it happened, I've wondered how everything would have turned out if I hadn't decided to stop when I did. It was all so arbitrary. I wanted to quit sooner, but didn't; I could have kept riding longer, but I didn't do that either. "Alice Childress" ended, and since the song was the only thing keeping me going, I stopped and got off. I leaned the bike against a tree and pulled the water bottle off its rack, and as I took a drink I saw something glinting in a patch of sunlight about twenty yards off. To this day I don't know what made me walk over for a closer look; maybe after what had happened the month before, I already knew what I was going to find. But then again, I kind of doubt that; knowing myself, if I had any idea what was out there, I would have climbed right back on my bike and fled.

The first thing I saw was her shoes, laid atop a stack of clothing. The shiny thing was the buckle on her Mary Janes, which were all the rage that spring, when every college woman seemed obsessed with dressing like Lolita. There was something plaid under the shoes, but that's all I remember, because the next thing I saw was the girl herself. They talk about death being a peaceful thing, but there was nothing peaceful about this, and nothing natural, either. Her eyes were bugged out and her tongue was lolling out of her mouth, all splotched and purple. She was stark naked, with big breasts that rolled to either side and made her look not only vulnerable but invaded, as though someone had taken her life and her dignity at the same time.

I'm not proud. I screamed my head off, before something made me clamp my hand over my mouth to shut myself up. In retrospect, maybe I was clued in by the fact that the scene was so obviously fresh. She was clean, not covered with leaves or mud; it had rained the previous night, but her clothes didn't look wet. Some instinct told me that she'd been put there in the past few hours—minutes even—and that meant that whoever did it could still be there.

I spun around, checking out every direction, but I couldn't see anyone. That didn't mean anything, though; off the bike path, the woods are thick with old-growth trees big enough for two people to hide behind. He— they—could be anywhere, waiting to swap one victim for another. I stared down at the body, picturing myself lying there in her place, with my sweatshirt and tights and sports bra folded . . .

A noise—a bird or an animal or something way worse—shook the trees and a branch went snap. Whatever it was, it sent me running, snagging my tights on the undergrowth. I was trying to watch where I was going and look around at the same time, and it didn't work; I went sprawling over a log and landed on all fours. As I scrambled back up I was sure I could hear something behind me but I was afraid if I looked back it would be all over. Five seconds later I was by my bike. I forced myself to wait long enough to turn it around before I jumped on and went barreling down the hill.

If I'd had time to think about it, I would have realized that even if someone was chasing me, there was no way he could catch me on foot when I was going twenty miles an hour, but all I could think of was getting away. I was coasting faster and faster, the trees whipping by in a gray-brown blur, my helmet swinging lamely from the handlebars where I'd left it when I got off. I must have hit a rock, because the next thing I knew I was somersaulting over the handlebars. I landed with a thud, and then I was no use to anybody.

What happened right after that is sort of hazy, which

the doctor tells me is perfectly normal for someone who flew ass over teakettle ten feet in the air. I was out for a while, how long I don't know, but somehow I got back on my bike and drove into town. The police station is on Spring Street, a half-hour ride from where I fell, and I have a very dim memory of thinking I had to get there. I know I could have just gone out to the road and flagged someone down, but at the time it never even occurred to me. I rode all the way to the cops, ditched my bike, and dragged myself inside.

There was a uniformed officer behind a heavy plastic partition. He took one look at me and disappeared, which in my altered state seemed the height of rudeness until I realized he was coming through a door to my left. Later, I found out he'd taken me for a battered wife.

"I need to see the police . . ."

"Ma'am, what's happened?"

"I need to report . . . a murder."

"Let's have you sit down."

"No, I don't want to sit down." I was swaying on my feet, and everything hurt. "Please, she's out in the woods. Someone has to go get her. Don't you understand? It's just like the other one. I found her. I found another dead girl in the woods. Please, you have to go get her."

The cop got it instantly; after all, we don't see a whole lot of murders around here. The previous body was hanging over everyone, and I was telling him there was another. "Can you wait right here?" I nodded, which was a big mistake, since it made the whole hallway spin and start to fade at the edges. I wanted to sit then, but I was afraid if I took a step I was only going in one direction, which was down. I heard a door open behind me.

"Miss," said a man's voice. "I'm Detective Cody. I need to ask you a few questions."

I turned around to face him, and that was it. I got a glimpse of reddish hair, and the next thing I knew I was keeling over in a full-out faint. The last thing I remember is someone catching me before I hit the ground, and the random thought that whoever he was, he smelled pretty good.

I woke up in the hospital, which was exactly where I belonged. You always see in movies where the hero gets really badly hurt but he has to go save the world so he refuses to stay in bed and checks himself out against the advice of his doctor. All I wanted to do was lie under the covers and have some male nurse bring me sugar-free Jell-O. But the first thing I heard was yelling from out in the hall.

"So when *can* I see her?"

"When she wakes up. I told you, she's had a damn good bump on the head."

"Don't you have to wake her up to make sure she doesn't have a concussion?"

"We've already ascertained that. She doesn't. But she's got two broken ribs, a sprained wrist, and thirty-two stitches. She needs her rest."

Jesus, I thought, *they'd better be talking about somebody else.* No such luck. "Doctor, that girl is a witness to a homicide. The last thing she said before she passed out was that she had found a body. Now, if she's telling the truth, it means there's a dead girl out there somewhere. The longer we wait, the more likely it is my crime scene will be compromised. That means the less likely we're going to be able to find this son of a bitch. It's going to be dark in a couple of hours. That means another night that somebody's parents are going to go to bed not knowing if their daughter is alive or dead. Do you really want that on your head?"

"Detective, I appreciate your situation, but I can't . . ."

"Five minutes. That's all."

Silence. I opened my mouth to call out that I was awake and all their manly arguing was for nothing, but when I breathed in I got a sharp jab that almost made me throw up. "Your word?" I heard the doctor say.

"Five minutes." There was a light knock on the door and before I could even try to answer they came in. "See, she's already awake."

The doctor had gray hair and a stethoscope around his neck, like something out of an ad for cough syrup. "Do you feel well enough to talk?"

"Uh-huh."

"I'm Dr. Krauss. This is Detective Cody from the Gabriel police. He wants to ask you a few questions. I told him"—he turned to the other man—"to keep it short."

"It's fine," I croaked. "I want to talk to him."

"I'll be back to check on you in an hour, and the nurses' station is just down the hall. If you need anything, just ring the bell."

As soon as the doctor left, the detective pulled a chair up by the bed. "I'll make this quick, I promise. What's your name?"

"Alex Bernier."

"Alex, I don't have a lot of time, so I'll get right to the point. The desk sergeant said you mentioned a body."

"Out in the woods. It was awful. I was riding my bike and I found her."

"Where?"

I told him. "It was just like they described the other girl last month, the one on Connecticut Hill. She was naked, and her clothes were next to her. She looked like she'd been strangled. She had these odd marks around her neck."

"Did you touch the body?"

"Of course not."

"Did you see anyone else out there?"

"I'm not sure. I thought I heard someone, or some *thing* anyway. Maybe it was an animal. But I got so scared I took off down the hill on my bike and then I crashed."

"How did you get to the station?"

"Bike."

"Six miles? Like that?" He aimed his little black cop notebook at the swath of bandages on my head.

"I guess."

"Hold on one second." He pulled a phone out of his jacket pocket and I could hear him giving directions to the crime scene. "Listen, I have to go. But I'll need to get a formal statement from you later."

"Okay."

"One more thing. I need your word that you won't discuss the details of this case with anyone."

"Sure."

"An officer will be in here in a minute to get your name and number. Your parents must be worried sick."

"My parents? They're in . . ." I tried to remember.

"Colombia. Or maybe it's Panama by now. They're on a cruise."

"So who are you staying with?"

"Huh?"

He looked at me like I was an idiot. "Who's taking care of you?"

"Taking care of me? What are you talking about?"

He stopped short. "How old are you?"

"Twenty-six. How old are you?"

His skin was tinging red around the scalp. "Never mind. Just never mind. Just tell the officer who we should call."

"Oh, man, my housemates. They must be going nuts." I tried to sit up, and thought better of it.

"Anyway, thank you for your help."

"You're welcome." He turned to go, and as he opened his coat to put his phone away I caught sight of a dark red splotch on his shirt. "Is that blood?"

He stopped in the doorway and looked down at the six-inch stain. "Yeah."

"Are you hurt?"

"It's not my blood. It's yours. From the police station."

"That was you?"

"Yeah."

"Good catch," I said, but he'd already bolted down the hall.

3

My friend Mad came to pick me up from the hospital. He drove his car, which made it quite an occasion, since Jake Madison pulls his ancient Volvo out of the alley behind his apartment roughly four times a year. Mad walks everywhere, not because he's environmentally conscious but because he believes deeply in not going to jail for DWI. It's no accident he lives 132 steps from the paper and 96 from our favorite bar.

"Shit, Bernier, you look like hell."

"Charmed, I'm sure. Now will you get me out of here?"

"You sure did fuck yourself up."

"Come on, Mad, it isn't nice to blame the victim."

The nurse came and though I'd had visions of being wheeled out like Cleopatra, in the end the elevator was tied up and I had to hoof it down three flights to the front door. Mad offered to do the gentlemanly thing and bring the car around but it seemed silly since he was parked thirty feet from the entrance. He did open the door for me, however, and when I sat down a spring jabbed my rear end right through my jeans.

"How many stitches you get?"

"Thirty-two, divided evenly among my knees, elbow, and pretty little noggin. How'd you like my bald patch?" I parted my hair to show him. "They shaved me. Cool, huh?"

"Is that gonna grow back?"

"Nope. I have to join the Hair Club for Women."

"You serious?"

"No."

"Bill wants to see you as soon as you're healthy." Bill's our city editor, a type-A kind of guy who thinks that any reporter who doesn't file twice a day owes him some sort of Japanese suicide ceremony.

"Is that how he put it? Or did he say he wants me there *now*?"

"The latter. But I told him you'd be there when you can make it up the stairs by yourself."

"That would be now."

"Fuck 'm."

"Have pity. He must be going out of his gourd with the new cops guy."

"Junior? Oh, not to worry. He's got lots of experience. He covered at least one drunk-and-disorderly at his college paper."

"You calling him Junior to his face now?" Mad crinkled his eyebrows. The new cop reporter had only been at the paper six weeks, and I hadn't worked with him that closely. But Mad was on cops for a while in his misspent youth, before he switched over to the science beat and stayed there, and he'd been appointed the new kid's fairy godfather. He was not thrilled. "I bet Bill'd give his left nut to have Gordon back. You hear from him?"

"That big-city shithead? He called to see if you were okay. He wants you to call him when you get home."

Gordon Band is a reporter for the *New York Times* who spent nine months in upstate purgatory as punishment for a particularly egregious newsroom meltdown. The paper had banned him for life, but no one seemed to recall this fact once he helped break one of the year's biggest national stories, dateline Gabriel. He'd blown town in February for the isle of Manhattan, and no one had heard from him since.

"How did he hear about what happened?"

"How does he hear about anything? It was on the wire."

"I was on the *wire*? Are you kidding me?"

"How hard did you hit your head? Of course it was on the wire. Front page of every paper in New York State."

"Even the *Times*?"

"Okay, not them. You can't expect them to give a damn who gets capped north of Westchester."

"Jesus, the cops are gonna kill me. You should have seen 'em when they figured out who I was. Chief Hill came into my hospital room personally to tell me to keep my mouth shut, that I wasn't a reporter, I was, get this, 'a material witness to a crime,' but by then I'd already spilled everything to Bill. So there."

"You filed from your hospital bed? You da woman."

"Did I tell you the first cop who talked to me thought I was in *high school*?"

"I heard."

"Man, poor Junior. What a way to get started. Multiple homicide. I wouldn't want to be covering it."

"Liar."

"Seen it, done it, been there. You know that. I've covered enough crazy killers, thank you very much."

"One's your limit?"

"Yep." I stared out Mad's window, which still had the outlines of fall leaves crusted on the outside. It had been nearly a year since Adam Ellroy died, and since Mad and Gordon and I nailed the killer. Nearly a year since I lost the only guy I've ever really loved, and I just barely escaped with my life. I was in no hurry to start dating again.

"So where to?"

"Huh?"

"You okay?"

"Fine."

"Where am I taking you? Home or into battle?"

"Home. I want to see my dog."

He parked on the street in front of my house, came around to open my car door, and before I knew what he was up to he'd swept me off my feet and into a bridegroom's carry like something off the cover of a Harlequin. He stood at the front door trying to figure out how to turn the knob and be manly at the same time when it opened from the inside and Shakespeare came running out. "Alex, you're home!" Marci said, a little too brightly even for her. "We cut class to make sure you were okay."

Mad dropped me on the couch, the dog jumped up on my lap, and about two seconds later I figured out what was up. C.A. was there too—she actually had lipstick on—and Emma came out of the kitchen, carrying a pitcher of martinis on a tray and wearing something best described as a sarong. I'd told them I didn't need a ride from the hospital, since Mad was picking me up. They'd been lying in wait, and they looked like a bunch of cats who'd just been handed a really good-looking ball of string.

Have I mentioned that Mad is a total babe? We're talking six-foot and change, obsessive gym goer, Nordic parentage, the whole thing. Truly, he's hard to walk down the street with. Sometimes I think that regular access to Mad is the main reason the girls let me live with them. Steve too.

"Oh, Jake, it was so very kind of you to collect Alex," Emma said. "And I thought you didn't have manners in this country."

"My pleasure."

"Sit down," C.A. said. "Ya wanna drink?" For her, this was Martha Stewart.

"You know it," he said, and Emma handed the glasses around.

"It's eleven o'clock in the morning," I said.

"The cocktail hour," said Mad.

"Don't you have to work?"

"I worked yesterday *and* the day before, thanks to you. Today's my day off."

"Well what about me? Don't I get a glass?"

"Oh, sweets, you can't drink," Emma said. "You just came out of hospital."

"How do you know? You're a goddamn veterinarian. How do you know I can't drink? What am I, a terrier?"

"It can't be good for you."

"But what if I want one?"

"Do you?"

"No. But a girl likes to be considered."

They turned their collective gaze back to Mad, who was in pig heaven. "That's such an interesting car you have out there," Emma said. "Such humble transport for a graduate of Harvard *and* Columbia Law School."

Mad smiled his wolf smile. "Stickers came with the car."

Emma didn't even look fazed. "Why, Jake, you *urchin*."

"So, Mad, what ya benchin' these days?" C.A. asked. "Two? Two-ten?"

"Two-thirty."

"No kiddin'?"

"How about you?"

She turned to Marci. "What do you weigh?"

Marci's eyes narrowed. "One-twelve."

"One-twelve."

Mad cracked up. "You wanna give me another go?" He rolled up his sleeve and leaned his elbow on the coffee table; C.A. did the same. Emma clapped her hands and made a happy little chirping sound.

"I have *got* to find my own apartment," I said to no one in particular. "And did I mention I have two broken ribs and a sprained wrist? Thirty-two stitches too. And a headache." When there looked to be no end to the arm wrestling, Marci came over.

"Listen, Alex," she said. "There was something I wanted to ask you. About . . . what you found in the woods."

I stared at her. If C.A. had asked the question I wouldn't have been the least bit surprised, but Marci is the last person who'd want to hear the gory details. "What do you want to know?"

"It's, um . . . the girl. When you found her, what did she look like?"

"You really want to know?" She nodded. "She was naked, and her tongue was lolling out of her mouth . . ."

"Stop. Oh, God, that wasn't what I meant. I mean, what did she *look* like? Did she look like me? Like the other one did?"

I thought about it for a minute. I wasn't sure how to answer her. Nobody who died like that could ever really look like someone alive. But I knew what she was asking. "She was about our age. Mid-twenties, you know, and white. But don't worry, Marce. Other than general stuff like that, she didn't look like you."

"Phew. That makes me feel better. I'm not sure why, but it does. I didn't really think some . . . maniac was hunting me, not logically anyway. It's all so silly, isn't it? But that other girl really had me all spooky, and when I heard about the second one I didn't know what to think. Thanks, Alex."

She pecked me on the cheek and practically skipped across the room to watch Mad finish off C.A. Even on his day of chivalry, he wasn't about to let some dame beat him. The two other girls looked positively feral with glee, and even C.A. didn't mind losing. "Victory is mine," he said. "And now which of you lovely ladies wouldn't mind getting the champ-een another drink?"

I sat there watching them, feeling the ache creep farther into my cranium. I'd had plenty of death last summer, and now it looked like a killer of a very different kind had set up housekeeping. He was out there somewhere, and he liked to turn live women into dead ones, and although no one had had the nerve to use the words "serial killer," it was just a matter of time.

But that wasn't the only thing on my mind as I stroked Shakespeare's silky snout. Yes, I'd been terrified when I found the body. I might even have been within feet of the killer, and within seconds of becoming girl number three. But there was something else. As frightened as I was, I had to admit that for the first time in nearly a year I actually felt alive. I'd spent the past eight months living in a netherworld between I'm-okay and everything's-fine. I hadn't gone on a movie date, hadn't slept with anyone, hadn't even cried about Adam too much because after the first few weeks even my well had run dry.

But I knew for sure that when I was running through the woods, when I was flying down the hill and pedaling back to town, I wanted to live. I wanted to pick up whatever pieces I had left, try to fit them together and make some sense of my life. I wanted to get back into the game. I just wasn't entirely sure how to go about it. And I was more than a little freaked out to realize that the only thing to shake me out of the doldrums had been the very thing that put me there. To wit: someone else's demise.

How creepy am I?

I was thinking about all this as I sat there, listening to the four of them drink and giggle and flirt. But I was also pondering another thing as well: I'd lied. The truth was, the second dead girl did look like Marci. Maybe even more than the first.

4

$\mathcal{S}$

WORD TO THE WISE: IF YOU HAVE A SPRAINED LEFT WRIST, don't try and drive a Renault Encore with a stick shift and no power steering. If I'd sprained my right one, it would have been impossible. Either way, I didn't have much choice but to take my own car, since Mad showed no inclination to stop snorting martinis with my roommates. I got to the *Monitor* around one and found the newsroom was its usual charming self. As I walked in from the back staircase past the darkroom I heard O'Shaunessey, the world's loudest sports editor, reaming out one of the photo interns. "I don't give a goddamn rat's ass if it's art. I told you to shoot the goddamn fucking football game, not the motherfucking thrill of victory on the quarterback's grandmother's goddamn fucking face. You didn't get one single goddamn picture of the goddamn *game*. What am I supposed to run tomorrow? *Shut* your mouth. If you say 'art' another son of a bitching time I swear I'm gonna . . ." It went on like that for some time. I kept walking. With O'Shaunessey, it ends as quickly as it starts. He'd be buying the kid a beer by the end of the night.

At one end of the city desk, the schools reporter was grilling whatever pour soul was on the other end of the phone. Lillian is in her early seventies; she came back to the paper two and a half years ago after retirement nearly killed her with kindness, and picked up her old beat when I moved over to politics. I have to admit she's way better at it than I was; her interviewing style is affectionately known as "silent but deadly." "Now, really, Mr. Superintendent, I understand how you feel. It's a terrible position you're in. My stars, it certainly is a pickle. But what can we do? The charges have been made . . . Now, sir, really. I don't want to pry. But you have children in that school yourself. A third- and a fifth-grader, isn't that right? Please put your professional position aside for a moment. As a parent, wouldn't you want—wouldn't you *deserve*—some concrete information about what's going on?" She must be working on the Cub Scout ass-grabbing story. If I knew Lillian, she'd break him in under three minutes. Someday I have to get her to give me lessons.

My desk is one over from hers. We sit in a block of four cityside reporters, schools and politics across from cops and science. It may sound odd that at a paper our size we have a full-time science reporter, but academia and research are big business, and this is a company town. Benson University is the major employer in the county, and every reporter at the paper covers it in some way. Mad does all the high-tech stuff, I do town-gown, the cops guy covers the various schoolboy antics, and so on.

When I got to my digs I found that somebody (or probably everybody) had taped a mock-up of Monday's front page to one of the poles that do their best to hold up the newsroom ceiling. The original headline had been SEC-OND BODY FOUND IN NEWFIELD with the subhead FIRST VIC-TIM STILL UNIDENTIFIED; POLICE WIDEN SEARCH. This one read BERNIER FINDS NAKED DEAD CHICK: "WHERE'S THE GUYS AT?" ASKS HORNY NEWSHOUND. I would have been pissed, if whoever did it hadn't also left me a very large chocolate cupcake.

I'd just sat down and started peeling the paper off the cupcake when Bill called me into his office. He did this by throwing a tennis ball at his Plexiglas window and catching it on the rebound, a habit that new hires tend to find alarming. I brought my cupcake with me. "Bernier, you look great."

"Is that on the record?"

"Okay, you look like hell."

"Mad's sentiments exactly."

"I was just talking to Junior here about the story." He jerked his tennis ball toward the kid, who flinched as though he was going to get beaned. Junior's real name is Franklin, and his regular expression is Bambi-in-head-lights. He's got pinkish skin, and freckles, and patches of acne that wax and wane with his deadlines. There's a newsroom pool going on how long he'll last; my betting slip says September 1.

"What's up?"

"Cops called a press conference for eight o'clock to-morrow morning."

"Eight? But that'll blow our deadline. TV'll get it a whole day earlier."

"That's the idea."

"They're not playing nice? What for?"

"Word on the street is they're twisting in their polyester over you flapping your gums."

"Flapping my . . . Give me a break. They didn't really think I wouldn't tell you anything. What was I supposed to say? 'No comment'? That's a hoot."

"Yeah, well, what they expected you to do and what they *ordered* you to do are on two totally different planets, capisce?"

"So good luck me ever getting another cop to open his mouth?"

"You got it. North Pole time."

"What's this press conference all about?"

"Word is they're going to ID one of the vics. Maybe one, maybe both."

"If the cops are freezing us, how'd you hear that?"

"Mad just called from the Citizen. Picked it up from one of the TV guys. Cameraman said somebody at the cops leaked it to his producer, dangled a carrot about how they were going to scoop our ass."

"How did Mad get there? I just left him swilling gin with my roommates."

"How the hell do I know? He was there with some limey chick." So Mad and Emma were living it up at the Citizen Kane, the local journalists' bar of choice. Fabulous. Well, maybe she could handle him. Or else she'd wind up dumping a pitcher of Molson over his head, like so many before her. "So it looks like the sons of bitches are yanking our chain," Bill went on. "I was going to send out Junior here to get somebody to spill it, but he assures me that there's not one single cop that'll give him the time of day."

"Well, actually, I . . ." Franklin began.

Bill shut him up with a look. "Meter maids don't count."

"Will you give him a break?" I said. "He just started. How many decent sources did any of us have when we first got here? Don't feel bad, Franklin. Right now I couldn't even get the meter maids to talk to me."

"You got that right," Bill said.

"That bad?"

"Fact is, when the chief called to screw me over with the press conference, he specifically said to make sure you weren't there."

"No way."

"Yep."

"So I take it you're sending me?"

"Of course."

"When again?"

"Tomorrow, eight A.M."

"Wow, they're really pissed. They know no A.M. reporter starts before ten. What a bunch of jerks."

"So tomorrow, bright and early."

"What about tonight?"

"What about it?"

"Are we really going to lie down and get screwed? Me, I like some romance first."

"You got a better idea? I'm up shit's creek here. My best reporter is drunk off his ass . . ."

"Thanks a *lot*."

". . . and my second-best reporter just did a Wicked Witch of the West down the side of a mountain. My cop reporter looks like he's dying for his mother's tit. Who am I supposed to send? Lillian? The cops aren't the goddamn ladies-garden-club bunch they've got over at the school board. We don't exactly have a staff of thousands here, you know. Hey, I got it. Maybe I could get one of the sports guys to go over, give me some play-by-play."

"There's a thought."

"Go home, Alex. Go get some sleep and let me figure out how I'm going to explain to our esteemed publisher that the world's smallest TV station is going to scoop us on the biggest story of the year."

"Come on, it's not that bad. It could be worse. They could be scooping us when they catch the killer. Then we'd all be out of a job."

"Junior, make sure Alex gets home okay. And for Chrissake, shut my door."

We went out by the back stairs, but when Franklin headed for his car I dragged him in the other direction.

"Where are we going? Alex, wait, will ya? Bill told me to get you home. You heard him."

"Just follow me."

"Where are we going?"

"Cop shop. You remember the way, right?"

It's a five-minute walk from the paper to the police station, but in my condition it took ten. When we went through the front door I had this wispy flashback of myself crawling in there two days ago, babbling and bleeding all over some cop's shirtfront. Lucky for my pride, there was a different guy at the front desk. When he saw me, he came around to the other side of the bulletproof glass.

"Hey, Joey. Can you tell Chief Hill I'm here to see him?"

"He isn't here."

"Of course he's here. You guys are working on the

biggest case since . . . since . . ." *Since last summer*, I thought, but there was no way I was going to say it. "Come on, I swear it'll only take a minute. I don't want to interview him or anything. I just want to talk to him for a sec." Even if the chief was pissed about me giving some facts to the paper, I didn't think he'd totally shut me down. Chief Wilfred Hill is pretty decent, for a guy who carries a gun to work. He was downright fatherly to me when Adam died, and he didn't have to be.

"Really, Alex, I swear he's not here. It's Monday. Rotary lunch day. You know."

"Oh, jeeze, I forgot."

"So he's at the Holiday Inn. Be back after three."

"Maybe you can bail me out. Word is you guys ID'ed the girl. Want to save my ass and give me a name?"

"There's like about zero chance of that and you know it. Your ass is plenty pretty, but I don't want mine in a sling either."

"How'd you like to be officer of the month? Editorial page guy's in my pocket."

"I *am* officer of the month. And you are getting nowhere, so you might as well go home and put a new Band-Aid on that head of yours. Nice bald spot you got there."

"So I'm denied?"

"Big time."

I was about to flee with my tail between my legs when I pulled another name out of the air. "How about that Detective Cody? Is he here?"

He waited a beat, like he wasn't going to tell me. Then he sighed. "Yeah, he's here. Whatcha want him for? He's not gonna tell you jack."

"Humor a poor bald girl."

"He's busy."

"And he's a detective, and he's a suit, and you'd just *hate* to make his life harder."

That got him. "Oh, all right. I'll go ask if he'll see you or if I should toss you out on your ear."

"What's the deal with him, anyway?"

"Hotshot from the Boston PD."

"No way. What the hell's he doing up here?"

"Only son. Transferred up to the woods to take care of his mom. She's sick or something."

"Decent of him."

He leaned forward. If I'd wanted to, I could've grabbed his gun. "Also, I hear his wife gave him the heave-ho."

"Ouch. So is he any good?"

"Bored off his ass until the dead girls. If I didn't know better, I'd say he killed 'em himself just to have something to do."

"You're joking."

"Whaddaya think? Course I'm joking. Oh, and get a load of this. He used to be a Navy SEAL."

"Macho man. I thought they only had those in Steven Seagal movies."

"Well, we got one. You want him or not?"

"You're the answer to a maiden's prayer."

He disappeared into the office to call Cody. "Would the chief really . . ."

"Jesus, Junior, you scared me. I forgot you were there."

"Sorry."

"What's the question?"

"The chief. Would he really take off in the middle of a

murder investigation to go to the Rotary lunch? Or was that guy lying?"

"Nope. First and third Monday of every month. Holy days of obligation. Rubber chicken, mushy peas, apple cobbler. Speeches by men in shiny suits. It's a Gabriel institution. Besides, what cop ever gave up a free meal?"

"Alex . . ."

"You gotta cover it sometime. It's a gas. The cops really strap on the feedbag. They serve donuts as hors d'oeuvres, but there's never enough of them, so the cops and the firemen practically end up pistol-whipping each other. One time Mad and I . . ."

"Alex . . ."

"What?" He made frantic stabs in the air with a bitten fingernail. I turned around, and there was Detective Cody.

"You've got two minutes," he said.

"Fine. Listen, I . . ."

"Not here. And just you. Your boyfriend can stay outside." He did an about-face worthy of Parris Island (or wherever it is you train a SEAL) and I followed him upstairs to his office. The cop sanctum sanctorum. The press is *never* allowed up here, or maybe they forgot to tell him. "Sit down." I obeyed even faster than my dog. "You did the right thing by coming here."

"I did?"

"So go ahead."

"Go ahead and what?"

"I assume you came here to apologize."

"For what?"

"For disregarding our direct request that you not discuss this case with anyone."

"Cops always say that sort of thing. Nobody ever follows it. If they did, we'd be printing nothing but horoscopes and Dear Abby."

"Miss Bernier, do you realize that by talking to the press, you disclosed information that might jeopardize our investigation? That might damage a prosecution, if one ever materializes from this mess?"

"Oh, get *off* it. Don't go yelling at me because you guys can't do your jobs. Well, guess what? I was just doing mine. I'm a reporter, Detective. That means I report. If I hadn't been the lucky stiff to find the body, I would have tried to track down whoever did find it, and get her to spill her guts. If she was like ninety percent of the human race, she would have spilled them. And I would have printed it. It happens all the time. What's the big deal?"

He looked like he wanted to throttle me, but it wasn't as threatening as you might think. Actually, with all that red hair, he looked like a very angry version of Opie from the *Andy Griffith Show*. "There is no excuse for the way you behaved. I stood in your hospital room and asked for your word that you wouldn't divulge any of the details of the case, and then you went ahead and did it anyway. Where I come from, they call that dishonor."

"Spare me the *Officer and a Gentleman* act, would you? When you talked to me, I was still all woozy. Besides, what did I say that pissed you off so much, really? All I told my editor was that it was just the same as the first girl, the clothes and the marks and the position and all. That's it. Big deal."

"Two young women are dead. I'd think that would bother you more than it obviously does."

"It does bother me. Of course it bothers me. If you want to know the truth, it scares the shit out of me, and all my friends, and my housemates too. And don't even *ask* about my mother."

"Listen, I have a hell of a lot of work and not a lot of time to do it in. If you didn't come here to apologize for making my life harder, then what is it you want?"

"I want to know who the dead girls were."

"So do we."

"I heard you already know. I also heard you're holding the names until tomorrow morning to screw us over."

"In that case, what makes you think I'd tell you now?"

"The chief's in a snit over me, and you know it. He's pissed and he's playing games. But I don't think you're the kind of guy who likes to play games." Actually, I had no idea what kind of guy he was. But it sounded good, so I kept going. "You know there's a whole lot of people out there waiting to find out who those girls were. Why should they have to wait almost a whole other day wondering if it's someone they know, someone they care about, just because I can't keep my big mouth shut?"

"Do you honestly care that much about the TV station getting the story first?"

"Goodness, how did you hear about that? I didn't mention it."

"Okay, the chief wants to teach you a lesson. You didn't answer me. Does it really get under your skin to come in second?"

"Principle of the thing. The information's available now. It should be out there."

"I'm surprised you're not trying to lift it off my desk. Can't all you vultures read upside down?"

"Yep. But I knew you'd never be that sloppy, so why embarrass myself? Listen, I can promise you this much. The next time this reporter finds a dead body, she'll keep her mouth shut."

"Comforting."

"So how about it? Will you give me the names or what?"

"Name. We're only releasing one."

"But you have both of them? Then why are you only releasing one? Next of kin?"

"Can't find any. But we have to try."

"Are you going to give me a name or do I have to see it on the evening news?"

"You talk faster than a used-car salesman."

"Thanks a lot."

"You're a very persuasive young lady."

"Young my ass. You're, what, thirty-five?"

"I'm thirty-two." He stared at me for a minute. "For the record, I thought the chief should have released the name yesterday. So I'm not just giving in to your charms."

"What a surprise."

"The girl's name is . . ."

"Wait. Hold on. Are you going to get in trouble for this?" To this day, I have no idea why I said that. It was not what you'd call in character for me to care if a source got in trouble for opening his mouth.

"Nice of you to worry. And no. The chief is the chief, but he's still spent his entire life up here. He hasn't had a whole lot of experience with homicides, beyond your average drunken brawl. He had the good sense to hand the investigation over to me, at least unofficially. And *that* is off the record."

"So what's her name?" I said, finally pulling out my notebook. "And are we talking about the first girl, or the second one?"

"The second. The girl you found is named Patricia Marx. That's M-A-R-X. She's from Syracuse. Age twenty-two. She worked at the Gap in the big mall up there."

"The Carousel. I know it well."

"She shared an apartment with another girl from the store. Her roommate wasn't worried when she didn't come home last Sunday night, since she'd stay at her boyfriend's house a few nights a week. Monday was her day off, but when she didn't show up for work on Tuesday her roommate called the Syracuse PD. Said the girl had never even been late for work without calling. We talked to the boyfriend. He never saw her on Sunday."

"He's not a suspect?"

"We're not ruling anyone out."

"Off the record?"

"Off the record, if he did it, I'm joining the Mounties."

"Any viable suspects?"

"That's all you're getting."

"Cause of death?"

"Strangulation."

"With?"

"Unknown. And I have to get back to work."

"Come on, can't you tell me anything else about Patricia Marx? I'm going to track her down eventually, but it'll probably take me all night. Give me a break. My wrist hurts. So do my ribs. I'm all taped up and everything." I pulled up my shirt just enough to show him my side. "Can't you at least tell me where she grew up? Or do I have to call every high school west of Albany?"

"Montour Falls. Now get the hell out of my office."

"Wait. There's something else I need to ask you about."

"I told you we're done here."

"It's not for me. It's for my roommate. I know this is going to sound crazy. But when the *Monitor* published that drawing of the first victim, she got all freaked out because she thought it looked like her. And then when I found the second body . . . Well, it looked even *more* like her. I told her it didn't, because I didn't want to scare her any more than she already was, but it probably wasn't the right thing to do. What if she's in danger? Do you think she could be?"

He stood up and started pacing, which wasn't easy in an eight-by-eight cubicle. He looked like an Irish setter cooped up at the SPCA. "Okay, Alex. This is off the record. Way off. What do you call it? 'Deep background'?"

"Agreed."

"If you've covered cops for any length of time, you know how the police work. We don't rule out anything lightly. We know that even though the obvious answer is usually the right one, it isn't *always* the right one. At this point, we think the same person killed both those girls. Common sense says it has to be. The M.O.s are too similar for it to be a copycat. There are a number of details that I couldn't tell you if I wanted to. But if you're asking me if you're right in thinking the two victims were physically similar to each other, they were. Both were small, five feet or under. Both wore their hair roughly the same way, shoulder length and parted down the middle. But beyond that, in terms of their facial features, you could say that they looked enough alike that they could be related."

"Do you think they were?"

"No comment."

"What about Marci?"

"Who?"

"My roommate."

"We're not sure that these two women were killed because of the way they looked. That's one theory, the obvious one. Or it could be a coincidence. There might be a whole other connection."

"So how do you figure it out?"

"We've got people on it."

"Who?"

"No comment."

"Who around here is possibly equipped to deal with this sort of thing? You said it yourself. The cops hardly ever see anything more mysterious than a hunting accident. So who are you bringing in? Don't tell me the Staties. Didn't you hear about that evidence tampering scandal a couple of years back? Practically the whole unit went to jail . . ."

"Oh, hell. No, it's not the state police."

"Sheriff's?"

"Give me some credit."

"Holy shit. The FBI's all over this, aren't they? Behavioral science, right?"

"That is not for publication."

"Why not? If Quantico's involved, people have a right to . . ."

"People have a right not to be scared to death for no good reason. You say FBI, everyone is going to think *Silence of the Lambs*. Hysteria isn't good for anyone."

"Maybe that isn't far off."

"You gave me your word."

"I realize that."

"Look. If I were your roommate, I'd be careful. I'd keep the doors locked. I wouldn't go out alone at night. Tell her to use common sense, look both ways before she crosses the road, and we'll catch the bastard. Now, you really need to leave." I was on my way out the door when he called after me, sounding at least five points higher on the decency scale. "Listen, Alex. I don't want your friend to be scared. How about if I send someone by in the next couple of days, do a security check on your place? It'll only take an hour. The officer can give you some tips about locks, that sort of thing."

"That would be great."

"And, Alex, be careful. Our file on you is thick enough already."

5

"HE REALLY LET YOU IN THE BACK OF THE COP SHOP? YOU gotta be shittin' me." Mad was sitting on a stool at the kitchen counter while I cooked, and with at least two dozen people spilling out into the living room, he had to shout.

"I shit you not."

"So what was it like?"

"Nothing fancy. Messy, in a . . . neat sort of way."

"What the hell does that mean?"

"You know, papers and files all over the place. But organized. Lots of framed certificates. They're big into framed certificates. 'Officially certified to kill you at a hundred paces,' that sort of thing."

"But what about the guns?"

"What guns?"

"You know, the guns, Bernier. The *guns*. What kind did they have?"

"Christ, I don't know. They don't have them hanging on the wall or anything."

"They don't?" He looked like a trick-or-treater with an empty plastic pumpkin.

"Oh, come on, Mad. You're a grown man. You didn't really think the cops kept an arsenal back there like the goddamn A-Team."

"I had fantasies."

"Poor baby."

"You got another bottle?" He dropped an empty magnum of something red into the recycling bin and it went *smash*.

"You just opened that."

"I had to share."

"Tonight's really sucking for you, isn't it?"

He looked over my shoulder into the living room. "Not totally."

I turned around to see what he was leering at. Emma. "You picking favorites?"

"Me? Never."

"Look, I don't give a damn who you're banging. But would you please not make my life a living hell?"

He kept looking over my head at her—this wasn't hard, since he's thirteen inches taller—and raised his wineglass toward her in a come-hither toast. "Me? Never."

"I would appreciate it if you didn't turn my living room into a singles bar."

"Me? N . . ."

"Oh, shut up, Mad. You know the drill. To wit: you drill her, she gets all grabby, you flee, I pick up the scraps."

"What if I have serious intentions?"

"You? Never. Now would you hand me the linguine?"

I threw four pounds of pasta into my big Calphalon pot with the built-in strainer. It's worth more than my car.

"Yo, who's got the vino?" O'Shaunessey said as he sauntered into the kitchen. "And how about some food action? Children are starving someplace."

I've been feeding most of the *Monitor* newsroom every Thursday night for the past couple of years. At this point, it's kind of gone beyond tradition into obsession. I start getting menu requests on Monday, and when there's some big story that keeps us at the paper until deadline, the thing has been known to start at midnight and go until four A.M. I warned my housemates about it when I moved in, and they said it was fine with them as long as they got to eat free. Journalists are creatures of habit, though, and my old roommate Dirk and his partner still have to put a sign on the door every Thursday that says BERNIER FOOD ORGY AT NEW LOCATION.

That night I was trying a new recipe for diavolo sauce, which, as the name implies, is hot as hell. I'm physically incapable of cooking for less than twenty people, so I'd quadrupled the recipe. This meant four full heads of garlic and eight teaspoons of dried pepper flakes. I tested the pasta to make sure it was done and had Mad pull the strainer out and shake off the excess water, since my left wrist was still out of commission. He mixed it up with the sauce, put it on the counter with a stack of bowls and silverware, and grabbed the six loaves of garlic bread out of the oven with his bare hands, as oven mitts are for wimps.

"Thanks for helping."

"Emma says chicks think cooking is sexy."

"I see." I went over to the far side of the living room and yelled that the food was ready. This kitchen is way smaller than my last one, and I learned the hard way that once the hordes start coming in, there's no getting out until they're done. Everybody made for the food so fast the house practically tilted. Along with all three of my female housemates, there was Melissa, a *Monitor* photographer who likes to shoot things from weird tilty angles, which makes them art; the Dixie-born business writer, Marshall, and his wife, Charlotte, who is presently out-to-here pregnant; the two guys who make up O'Shaunessey's entire sports staff; Wendell, the photo editor, who spends most of his time at the local Buddhist temple but occasionally eats with us if we promise to cook vegan; Maggie, who just got promoted to anchor for the local TV news but would give a major organ for a slave job at CNN; a couple of radio reporters; and various interns, spouses, and significant others.

Okay, it was a mob scene. But it was *my* mob scene.

Everybody eventually settled throughout the living room, and those who got stuck on the floor had to eat with one hand and fend off dogs with the other. Shortly thereafter most of them were begging for Kleenex and gulping down their wine. I was wondering if maybe I'd put just an eensy bit too much pepper in when the doorbell rang and Marci got up to get it. The dogs glanced back and forth between the door and the food and decided to stick with a sure thing.

"Hey, where's Junior?" I asked. "Anybody seen him? Don't tell me he's bailed already."

"Man, he better not," O'Shaunessey said. "He lasts six more days, I'm up three hundred bucks."

"Right, but if he lasts two weeks, *I'm* up three hundred

bucks," said Melissa, who's way less sweet than she looks. "And since I started the pool, it seems only fair."

"Flag on the play," O'Shaunessey said, and threw his napkin at her. "The fix is in. Clearly."

"Nah," Mad said. "He's still back at the joint. Bill's got him working on some goddamn timeline, history of homicides in Walden County or some crap. Probably never run it. He's just trying to torture the kid. Says it's for his own good."

Melissa snorted. "Right. Twelve hours down in the morgue. That's bound to teach him something. If the rats don't get him, the asbestos will."

"Who was that at the door?" I asked Marci when she got back.

She shrugged. "Some old man. He had the wrong house. I think he may have been looking for whoever lived here before us."

"You mean the biker fraternity?"

"Well, no, probably the people before them. He said he hadn't been back in a while. I offered to let him use the phone but he said he didn't want to disturb us."

"So screw 'em," O'Shaunessey said cheerfully. "Who's for seconds?"

All our Thursday night dinners have one thing in common: you know they're over when we run out of booze. It's a good thing Friday is recycling day, or we'd spend the rest of the week tripping over empties. That night, the party broke up around eleven, which is on the early side. Mad usually sticks around until I evict him, but that night he and Emma repaired to his lair at ten, presumably to act out his Princess Di fantasies.

The guests always do the cleaning—I'm hospitable,

but I'm not crazy—and I was putting away dry dishes when the doorbell rang again. I opened the door, and there under the porch light was just about the last person I would have expected.

"First rule of home security," said Detective Brian Cody. "Keep the front door locked." Two of the dogs started barking and lunging at him and I told them to heel. This did no good whatsoever, so I grabbed their collars (my left wrist didn't thank me for it) and yelled at him to come in. He was wearing jeans, ratty sneakers, and a black leather jacket over a navy Red Sox sweatshirt. It looked a lot better on him than the suits had. Then I noticed he had the *Monitor* folded under his arm. Uh-oh.

"What are you doing here?"

"I promised you a security check."

"I thought you were sending someone."

"I wanted to talk to your friend Marci, get some basic information just to be safe, so I decided to come over myself."

"At eleven?"

"Is it too late?"

"Nope. I'm a night owl."

"Good guard dogs you've got there. Yours?"

I shook my head. "That lump on the couch is mine. Her name is Shakespeare. She's part German shepherd, part beagle. She'd play fetch with a rapist. The big black poodle is Tipsy. He belongs to my roommate Emma. The shepherd is C.A.'s. He's a purebred, real champion stock. Her mom's family's really into the dog-show thing. Name's Nanki-Poo."

"That's humiliating."

"I know. C.A. hates it. She got him from her grand-mother when the dog was already three, so there was no changing it. Believe me, she tried. I guess her grandma's all freaky for Gilbert and Sullivan."

"So she named it after the fellow from *The Mikado*?"

"How'd you know that?"

"My mom's all freaky for Gilbert and Sullivan."

"Oh." We stared at each other for a while. I could see the outline of his gun under his sweatshirt and hoped there was nothing particularly incriminating in the living room; good thing I wasn't wearing Adam's HEMP IS HEAVEN T-shirt. "Are you going to come in, or would you rather just loiter here in the doorway?"

"Loitering is underrated."

"Want a beer? Or are you, I don't know, on duty or something?"

"Thanks for the offer, but I might as well get this over with and let you get back to whatever you're doing. Can you go get Marci? It will only take a couple minutes."

"It'll take less than that. She's not here."

Insert more uncomfortable silence. "I guess I should have called first. But I was on my way home from the station and I saw your lights on, so I figured I'd stop."

"Decent of you."

"No trouble. I can come back some other time." He turned and started down the front steps.

"You sure you don't want a beer? We've got Guinness." That stopped him.

"I probably shouldn't."

"Why not? What is it, sleeping with the enemy or something?"

He turned around, and his cheeks were tinged the same

shade of pink I'd seen in the hospital room when he took me for a tenth-grader. I wondered again how a guy this easily embarrassed had managed to get through basic training. "Ex . . ." He cleared his throat. "Excuse me?"

"'Sleeping with the enemy,' you know, it's an expression. It was a joke. A really bad one."

"Oh. Right."

"So do you want a Guinness or don't you?"

He cocked an eyebrow. "No strings attached?"

"Huh?"

"Just a beer and nothing else?"

"What, are you afraid I'm gonna jump your bones? Those Boston chicks must be pretty hot."

"Come on, I didn't mean . . ."

"Oh, I get it. You're afraid I'm going to pump you. I mean for info."

"Crossed my mind."

"Oh, Christ, Cody. I was just trying to be nice, say thanks for you coming by to protect our virtue."

"No digging about the case?"

"Not unless you want to unburden yourself."

"You got Guinness stout?"

"How the hell do I know?"

I got him a bottle out of the fridge from Emma's private stock, and we sat on stools at the kitchen counter. "Where is everybody? I thought you lived with a whole houseful."

"Steve is out counting the little birdies, which is where he is most nights. Emma is disporting herself with my friend Mad, and the other two just took off for the vet library. That's everybody."

"It's good there are so many of you. Safer."

"I guess. What about you, Detective? Do you live alone?"

"Yeah. And since you're serving me the good stuff you could call me Brian."

"Wait, I thought you lived with your mother."

His bottle stopped an inch from his lips. "Now *that's* a crock. Where did you hear that?"

"Apparently from someone who didn't know what he was talking about."

"For the record, I live *near* my mother. I do not live *with* my mother."

"It's an important distinction."

"I'll say."

"You know, it totally freaks me out you thought I was in high school."

"It was the cuts and bruises. They made you look vulnerable. The pigtails didn't help."

"I have *got* to stop dressing like Buffy the Vampire Slayer."

"Who?"

"Never mind. So I hear your wife left you."

"Are you always this shy?"

"Always."

"Where'd you hear about my wife?"

"Sources. Hopefully, more reliable than the other one."

"Well, that much is one hundred percent true."

"What happened? She didn't like being a cop's wife?"

"No, she loved being a cop's wife. Loved it so much, she traded up. Dumped me for my lieutenant."

"Isn't that—I don't know—unethical? On his part? Can't he get in trouble?"

"He might, but only if I made a stink. Which I didn't."

"You just did the honorable thing and retreated to a nothing police department in the middle of nowhere."

"I don't hate it here. I already told you, my mom lives in Gabriel."

"You didn't grow up here, did you? You sure don't sound like it."

"Me? No way. I grew up in Southie. That's South Boston."

"I know what Southie is. I grew up in Western Mass. The Berkshires."

"Another world out there."

"We all root for the Yankees and plot secession."

"And we'd just as soon have you fall off into New York."

"No kidding. How did your mom end up here?"

"After my dad died, she married a guy who got a job running the grounds department at Benson. He died last year, so she was by herself. But she had her friends here, and her church, and she didn't want to move. So here I am."

"Doomed to be bored off your ass."

"Hardly. Not now, anyway." He picked up the paper from where he'd dropped it on the counter. I'd assumed it was that day's, but it turned out to be from Tuesday. My story had run above the fold under the headline POLICE IDENTIFY SECOND VICTIM. I'd filed it ten minutes before deadline Monday night, then fallen asleep on the couch in the managing editor's office. Cody unfolded the paper and shook his head. "How the hell did you pull this off?"

"What do you mean? How did I get you to talk?"

"You did not 'get' me to talk. I did the only logical thing under the circumstances. Pissing off the local daily is very shortsighted. It feels good at the time, but when you need a favor two weeks later, it comes back to bite you on the ass. I meant, how did you get these pictures? And how did you get all these people to talk to you—her roommate, her boyfriend, her *parents*, for God's sake?"

"That's not my story. The cop reporter wrote it."

"Do you think for a minute I believe that frightened adolescent wrote this?"

"Okay, you got me. We co-wrote it. And if you really want to know, the photo on the jump page came from her high school yearbook. That's a no-brainer. We just sent the photo intern to the local library. The one that ran on page one—that posed sort of glamour shot—we got that one from her boyfriend. He kept it in his wallet."

"But why do people let you invade their privacy like that? That's what I can't understand. If I was that poor girl's boyfriend, I would never talk to you people in a million years."

"Most people think they'd feel that way. But when push comes to shove, they'd rather talk about something than just sit on it."

"I don't buy it."

"Then maybe you're the one person out of a hundred that can handle silence. Most of us can't. It makes my job a lot easier. I bet it does the same thing for yours."

"Food for thought."

"Fact is, most people *need* to talk about themselves. Makes them feel like they're worth something."

"Only if they've got something to prove."

"And you don't?"

"I'm not real big on spilling my guts."

"So why'd you tell me about your wife and all?"

"Damn good question." He thought about it for a minute. "I guess . . . because you asked so straight. Frontal assault."

"The best kind."

"But there's a big difference between talking over a beer and spilling personal stuff to the newspaper. It's not like my lousy marriage is going to end up in print."

"You hope." He shot me a startled look. "Relax, Cody. I'm just joking. And for the record, though it's absolutely, positively, and completely none of my business, it sounds to me like that wife of yours was a flake and a half."

"You're not wrong." He drank down the rest of his beer. "All right, let's take a look around this place." He got up and went straight for the front door. "What you have here is a lock so cheap any two-bit break-in artist could pick it. Which doesn't much matter, because any-one with a brick could break the glass, reach in, and turn the latch. What you want is a Medeco lock, the kind you can deadbolt from the inside with a key. They cost a mint, but when you move out you can take it with you. And you don't want to leave the key hanging in the lock, or you've defeated the purpose. Got it?" I wrote it down. He sur-veyed the house, and, in the end, calculated eight separate points of entry that any idiot with a stepladder and an urge to maim could use to get at us. Put security bars on the first-floor windows, he said, and plant prickly bushes underneath them. Close and lock the ones on the second floor, since it wouldn't take much to climb the trellis to the garage roof and get in that way. Have the landlord fix the broken light fixtures outside the back door. Install motion-sensitive floodlights. Et cetera, et cetera.

"Sounds like living in a prison."

"It's living in the real world."

"How about you just catch this guy?"

"We're working on it."

"He's crazy, isn't he?"

"I don't believe in crazy. I believe in evil. How else do you describe someone who kills women, and leaves them lying in the woods like some sort of . . ."

I thought of what I'd found on Saturday. ". . . sacrifice?"

"Exactly."

"Do you have any leads at all?"

"A few. And you know I can't say anything."

"What if I promise to be a good little girl and keep my mouth shut?"

"You wouldn't know how."

"Look, I'm not asking you as a reporter. I'm asking you as the poor schmuck who found Patricia Marx in the goddamn woods." I stared him right in his baby greens, and for a minute I thought he was going to open up. Fat chance.

"I'd better get going before I say something I'll regret later. You're damn good at what you do. Too good for my taste."

He moved toward the front door, fast enough to upset the unfortunately named Tipsy and Nanki-Poo. They lunged for him, and I grabbed them by their collars again to give him enough time to get out. After informing the dogs that they were both very bad indeed, I followed him outside and shut the door behind me. "Sorry about that," I said, and reached out to shake his hand.

"I don't mind. Like I said, they're good guard dogs." He went to shake, but all of a sudden he grabbed my wrist and held it up to the light. For a minute I thought he was going to try some gentlemanly hand-kissing thing, but he was just trying to get a good look at my palm. He stared at it, and rubbed at the marks that were already fading.

"What's the deal?"

"Which dog were you holding with your right hand?"

"Jesus, I don't know." I thought about it. "It was Nanki-Poo. The German shepherd."

"Go get me his collar."

"Why?"

"Just do me a favor and take it off him."

I went back in the house, took the collar off the dog, and snapped off the license tags. "Here. Now what's going on?"

"I'm sorry. I can't tell you. But I've got to take this with me. I'll give it back." He started down the driveway.

"Wait. Hold on. What am I supposed to tell C.A.?" I looked down at my hand. The marks were just faintly visible. "Oh, my God." I ran after him. "It's the marks on the girl's neck. The diamond-shaped marks. She was strangled with a goddamn dog collar. Wasn't she?"

"I can't talk about this."

"Come on."

"I'm sorry," he said, and he was gone. I locked the door behind him and C.A.'s dog looked up at me, naked and wondering where his next biscuit was coming from.

6

"A DOG COLLAR? A MOTHERFUCKING DOG COLLAR?"

"Ssh. Mad, for Chrissake, can you keep your voice down?"

"Who's gonna hear in this place?"

"Are you kidding me? Everybody. You know better."

We were in the Citizen Kane, our favorite spot for bringing journalistic stereotypes to boozy life. It was around nine on Friday night, and the place was just beginning to fill up. Lately, our turf has been invaded by students from Bessler College, which is located on the opposite side of town from the behemoth that is Benson. Bessler is a small liberal arts school that has amazing theater and music departments; too bad the rest of its student body is a bunch of beer-swilling numbskulls. Every once in a while one of them manages to drink himself right into a coma and the college president has to go to the funeral and try to keep a straight face. Mad calls it "natural selection."

"Okay, okay, I'll be quiet," he said. "So what the hell happened?"

"I told you. Mr. Hunky Cop was standing in the doorway, and when he saw the pattern the dog collar made on my hand, he got all hepped up and split. Bat out of hell. Back to the cop shop, I assume."

"And it was the same pattern as on the girl's neck?"

"I'm pretty sure. It's kind of weird. I didn't think I remembered that much detail; I was scared shitless. But when I saw the marks on my hand it just sort of flashed back. I could see her lying there with these bruises around her neck."

"What did they look like?"

"Diamond-shaped, evenly spaced but with sort of a groove at the front. And deep. Angry."

"Angry?"

"Really vicious. Cut in really deep. Bloody."

"Why do all the cool things happen to you?"

"Shut up, Mad. It was awful."

"It's a guy thing. We love this blood-and-guts shit. I'm thirty-four years old and I've never even gotten a peek at a really interesting corpse."

"Mad . . ."

"I know. I'm an asshole."

"Clearly."

"Sorry."

"No problem."

"You seem to be taking this pretty well, Bernier. You find the stiff, you run for your life, and none the worse for wear."

"Yeah, right. Two cracked ribs, one sprained wrist . . ."

"Besides that. You don't seem any too freaked out."

"Are you nuts? Of course I'm freaked out. I'm plenty freaked out. It's just . . . I don't know. Nothing could be as bad as last year."

"I get your drift."

"You see the man you love in a body bag six hours after he's out of your bed, everything's pretty much a cake walk from there."

"No shit."

We sat there for a while, Mad drinking his Molson and me swirling the limes around my gin and tonic. Mad loves to talk, but he's also one of the only people I can just sit with and not feel weird. "Oh, fuck, Mad. I still really miss him."

"I know you do. But it's okay."

"How is it okay?"

"It's okay to miss him, because he was worth missing. That means missing him is the right thing to do."

"Wow. Mad, that was positively poetic."

"Well, it's true."

"You going to start singing Carpenters songs now?"

"Hey, I'm a sensitive new age guy, *baby*. Don't you forget it."

"Rainy days and Mondays always get you down."

"I'm serious, Alex. Okay, mostly serious. But you know Adam wouldn't want you to live in the dumps for the rest of your life. It's almost been a year. You've got to deal."

"I'm dealing. At least now I've got something to take my mind off it. Awfully nice of that guy to start strangling women with dog collars and making me feel better."

"What would scumbags like us do if everybody started being nice to each other all of a sudden?"

"We'd be out of business. Cops too."

"Speaking of cops, what was Cody doing at your place last night anyway? That detail seems to have been overlooked, eh, foxy?"

"Do you ever listen? I told you, he was doing a security check. For Marci."

"A likely story. He couldn't send a uniform?"

I shrugged. "He wanted to talk to her himself."

"So did he make the moves on you?"

"Hardly."

"Did he get lucky?"

"You *mutant*."

"Did he get to play sink the salami? Take Mister One Eye to the optometrist? Make you smoke the bone?"

"Mad, I swear if you don't shut up I'm going to hurt you. I don't know how, but I'm going to do it."

He stood up, neatly avoiding the feet that were trying to kick him under the table. "And now to drain the snake. I shall return."

I put my head down on the tabletop, which proved to be mercifully free of beer. I wasn't all that tired, since Bill had given me the day off and I'd spent most of it in bed with Shakespeare. But I could feel another headache coming on, and I was starting to wonder if I'd really messed up my noggin with that trip over the handlebars. Closing my eyes turned out to be a bad idea, though, because all I could see was the dead girl. She had those marks around her neck, and her palms and knees were bloody just like the girl before her. I tried to picture her alive, and couldn't.

What had he done to her? He'd strung that collar around her neck, and at some point she'd had to crawl around on her hands and knees. Was she trying to get away? Or did he force her to crawl around like a dog, just to humiliate her?

Like a dog. Jesus. Could that be it?

No way. The thought was just too creepy. But frankly, nothing seemed too creepy to match what I'd found in the woods and what the other guy had found on the mountain. If you're going to abduct a girl and torture and kill her, does it really matter why? Does anybody care about your inner dialogue? Does your personal history dictate whether you wring her neck or slit her throat?

"Hey, you know, you got really big tits."

I looked up to find two college guys, each just slightly smaller than the new Volkswagen Beetle. They were bleary-eyed and standing close together, like they were holding each other up.

"Didn't ya hear me?" said lout number one. "I said, 'Man, you got really nice tits.' We saw ya through the window here." He gestured with his beer mug and I felt a splash go down my neck.

"Yeah," said his companion. "He said, like, 'Look at that girl with that great rack,' and I said, like, 'Dude, it's your *duty* to go in there and tell her how you feel.' And he said, 'Dude, you are *so* right.' And . . . here we are." He said it like he was Lindbergh describing his trip across the Atlantic. I didn't know whether to laugh at them or reach for my Mace. Oh, hell. If you live in a college town, sometimes you have to suffer for all the good coffee and reasonably priced drugs.

"So whaddaya say?" said the first guy.

"Yeah," said the other. "Whaddaya say?"

"Is there a question? Because if there is, I believe I may have missed it."

They looked at each other. "Huh?" said lout number two. "My friend here just wanted to express himself, that's all."

Where do these guys come from? Failed government experiments?

"Yeah," said his buddy. "I expressed myself."

"I see."

"'Cause we were sorta wondering," said the first one, "if maybe you wanted to . . ."

"No. No thank you."

"Ya sure?" said the second. "We got a whole case of Mad Dog back at the . . ."

"It's a charming offer, really. But you boys have a lovely night."

They looked at each other, seemed to come to some manly understanding, and turned to go. Just as they were walking down the steps to the main part of the bar they encountered Mad, who'd finally reappeared. "Dude," the second guy said to him. "That girl is *deep*."

"You have no idea," Mad said, and the two undergrads toddled off toward the pinball machines.

"Where the hell have you been?"

"I didn't want to interrupt."

"You might have rescued me."

"And validate the dominant male paradigm? I'd never."

"This bar is going to hell."

"Right. All those horny nineteen-year-old girls with fake IDs. It's a tragedy."

"Why doesn't somebody start picking these guys off for a change? They wouldn't be missed. Who can even tell them apart?"

"You're suggesting a serial killer who preys on dumb jocks?"

"Sounds good to me."

"Their parents might mind."

"They might just as soon save the tuition."

"Good point. Oh, hey. I forgot to tell you. O'Shaunessey won the pool. Junior packed it in today."

"No kidding? Melissa's gotta be pissed. Five more days and she was in the money. But I guess one night down in the morgue was enough for him."

"Yeah. Plus, he got a little push."

I gave him the fish eye. "Push?"

"O'Shaunessey told him if there was another murder, he was going to have to go cover the autopsy. Said he'd have to go to the *real* morgue, not just the newspaper kind."

"And he fell for it? As if they'd ever let a reporter within a mile of the place. What a dope."

"See what happens when you go to journalism school? They take out all your brain cells."

"You mean he just took O'Shaunessey's word for it?"

"Well"—Mad smirked into his mug—"I kind of backed him up. Told him all about what it was like to cover my first autopsy. I thought the kid was gonna hurl." He reached into his shirt pocket and threw five twenties on the table. "My percentage."

"Wait until Melissa hears about this. She'll demand a recount."

"Nothing she can do about it. Fair is fair. Nobody ever said you couldn't help things along. Besides, he'll be much happier back in Iowa covering the corn beat."

"He was from Wisconsin."

"Dairy. Whatever."

"So what's Bill going to do? We need a cop reporter, especially now." Mad wiggled his eyebrows at me and I got a sinking feeling in the gut area. "No way. You do *not* mean me. Who's going to cover the city?"

"Relax. Don't get your crotchless panties in a twist. You're not covering cops. I'm covering cops. You're ghosting."

"Oh, *fuck*. You mean on top of covering my own beat, I also get to be your slave? Do your dirty work? Be your girl Friday?"

"That about sums it up. But only on the murder case. Bill just wants you to keep your eyes and ears open. I told him you were uniquely qualified for the job."

"Mad, I am uniquely *un*qualified for the job. I found the second body. I'm not what you'd call involved."

"You broke the story about Patricia Marx."

"Under Junior's byline."

"And now you can break the rest under mine."

"What a treat."

"What's the problem? I thought you were all hot for this story. You went charging off after Cody, got him to ID the victim for you. I thought you'd be psyched. Come on, it'll be a hoot. How often are we going to get to cover a genuine psycho in this stinking town? And besides, now you're all chummy with the investigating officer. It's a reporter's dream come true."

"Is that what you told Bill? That I was 'chummy' with Cody?"

"More or less."

"What did he say?"

"He said to use a condom. I'm *kidding*. Lighten up, will you?"

"Sorry. I'm in a bitch of a mood all of a sudden. Maybe I'd better remove myself from society."

"What's your damage? A couple of frat boys put you off your gin?"

"Nah. It's what I was thinking about before they showed up."

"What?"

"It's probably nuts. But I was thinking about the whole dog collar thing, and how the girls' hands and knees were all fucked up. And I just got this image of what they might have gone through. I mean, what if he didn't just strangle them with that thing? What if he dragged them around like that, made them crawl?"

"You mean he made them, what, act like dogs?"

"I guess so, yeah."

"I'd say he's one sick motherfucker."

"You got that right. Jesus, Mad. How could this happen?"

"We're a nasty species. Been preying on each other for a long time."

"I mean, how could this happen *here*? Seems like a lot of evil for a small town."

"Yeah, but this is no ordinary town. You know that. We attract nuts from all over the place, and not just the good kind."

"That's not very comforting."

"Is that what has you so upset? The end of your little fantasy that Gabriel equals paradise?"

"That, and . . . I was picturing what happened to that girl, and I guess it got to me. It seemed so . . . well, like you said, *psycho*. And then I started thinking what difference did it make, since the guy is obviously a monster to begin with. What do the details matter?"

"The devil's in the details, and you know it. But, Alex, keep in mind that we don't really know what the physical evidence is. All we know is what the cops have released, what a few lame-ass witnesses have said, and what you've managed to charm out of the local goons. We don't know squat. It was only a fluke we found out about the dog collar. None of the other news guys have it."

"That's just what I mean. What are we supposed to do with that? We can't run with it."

"The hell we can't."

"Who's the source?"

"You are."

"Oh, *please*."

"So it's unattributed. 'Police refused to comment on whether the victim may have been offed like a pooch.' I love that shit."

"But what if it queers the investigation?"

"I can't believe you're talking like this."

"Okay, neither can I. But it seems out of bounds somehow. Cody just happened to be in my house when he figured it out."

"Too bad for him."

"Do we really want to piss him off beyond all reason?"

He sighed, eyeing me with the pity he reserves for teetotalers and the overweight. "You win. But what if I get it on the record from somebody else? Will that satisfy your newfound . . ." He cast about for the right word, and it came out in a growl. "Scruples?"

7

ANOTHER JOY OF LIVING IN A COLLEGE TOWN IS ALL THE free entertainment. And I'm not just talking about the various paeans to wretched excess, like the annual rite of spring in which the architecture students build an enormous papier-mâché gopher and drag it through campus while the engineers sing songs and pelt them with beer bottles. No, I'm fond of the more impromptu, entirely unsanctioned outbreaks of mirth: the arcane fraternity rituals performed in drag, the couches that are routinely pelted from third-floor balconies, and, of course, the streaking.

Benson also offers near-constant opportunities to observe the current state of campus protest. Last year, the hot topic was gay rights, after a couple of freshmen got bashed within an inch of their lives and activists took to the streets in droves. All the agitating worked—the university gave in to most of the demands—but that was pretty much the exception that proves the rule. When it comes to activism, there's an awful ache about the place;

call it the agony of having missed the party by several decades. Sure, they dress like the sixties are still upon us, with their braids and their tie-dye and their anklets made out of hemp. But there's a certain desperation to it all, and it isn't pretty.

In the more than two years I've been at the *Monitor*, I've covered rallies, marches, and sit-ins (sits-in?) on the following issues: gender equity in sports, nasty labor practices at the company that makes Benson T-shirts (from what I hear, "sweatshop" would be too nice a word), the university's investment in tobacco companies, a teaching assistants' union, disabled access to the football stadium (there isn't any, unless you sit on the field), a pomology professor accused of sexual harassment, and the crappy food in the dining hall. I always seem to get good quotes out of the protesters, which is either proof of my journalistic acumen or their willingness to mouth off to anybody with a notebook. One of them once told me that they trust me because I'm quote, "too young to be the man." (And I thought I was just too girlie.)

I mention all this because in what turned out to be a brief lull between the discovery of the second body and the third, I got caught up covering the latest social action up on the hill. This time, the hot topic was animal rights, and the protest forces were hitting it from all angles. They'd stormed a trustee meeting, demanding that Benson divest from companies that do animal testing. They'd raided a mink farm forty miles away. They'd trashed a bunch of labs up at the vet school and, over at the Ag school, liberated some cows from the experimental dairy herd. So far, nobody had been arrested, and the talk was that the group had some friends on the inside who helped them get into the buildings and avoid security. It wasn't much and it certainly wasn't violent, but it was enough to have anybody even remotely involved in animal experiments feeling itchy. An entomologist I knew even put triple locks on her office because she was terrified the "loonies" (her word) would try to free her tarantula collection. And, she lamented, only half of them were poisonous.

But unlike most campus causes, this one seemed to have a fair number of opponents among the student body itself. Benson has world-class animal science departments, and their grants pay a lot of people's salaries. Plus, there are plenty of grad students (and undergrads too) up there for the sole purpose of doing the very things that the so-called Benson Animal Anarchists object to, whether it's dissecting frogs or twiddling with equine DNA. It didn't help that of the five hundred animals they'd freed from the shackles of the mink farm, almost all of them died (either run over by cars or eaten by their closest friends) and one of the liberated cows wandered into the road and caused a near-fatal accident.

Maybe because their profile wasn't what they might have wanted—or because graduation was coming up and most of the group was off to law school—they decided it was time for something more dramatic. So there I was, hauled out of bed at seven on a Wednesday morning a week and a half before Memorial Day, watching the campus police try to unlock the front doors of the biology building. Gabriel is an eight-to-four town, and there was already a crowd of office workers, professors, and early-bird students waiting to get inside. Through the glass doors, I could see four beleaguered-looking people in lab coats who'd apparently been trapped there overnight, and it didn't look like they were going anywhere soon. The handles of the back doors had been chained together with titanium bike locks, and in front the door locks had been glued shut with the industrial-strength stuff abortion protesters use to close down clinics. From what I could tell, there was no opening them without a battering ram. It was going to be a long day.

Melissa was wandering through the crowd snapping pictures, wearing the photo-safari vest that makes her look like Meryl Streep in *Out of Africa*. The campus cops were not happy. At least nobody was chanting.

"Hey there, Miss Alex," she said. "What do you make of this spectacle?"

"Drag. Nobody's chained to anything."

"Not yet."

"Get any good shots?"

"Fat cop with a hacksaw."

"Pulitzer time."

"I wonder what they're after."

"All of bio's in this building, so take your pick. I'm betting fetal pigs."

"Heads up. Here comes the flack brigade."

I turned around and saw the new vice president for university relations and two of his assistants coming our way. Phil Herzog got hired after his predecessor was shipped off to minimum-security work camp for drunk driving. The new guy was considerably less of a jerk but every bit as unhelpful. That part is inevitable, though: our job is to report the news, and his is to filter out all the bad stuff and leave us with the vanilla-pudding dregs that make parents and donors sleep at night. It's not what you'd call a mutually satisfying relationship.

Melissa slipped off, leaving me to deal with Herzog and his crew on my own. But when they were twenty feet away and closing, they and everyone else in the crowd stopped to stare at the line of marchers coming down the middle of the main campus street. There were only about two dozen of them, but they'd already jammed up what passes for rush-hour traffic around here. They were making some horrible noise, and it took me a minute to realize it was coming from four boom boxes playing recorded sounds of screaming animals, presumably at the slaughter. Lovely.

The campus cops started barking into their walkie-talkies, calling for backup before they were drowned out by the animal screams. The marchers finally drew up in front of the building and spread themselves at various points on the front steps with the precision of a ROTC drill team. As it turned out, there was a good reason they weren't chanting. They had their mouths covered with duct tape, which made for dramatic effect but was going to hurt like hell when it came off, and they were wearing identical T-shirts that said STOP VIVISECTION.

That was it. They all just stood there and stared straight ahead with those horrible recordings blaring one on top of the other, out of synch and sounding like teatime at the abattoir. I caught sight of my friend Nicky from the NPR station in Binghamton, who was trying to set sound levels on his recorder, and he gave me a look that translated as *what am I supposed to do with these nutbags*? I shrugged back. Nothing happened for a couple of minutes, and I was wondering how long the standoff could possibly go on when one of the campus cops had enough. He was a guy in his fifties, red-faced from carrying an extra sixty pounds, and as he stepped from behind me I heard him say four words crowded into one.

"Sonofabitch."

He ran up to the closest kid with a tape player and went to pull it out of her hands, but she held on. He might have chosen a woman because he thought she'd be easier to handle, but if he did he chose wrong. He tried to grab it again, and she wrapped her arms around it tighter, all the while staring straight ahead. He tried to pick her up and the radio along with it, but she collapsed into a heap on the steps and became total deadweight; somebody had obviously given them a primer on civil disobedience.

"Turn off that goddamn noise!" he shouted, and was about to move on to the next nearest protester when two other campus policemen intercepted him. They talked to him for a minute and the three of them seemed about to walk away when the first cop threw them off, whirled around, and rushed a skinny kid perched on one of the middle steps. He took a swing at him but the kid was too fast, and when the punch didn't connect the cop lost his balance and nearly toppled over. But he recovered and grabbed the radio with more agility than you'd think he could manage, lifted it over his head, and pitched it down the stairs. One out of four screaming pigs went quiet, and most of the crowd looked like they wanted to kiss the guy.

He started toward the next radio, his face even redder than before, but all of a sudden he stopped and just keeled over, splat. The EMTs—who always seem to be lurking on the sidelines at such occasions—leaped into action, giving CPR and loading him into an ambulance. The protesters never even looked. I was starting to write the lead in my head. *A Benson University public safety officer collapsed during a campus protest in front of a blockaded Dew Hall Wednesday morning. Student activists, clad in identical anti-vivisection T-shirts and wearing duct tape over their mouths, stood around like a bunch of twits while the old guy croaked.*

The dean of students showed up with a megaphone and talked about how the protesters' concerns would be addressed, but first they had to disperse and let them free the people locked inside the building. It was a lovely speech, but nobody could hear it over the recorded screams of animal torture. The vice president for research picked up the megaphone and started calling for "civil discourse," but by then the Gabriel city cops were involved and there was no more Mr. Nice Guy. Working in pairs, they handcuffed the protesters with plastic strips and carried them to a bus, which whisked them away, boom boxes and all. So much for getting some quotes.

The doors were still locked by the time I left an hour later; they finally had to bring in a glazier from the buildings and grounds department to cut through one of the glass panes and let the people out. Herzog had told me that they were going to charge the perpetrators with unlawful imprisonment, vandalism, and malicious mischief. But since there was no way to prove that the protesters had anything to do with sealing up the building like a giant brick Tupperware, in the end all they got hit with was disorderly conduct—and only the four kids with the noisemakers, at that.

I was in the newsroom working on the story and eating

a bagel with green olive cream cheese when Mad came over and deposited an envelope on my desk. It was addressed to "Police Reporter."

"Guess who dropped us a line."

"Junior's Aunt Thelma?"

"I hope not. Open it."

It was one typed page, single-spaced with no margins—the format of choice for raving lunatics with something to share. For years, we've been getting letters from God that start like this: "This is the Lord your Savior, speaking to you through my earthly son, Jethro." Return address, Texarkana.

This one was obviously different. For one thing, there were no typos, nothing crossed out or whited over. And for another, it was signed *The Devil's Disciple*. The text went like this:

You think I have only killed two but there are many many more. They thought they could look down on me but I am the one. I am in control. I decide who lives and who dies. I have the power. I will determine when to be merciful and when to take my vengeance on the ones who have disobeyed.

They cannot hide from me. I watch them in secret as they walk pretending they do not fear me. But I can smell it. They are afraid of me and they should be. In my mind I can see them under me, and my hands around their necks, and I watch as

the life God gave them is taken away by
something much much stronger.

They lock their doors at night. They hud-
dle together and hope I will go away. But I
will stay until my destiny is fulfilled and
my job is done. How many will there be?
How many does the master crave? That is
the question and only I know the answer.

I will act again soon.

I dropped the paper on the desk like it was crawling
with cockroaches. Even insect-free it gave me the willies.
"Is this what I think it is?"

"Looks like it."

"You think it's for real?"

"Like I'm the expert?"

I read through it again. It was less scary the second
time around. "You know what, Mad? I don't know if I
buy it."

"Huh?"

"It sounds to me like whoever wrote this has been
watching too goddamn many *X-Files*."

"You mean it's a fake?"

"It's just so, I don't know . . . predictable."

"You're criticizing a serial killer for bad writing?"

I shrugged. "What are we supposed to do with this
thing?"

"Damned if I know. Bill's out, so let's ask the boss."

We knocked on the managing editor's office and she
opened the door wearing her dojo whites, sweaty from
practicing tae kwon do kicks. Nobody messes with Mar-

ilyn, and not just because she has a black belt. Mad handed her the letter and repaired to the corner to do combinations on the punching bag that was still swinging from the ceiling. She read the page in under five seconds. "Motherfuck."

Mad kept hitting the bag. "My" [*pow*] "words" [*pow*] "exactly."

"Oh, crap." She picked up the phone. I flopped down on her office couch and she threw a cappuccino-flavored PowerBar at me. "Chief Hill, please. Marilyn Zapinsky from the *Monitor*. It's important." He came on the line right away. Impressive. "Chief, you might want to send one of your boys over here. There's something you ought to see. It's a letter purporting to be from the killer. Might be a crock, but I figured we'd play it safe. What? No, I haven't made any decisions about printing it yet ... Whoa. It came to *my* newsroom, mister. If I want to run the goddamn thing I'll run it. I called you up in the spirit of cooperation. Huh? Evidence, schmevidence. I can photocopy this sucker faster than you can zip up your fly." She listened again. "Why, that's *much* nicer. Tell him to come right up to my office. And good day to you, sir."

She hung up and I bowed my head. "Mistress Marilyn, I kneel in adoration of your power."

"It's all in the attitude, sister."

"That man would pay big money to have you walk on his back with spike heels."

"He can't afford me."

"So who's he sending?"

"Your hero, Detective Cody."

"Oh, joy."

"And a prints guy."

"What for?"

"They're dusting us for elimination prints. Apparently we should have known better than to handle the letter. We've probably smeared it all to hell and destroyed their evidence. But they're going to check it anyway."

"Why do I doubt the killer would do us the favor of running his mitts all over the thing?"

"Because you have common sense. But these guys are cops, and we have to make allowances. Now be a good girl and go xerox this thing before the stormtroopers get here. Five copies should do the trick. No," she called after me, "make that ten."

8

WE DIDN'T RUN THE LETTER THE NEXT DAY. A WEEK WENT by, then another, and the copies still sat in a heap on Marilyn's desk. It wasn't that she was knuckling under to the cops—she'd "sooner chop off a tit," as she so eloquently put it—but because she had her own kind of qualms. Our fearless leader has never been one to do things by committee, but this time she decided to keep us informed. She'd read the letter a hundred times, and it bugged her too. Yes, it was properly twisted, but it was all too general; there were no details, nothing in there that some wacko couldn't have written just by reading the paper. And, she told us, she was damned if her newspaper was going to turn into a playpen for every sicko with a typewriter. "Except," she added, "you guys."

Then the next one came. It was addressed to me, which did not enhance my personal calm. I'd gotten a number of threatening letters the year before when we were investigating Adam's murder, and although this one came to the paper rather than my house it brought back nasty memories. I told myself he'd probably picked my name because at that point I was the only female reporter under sixty-five working on the city desk. Or maybe because I'd found the second body. Or maybe because he liked my movie column. I'm still not sure which was the least comforting.

The second letter was as neat as the first, and as soon as I realized what it was I didn't touch it with my fingers. I nudged it the rest of the way out of the envelope with the eraser end of a pencil, just like the cops do on *Law & Order*, and laid it flat on my desk.

You are weak so you do not understand. I have sent you my words and you will bring them to the world. You cannot eclipse my destiny. I will take lives when and how and as I see fit. I will act in the darkness and though they may struggle in the end they will yield.

Read my words carefully or you will pay the price. I have the power over life and death. The world has seen me use my power and I will use it again soon. The master in his dark force can show mercy. But only if those who serve him do obey.

You will hear my words with fear and humility. These words must be put forth for all the people to read. If they are not put into print one week hence I will act. I will take another life and another and another. You have no power and you must obey.

My next sacrifice may be any one of the weak.

It may be you.

"Yo, Alex, whatcha reading?"

In the midst of the love letter from Charles Manson, Mad's big baritone scared the bejeezus out of me. I jumped up and knocked over my can of Diet Pepsi, which proceeded to coat everything on the desk in a fizzy brown pool. "Mad, oh, *shit*. Help! Go get some paper towels or napkins or something." I picked up the letter by the corner. It was so wet it was translucent, and a little fountain of soda dripped from it onto the desk. Mad came back with a wad of white cotton and started swabbing. "Careful, you're ripping stuff. What the hell are you using?"

"The men's room was out of paper towels. Ditto the ladies'. I found these under the counter."

I picked up one of the sopping rectangles from the desk. Even under the circumstances, I had to crack up. "Mad, these are Kotex."

"Huh?"

"Sanitary napkins. The kind you use with pins and a belt. Like from 1960."

"Oh, Christ," he said, and dropped the wet wad into the garbage. "There are some things a man wasn't meant to know."

I finished cleaning up the mess while he stood around looking scared somebody was going to lop off his member. I threw away a stack of mushy press releases I should have tossed months ago and inspected the letter I'd laid on Junior's old desk. It was still in one piece and legible, but the fingerprint situation wasn't promising. I had no idea what I was going to say to Marilyn, much less Detective Cody. I crawled into her office and confessed, and an hour later we were sequestered there with the cops.

"You people are unbelievable." This from Chief Hill. And I thought he liked me.

"I'm sorry," I squeaked out, wishing Mad hadn't left me to take the heat alone. "It was an accident."

"Accident, my keister. If you worked for me you'd get the sack."

"You still have the contents of the letter," Marilyn said. "The only thing you've lost is any fingerprints that might have been on there, and you know damn well there weren't any."

"We have no way of knowing . . ."

"Come on, Chief, did you find any prints on that first letter besides ours?" He didn't say anything. "I didn't think so."

"If you'll permit me, Chief, I think we have something more serious to talk about," Cody said from the corner of the room, where he'd been watching the two bicker with what I could have sworn was the hint of a grin. "This second letter is obviously a threat. I think we have no choice but to consider it in that light."

"Go on," Marilyn said.

"Let me ask you an honest question, and I'll expect an honest answer. We all know you could have run that first letter. Why didn't you?"

Marilyn stared at him with that assessing look of hers. I bet it was the same one she used on Oliver North when she was covering Iran-Contra for the AP. "Damn thing didn't sit right."

"Why not? No offense, but you've run more with less."

"I damn well do take offense. Despite what you seem to think, Detective, we aren't in this business just to sell papers. There's such a thing called journalistic ethics. And we have no obligation to give equal time to all crackpots."

"And you think your letter writer is a crackpot?"

"I've done my research. I know which papers went for this kind of thing and why. And even if this *is* the real thing, I have no intention of dragging my newspaper through another Son of Sam catastrophe."

"I'm glad to hear it."

"Christ Jesus," the chief said. "What does the Son of Sam have to do with this?"

"Nothing," Marilyn said, with a wistful look at her punching bag. "But maybe everything, damn it all."

The chief was starting to look annoyed. "I can skip the mystery. Just tell me what you're up to."

"The Son of Sam," Cody said. "David Berkowitz. Originally known as the 44-caliber Killer, for his gun."

"I can also skip the history lesson," the chief said. "What's your point?"

Marilyn picked the Thurmon Munson baseball off her desk and rolled it around in her hands as she spoke. It had taken me a while to realize that her collection of sports memorabilia didn't include anyone who made it to a normal life span. "Toward the end of the Son of Sam case, Berkowitz sent a letter to Jimmy Breslin at the *Daily News*. You gotta remember what it was like down there back in '77. New York was paralyzed, and it's a pretty tough town. This was before local TV news amounted to much, no Internet or CNN, and the papers were falling all over each other covering the story. Cops wanted the city to see they were working their asses off looking for the guy, so they let reporters swarm all over the place. We're talking cameras in the squad room."

The chief looked vaguely horrified. "Lady, if you think your reporters are getting within a hundred yards of my . . ."

"Like I was saying," she cut him off, "first Berkowitz leaves this rambling note next to two of his vics. The cops release it eventually, but not the whole thing, and I guess that pisses him off. He sends his next letter straight to Breslin, and based on the first one the cops verify it's for real. The *News* teases it for a couple of days to build things up, then they print the letter and wham, the first edition sells out in an hour. The paper isn't stupid. They couch the whole thing as a plea for the killer to turn himself in. But three weeks later Berkowitz shoots somebody else."

"That's it?"

"No. A month later it's the anniversary of his first kill, and Breslin writes a column practically daring him to make a move. Two days later he shoots a couple of kids. Lots of people thought Breslin had goaded him into it, practically accused the paper of being an accomplice to murder just to up circulation. The shrinks weren't so sure, but either way it wasn't what you'd call our finest hour. Sold a lot of papers, though."

"How do you know so much about it?" the chief asked. "What'd you do, teach a course on this crap?"

Marilyn shrugged. "How do you know all the dirt on Rodney King? It's not likely to happen here, but you gotta keep your eye on the pitfalls."

Cody spoke up. "And you're saying you don't want the *Monitor* in that kind of mess."

"Right. And there's another thing. With the Son of Sam, there was enough in the letters to prove the writer was who he said he was. Same goes for the Unabomber."

"But not this one?" Cody asked.

"Don't insult my intelligence, Detective, and I won't insult yours. Maybe the nut who wrote these is your guy. But like I said, he could just as well be some copycat crank."

"That doesn't mean he won't kill people."

"That's true, too."

"Then the question is, where does it leave us?" He held up photocopies of both letters. "We've gotten his message now, and it's loud and clear. He says that if you don't print his letters within a week, there's going to be another murder. What do you intend to do about it?"

"Look, Detective, I don't want another body in the woods any more than you do. But my paper is not going to be held hostage."

"So you'd let a girl die in the name of your so-called ethics?"

"Hold on," I said. They both looked at me as though they'd forgotten I was there. "Do you think the killer wrote these or don't you?"

Cody and the chief glanced at each other, exchanging some sort of cop semaphore. Finally Cody sighed. "This is off the record."

Marilyn muttered under her breath. "No shit."

"Normally we wouldn't tell you this sort of thing. But like it or not, you're in the loop. Whoever wrote this put you there. All right, the truth is, we're not sure whether this guy is on the up and up. At first glance, I'd kind of doubt it. There's almost a whiny quality to these letters, like the writer really has something to prove. And let's face it: the killer already *has* proven something. He's proven he can kill people, dump them in the woods, and get away with it, at least for now. Experience tells us that the vast majority of these maniacs don't even write letters. For the Ted Bundys of this world, the crime is its own reward. They're in it for the kill itself, not to crow about it afterward."

"So what's your point?" Marilyn said.

"My point is, conventional wisdom says the letters could very well have come from a crank. But the truth is that there is no such thing as conventional wisdom when it comes to this kind of killer. Some serial killers do write letters. Just because my first instinct is that these letters aren't the genuine article doesn't mean I'm right. That, we won't know until we catch the guy. And if you know about Berkowitz, then you know that the psychologists are split on how much the newspaper coverage had to do with his crimes. Some think it encouraged him. Others say that if he hadn't had all the publicity to feed his ego, he would have killed even more people to get himself good and noticed."

"But where does that leave us?" I asked. "I mean, what would you have us do?"

"Not that it's up to you," Marilyn interjected.

"Look, lady, I could get a court order . . ." Chief Hill began.

"You damn well could not, and you know it," she shot back. "Ever heard of the first amendment?"

"Shouldn't your publisher be in on this?"

"He's on vacation. Far, far away. I'm all you've got." Thank God for small favors. Chester, our publisher, got where he is by rising through the ranks of classified advertising. He's spent about fifteen minutes in a newsroom in his whole miserable life, unless he's contemplating redecoration. He's an idiot, and he also happens to be the owner's son-in-law—not that his marital state keeps him from chasing the occasional miniskirted intern.

"Let's try to keep this civil," Cody said. Where was all this diplomacy coming from all of a sudden? Did they teach that in the SEALs, right after how to kill people with your pinkie? "We know you're not the bad guy. You're just trying to do your job like we are. For once, maybe we aren't on opposing sides. We both want to make sure no one else gets killed."

"A minute ago you accused me of being willing to let a girl die."

"I'm sorry. I really didn't mean to imply that. I was just trying to make a point that we have to work together. Now, we know that you could run those letters or not run them. It's your newspaper, and the final decision will be up to you. But I hope we can work together to try and establish the most responsible course of action. We want to catch the killer, and do it before anyone else gets hurt. If you help us, and we put him away—well, that seems to me to be the most newsworthy story of all."

Was he really trying to finesse Marilyn? And what's more, was he getting away with it? This was unprecedented. "Lay out the options," she said finally.

"Chief?"

"Go ahead, Cody. You've got it on the ball."

"Okay, I'll give it to you straight. This may be life-or-death serious, and there are a hell of a lot of variables. Either this is our guy or it isn't. Either he's serious about his threat or he isn't. To begin with, let's say it's him. If you don't run it, he could go out and kill someone to teach you a lesson. If you do run it, he could get an even bigger kick out of his power trip and pursue his career with a vengeance. Now, if he *isn't* our guy and you don't run it, he may crawl back into his hole and we can write him off. Or else he might try to make his bones so he really can feel like a big man."

"But what if we do run the letter, and the writer was a fake?" I asked. "Don't we look like idiots?"

"Maybe. But that might not be the worst part of it."

"Meaning?"

"Meaning if the real guy sees some creep taking credit for his labors, he might step up his own efforts."

"So you're saying that pretty much no matter what we do, someone else is going to die? I mean, that seems to me like what you're saying—that there's no way out of this."

"No, Alex, I . . . Okay. You're right. I'm saying there are pitfalls everywhere you look. Make the wrong decision and it could cost someone her life. Killers kill. That's what they do."

"Yeah, and cops catch them," I said. "That's what *they* do, remember?"

"I remember," Cody said, sounding so straight-ahead earnest he might have been taking the Cub Scout oath.

"Look, I don't mean to sound like a sissy or anything. But might I point out that the second letter was addressed to yours truly? And at the end he mentions in passing that the next victim might just as well be me? Am I crazy, or is this grounds for just a little bit of hysteria?"

"I've been thinking about that, Alex," Cody said. "Don't be scared. It's probably just an empty threat. From what Quantico tells us, these guys almost never warn their victims beforehand. It's practically unheard of. That's one of the reasons we tend to think he isn't for real. In any case, we can protect you."

"How?"

"We're assigning you a plainclothes detail. They'll watch you whenever you're alone, until we catch this guy. Same goes for your roommate Marci, since she has such a strong physical resemblance to the other victims."

"Isn't that kind of excessive?"

This time the chief answered. "Believe it or not, Bernier, I've gotten kind of attached to the idea of you not getting killed. And besides, having you get offed on my watch, after you'd been threatened and all, is the kind of public relations diarrhea I don't need."

"Come on, Chief. I know your budget. Who's going to pay?"

"Mayor's discretionary fund."

"So as long as you don't need to plow the streets next winter, everything will be just fine."

"I don't like it," Marilyn said. "No, I don't mean the guards, Alex. At this point, that's probably the better part of valor. I mean letting you guys tell me what to run and what not to run. Hold on, Cody. I heard what you said. And right now I'm not in a position to know if it's a song and dance, but if it is, it's a good one. So although I would like to say for the record that in no way is this a precedent, I'm going to leave it up to you. I know what makes good copy, but I have no idea how to untangle that mess of what-ifs you just spun. And I sure as hell don't want to think afterward that I got some girl killed. So if you think we should run it, we'll run it. If you don't, we won't."

"That's a very smart decision, Ms. Zapinsky," Cody said. "And a very responsible one too. We'll get back to you with our recommendation by the end of the day."

"Thanks a lot. Now if you wouldn't mind, get the hell out of my office so I can hang myself in peace."

9

WHEN YOU'RE FEELING ALL FREAKED OUT, NOTHING RE-
turns you to your right mind like banana bread. I mean
the baking of it, not necessarily the eating, though that's
pretty satisfying too. There's something cathartic about
the process, all the mashing and puréeing and sifting and
egg-cracking. It allows you to be both destructive and
creative at the same time, and your friends thank you afterward. Halfway into the week the letter writer had
given as his deadline-with-a-capital-DEAD, I was home
in the midst of a baking orgy when the doorbell rang. I
wiped the fruity sludge off my hands and opened up to
find a very irked Detective Cody on my front steps.

"What the hell is wrong with you, Alex? Do you have
a death wish?"

"Huh?"

"You didn't even ask who I was before you opened the
door."

"Oh. Sorry."

"Aren't you the least bit concerned about your own safety?"

"The door was locked this time, wasn't it?"

"You've accomplished a great deal. Are you here alone?"

"My housemates just went to the store for a sec. They're coming right back."

"Alex, goddamn it, you're supposed to call for an escort if you're alone."

"But they're coming back in, like, twenty minutes."

"If I had my way you'd have round-the-clock surveillance, but at this point, we can't justify the money."

"Not until my head is actually separated from the rest of my body. I know."

"Don't joke."

"What are you doing here anyway?"

"I was on my way home and I noticed yours was the only car in the driveway, and no cop car either."

"Hmm. That's very interesting. You said that the last time you were here, that you stopped by on your way home. But you know what, Cody? I did a little investigative reporting, and I found out your apartment is on the other side of town from the station house. So what gives?"

Those freckles of his started a slow burn. "You caught me. Uncle. I was checking up on you."

"I didn't know you cared."

"You're my responsibility."

"How do you figure that?"

"You fell over. I was the one who caught you."

"So it's a karma thing."

"Yeah. You got another Guinness for me?"

I went into the kitchen and when I got back to the living room I could see him casting about for a place to sit that didn't look like it was going to sprout a tail. He finally settled on the arm of the couch next to Shakespeare, who looked up long enough to see if he happened to be carrying a steak. "Am I interrupting you? If you're in the middle of cooking, I can entertain myself until your roommates get back."

"I just threw four loaves of banana bread in the oven. It takes over an hour, so there's nothing I can do with the rest until then."

"How many are you making?"

"Eight."

"You feeding an army?"

"At the *Monitor*, it'll last an hour."

"Smells good." He reached into his jacket pocket. "Mind if I smoke?"

"You smoke? But you're such a square."

"Not much. Only when I have a beer. I smoke, I drink."

"You didn't last time."

"I was trying to be polite. So can I smoke?"

"Outside. It's a nonsmoking house. Emma smokes Dunhills sometimes, but only out on the back porch."

"Are you serious? Look at this place. I've never seen so much dog hair that wasn't connected to a dog. I've got clumps on my tongue. And I can't smoke in here?"

"We all have our foibles."

"It's freezing out."

"So don't smoke."

"Is my mother paying you?"

"No, but if she'd like to, I could use the money."

"Okay, you win. Sorry if I'm being rude. I'm just jonesing for nicotine."

"Is this a cop thing?"

"No. Maybe. Probably it's the case."

"Can you talk about it?"

"Course not. You don't smoke?"

"Used to. A lot. But now I equate smoking with hysteria."

"How so?"

"When I got upset about a guy, I'd smoke. Then I got so upset over a guy, no amount of nicotine did any good. So I figured, what's the point? Packed it up. Haven't smoked since."

"And you don't crave it?"

"Nope."

"Lucky. So who was the guy?"

"How do you men in blue like to put it? 'No comment.'"

"Not very sporting."

"It was somebody who died, okay? Now drop it."

"Adam Ellroy?"

The name hit me like a sockful of nails. All of a sudden I wanted to punch him, and for no good reason. "If you already knew, why did you ask?"

"I don't know. I guess I just wanted to see if you'd tell me."

"Power trip?"

"Maybe."

"Is *that* a cop thing?"

"Yeah."

"Too bad. Because I'm much more interested in scoping out other people than spilling my own guts."

"You already know my life story. Now it's your turn. Cops like grilling people too, you know. Best part of the job."

"Why are you so curious?"

"Truth? I have no idea. I just am."

I got up and went to the coat closet, pulled a beach towel off the top shelf, and spread it out on the couch to cover the dog hair. "Here. You might as well make yourself comfortable while you're guarding my honor. Besides, I'm not sure the couch arm was made to stand up to a man your size." He moved over and Shakespeare promptly stood up, turned around, and settled with her head on his lap.

"Nice pooch."

"Love of my life."

"Is this the part where you tell me she doesn't usually take to people this quickly, so I must be special?"

"Shakespeare? Hardly. She'll shake paws with cops or criminals. Not what you'd call discriminating."

He scratched her behind the ears. "Zeke would like you."

"Zeke?"

"He's my dog."

"What kind?"

"Lab and something. Maybe husky. He's a mutt."

"How old?"

"Four."

"And you got custody in the divorce?"

"Damn straight."

"Gee, Cody, I'm getting a newfound respect for you. Do you have a picture?"

"Of my dog? You mean in my wallet?"

"Sure."

"Nah. I used to carry one, but my ex said it was idiotic."

"No wonder the marriage was doomed."

"Yeah, well, it was probably doomed anyway."

"So how come you got hitched?"

"I thought I was supposed to be grilling you."

"Good luck."

"Okay, what say I trade you one for one? I spill some hideously painful personal detail, then you."

"So let me get this straight. Is this the point when we bond by sharing details of our empty lives?"

"Works for me."

"Deal. But only if I think you came across with something sufficiently hideous."

"That's tough but fair."

"So go. Hand me your tale of woe."

"And you won't call me a nancy boy behind my back?"

"Not unless you cry."

"I'll try not to. Anyway, it's not even that interesting. Her name was Lucy, we met in college . . ."

"You went to college?"

"Cops can't go to college?"

"Sure they can, I guess. I never really thought about it."

"Well, lots of us do nowadays. Some of us even know which fork to use."

"Sorry. No offense. You were saying?"

"I went to U-Mass on a Navy ROTC scholarship. After graduation, I owed the service four years, and I was damned if I was going to spend it sailing around in a circle, so I applied for the SEALs. I probably would have gone career except my ex said she wouldn't marry me unless I got out. What she really wanted was to be married to a cop."

"Isn't that weird? I mean, I thought being a cop's wife was supposed to be so stressful and all."

"It's a lifestyle. Her dad was a cop, and both her brothers. She wanted me in the family business."

"And you just went along?"

"Seemed like the thing to do."

"So you chose a career to please a girl who wound up dumping you anyway?"

"Truer words were never said."

"That's awful."

"It might have been, I guess. But the fact is I love what I do, and twenty years in the navy would have been about fifteen years too long. So there you go. Sometimes you make the right choice for the wrong reason."

"So how did she tell you?"

"Ah. You want gory details."

"Naturally."

"She fixed us breakfast, ate some pancakes, and told me she was leaving me while I was washing the dishes."

"What did you do?"

"I threw up. Then I moved in with my partner. Slept on his couch for a month while I thought things over, and in the end I decided to get out of Dodge."

"Why?"

"Like I told you before, she was banging my lieutenant. He was married too, and kids. Man, what a mess . . . I guess I just didn't want to stick around for the cleanup. And besides, my mom needed the company."

"What happened to the ex?"

"They shacked up for a while, but he ended up getting back with his wife. Last thing I heard she was seeing a captain, sleeping her way up the chain of command. I figure sooner or later she'll wind up with the chief of police."

"You miss her?"

"Nah."

"You with anybody else since her?"

"Nah."

"Why not?"

"A boy's best friend is his mother."

"You realize that's from *Psycho*." He laughed, a deep chuckle that seemed to clear the dregs of memory. "Pardon me if I don't go take a shower now."

"Your turn."

"Do I have to?"

"Unless you want me to call you a chicken."

"You want another beer?"

"Quit stalling."

"This is perverse. But okay, a deal's a deal. Here goes. When I was working at a paper in western Mass, I met this guy. His name was Adam Ellroy. I fell for him like a ton of bricks, but in the end he went back to California to the love of his life. I move to Gabriel, she winds up giving him the shaft, and he comes back east to get away from it all. We sort of get back together, and the next thing I know he's dead at the bottom of the gorge. Everybody thought he'd offed himself, but I couldn't let it go. So I didn't."

"And you and your crazy friends tracked down the killer. GPD's still smarting about that, you know."

"Really?"

"Really. To put it in your parlance, you scooped them."

"Goodie for me."

"But you're leaving out the best part."

I took a swig of my beer. I knew what he was going to say. "Which is?"

"That the person who killed him turned out to be . . ."

"Stop. Just drop it."

"Alex, come on. You should be proud of yourself. I heard you really kicked butt."

"Can we talk about something else? I'm willing to share every detail of my miserable love life. Want to hear about how my college boyfriend dumped me for a two-hundred-pound lesbian? It wasn't pretty."

"This really gets you."

"Are you crazy? Of course it does. It was the worst thing that ever happened to me."

"But you did the right thing. You nailed the son of a bitch. You avenged your friend's death. You got justice for him."

" 'Avenged'? How melodramatic."

He stopped and stared at me. "There's something I don't know about this."

"There's plenty. Look, I'm not as tough as you are, okay? Can we just drop it?" He looked disappointed in me. Why the hell was he so interested in all this, anyway? And why did I care what he thought? "Listen, last year was a goddamn nightmare, okay? I nearly got myself killed. But I was lucky. I only got myself just short of raped."

"Fuck." He said the word under his breath, and I realized I'd never heard him really swear before.

"And for your information, I've barely even talked about it in the whole goddamn year since it happened, not that I don't *think* about it every five seconds. My parents wanted to pay for a shrink, but I didn't see the point. What am I supposed to do, somehow 'come to terms' with the fact that one of the best people I've ever met is stone-cold dead, and the guy who did it is reading the *New Yorker* up in Dannemora? The only thing I regret is that I didn't kill the bastard when I had the chance. I could have, you know. I hit him, just enough to knock him out. But when he was lying there unconscious and I was waiting for the cops to come, I could have killed him, and no one would have been the wiser. They would have called it self-defense. Sometime I picture myself hitting him over and over, watching his brains spill out on the carpet . . ." I was seeing it then, feeling my arm swing down hard. I got a jolt of pure hate that fueled what I can only describe as blood lust. Then I snapped out of it. "Christ. Maybe I do need a shrink. You must think *I'm* the homicidal maniac."

"Actually, I'd only think you were a maniac if you *didn't* want to kill him."

There were tears prickling at my eyes, and I swiped at them, hoping he didn't notice. "Would you have done it? If someone murdered someone you love, would you kill him if you had the chance?"

"I don't know. I hope I never have to find out."

"Have you ever killed anyone?"

"Yes."

"More than one?"

"Yes."

"Are you sorry?"

"No."

"Line of duty?"

"That's right."

"Cops or navy?"

"Both."

"What did it feel like?"

"It felt like work. It wasn't personal."

"Which is why it bothers me more *not* to have killed someone than it bothers you to have actually done it?"

"That's very perceptive. And probably true."

"Great. If I hadn't given you my speech about the evils of smoking, I'd probably be asking you for a cigarette right about now. See? I told you I equate smoking with hysteria."

"I'm sorry I pried. I didn't want to upset you. Really, I apologize. I suppose I thought that . . ."

"If I could dish it out, I could take it?"

"Yeah."

"You'd think," I said. "But it ain't necessarily so."

10

THE WEEK WOUND DOWN, AND THE DEADLINE PASSED without the killer's letter appearing in print. Or was he the killer? That was the question, and the cops had come to the conclusion that the answer was no. Or rather, probably not. All week, I'd been playing mind games with myself about what exactly the letter writer had meant. Did he mean a week from when he *mailed* the letter, which we had no way of knowing? Or from when we got it, which *he* had no way of knowing? And could the cops be wrong? My desk is right across from the police scanner, which sits on what used to be Junior's desk—much longer ago, it was Adam's—and I constantly had an ear cocked for something horrible.

Not that I spent much time in the newsroom. After that episode at the bio building, the animal-rights movement on campus exploded. The town's hippie weekly ran an editorial calling it "a watershed in the history of nonhuman rights on this planet" and deeming the screaming pigs "a moving elegy for the millions of lives lost every day in homage to the supremacy of *Homo sapiens*."

Have I mentioned that I haven't eaten meat since I was twelve?

Anyway, that editorial rallied the town's socially conscious legions, who are always up for a good march. Before you could swing a fistulated frog around your head they'd pledged solidarity with the students, and by Friday there were five hundred people in front of the university administration building, chanting enough to make up for the last silent protest and maybe four more afterward. They'd erected a great pile of products made by companies who do animal testing, and a few diehards were about to light it on fire when someone pointed out that the fumes could kill everyone within a hundred yards. They'd held up placards of monkeys getting electrocuted and bunnies with their brains exposed, and although I'm supposed to remain all journalistic and unbiased, it made me want to dissect somebody.

The fracas netted me a page-one story, which jumped to page four and ran with two sidebars. One was a rundown of the various fields on campus that do animal testing, listed in bulleted paragraphs—the sort of journalistic Chicklets that readers have come to expect these days (thank you very much, *USA Today*). The other sidebar was a profile of the leader of Benson Animal Anarchists, a former biology grad student named David Loew who'd shucked off his life after a bona fide crisis of conscience: he'd been in the midst of his dissertation research when, for no particular reason, it occurred to him that over the course of his experiments two hundred lab mice were going to die. "It just struck me," I'd quoted him as saying, in the elevated language he seemed to favor. "For me to earn this PhD, this mere piece of paper, two hundred lives would be sacrificed. And I thought, with all of the other researchers on campus, all of the degrees they grant, there had to be many other people doing the same thing—thousands and thousands of deaths in the name of science. But they were just lab animals, so no one cared. And all of a sudden, I cared."

It was his "personal epiphany" (his words, not mine), and it flipped him to the other side with the zeal of a true convert. He'd dropped out and gotten a job stacking soy milk and nutritional yeast at one of Gabriel's four health food stores. He'd also cut off contact with his parents who, as luck would have it, owned a half-dozen Burger King franchises outside Milwaukee. He wouldn't speak to them again, he told me, "until they agree to divest from the economy of death." Nice.

"Whoa, *man*," Mad said. "How'd you like to be that guy's mother?" We were back in our window seat in the Citizen Kane, unwinding after a particularly migraine-inducing workday. Mad had been gentleman enough to allow me the evening's first tirade. "What does he send her for Mother's Day? A funeral wreath?"

"Maybe a card with pictures of penned-up veal."

"This story's really driving you up the wall."

I raised my glass. "As well as driving me to drink. And get this. You know what I realized today while I was writing my story? The acronym for Benson Animal Anarchists spells out BAA. Like a sheep. Like I bet *that* was an accident."

"That's almost as bad as that gay rights group last year. What was it called—the one that got their own building?"

"The Benson Gay and Lesbian Action Detail. B-GLAD. As in, 'be glad you're different.'"

"That cutesy shit makes me want to kill somebody."

"I don't think that was the effect they were after."

He picked up my drink and sniffed it. "What is that putrid concoction, anyway?"

"Midori sour. Sour mix and melon liqueur. It's yummy. Want a taste?"

"No way. It could turn a guy all queer."

"Mad." I looked around to make sure no one had overheard.

"Don't worry, Bernier. The P.C. police aren't on duty in here, thank the fucking Lord."

"Someday you're going to get your ass kicked for talking like that."

"And the broccoli-crunching sissy who tries it is going to get his ass kicked right back, only worse." He started to roll up his sleeve.

"Oh, Mad, not *again.*"

Undeterred, he pulled back his blue oxford to reveal a chiseled bicep and proceeded to flex. "Behold. Witness the power of physical exercise."

"Okay, fine, I behold the power. I'm in awe. Now would you please put your shirt back on? People are starting to stare."

"And well they should." He rolled his sleeve back down. "You want another round?"

"Oh, God, yes."

"What do you call that swill again?"

"Midori sour."

"You chicks are a pain in the ass." He was about to get up when Mack the bartender saw us, anticipated our desires after several years of second rounds (and third rounds, and fourth, and give-me-your-keys), and delivered the drinks himself. Mack also owns the place, and Mad and O'Shaunessey are putting his kids through college.

"Okay, manly one, it's your turn. How was your day on the cop beat?"

"You little vixen. You're just thrilled that this baa-baa story is keeping you from my clutches, where you belong."

"And you could just as well be covering it yourself, Mr. Wizard. It's turning into something way more up your alley than mine. Or aren't you the science reporter anymore?"

"Rolled up my alley today, actually. Bill wants me to do some big package on the science of animal testing, nitty-gritty kind of thing. Wire might pick it up."

"And he wants you to write the whole damn thing while you're working on the murder story."

"I can handle it, baby. I'm a reporting *machine*." He reached for his cuff button.

"Mad, I swear if you try to roll that sleeve up again I'm going to staple it to your wrist."

He smirked. "Your friend Emma doesn't mind a man showing a little muscle."

"Are you about to kiss and tell?"

"Nah."

"So did you file on the cop thing or what? I didn't see anything on the story budget."

"Don't rub it in. I haven't gotten jack. Everybody's sniffing around, trying to break the name of the first vic.

But you know what? I'm starting to think the cops don't even know."

"You think? Last I heard they were waiting to notify next of kin. But that was ages ago."

"Right. And once you ID somebody, it only takes a couple of days at the most to track down their family or else figure out they haven't got any. You just get the local cops on it and that's that. So you know what I think? They thought they knew who she was and it turned out they were wrong. But nobody's talking."

"They'd hardly advertise their own mistake."

"Why don't you ask your friend Cody?"

"He's not my friend. And he wouldn't tell me anyway."

"Anybody else you know might crack?"

"Zippo. So what are we gonna do? Sit here and get shit-faced until they call the next press conference?"

"I've had worse offers."

"Come on, we're smart kids. We went to college. Let's think about this for a minute. How can it possibly be so hard to identify a dead girl?"

"I'd rather think about that cute little number out there."

I peered through the plate-glass window to check her out. There were a dozen girls slacking en masse on the Gabriel Green, our beloved pedestrian mall that, contrary to its name, is entirely paved. "Which one?"

"Red tank top."

"The one with both her bra straps showing?"

"That's the one."

"Mad, that girl isn't a day over fifteen. She was born during the *Reagan administration*, for Chrissake."

"Cool. I enjoyed the eighties."

"Can we please talk about the story? Come on, let's just brainstorm a little. Then I'll go home to my dog and you can get arrested for statutory rape."

He sighed into the bottom of his beer mug. "Have it your way."

"Thank you. Okay. Here's what I'm wondering. How can a girl just get lost? I mean, think about how the first girl was described. Healthy, nice clothes, good teeth, expensive boots. People like that don't live in refrigerator boxes. They have families. They have jobs. They have *connections*. When they go missing, somebody looks for them, right?"

"And since the cops have had weeks to scour every report of every missing girl in the U.S. and Canada, she wasn't one of them."

"That's what I'm thinking."

"So if the cops couldn't find her, how can two lazy drunks do any better?"

"Come on, Mad, we're just free-associating. Don't you want to play?"

"Do I have to watch you drink another goddamn Missouri sour?"

"It's Midori, and why yes, I'd love another one. Thanks very much."

He rolled his eyes and waved to Mack. "Okay, I'm listening."

"Let's think about this logically for a minute. Why in the world would a girl like our victim not be reported missing?"

"You want me to answer that?"

"Please."

He rubbed the back of his neck. "All right. Okay.

Lemme see here. Well, what if she's all alone in the world? No family, no friends, no job, no nothing. There'd be nobody to miss her."

"Sure, but let's face it. Even the guys who collect cans on the Green have at least one friend who'd worry about them if they disappeared. This girl had resources. She wasn't dressed like some transient."

"What if they weren't her clothes?"

"Man, I never thought about that. What if that's true? But wait. She wasn't starving or anything, and the description said her teeth had been straightened. Doesn't a few thousand dollars worth of braces mean she was at least middle class?"

"Maybe she hit the skids."

"Yeah, but let's not forget that this guy seems to have a pattern. His victims are physically similar, and the second girl was no hooker. She worked at the Gap, for Pete's sake. You can't get more middle class than that."

"How come all my ideas get shot down?"

"Sorry. I'm just trying to be logical. It doesn't come naturally."

"Well, you're probably right anyway. Which brings us right back where we started."

"How does a regular, decent girl fall off the radar?"

We thought about it for a while. It was getting on nine o'clock, and the lull following the after-work crowd was ending as Bessler students straggled in the door in twos and threes. Several of the girls sized up Mad with looks so brazen they seemed to come from another, sexier planet than the one I live on. These days, the only things I can summon up that much lust for come topped with melted cheese.

"I got it," Mad said. "How about this: what if she wasn't the only victim? What if her family was offed too? There'd be nobody to report her missing."

"And also nobody to report that a whole *family* had gone missing?"

"Oh. Right. I didn't think about that."

"Minor detail."

"This is no fun. Why don't we do this on company time? Why are we wasting valuable booze-and-babe time?" He leered at a gaggle of flat-chested blondes drinking screwdrivers at one corner of the bar. One of them caught his eye and gave him a look that I'd swear said *lose the chunky brunette and come on over.*

"Okay, I'm no match for your sloth. Have a lovely evening. But would you do me a favor and at least make sure her fake ID *looks* convincing? Maybe the judge will be more sympathetic if you card her before you bang her."

"Don't worry about me, sister. It only takes two to tango, and I'll make sure she has nothing to complain about afterward. No witnesses, no case."

I got up to leave and was halfway down the window seat steps when I stopped cold. "Wait a second."

"Get lost, Bernier. You're cramping my style."

"No, listen. What if that's it?"

The blonde was looking at him. He was looking back. "Huh?"

"What if there were no witnesses? What if the person who would have reported her missing was the one who killed her?"

That got him. "Jesus. You think?"

I sat back down. "It's one way that might explain things."

"A damn nasty way."

"Yeah, but not a particularly surprising one. Crazy killers make good copy, but statistically a woman is a lot more likely to be killed by her husband than by some stranger."

"Could it really happen, though? Wouldn't someone else miss her? Her family and friends?"

"You'd think. It would depend on the circumstances—who's still alive, how close people are. Take, I don't know . . . Melissa. Her parents are both dead. She hates her brother's guts. Let's say I want to off her. I tell everybody, 'Oh, Melissa had a meltdown and went to stay with her relatives in Greece for a while.' Would they buy it?"

"About Melissa? You bet. From you? Sure."

"From someone *close* to her, right?"

"Right. But what about the, you know, corpus delicti?"

"You make sure there's no easy way to identify her. As far as I know Melissa has never been fingerprinted, so you probably couldn't ID her that way. You dump her someplace she might never be found, or at least not for a while. You do it far away from home, so it's unlikely that even if she is found and the media runs a sketch like we did, there's no one around who would recognize her."

"Which would mean that both the killer and the first victim don't come from upstate New York, or even anywhere in the Northeast."

"If my little theory is right." I caught Mad peering over my shoulder toward the bar. "She still there?"

He shook his head. "I guess she wasn't interested in a three-way."

"Poor dear."

"Hold on a minute, Bernier. Oh, fuck, I can't believe you got me interested in this. But I think you're blowing off a major point—like the, you know, *physical evidence*. I mean, don't forget what this guy did to her. He strangled her with a dog collar, for Chrissake. He probably made her walk on a goddamn leash. He left her naked with all her clothes folded next to her. Those are not the actions of some guy who wants to smoke his wife so he can shack up with his secretary."

"I'm not saying it wasn't a crazy person, Mad. I'm just saying maybe it was a crazy person she knew."

"Man, and I thought *I* was a sick bastard."

"Because you're a skirt-chasing alcoholic? Come on, Mad. Your neuroses are relatively benign. This guy puts nuts like us way on the sunny side of normal."

"Nice of him."

"You know, I wonder if we're onto something with all this."

"Think you should share it with your buddy Cody?"

"I'm sure it's already occurred to him."

"Do I detect a note of admiration?"

"He's a decent cop."

"But is he any good in the sack?"

"Do you have any idea how old that joke is getting?"

"Sorry. I'm not at the top of my form."

"Riddle me something else. Are we saying that this guy killed someone he could cover up and then, like, branched out? Came here to dump the body and started murdering strangers? Just for the fun of it? And wrote letters to the paper just to scare people even more?"

"Damned if I know."

"Jesus, Mad. If we're anywhere near right, he started off as an amateur, and he's turning into a pro."

We stayed there in the window seat for a while, mulling the nasty possibilities over and over again. None of it put me in the mood to take any stupid chances, so when it came time to leave I used the bar phone to make sure someone was home, just like the cops had told me to. The machine answered. *You have reached Steve, Emma, Marci, C.A., Alex, Tipsy, Nanki-Poo, Shakespeare* . . . I hung up. The message was in Steve's voice, calculated to fend off mashers, but it actually made us sound like his harem. I gritted my teeth, put a finger in my other ear so I could hear over Roger Daltry singing "Pinball Wizard" at top volume, and dialed the police station for an escort. It felt like I was thirteen years old again, asking Dad to pick me up at the Cinema Four.

I sat back down next to Mad, who was in no shape to drive anybody anywhere. Five minutes later there was a rap on the window, and I turned to find Cody on the Green, motioning at me to come out. He didn't look happy. "I think my ride's here," I said, and pecked Mad on the cheek. He waved me off and went back to his pitcher. When I got outside, I saw that Cody was wearing his jeans and leather jacket ensemble, so he wasn't still on duty. "What are *you* doing here?"

"You know, every time we run into each other, that's the first thing you say."

"I meant, are you supposed to be my escort? And how did you get here so fast?"

"I was on my way out of the station house when you called. Alex, we need to talk."

He sounded more serious than I'd ever heard him,

which was quite an accomplishment considering his flair for gravitas. "What's going on?"

"Where's your car?"

"Behind the *Monitor*. But I know better than to drive after three drinks."

"I'll take you home then."

"I tried there already. Nobody's home. That's why I called for a baby-sitter. So maybe we should call a uniformed . . ."

"Your roommates are on their way there. Some of them, anyway."

I stopped in my tracks. "How do you know? What is it? Come on, Cody, tell me."

"Have you been home lately?"

Another odd question. "This week, not much. Just to sleep and shower. The animal-testing story has had me running all over the place. Why?"

"I'd left word with the desk sergeant that I was to be informed if anyone filed a missing persons report on a girl who came even close to fitting the killer's profile. They just paged me. Something's come up." I didn't have the guts to prod him. I waited until he started talking again. "One of your roommates filed a report. Seems one of the girls hasn't been seen since Wednesday night. Missed class yesterday and today. Her family hasn't heard from her."

The three Midori sours started churning in my stomach. "Oh, my God. We were wrong. We must have been wrong. We didn't publish that goddamn letter, and he went out and did just what he threatened to do."

"We don't know that. There may be a perfectly logical explanation."

"But your people were supposed to watch her. They were supposed to guard her like they were guarding me. Oh, Jesus, poor Marci . . ."

"Alex, it isn't Marci who's missing. It's C.A."

I gaped at him. "C.A.? That's impossible. No one messes with C.A. She was raised in the army, for Chrissake. She knows how to protect herself."

"Like I said, she could walk in the door tonight. But she's been gone more than twenty-four hours, and your friend Marci called the police."

I felt my shoulder muscles relax. "Marci does have a hysterical side. She's been known to overreact."

"That very well may be the case. But there's something else odd."

"What?"

"Her dog is missing too."

11

I KNEW SHE'D BEEN ABDUCTED. I WAS SURE FROM THE minute I looked through her stuff, because it was obvious she hadn't gone willingly. For one thing, her dad's army duffel was still on the top shelf of her closet, and none of us had ever seen her travel without it. We couldn't find any of her clothes missing except the ones she'd been wearing. And most importantly, her dog's medication was still in the bathroom cabinet.

"What kind of medicine is it?" Cody asked. All five of us—Steve, Marci, Emma, Cody, and I—were sitting in the living room. Marci looked as though she'd been crying all night, and Emma was drinking a martini out of a jumbo plastic cup. With Steve there, it struck me that it was the first time in a long time all of my housemates had sat down together. Then I remembered C.A. was gone, and I felt like crying myself.

"It's enrofloxacin," Emma said. "It's an antibiotic. Nanki-Poo has prostatitis, so he's got to take it for three more weeks."

"Can he live without it?"

"Live? Oh, certainly. But the infection will come back, and then you have to begin the course of treatment all over again."

"What I need to know is, would C.A. have left this behind? Forgotten it, maybe?"

"I wouldn't think so. The dog's been taking it twice a day for three weeks already."

"Could she have another bottle of it with her?"

Marci shook her head. "It's expensive. We get a vet student discount, but only one bottle at a time."

"What kind of car does she drive?"

"Like I told the policeman before, she doesn't have a car. She rides her bike everywhere." Marci started sniffling, and Steve got up to hand her another box of Kleenex. As he crossed the room, I noticed he wasn't too overcome with grief to check out the pecs beneath Cody's plaid cotton shirt.

"We're going to do everything we can to find her," Cody said. "We have officers out canvassing, both downtown and up on campus. We've sent out alerts to the surrounding counties. Marci, I want you to know you did the right thing by contacting us immediately. The earlier we get the report, the more likely it is we'll find someone. You said her parents were coming into town?"

"They said they were coming the moment we called them," Emma said. "They were so very certain it wasn't like her to go off without a word."

"Her father's a colonel," Steve interjected. "We used to joke about how he was, you know, 'a full bird,' because I'm an ornithologist . . ." He got up and retrieved the Kleenex.

"Her mom's so upset," Marci said. "Not just C.A. gone, but poor Nanki-Poo . . ."

Cody looked a little put off. "They're upset about the *dog*?"

"No doubt it will seem quite senseless, Detective," Emma said by way of explanation. "But when he was younger, the dog was one of her grandmother's show champions. She only let C.A. have him because the dog really bonded to her one summer. They were flying him back home to Ohio in a few weeks."

"Why?"

"C.A.'s grandmother was insisting that she breed him one last time before the neutering. I gathered that there was a certain female coming into heat that she'd matched him up with."

"Neutering?" The word seemed to make him a tad uncomfortable.

"I'm sure this is far more information than you wanted, but Nanki-Poo suffered from a condition called prostatic hyperplasia. It's quite common in older dogs who haven't been neutered. It can lead to chronic infections, and sometimes the animal has trouble . . . hmm . . . 'lifting his leg,' as they say. It's quite treatable, of course, but only by castration."

That particular word seemed to bother him even more than the last one. No wonder women like to say it so much. "And C.A.'s family asked her to hold off on the operation until he could, um, father one more litter?"

"That's right."

Cody rose. "Please let her parents know we'd like to talk with them as soon as they get here. And if you remember anything, anything at all that might help us find her, don't hesitate to call. Middle of the night, it doesn't matter. Alex, will you walk me out?"

We went to his car, but he made no move to get in. "Are you going to be all right?" he asked. "You look pretty ragged."

"I'm okay. I like C.A., but the truth is I barely know her. Marci and Emma and Steve are much closer to her than I am. But I'll be honest with you, Cody. I have a terrible feeling about this."

"I'll be honest with you too. So do I."

"Do you think you'll find her alive?"

He seemed about to backpedal and say something comforting, then pulled himself up short. "I don't know."

"What are the odds?"

"I wouldn't want to guess."

"I just can't help but feel like we're responsible somehow. If the paper had run that miserable letter, maybe this wouldn't have happened. We were warned, weren't we?"

"We rolled the dice. Quantico made its best prediction, and we followed it. The FBI profile said it was a hoax. But it's not an exact science. I wish it were."

"You've got to find her. Please, you've got to."

"We're doing everything we can. But, Alex, don't do this to yourself. You have to remember that whoever killed those girls doesn't play by the rules. I don't know if he took your friend or not. But I do know this much. He's a killer. Don't think running that letter or not running that letter would have made a damn bit of difference. This guy is going to kill whenever he gets the urge. Now, I hope to God he didn't take your friend. But if he did, there's no way it has anything to do with you."

"How can you possibly know that? I found the second

body. He was there then, Cody. I could *feel* him. And then I got that letter. Maybe this was no accident, no random abduction. Maybe he took C.A. because she's my house-mate. Maybe he's playing with me. Maybe . . ."

I could feel myself edging into hysteria, and Cody knew it too. He grabbed my shoulders and shook me gently. "Ssh . . . come on, that's enough. We don't even know if she was taken by the same person, or if she was taken at all. I know it's hard, but you have to keep your head together. You can't let the fear get the better of you. Alex, listen to me. I can't promise you we'll find your friend, but I promise you this much. Nothing is going to happen to you. I'll protect you. I swear. Do you believe me?"

I looked up at him. He had so much muscle, it would have taken a backhoe to dislodge him from my person. "At this point, I think it would be a fatal blow to your ego if I got snuffed."

He cracked the beginning of a smile. "Good. Because there's something else I want to talk to you about, and I need you to focus if we're going to move quickly."

I took a steadying breath. "Okay."

"We think that whoever took the first two girls kept them alive for a while so he could . . . mistreat them. We're not sure how long, maybe just a day or two. But if we're dealing with the same person, then your friend's best chance is for us to get her face in front of as many people as we can, as fast as we can. We're setting up a po-lice hotline, and we want you to run her picture in the paper. Tomorrow. Can you do that?"

I shook off the tears that still threatened to pounce. "Give me your cell phone." I dialed Bill's direct number in the newsroom. It was eleven, and the editors would be going insane in anticipation of the one A.M. press run. I couldn't have picked a worse time to talk them into messing with page one, but they did it. Two minutes later I was in the car with Cody, delivering a head shot of C.A. to the newsroom. On the way I called the news director of the local TV station at home and talked him into cutting a missing persons bulletin first thing in the morning, to run as a public service announcement whenever the cable stations had airtime.

When we got to the *Monitor* Cody waited while I ran inside to have the photo scanned on one of the newsroom layout computers. I was on my way out the door when Bill yelled after me. "Bernier, where the hell do you think you're going?"

"Over to the . . ."

"Fuck it. I need a goddamn story to go with this picture. You got me to rip page one, remember?"

It was obvious enough, but I hadn't thought of it. "But I have to . . ."

"I have no cop reporter. Mad is nobody knows where. Everybody else filed and went home like good little children. You're here. So write."

"Okay. Just let me go over to the . . ."

"Bernier, I have no fucking page-one story. Do not take a step until you file one, or I'm dropping in the old one. *Now*."

I sprinted across the newsroom to my desk, opened up a new file, and started typing. I stopped long enough to call Cody. "I'm still up here. I need to write a story to go with the picture. Can you give me ten minutes? Yeah, I can do it in ten. But listen, I need you to do me a favor. Call the Benson student paper." I gave him the number.

"They're on pretty much the same deadline as us. Ask to talk to the city editor—no, wait, they call it the news editor. Tell her about C.A. and that we'll be bringing by a photo in twenty minutes. Oh, and if she gives you a problem, mention that the *Monitor* already has the story and is running it on page one tomorrow morning, picture and all. Wait, before you go, give me a quote. Something about the investigation." I typed as he talked. "Okay. Fine. I'll call you back in five to check facts on this thing."

I pounded out the story, called Cody back to confirm everything, and filed it with Bill. He read it with speed-bag jabs of his pinkie on the SCROLL DOWN key and slapped on a headline: VET STUDENT REPORTED MISSING. "Fine. Get out of here. And, Alex?" I stopped. "Sorry about your friend."

For Bill, that was a Hallmark card wrapped in a valentine. "Thanks."

I met Cody in the back parking lot. He was sitting on the hood of his car, smoking a cigarette. "Give me one of those goddamn things."

"Alex, believe me, you don't want to . . ." I shut him up with a look, and he even held out his lighter.

"Let's go. The student paper office is just down the street. They aren't owned by the university, you know. They're independent. That's why they don't suck."

"I'm not taking you anyplace until you promise me one thing."

"Okay, I swear I won't take up smoking again forever."

"Not that. Jesus, Alex, look at this place." He gestured at the *Monitor* parking lot, with its Hoffa-era loading dock, Dumpsters, delivery trucks, and trailer full of spare parts for the pressroom. If some crazy killer wanted to play hide and seek, this was the place for it. "Promise me you won't come out here alone at night. When you leave work, I damn well want you to have an escort. Get some-one from the paper to walk you to your car. Drive with your doors locked. Call home first to make sure some-one's there. If no one is, call the cops."

"Deal."

"You swear?"

"What did you expect me to do, argue? I'm not stupid, and I'm definitely not suicidal. I'm as attached to living as the next guy."

"Okay. Let's go."

We waited while they scanned C.A.'s picture at the Benson *Bugle*, then dropped it off in the mailbox at the TV station. "They'll take a shot of it to use on the air in the morning. We can get it back then if we need it."

"You really thrive under pressure, don't you?"

"Let's just say I work well on deadline."

"Where to now?"

"That's it. Unless you count how badly I need another drink."

"Then let's go scare one up."

"You must think I'm a total lush."

"Doesn't it go with the job?"

"Supposedly. But don't they need you back at the cop shop?"

"I'm in first thing in the morning. We've got people looking for her, but there isn't a whole lot you can do overnight. You can't exactly go knocking on people's doors at one A.M. asking if they've seen her. And if I don't get some sleep I'm not going to be any good to anybody."

"Then you can just drop me home."

"Probably should, but the truth is I'm wide awake. And anyway, I think we both could use some winding down."

I looked at my watch. "Bars close in twenty minutes."

"Your place?"

"Everybody's either crying or drunk. I don't think I can deal. I just feel like I need a couple of hours to . . ."

"Not think about death?"

"How did you know?"

"Occupational hazard. How about we go to my place then?"

"Won't that be a little . . . weird?"

"Sleeping with the enemy again? Unchaperoned?"

"Sounds silly when you put it that way."

Cody lived on the top floor of what used to be a big one-family house six blocks from the police station, on the outskirts of what passes for the ghetto around here. The house was well kept up, though, and the yard was free of forty-ouncers, possibly because it was surrounded by a spiky wooden fence.

"We ought to be quiet. Landlords have little kids."

He unlocked the door at the top of the stairs to reveal a comfy-casual living room with an overstuffed couch, a matching chair, and stacks of newspapers overflowing the coffee table. It took me a second to realize there was also a very fluffy gray-and-white dog by the door; he was sitting there so quietly, I hadn't even noticed. "This is Zeke?" I let him sniff my open hand. "What a hunk." I bent down and kissed him on the snout, leaving a pucker of brick lipstick on his muzzle. "Doesn't he move?"

"Zeke, okay," Cody said in the commanding voice they teach you in dog school, and that I'd never been able to manage. The dog stood up, did a yoga stretch, and followed us into the kitchen. "Want a beer? I don't think I have any wine in this place."

"Do you have anything stronger?"

"What did you have in mind?"

"I'd sell my soul for a gin and tonic."

"I think I can swing that. No limes, though." He held up a plastic lemon.

"Primitive, but adequate."

He mixed me a drink, let the dog out, and opened up a Sam Adams. We sprawled on the couch, and he lit us each a cigarette. "When this pack is empty, we're both through. Agreed?"

"When you catch this bastard, we're through. How's that?"

"Dangerous thing for me to say—'I'll clean up my act when this case is over.' Because there's always another case, so there's always another excuse to keep up the bad habits."

"But this is the first time you've even thought about quitting. Hardly a string of broken promises."

"Good point. All right. It's a pact."

We sat there for a while without talking, just listening to the Eagles on his stereo. The gin and tonic didn't turn out to be half bad, even with the faux lemon; you have to respect a guy who keeps Tanqueray and Schweppes around the house. Maybe Cody was more civilized than I'd figured.

"Cody, listen. I don't really want to talk about C.A. Not talking about it seems very much the point right now. But there's something I wanted to tell you. And before I do, let me just make it clear that you don't have to tell me diddly if you don't want to. I'm not trying to dig here. But let me ask you one thing off the record. Have you ID'ed the first victim yet?"

He seemed to be debating whether or not to tell me anything. Finally he just said, "No."

"And you've checked all the missing persons reports for the U.S. and Canada? And runaways that would have been the right age?"

"Of course."

"Well, Mad and I were brainstorming at the bar tonight, trying to figure out how that could possibly be— how a girl you'd think would have friends and family could just disappear without anyone reporting her. And we were thinking—you've probably thought of this already—but we were wondering whether she might have been killed by the same person who would have filed the report in the first place. I mean, how else can you explain a person just getting . . . misplaced like that? How could there be no one left to miss her?"

"That's what we've been trying to figure out. Off the record."

"So maybe once you figure out who *she* is, you'll also know who *he* is."

"It's possible. And I think we'd better change the subject."

Then the doorbell rang. "Who could that be at this hour? Jealous girlfriend?"

"Jealous boyfriend." He jogged downstairs, opened the outer door, and came back with Zeke.

"Do not tell me the dog rang the doorbell. How the hell did you teach him that?"

He grinned. "Basic training principles. Positive reinforcement. Discipline. And a whole lot of hot dogs."

"He's fantastic."

"Zeke, sit." The dog did. "Lie down." He did that too, then rolled over, begged, gave both paws, and spoke. Cody looked absurdly proud.

"Show-off. Does he play dead too?"

"Never. He has his dignity."

"You can leave that jar of biscuits there? And he won't eat them all?"

"Of course not."

"And where's all the dog hair, anyway? Doesn't he shed?"

"I brush him. And he's not allowed on the furniture. He sleeps on his bed in the corner."

"Wow. My dog would consider this a fascist state."

"You just have to establish who's the alpha male. Want another drink?"

"God yes." He went back into the kitchen, and I stretched out on the floor with Zeke. "Does he really sleep in the corner all night? All by himself?" Cody didn't answer. "Or is there an occasional breakdown in discipline?"

"My ex didn't care for dogs in the bed," he said from the other room. "Or anywhere near her, for that matter."

"Jesus, Cody, how did you end up with this chick?"

"I was young and stupid."

"You still didn't answer my question. Does Zeke really get exiled to the living room?" He came back and handed me my drink, filled up to the very brim. "Well?" He wouldn't look me in the eye.

"Okay. Maybe, once in a while . . ."

"He sleeps with you every night, doesn't he?"

"Yeah."

"Cody, you big *softy*. Words can't express how much I approve."

"My sheets smell like his feet."

"What could be better?"

"You are one strange lady. You drunk enough yet?"

"Not quite."

"Are you going to drink all my gin?"

"I might."

"What if I take advantage of you?"

"I'll take my chances, Boy Scout."

12

FOUR DAYS WENT BY, AND NOTHING. NO SIGN OF C.A., AND no sign of her dog either. We'd even run a picture of Nanki-Poo as a second-day story—"vet student and pooch still missing," that sort of thing—but so far none of the calls to the hotline had panned out, at least as far as I knew. I hadn't asked Cody if they had any leads, but I had a feeling if they did, he'd break protocol and tell me.

There was some good news, though. The animal-rights story died down for a while, which helped me hold on to my sanity for the time being. With my roommate missing and creepy letters coming to my newsroom cubbyhole, I wasn't sure I could handle more pictures of fetal pigs. Mad and I were supposed to be covering the murders together (him officially, me not), but Bill had an attack of humanity and sent me out on a few quick-hit stories. I did a piece on some Benson students who were building bicycles out of spare parts and giving them to needy kids, and one on a guy who does a cable-access show on the JFK assassination (one conspiracy theory per episode), and another on a cop who was retiring after twenty years of directing rush-hour traffic at Gabriel's most hated intersection, a notorious eight-road snarl nicknamed The Octopus.

That Tuesday, I wasn't working on anything much more exciting. My assignment for the day was a piece on a couple battling the landmarks preservation commission for the right to fix half the roof on their house. The roof was white, and part of it was leaking, but the commission told them if they replaced it they could only do it in the "historically faithful" color now required of the whole preservation district, which was dark brown. (The white roof had, apparently, been put on during those crazy fifties.) The couple wanted a variance so they could fix the roof. The commission told them to go to hell, so they were appealing. My original story, by the way, included the phrase "Oreo cookie" to describe one possible architectural outcome.

I was looking up the number of the head of the city planning office when the scanner went off. "Emergency control to Gabriel monitors. Report of a body in Blue Heron Wood, approximately a quarter mile southeast of the main entrance. Subject is a female Caucasian, appears to be . . ."

The announcement just stopped, as though the dispatcher had been cut off. I'd been sitting on top of that scanner for nearly four years, and I'd never heard it happen before. Sure, sometimes the dispatchers trip over their own tongues and start over, but this sounded like the microphone had actually been snatched from her.

"Mad, did you hear what I just heard?"

"Yeah."

"It's C.A. It's got to be."

"Take it easy, Alex. Don't jump to . . ."

"Did you ever hear anything like that? They found another body. There's no way they'd want that over the regular dispatch radio. The announcer must have screwed up, and somebody grabbed the mike."

He didn't try to argue with me. "I'll tell Bill."

We ran out to the parking lot and jumped in my car. My left wrist was getting better, but it was still weak and I didn't dare drive too fast. Blue Heron Wood is Benson's ornithology preserve, thirty acres of land five miles from central campus. There's a study center overlooking a pond, and trails that intertwine throughout the property. It's one of the few parklike areas around Gabriel that doesn't allow dogs, because they'd scare off the birds. I'd spent a fair amount of time there, though, because the trails are perfect for cross-country skiing—and, well, I brought Shakespeare anyway.

"Where are you going?" Mad asked when I drove past the road leading to the main entrance. "You missed the turn."

"No point in trying to go in the front door. Cops'll be all over the place. We won't get within five hundred yards."

We took a left a mile farther and skirted the preserve's outer edge. Blue Heron is much wider than it is deep, and by parking along the road on the far side we'd be just as close to the location the dispatcher had described as we would have been by going in the front.

We started hiking in, picking our way around the gopher holes and fallen trees. The undergrowth was dense, and nobody seemed to have done any previous bushwhacking that might have helped us out; most people crunchy enough to visit the preserve have the good manners to follow the signs and stay on the trails. Worse, we really weren't dressed for it. It was the warmest day of the season so far, and I was wearing a short-sleeved mini-dress with brown leather sandals whose major fashion statement was clunky two-inch heels. Mad was wearing his usual uniform of khakis and a blue oxford, but his footwear—his only vice, if you don't count booze and women—consisted of an expensive pair of black wing tips with leather soles, which were getting ruined.

It was slow going, but after twenty minutes of slogging we got to the spot I'd been aiming for. There was nothing in sight—no cops, no ambulance, and certainly no body. I looked around, trying to get my bearings.

"I thought you knew where you were going," Mad said, sitting on a log to inspect his shoes. When he got up, there was a muddy streak on the seat of his khakis. I decided not to tell him.

"I haven't spent much time here when it wasn't winter. It looks different with leaves on the trees. But the trail has got to be around here somewhere."

"Look, Alex, maybe this isn't such a great idea. They must have sealed off the park by now. If the cops catch us, we're going to be in deep shit. I'm still not off the hook with those goons for punching out that cash machine . . ."

"Go back if you want. I just have to know if it's her."

"Aren't you going to find out soon enough?"

"I thought you were dying to see a dead body. Now's your chance."

"Maybe I'm not so hot for it after all."

"I'm going ahead. You can do whatever you . . ."

"Shh. I think I heard something."

We listened for a minute. "I don't hear . . ."

"Shut up," he whispered, and pointed off to our left. "Over there." I still didn't hear anything, but I crouched down next to him. We were at the edge of a small clearing, and the long grass tickled my naked legs. "Look." Sure enough, off in the distance were two people in dark blue windbreakers with yellow lettering on the back. I couldn't read it from that far away, but I knew what it said: GPD.

"They're searching," I whispered back. "They can't have found anything yet."

"You don't know that. They might be sweeping for evidence."

"So what do we do?"

"Try not to get caught." I crept forward, glad I'd worn my brown dress instead of the fuchsia; at least I had some decent camouflage. "Alex, where are you going? Get back here." I pretended not to hear him. "Would you just stay put? Oh, *Christ*," he growled, but I heard him follow.

"Listen," I said when he caught up. "I think I know where we are. There's a trail off to the right that winds around the edge of the pond and goes back to the main parking lot. It's like the main drag."

"So let's stay the hell away from it."

"No, let's take it. Think about it. The body's got to be deep in the woods, just like the other ones. The main trail is the last place the cops'll be. And besides, if we run into them, we're just two people taking a walk."

"Just two reporters taking a walk through a crime scene. Right. They won't suspect a thing."

We made our way through the dense woods without speaking. Birdcalls filled the silence despite our intrusion, or maybe because of it. I wondered if the preserve's rightful owners were warning each other of interlopers, and what their calls might have sounded like when a killer was dumping a dead human being in the birds' backyard.

After a couple of wrong turns, we finally found the trail. We walked along for ten minutes without running into anyone, when Mad stopped. "How far away from the main entrance did the dispatcher say the body was?" Mad asked.

"A quarter mile."

"That's what I thought. We should be around there by now, and there's nobody."

I glanced around, trying to make out landmarks through the trees. "Shit, Mad. I think I sent us in the wrong direction. We're probably back close to the car."

He gave an exasperated sigh. "Then let's turn the fuck around." We retraced our steps to where we'd found the trail and kept going in the right direction.

"Hold on," I said. "I have to stop for a sec." I sat on a flat rock and dug out a pointy twig that had lodged itself between my foot and the sandal.

"I'll be right back. I just want to see what's around the corner." He took off down the path. The forest was quiet once his footsteps faded; even the birds had taken a break. I sat there inspecting my foot for splinters, and wondering what the hell I was doing in the woods looking for my roommate's corpse. Why couldn't I wait for the cops to report the identity of the body? Did I feel guilty because of the disaster over the letters, which had seemed so lame but obviously weren't? Or was I just hoping that it would turn out to be another girl—somebody else's roommate, instead of mine?

"What are you doing here?" The voice, male and authoritarian, made me snap to attention and look around. But there was no one there; the question had come from around the bend, though the voice was forceful enough to sound closer.

"Nothing, Officer," I heard Mad say at the top of his lungs, presumably to warn me. "I was just going for a walk."

"The preserve has been closed for the day. You'll have to leave immediately."

"Why? What's going on?"

"There's been an accident. Please turn around and go back the way you came. If you take a right at the first fork it will bring you back to the main entrance."

"But what's . . ."

"I'm sorry, sir, I can't . . . Wait a second. You're that jerk from the newspaper." Mad didn't say anything. I cringed behind a tree, but bravely. "Nice try, you little prick. Now get the hell out of here before I bust you for fucking with a crime scene." Ouch. So much for the civil servant routine.

They came around the corner, and I continued my very successful cringing. I peeked when they passed by and saw that the cop who had called Mad a "little prick" was about half a foot shorter than him, but twice as wide. Apparently the guy was determined to bring Mad right to the car; I hoped he'd have the presence of mind to come back and get me.

Mad and his escort disappeared down the path, and I

sat there trying to figure out what to do. I still couldn't hear anything from the direction the cop had come from, so I figured he must have been one of a legion of uniforms searching the woods for evidence or just evicting stragglers. I stood up and nobody leaped out to slap the cuffs on me, so I kept going. The path straightened out for about a hundred yards, then curved to the left. I was almost to the bend when I heard voices behind me, just around the previous corner, and guessed it was probably cops. I broke into a trot, hoping to get around my corner before they got around theirs. *Screw this*, I thought. *I'm going back to the car, and whenever the cops figure out . . .*

I'd rounded the corner by then, and a second later I wished I hadn't. Because when I looked up, I saw the body of Cathy Ann Keillor. She was lying across the path, laid so straight and precisely it might have been a geometry lesson. Her eyes were closed, and from the chin up she looked as though she'd died in her sleep. But the fiction ended there, because her neck had the same diamond-shaped marks as the others.

And it got worse. Even from fifteen feet away, I could see that there was something wrong with her stomach. It had been sliced open and sewn shut again, and lying in a triangle on her abdomen were three grayish-pink blobs that I didn't recognize. I still wish I'd never found out what they were.

I'm not sure how long I stood there gaping. It was just about the most horrible thing I'd ever seen, second only to the memory of my lover's body on a bridge, broken and faceless . . .

"*Alex.*" I looked beyond what used to be C.A. to see

Brian Cody, standing in a crowd of uniformed police and crime-scene workers. There was Chief Hill, a woman taking pictures of the body, a man I recognized as the Walden County coroner, two cops unrolling yellow tape, and a cadre of other people wearing latex gloves and looking grim.

Cody came stalking toward me, slowing down only to cut through the woods to avoid walking over the corpse. He was furious. "What the hell are you doing here?" He grabbed me by the arm so hard he nearly dislocated my shoulder. He asked the question again, even harsher than before. But I couldn't answer, just gaped at him and then back at the body. My silence made him grab the other arm, which at least made the pain symmetrical. "You're not supposed to see this. Do you understand me? *You're not supposed to see this.*"

The whole crowd of cops and civilians was staring at us. Cody must have realized it, because he didn't say another word to me. He just pushed me away, got a handle on his temper, and told one of the uniforms to take me home. I was in the back of the squad car and halfway down the hill when I realized that I was going to have to tell Marci and Emma and Steve what had happened to C.A., and that's when I finally started crying. The cruiser dropped me in front of my house and, obviously on orders, parked itself there.

I'd barely gotten in the front door when the phone rang, and I hoped to hell it wasn't one of my roommates. It wasn't. The voice was oddly distorted, almost fake, and it asked just one question. "Well, Alex," it said, "what do you think of my handiwork?"

13

It's called an ovariohysterectomy. That's the technical term for what was done to C.A., the removal of the ovaries and the uterus. I know it sounds horrible, and it is, but it's also one of the most common operations performed today—by veterinarians, at least. I had it done to Shakespeare when she was six months old. You might know it better as "spaying."

Mad got the details through a source in the medical examiner's office. He had to call in a lot of chips in exchange for the information, even off the record, but he did it as a favor to me. I've been told more than once that I'm obsessed with finding things out, even if knowing only hurts me in the long run, and I guess this was a pretty good example. Like I said before, from where I'm sitting now I'd just as soon not know what happened to C.A., because it's so damned awful. It speaks of a person who must hate women with a passion—no, with a vengeance. But at the time, I just had to know.

The only thing that made it any easier to deal with was

the fact that she hadn't been alive by then. C.A. had died just like the other two, strangulation; the mutilation had been postmortem. But why? The symbolism seemed obvious—taking not only life but the potential for life. But it hadn't happened to the other two women, so why C.A.? Did it have something to do with her personally, something she'd said or done after the bastard abducted her? Or was it just the killer's next logical act (as though logic had anything to do with it)? And what would he do next time?

Those were the questions I asked myself as I stood at Marci's bedroom window, staring down at the police car parked outside our house. It had been there for forty-eight hours, that one or one just like it. They changed in eight-hour shifts, regular as the guards outside Buckingham Palace. I wondered what the neighbors must be thinking.

"Are you certain about this?" Emma said to Marci, who was filling her fifth suitcase with sweaters and pastel dresses. "Perhaps you'd best give it a bit more thought. Don't you think you'll feel calmer in a day or so?"

"No," Marci said. "I can't stand it. Every time I think about C.A. I just . . ." She reached for her umpteenth Kleenex and sobbed into it. "It's so awful . . . what happened to her. My mom told me to try to stop thinking about it, but I just *can't*."

Marci didn't know the half of it. I'd told my roommates that C.A. had died like the others, but that was it. They didn't need to know the details of what had been done to her, and I was sure the police weren't going to release them. The story Mad wrote for the previous day's paper just said "mutilated."

"But you'll be back next semester, right?" I crossed from the window to the bed, which was covered with what was left of Marci's wardrobe. "You're just taking a leave of absence, right?"

"I think so," she said. "I hope so. I just feel like I need to get someplace . . . safe. Besides, my folks said if I didn't go home they were going to come and get me. They just can't believe something like this could happen in Gabriel . . ."

Marci's parents had met at Benson vet school and were the most loyal, duck-pant-wearing alums you could imagine. Now they were forming a parents' committee to pressure the university for more security. They didn't have a clear idea of what their demands would be, but they were talking about withholding tuition payments to get them, and I was going to have to do a story about it when I finally went back to work on Monday.

"Is that policeman still out there?" Emma asked.

"Yeah," I said.

"I don't suppose he'd like to help us carry suitcases."

"Probably not in his job description."

"It is where I come from."

We gathered as much stuff as we could handle and went downstairs to Marci's Honda. The cop rolled down his window as we passed the cruiser. "Somebody leaving?"

"My roommate Marci. She's going home to her parents in Pennsylvania." He nodded and rolled it back up, all business. Through the tinted window, I saw him reach for the radio.

"I do wish she'd reconsider," Emma said as we loaded up the trunk.

"I don't. I mean, I don't know Marci that well, but she doesn't strike me as somebody who can roll with the punches. And even though she and C.A. drove each other nuts, they lived together a long time." Marci and C.A. had shared an apartment as first-years after being matched by the university, presumably because they both checked "neat" and "pet owner" on their housing applications. Their similarities ended there, but they must have enjoyed the friction on some level, because they'd been rooming together ever since. "You know more about this than I do, but it seems like vet school is a lot of work, and there's no way Marci can concentrate right now."

"Better to take leave than to come a cropper."

"Yeah, whatever the hell that means."

"You didn't tell her about the dreadful phone call?"

"She was leaving anyway. She didn't need to know. It'll only freak her out worse."

"What did the police say?"

"Last thing I heard they were going to check the LUDs on our phone, try to figure out where it came from."

"The whats?"

"The LUDs. It's some damn cop-show thing. They have the phone company figure out who called who. Don't ask me what it stands for. Meanwhile, the caller ID guy is coming today."

"And if we don't recognize the number, we shan't answer?"

"That's the idea."

We finished loading Marci's car and sent her off with a promise to let her know when the killer had been caught. "I know I'm a coward, but please don't tell me if anybody else dies," she'd said as I put a spare box of

Kleenex on top of the cat carrier that was strapped into the passenger seat. "I can't take the stress, I really can't. I just want to know when they catch the guy, okay?"

With Marci safely on the road, Emma and I collapsed in the living room with our dogs. It was three o'clock on a Thursday afternoon. The rest of the day stretched ahead, ugly and long.

"Where the hell has Steve gone to?" I asked. "I thought he was going to be here to see Marci off."

"Still up at Blue Heron. The police haven't allowed them to reopen the preserve as yet, and I gather he's been conscripted to give talks to amuse the tourists."

"The house seems so . . ."

"Empty. Yes, I know."

"Marci's gone for now. C.A.'s gone for good. We don't know if her dog is dead or alive. Last one left at 357 Roscoe Street, turn out the lights."

Emma looked grim. "Do you fancy a drink?"

"It's getting to be a bad habit."

"Nonsense." Emma got out her martini pitcher and started mixing.

"Are you going to rat on me if I smoke in here?"

"Rat on you to whom exactly?"

"Good point."

"But put away those disgusting Marlboros and let me find my Dunhills. I must have a pack around here somewhere."

"They're all the same to me."

She gave me a long, assessing look. Apparently, Emma sees bad taste as the first sign of insanity. "Poor Alex. It must have been horrible for you. I don't think I've said that to you, how sorry I am that you had to go through such a thing."

"Seeing what happened to C.A.? I pretty much asked for it, running around in the woods like an asshole."

"I'm sure you had your reasons. But that doesn't make it any easier for you."

"Hey, don't worry about it. I'm starting to consider a second career as a coroner, or maybe a bloodhound. The way I attract corpses, it seems like fate."

"Don't joke. I know you're just doing it to cope, but you shouldn't. At some point, you're going to have to admit to yourself how you're really feeling, and it may as well be now."

"Jesus, Ems, are you a veterinarian or a shrink?"

"You know that I'm right."

"Yeah, but I don't feel like dealing right now. Can't we watch one of your Monty Python videos or something?"

She thought about it. "As therapy goes, that might not be too shabby."

"Thanks. Can we do the one where they sing that lumberjack song?"

"Whatever you'd like."

She got up and was about to go to her room for the tape when the doorbell rang. She answered it, and two minutes later Detective Cody was in my living room. I hadn't laid eyes on him since our run-in at the crime scene, and it looked as though he had hardly slept in the intervening two days.

"Where did Emma go?" I asked.

"Her room. I asked to speak to you alone."

"What's going on?"

"Can I sit down?"

"I guess," I said warily. "Do you want a drink?"

I motioned at the pitcher of martinis on the coffee table. Cody made a sick face and shook his head. "I haven't eaten much lately."

"Me neither."

He sat at the far end of the couch and pointed at the pitcher. "You been hitting those hard?"

"No. Emma just mixed it. Martinis and Monty Python. Guaranteed to cure what ails you."

"How are you doing?"

"Shitty."

"I'm sorry to hear that."

"What do you expect?"

"Honestly, Alex, after what happened the other day I don't know what to expect. What the hell were you trying to prove? Did you think you could just march out there in the middle of a crime scene?"

"I . . ." I could feel myself tearing up, but I was damned if he was going to see it. "I was just trying to cover the story."

"That's bullshit and you know it. There were lots of people there covering the story, and they were all outside the front gate where they belonged." He stood up quickly enough to wake up Shakespeare, who'd been asleep on my lap. The dog surveyed the situation and promptly went back to sleep. "A press pass doesn't give you permission to trample a crime scene. You could have destroyed evidence without even realizing it. Christ, Alex. You could even have put yourself in danger. Who knows whether this guy was still out there?"

"Did you come here to yell at me? Because you can just get the hell out of my house." My voice was starting to crack. "It's been a real bitch of a week, and I don't need you coming over here . . ."

"I'm sorry," he said, his anger blowing over as fast as it started. "Oh, hell. This is exactly what I promised myself I wouldn't do."

He sat back down on the couch and started petting Shakespeare. The silence stretched into weirdness, and finally I couldn't stand it anymore. "So why did you come?"

"Believe it or not, I came to say I was sorry."

"For what?"

"For shouting at you like that at the crime scene. For blowing my stack and embarrassing you in front of the whole Gabriel PD. For not even thinking for half a second that the sight of your roommate's dead body might call for a little . . . sensitivity. Take your pick." I didn't know what to say. "I'm not real good at apologies." He smiled a little. "My mom says I have to learn how to say I'm sorry. I guess this is good practice."

"Well . . . thanks."

"You're welcome."

"Can we start over here? Can I rewind and ask you how you are, without all the hollering this time?"

"Sure."

"So how are you?"

I cracked a grin to match his. "Still shitty."

"I guess that's to be expected."

"Good answer."

"I'm sorry about your roommate."

"I'm sorry I trampled your crime scene."

"Okay, we're even." He took a deep breath. "How are the rest of your roommates doing?"

"Marci left for home, but you probably already heard that from the cop watching the house." He nodded. "She was pretty crazed. Kept talking about how it was supposed to be her, that maybe the guy took C.A. by accident."

"I doubt this guy does anything by accident."

"That's what I told her, but she still felt like it was all her fault."

"Sometimes guilt is as good a way to cope as any."

"Wise man."

"You see a lot of it in my line of work. Guilt, I mean."

"Listen, can I get you something to eat? It's strange, but I'm actually hungry all of a sudden."

"You sure you don't mind?"

"I'd kind of enjoy it. Cooking's the only thing that keeps me out of the shrink's office."

"What did you have in mind?"

"Maybe an omelet. Nothing fancy."

"Sounds fine."

"Don't you have to go back to the cop shop?"

"I've been there for two days straight. I'm off until tomorrow morning."

"What about Zeke?"

"He's been at my mom's. But it's nice of you to ask."

We went into the kitchen, and he sat on a stool at the counter while I pulled eggs, onions, mushrooms, tomatoes, and a block of cheddar cheese out of the refrigerator. I put the teakettle on the stove, diced the onion and sautéed it in olive oil while I sliced the mushrooms and shredded the cheese.

"Can I talk while you cook? There's something else I need to tell you."

"Sure."

"It's about the phone call you got."

I stopped in mid-slice. "Are you about to ruin both our appetites?"

"I hope not. Listen, Alex. We traced the call to a cell phone belonging to a philosophy professor at the University of South Dakota."

I stared at him. "The killer is a *philosophy* professor?"

"No. First off, it's a woman. Plus, she was two thousand miles away when the girls were killed. She had nothing to do with any of it."

I threw the sliced mushrooms in with the onions and stirred. "So what gives?"

"Last fall, the professor was at Benson for a conference. Three days of debating whether the universe exists, or some such junk. Anyway, she used her cell phone while she was here. Our best guess is that it was cloned."

"So why didn't she report it stolen?"

"It doesn't work like that. I don't understand the particulars, but the techies tell me that you just have to be within a few hundred yards of the phone while it's working. You use a device to read the code number, and then you can program any old cell phone so you can make calls and somebody else gets the bill. Bad guys love them, because they're untraceable. And when the owner realizes what's up and tells the phone company, zap, they just ditch it and clone another one."

"Nice racket," I said, and cracked four eggs into a bowl.

"I'll say."

"Why don't they make the phones so you can't mess with them?"

"They keep trying, and the bad guys just keep figuring out ways to outsmart them. That's one thing that's strange about this. The professor had the latest technology, the most sophisticated encryption around for general use. Don't ask me why she needed it in South Dakota, but that's what she had. And according to the manufacturer, this is the first time it's been cloned. They're not happy about it."

"And you think the killer copied this lady's phone while she was in Gabriel?"

"More likely, he bought it from someone who did. It would take a lot of technical know-how."

"So it doesn't really help you, does it?"

"Sure it does. It's finally something we can run with. If we can track down whoever cloned that phone . . ."

"He might be able to lead you to the killer."

"Exactly."

I put the onions and mushrooms aside and poured the beaten eggs into the pan. "Can I ask you a question?"

"Shoot."

"Why are you telling me all this?"

"I figure I owed you one."

"For yelling at me the other day? I didn't really blame you, you know."

"For a lot of stuff. For not trying to print the detail about the dog collar, for one thing. For not insisting on running the letters when we didn't know if it was the right thing to do."

"You're welcome. But the reasons you're grateful also happen to be the reasons I'm turning into a crappy journalist."

"Who says?"

"I say. I seem to be lacking that killer instinct these days."

"Alex, you're right in the thick of this. You can't be expected to treat it like a normal day at the office. You found the second body, for God's sake. Then you had to see your roommate like that . . ."

"And why is that? Just tell me that, Cody. Why do you think it is that it was *my* roommate who ended up dead, after *I* was the one who found the body? Why am I getting notes and fucking phone calls? How did this bastard know when to call me, like he knew the minute I walked in the door?" I was losing my grip all of a sudden, and I couldn't stop. "Why is there a goddamn police cruiser parked outside my house? Why am I so goddamn fucking *scared*?"

Cooking and hysteria are not a good combination. I tried to flip the omelet, which I can usually do in one flick of the wrist, and it ended up half in the pan and half on the stove. The part that fell into the gas burner caught on fire, and I had streaks of raw egg dripping down the front of my T-shirt. "Oh, *shit*." I tried to rescue the omelet, but since I forgot to turn off the burner I only succeeded in singeing my fingers.

"Jesus, Alex, what did you do to yourself?" Cody grabbed my wrist and ran my hand under the cold water. I was crying then, and not just because my fingers hurt. "Oh, come on," he said. "Don't cry. Come on. It'll be okay." I was really losing it, and Cody could tell. He patted my hair like I'd seen him do to Zeke, cupped my face in his hands, and murmured things that were supposed to sound comforting. "Take it easy, Alex," he said. "Just breathe. I promise, everything's going to be fine. We're going to find this guy."

"But . . . But . . ."

"But nothing. I don't care who this son of a bitch thinks he is. We're going to put him away."

"But . . ." I cast about for what I was going to say and wound up with nonsense. "But I ruined your omelet."

He stared at me like I was truly nuts. Then he just up and laughed, more deeply than I'd ever heard him laugh before. "You're right. It's a capital offense."

I felt myself starting to calm down. Unfortunately, when the hysteria moved out it left a hole that filled up with old-fashioned humiliation. I may even have blushed. "I throw myself on the mercy of the court."

He was still laughing. "You're lucky I don't slap the cuffs on you."

I turned away, ostensibly to clean up the stove but actually because it was the closest thing to crawling into a hole that was presently available.

"Alex? Can I ask you something?" he said after several minutes of silence. I turned around, and there was something in his eyes I hadn't seen before. For lack of a better word, I'll call it intensity. "After your . . . After Adam died. Have you been with anyone else since that happened? Are you with anybody now?"

I wasn't even tempted to give him the standard answer, which goes something like this: *Are you out of your mind? Considering my track record, I'd just as soon get me to a nunnery.*

"No."

"Good."

"Good?"

"Yeah."

I won't try to fib. I'd sensed the chemistry all along, but I'd mostly put it down to the high-tension situations in which we'd always met. It hadn't really occurred to me that he might be tuned into it too, or that he might do something about it. Also, I'd never been attracted to a redhead in my life. Despite these issues, Detective Brian Cody leaned over, put a hand on the back of my neck, and kissed me. Very softly, in fact.

I might have slapped him across the face and called him a rat for taking advantage of a girl on the downside of crazy. I might have filled him in on my plans for the convent. Instead I kissed him back, openmouthed and hard, with the kind of gusto you get from spending an entire year sleeping with no one but a forty-pound dog.

He was a good kisser, there was no denying it. You can always tell when you're kissing someone who you have no business locking lips with—the rhythm's all wrong, and you wind up clashing teeth and drooling on each other. It wasn't like that. His mouth was warm and strong, and it kept coming up against mine just when you'd want it to. We kept going like that for a while, and I half hoped and half dreaded that Emma was going to walk in and bust us up. But that sort of timing only happens on nighttime soaps, and in the end Cody and I had to stop kissing and deal with each other.

"Wow," I said.

"Wow is right."

"Where did that come from?"

"I'd say, wherever it's been loitering for the past several weeks."

"Oh."

"I'd probably better go," he said, but made no move to go anywhere.

"Don't you want your omelet?"

"No, I don't want my damn omelet. What I want is to drag you back to my apartment and rip your clothes off."

"Really?"

"Really."

"My bedroom's closer. Just upstairs."

He looked slightly shocked. But only slightly. "What about your roommate?"

"She's very discreet. And besides, she's on the first floor."

"Are you serious?" I kissed him, long and hard, and it really set him off. The next thing I knew, he had me bent so far backward over the stove I was practically lying in the omelet pan. "Are you sure this is what you want?" he said against my lips. "Are you sure this is a good idea?"

I pulled away from him, but only long enough to grab his hand and lead him to the staircase. "Probably not," I said. "But you know what I've been realizing lately? Life is too fucking short."

14

They say when you fall off a horse, you're supposed to climb right back on. Now, I don't mean this as some sly description of what Detective Cody and I were up to in the boudoir, but rather in reference to the far less alluring subject of my mountain bike. For obvious reasons (sprains, stitches) I hadn't gotten back on the thing since the day I fell off it, cracked my head open, and landed in the arms of a certain member of Gabriel's finest. Frankly, I didn't care if I ever saw it again. But three hundred bucks is a lot to blow on something you used exactly six times. And besides, if I didn't bike I'd have to take up jogging again or my pizza habit was going to return me to my college-era physique. This was not tempting.

So on Saturday, to prove to myself that my biking career wasn't totally over, I drove to the Y to spend what I hoped would be a very few minutes on the Lifecycle. It was the first time I'd left the house since we saw Marci off, and just going outside felt good. It had rained off and on all day Friday, and when I went out the sky was still that shade of gunmetal gray that inspires so many Gabrielites to contemplate their own demise. The police car didn't follow me—driving three miles to the gym in daylight was deemed insufficiently dangerous to my person—and on the way up the hill I got this weird jolt of giddiness, like a teenager breaking curfew.

Or maybe like a kid who'd been at the cookie jar for eight hours straight. Because that was how long Cody and I had desported ourselves in my bedroom, pausing only to make the omelet that had gotten me into so much trouble in the first place. When we finally ate it off a tray in bed with a stack of English muffins, some clementines, and a Hershey bar, he was wearing my Walden County SPCA T-shirt, and I was wearing nothing.

He hadn't spent the night, since there was a uniform parked outside who was probably already wondering what the hell Cody had been doing there all day. He wanted to, though, and that in itself was good for a girl's self-esteem. I guess neither one of us wanted our little interlude to be over, because we were having so damn much fun. He was a different guy for those eight hours, funny and sweet and all fired up, and maybe we both knew that once we went our separate ways that would be that. We finally called it a night at eleven, after doing the deed more times than I'm willing to admit. Suffice it to say that when I climbed on the Lifecycle two days later, I was not what you'd call entirely comfortable.

So there I was at the Y, pedaling away at a pace that would inspire Jake Madison to compare me to his grandma. I was listening to my beloved Edith Piaf mix tape on my Sports Walkman, which had survived its trip over the handlebars strapped to my back. I wondered whether I should write a letter to Sony, maybe get myself into one of those testimonial ads. *Hi, my name is Alex Bernier, and I'd like to say that if you're ever flying down a mountain being chased by a serial killer, your Walkman won't let you down. You may not survive, but your Sony will!*

I was contemplating what a career in advertising might pay when someone poked me in the arm. I looked up from the handlebars, and there was Gordon Band. He was moving his lips, but what he was saying sounded very much like the lyrics to "*La Vie en Rose*." I pulled off my headphones.

". . . and can you please lose those goddamn . . ."

"Huh?"

"I said would you please take those goddamn headphones off."

"I just did."

"*Thank* you."

"What are you doing here?"

"Looking for you."

"How did you find me?" He looked insulted. "You went to my house and Emma told you I was here. Nothing for a newshound such as yourself."

"Can we get out of here?"

"Sure. Where do you want to go?"

"Anywhere people aren't sweating." Gordon is no fan of exercise, and he has the body to prove it. Jab him in the stomach, and he feels like the Pillsbury Doughboy. "Do you have any idea how anti-evolutionary this is?" He looked around at the spandex-clad legions. "Human beings were not meant to expend energy for no good reason."

"It's lovely to see you too. How long has it been? Four months? We'd given you up for dead."

"Sorry."

"What are you doing up here, anyway?"

"I heard what happened. I wanted to make sure you were okay."

"Right. And you're donating a kidney on the way back to Manhattan."

"Come on, let me buy you a cup of coffee."

"After not answering nine messages? You're buying me breakfast."

We went to a bagel place a quarter mile from the gym, a little gourmet deli that sells so many different kinds of olives, even an urban guerrilla like Gordon feels at home. I ordered a Long Island bagel with chive cream cheese and tomato, half a cantaloupe, and a large cup of the darkest, nastiest coffee they had, and when the time came he opened up his wallet with reasonable grace.

"So how the hell are you?" I said when we settled into a booth. "You still seeing that radio chick? The one you stayed with when we went down to the city last summer?"

"You mean the one who dumped me for that asshole from *Nightline*?"

"Oops."

"Forget me anyway. How are you?"

"I've been better. Once upon a time."

"Didn't you get the message I left with Madison? I'm not the only one who sloughs people off, you know."

"Yeah. Thanks. It was nice of you to check up on me. I'm sorry I didn't call back. Things have been kind of crazy."

"There's an understatement. What's happening to your little rural paradise, anyway?"

"You sound like Mad."

"Drunk and surly?"

"Just surly."

"So come on, I'm dying here. What the hell is going on?"

"I don't feel like talking about it."

"You? You always feel like talking about *everything*."

"Yeah, well, this is kind of close to the bone right now."

"That bad?"

"I'm in this up to my ears. It's fucking déjà vu all over again."

"Are you okay? Physically, I mean?"

"I'm still kind of sore. Nothing serious."

He took off his little round John Lennon glasses and wiped them with a napkin. "Holy shit, Alex. I just about flipped when I saw your name in that wire story."

"I didn't know you cared."

"What kind of a jerk do you think I am?"

"Don't tempt me."

"So what happened to you, anyway? The AP didn't have much, and all I could get out of Madison was that you fell off your bike."

"Falling off my bike has been the high point of my month."

I didn't elaborate, and after a minute Gordon brought out the big guns. "How about something dessertlike? Want to split one of those big chocolate-chip cookies?" He pointed at the glass case with an expression resembling desire. On Gordon, it looked like a toothache.

"Worming your way back into my heart through my tummy?"

"If that'll work."

"Come across with the pastry and we'll talk."

Five minutes later the cookie was history. Gordon and I slouched across from each other in the booth, feet up on the opposite seat. "It's weird being back up here."

"Just like old times?"

"I hope not."

"Don't you miss the simple country life? Just a little bit?"

"No."

"Infidel. Heretic. Unbeliever."

"I miss you, though."

"And well you should."

"You look great."

"You know, everybody's been saying that to me lately, in exactly the same tone of voice. They say, 'You look great,' but what they really mean is, 'You look like something the cat dragged in and sat on, and I pity you.'"

"You sound fried."

"I'm positively crispy."

"Don't you think it might help to talk about it?"

"You're just dying to hear the gory details, aren't you?"

"Of course."

"Then you better get me another goddamn cookie. Peanut butter this time."

He delivered it, and after I washed down half with the rest of my coffee I took a deep breath and started from the beginning. I told him everything that had happened so far, with the exception of my tryst with a certain homicide detective. Gordon must have been following the story pretty closely over the wire, because he didn't look at all that surprised until I told him about C.A.

"Cathy Ann Keillor was your *roommate*?" he said, his eyebrows rising over wire frames. "Holy crap, Alex. Let me get this straight. You found the second body. Your roommate was the third body. And this putz sent you letters *and* called you at home?"

"That's about the sum of it."

"So why aren't you hiding out in . . . I don't know, Vancouver or something?"

"Why Vancouver?"

"Wherever. Off the end of the planet."

"Someplace they don't deliver the *Times*?"

"Right."

"Interesting question." I thought about it for a minute. "Maybe I don't feel like getting chased out of my own town."

"Tough little country girl."

"Shut up. Jesus, I don't know, Gordon. Truth is, once you've been as scared as I was last year, it kind of gives you calluses. I don't think anything could get to me that much anymore, or any*one*, for that matter. Kind of makes me sad."

"Why?"

"Because I'm twenty-six years old and I feel like I'm all used up."

"Bullshit."

"Thanks a lot, Mr. Sensitivity. You're damn good at trampling over other people's feelings. I bet you fit right in down there in your West Side hellhole."

"Yeah, I'm a pig in shit."

"That's frighteningly accurate."

He stared at me for a second, then laughed in a violent snort. "You always did have my number, Bernier."

"Welcome home, Gordon."

"This is *not* my home. But I'm willing to think of it as my cabin in the woods."

"So come on, what's going on with you? How's life down there at the Pink Lady?"

"The *Gray* Lady."

"Pink is prettier. You covering some cool stuff?"

He didn't say anything, just started scratching his head in that Gordon way of his, attacking the follicles so the hairs stood up straight when he was done. I could tell he didn't want to answer, but he finally did. "Stringing night cops."

"You mean you're the fourth guy in line to cover a car fire in Queens at three o'clock in the morning."

"Boss's really rubbing my nose in it."

"The same guy you decked in the city room?"

"That's the one."

"But you'd still rather be a peon at the *Slimes* than cover a serial killer for the *Gabriel Monitor*." He stared more, scratched harder. I got the feeling there was something he wasn't telling me. "Gordon, what the fuck are you up to?"

He focused on his plate for a long time, like he was counting the holes in the Swiss cheese on his bialy. Finally he looked me in the eye. "I'm covering a serial killer. For the *New York Times*."

I was speechless, which doesn't happen often. When I finally thought of something to say, it wasn't all that eloquent. "You *jerk*."

"Give me a break. What was I supposed . . ."

"You fucking weasel. So *that's* what you're doing up here. I can't believe you're up here covering this thing. Don't you think you might have mentioned that before you got me to spill my guts? Jesus Christ, I told you all sorts of shit that hasn't run in the papers. Like how this son of a bitch cut my roommate open and took out her major fucking organs. Man, I am such an idiot . . ."

"Take it easy, Alex."

"Take it easy my ass. You knew what you were doing, and I fell for it. I can't believe I let you finesse me like a *source*. 'Talk about it, Alex, you'll feel better.' You are such a prick."

"What did you *think* I was doing up here?"

"Did you bring your tape recorder? Have you been recording this?"

"Of course not. I can't believe you'd even think that."

"It would hardly be out of character."

"I didn't have to tell you about the *Times* thing, you know. I just didn't want you to find out from somebody else."

"You could have told me *before* you grilled me."

"Then you wouldn't have said anything."

"You bet your ass."

"Come on, Alex. You know I can't use anything you said on the record. I have to get it all confirmed someplace else anyway. What's the big deal?"

"The big deal is that I'm supposed to be your friend and you just *screwed* me. Jesus, Gordon, what happened to all those fancy ethics of yours? I seem to remember you lecturing me plenty last year. And now you come up here and trick me just so you can get some stupid scoop?

Well you know what? I hope you win your fucking Pulitzer, and I hope you choke on it."

I stood up, but he didn't move. And when I stopped wanting to kill him long enough to look at him, I could tell he was actually upset. It was the first time I'd ever seen Gordon express an emotion that wasn't either journalistic blood lust or generalized disdain, and I got the feeling he was worse off than he was letting on. I sat back down. "You look like hell, you know."

It was true. He had big circles under his eyes, and since Gordon is so pale he's practically transparent, he resembled a sad Jewish raccoon.

He reached up to loosen his collar, only to realize he was wearing a T-shirt. He let out a strangled sort of groan and put his head down on the table for a minute. Then he twisted his neck just enough to talk over his elbow. "What you see is what you get."

"What's your damage? I mean, you're back in the city, getting mugged every Saturday night. What's the problem?"

"I fucked myself but good."

"By coming up here for six lousy months? You weren't out of the loop for *that* long."

"Yeah, but you know how it is. You can bust your ass for years, but step out of line for a second and there's ten guys killing each other to fill your slot. I don't have to tell you how fierce the competition for jobs is, especially for white guys. When I got canned, I was up for doing investigative shit. Now I'm back at the bottom of the sludge heap."

He banged his head lightly on the table, loud enough to make a statement but not so hard as to shave any points off his 160 I.Q. "Jesus, Gordon, cut it out. Come on, sit up and calm down."

He stopped banging. It seemed a good sign. "My life is a living hell."

"I don't get it. If they hate your guts, why'd they hire you back in the first place?"

"Good fucking question."

"So how did you get this story? Just because you know people up here?"

"I promised I could deliver the merchandise."

"That's it?"

"I also begged."

"That I'd pay to see."

He finally sat up. "You're really pissed at me, aren't you?"

"Why? Just because you're a manipulative schmuck who ignores me for four months, then shows up to pump me like I'm some idiot beat cop?"

"Come on, Alex, please don't be mad at me. My wires are crossed."

"Are you pleading insanity? *Non compos mentis?* I don't believe it for a minute."

"I'm desperate."

"Really? I think I like the sound of that."

"I don't have what you'd call a well-rounded life, you know. I don't have a passel of people eating at my house every Thursday night. Women don't exactly throw themselves my way. My career is pretty much it."

"You could get a cat."

"Now you're just being mean."

I sighed. He was right. "So what are you going to do?"

"Start seeing my shrink three times a week instead of just two."

"I mean about this story. What are you going to do with the stuff I told you?"

"You want me to sit here and promise I'll forget it all? You know me better than that."

"I want you to tell me the truth."

"The truth is, I'm going to bust my hump to write the best goddamn story my wanker of an editor has ever seen. One of those eighty-inchers, jump off the front of the metro section, two sidebars. 'Murders strike fear into upstate town,' by Gordon Band. We're talking simile, metaphor, onomatopoeia, all that writerly shit. And when they catch the guy I'm going to crawl up his ass and suck on his brain."

"There's a lovely image," I said, but he wasn't listening.

"Page one, above the fold," he went on. " 'Inside the mind of a killer.' I love that shit. And *that's* going to win me my fucking Pulitzer."

"Speaking of minds," I said, "I think you're losing yours."

15

THE WACKOS REALLY STARTED COMING OUT OF THE WOOD-
work then, and I don't just mean Gordon. Gabriel has
more than its share of what you might call "alternative elements" if you were feeling generous, and "unemployed
freaks" if you weren't. They roam the Green in packs—
when they have enough energy for roaming—and although it's amusing, sometimes it isn't pretty.

The Green's storefronts are evenly divided between
the hippie (selling cheap scented candles and used
clothes) and the yuppie (selling pricey scented candles
and new clothes that *look* used), and the local crunchy-
slacker population likes nothing better than to mock the
professorial wives as they sally forth to stimulate the
local economy. They mutter things like "cultural imperi-
alist" at them, and it can get nasty. Last fall, the wife of a
chaired professor at the business school was actually
charged with assault after she pummeled one guy with
her Dooney and Bourke handbag, screaming "socialize

this, you little pisher." When the DA tried to get an indictment, the grand jury gave her a standing ovation.

I mention this by way of explaining that although a certain number of psychics and soothsayers always flock to a big murder investigation, in this case they didn't have much of a commute. Besides the usual hippie contingent, our fair town is already home to a glorious tapestry of tarot throwers, aura photographers, dowsers, channelers, gurus, shamen, spirit guides, and readers of everything from palm lines to the grunge at the bottom of your latte.

And on Monday, I had to talk to all of them.

They'd staged an event on the Green—you couldn't call it a sit-in, because you can sit on the Green all day and no one gives a damn. They just called it an "Awareness" with a capital "A," and although I should have asked them what they meant by it, frankly I was just as happy not knowing. Apparently, "their gathering was intended to protest the police's perceived indifference to their possible contributions to the investigation." At least, that's the way I put it in my story; the truth was that they were as frothing mad as you can get and still claim a connection to the Great Goddess.

"Those pigs don't know shit," one young lady was telling me. "We went trying to help them, man, and they just gave us some mumbo-jumbo fucking crap about *procedure*, man, like they don't even give a fuck that people are *dying* here, man."

I scribbled it all down and tried to figure out if it would make any sense with the expletives deleted. I'd done six interviews so far, and I hadn't gotten a single quote my editors would let me run in a family paper. At least I was learning that, along with peasant blouses and cutoffs, the word "pig" was coming back into fashion.

My latest interview subject was dressed for a day at the Renaissance Fayre, in a dark purple dress with a thin white underblouse and some sort of corset laced up the front. She didn't have much of a bosom, but the extra support gave the effect of two big potato rolls on a tray. If I tried to wear the thing, I'd put somebody's eye out.

She was in her mid-thirties, with dyed black hair that didn't match her coloring, and dark purple eyeliner that did, at least, match her dress. Her name—first, last, and only—was "Guenevere," and when I asked her how she spelled it she said it was the same way Malory did in *The Morte Darthur.* That shut me up.

From what I gathered, Guenevere and her compatriots had tried to tell the cops about the visions they'd had of the killer, and they weren't exactly satisfied with the response. The police had listened very politely, written everything down, and shown zero enthusiasm for following up their leads. So they'd returned to the cop shop en masse to plead their case, wouldn't take no for an answer, and nearly got themselves arrested. I was starting to picture how Cody must have spent his weekend.

By Monday, they'd worked themselves into a tizzy. They decided the public had a right to know about the GPD's lack of enlightenment, so they took over the Green to air their theories about the murders and gather signatures, of which they had precisely twelve. Even the Awareness organizers weren't quite sure what the petition was for.

Believe it or not, the sight of two dozen rabid psychics doesn't raise too many eyebrows around here. Gabriel has its conservative and ultra-liberal extremes, but most people fall somewhere in the middle; this is a town full of leather-wearing vegetarians, and lawyers who belong to the Green Party. The general consensus among the spectators I interviewed was that the incense contingent couldn't do any harm—and besides, the cops could use all the help they could get.

I stuck around for a couple of hours and managed to scrape together a couple of quotes that didn't contain the f-word. I was on my way back to the paper when I ran into Guenevere, who was sitting on a bench rolling a cigarette.

"You're not into it, are you?" she said as I passed.

"Into what?"

She stretched her arm toward the pavilion where her friends were gathered. The gesture was broad and dramatic, like something from *Swan Lake*. "The scene. You're not into the *scene*, man."

"Huh?"

"You don't *subscribe*."

"You mean you think I don't buy it?" She nodded and lit her cigarette. "Well, you're probably right."

"You gonna give us a fair shake?"

"You mean in the story?" She nodded again. "Of course."

"How come?"

"Because it's my job not to take sides."

"Nah, I mean how come you don't believe?"

Because it scares me to meet a woman who washes her hair even less often than I do, I thought. But I just said, "I don't know."

"Aren't you spiritual?"

"Um . . . no."

"Come on, take a load off." She patted the bench beside her.

"I have to get back to the paper."

"Just sit down here for a sec. Think of it as research, man."

"You know, I don't know how to tell you this, but I'm not a man."

She chortled herself into a racking smoker's cough. "That's a good one, man," she said when she caught her breath. "That is a *good* one. Come on, just give me your hand for a sec."

"Why?"

"I want to tell your future."

"That's okay. Sorry to be all bourgeois and everything, but I'm one of those people who'd just as soon not know."

Her eyes widened and she nodded solemnly, as though I was suddenly speaking her language. "I gotta respect that. Gotta respect it. You can't force the future on anybody." Then she grabbed my wrist anyway.

"What are you doing?"

"Reading your *past*."

"There's a treat."

She stared at my hand for several minutes, tracing the lines with her fingers and mumbling under her breath. I wondered how long I was going to have to sit there, and whether I'd ever be able to live it down if someone from the newsroom walked by. Then she looked up, and I saw that she had tears in her eyes. Actual tears.

"You poor thing," she said.

"Me?"

"So much death," she whispered, and I noticed she'd dropped the hippie vernacular. "So much death."

"Jesus, I heard you the first time."

"I hope I'm wrong."

"That makes two of us." She took a long drag of her cigarette. She really looked shaken. "Hey, come on, it could be worse. At least it's my past, not my future."

She shook her head. "No," she said. "It was both."

On that happy note, I went back to the newsroom and started working on my story. I typed in all my notes, which I rarely do since it's usually a waste of time, but at least it was a way to avoid calling the cops. I had to give them a chance to respond, but I knew just who the call was going to get referred to: one Detective Brian Cody. And since I hadn't heard from him since he crawled out of my bed and hit the road, I was in no hurry to make more of an ass of myself than I already had.

This, of course, is why your mother tells you not to get involved with people you work with. "Don't hunt quail where you get your mail" is her expression, but Mad puts it a bit less eloquently: don't shit where you eat. Not that it's ever stopped him.

And in case you're wondering . . . No, reporters are not supposed to cover people they're sleeping with, or sleep with people they're covering. Clearly, I wasn't behaving well. So much for that guest lectureship at Columbia J-school.

Okay, I thought. *If 'tis done, 'tis best done quickly. But 'tis even better done from the phone down the hall in the library, just in case I decide to cry.*

I shut the door behind me, dialed the station house, and

was transferred to Cody inside of three seconds. I tried to gird myself. *Be professional. Be detached. Just get your quote and leave him to fester in his miserable pit of . . .*

"Alex, I'm so glad you called."

His voice was warm, and it threw me for a loop. I'd been expecting the distant-and-awkward treatment. I pulled him out of the mental pit I'd dropped him in a second before. Provisionally, at least. "You are?"

"Course I am." He lowered his voice so it came out all rich and husky. "God, I miss you."

"Yeah?"

"You probably think I'm the world's biggest jerk."

"Oh, uh . . . no. Why would I think that?"

"Because I haven't called you."

"Well, um . . . I haven't called you either."

"Yeah, but I'm the guy. I'm supposed to call."

"So why didn't you?" I couldn't believe we were having this particular conversation with me in the *Monitor* library and him at the cop shop; I was willing to bet it was the first chat of its kind conducted between these two phone numbers. I wondered which one of us would be the first to get the sack if we were found out. The chief would be mightily pissed, but in the end I decided Marilyn would decapitate me with one mighty karate chop.

"You wouldn't believe the weekend I had," he was saying.

"Oh, yes I would."

"These crazies kept coming around the station waving crystals at us . . ."

"I know. That's why I'm calling. I'm writing the story."

He was silent for a minute. "I thought you called . . . you know, because you wanted to talk to me."

"I did want to talk to you. But I was waiting for you to call me."

"Why?"

"Because you're the guy."

He chuckled. "Fair enough."

"So can I ask you a couple questions for the paper?"

"Only if I get to ask one first. Will you have dinner with me tonight?"

"Do you have time?"

"A man has to eat."

"I could cook something at my place."

"Nope. I'm taking you out."

"Is that smart? What if someone sees us?"

He laughed again. "We'll go someplace dark."

He gave me the info I needed for the story, and I walked back to the newsroom looking way too happy. It had been a damn long time since I'd actually had what might be described as a date, and I was positively giddy at the prospect. I felt as though I should go get my hair done, or at least try to pull the dog hair off my sweater with some masking tape.

I filed the story at six and blew out of the newsroom before Bill could assign me anything else. I then spent some time trying to make myself look like a girl. Cody picked me up at seven, right in front of the cop who was guarding my house. "What did you tell him?" I asked as we rounded the corner at the end of my street.

He reached across the gearshift and put his hand on my knee. I was wearing a short velvet skirt with no stockings. Cody didn't seem to mind. "You're interviewing me."

He ran his hand up my thigh, and the skirt went with it. I reached under his collar to scratch the back of his neck. "Best interview I've had in a while."

"Keep that up and I'm not going to make it through dinner."

"You started it."

We managed to get to the restaurant without cracking up the car, but when we parked he grabbed me instead of the door handle. He kissed me, hard, and if we'd been anywhere near our respective domiciles, dinner would have fallen by the wayside.

"We're steaming up the windows," I said finally.

He lifted his head from my cleavage long enough to take a look. "I'm not behaving like a gentleman, am I?"

"Like I'm behaving like a lady?"

"Yeah, but I think I'm living up to every macho-man stereotype there is."

"You mean, like, sleep with the girl, don't call her for four days, then jump her bones before you've even bought her a decent meal?"

He laughed so hard I thought he was going to choke on my bra strap. Then he unwrapped himself from my person. "Come on, let me buy you a decent meal."

"On one condition."

"Name it."

"You have to promise to jump my bones later."

"I'd bet my shield on it."

We went into the restaurant, and when he got a load of the place I could swear I saw Cody pat his gun. I couldn't blame him; if the New York mafiosi would only commute five hours to cap each other, Albertini's would be the perfect place for it. It's three miles out of town in a low-slung brick building shadowed by enormous trees; you risk turning an ankle just walking from your car to the front door. Inside, as I'd promised Cody, the ambiance is on the dark side of inky. The checkered tables are set far apart from each other, the only light comes from candles in brass holders, and the waiters never seem to look you in the eye. There's no table-hopping at Albertini's—it would be considered unseemly—and if it's your birthday nobody's going to stick a candle in your tiramisù and sing to you. The food is great, but the restaurant is never full, probably because they only accept cash, which weeds out all the college students eating out on daddy's Visa.

Cody and I were ensconced at a corner table, on the dining room's even-darker margins. It was a good bet that most of our neighbors were stepping out with persons other than the ones they married.

Cody looked around, leaned across to me, and hummed a few bars from the *Godfather* theme.

"Remind you of the North End?" I asked.

"I was just thinking that."

"Do you miss Boston a lot?"

"Nah," he said. "Well, actually, yeah."

"You thinking about heading back?" I got an icky feeling in the pit of my stomach.

"Maybe. But not for a while."

"Could you get back into the Boston PD?"

"Yeah. A lot of guys there owe me one."

"Because you took a bullet for them?"

"Because I overlooked the fact that they were banging my wife."

"Ah."

"Alex, will you do me a favor?"

"Right here in the restaurant? Don't you think we might get arrested?" I thought I'd made him blush, but it was too dark to tell for sure. "Okay, sorry. What is it? Come on, I'll be good."

"Will you explain this town to me?"

"Tall order. Gabriel kind of defies explanation."

"But I have a feeling you've given some thought to the subject."

"Are you asking for business or pleasure?"

"Both. Pleasure, because I need to figure out whether I'm really going to fit in here in the long run or if I should just stay as long as my mom needs me and go back to Boston. Business, because, well . . ."

"You don't have to tell me if you don't want to."

He grabbed my hand across the table. "That's just it. I *do* want to tell you. I mean, we're not supposed to discuss cases outside of work, but the truth is, everybody goes home and bounces things off their wives or girlfriends or whatever. Half the time, that's where it falls into place, where it makes sense all of sudden—the real world, not the goddamn squad room. At least that's how it always was for me."

"Do you talk about things with your mom?"

"Some cases, yeah. Not this one."

"And you feel cheated because my job makes it so you can't talk to me about anything?"

"I wouldn't call it cheated. Maybe frustrated."

"So maybe you're messing with the wrong girl."

"I'm not messing with you."

"You know what I mean. Let's face it, we're wreaking havoc on the ethics of our respective professions."

"Technically."

"And that doesn't bother you? Come on, Cody, you're just about the most morally upright person I've ever met."

"Alex, it's been a long time since I met a woman I even wanted to cross the street for. You're an incredible pain in the ass, but I'm . . . I don't know, fascinated."

"You do talk pretty."

"I'm a good guy, Alex. I'm not the kind of guy who'd cross the line professionally. And even though you're ambitious as hell, I've never gotten the idea you'd expect me to. I think you want to win fair and square. You wouldn't want to get a story by . . ."

"By screwing the source?"

"I wasn't going to put it like that, but yeah."

"So you think we can keep our social and professional lives separate?"

"We could give it a go."

"In the middle of a murder investigation?"

"Story of my life."

"So how do you want to handle this?"

He took a deep breath and started to eat his salad. The waiter had slipped them onto our table so slyly we'd barely even noticed. "You know, Alex, back in Boston this wouldn't be all that odd. Lots of reporters get loaded in cop bars, and I knew more than a few who got hooked up romantically. The only thing you had to watch out for was that you weren't both working on the same case. But Gabriel is such a small town . . ."

"That it's impossible to keep things separate."

"Right. And in our case, you aren't just a reporter covering a story . . ."

"I'm not covering it officially, you know."

"Yeah, but you're covering it, and you probably shouldn't be. What I was going to say was that you're not just involved as a reporter, you're also a witness."

"And you're tampering with me."

"As often as you'll let me."

"So we've both flushed our ethics down the john."

"And you thought I was such a solid citizen."

"But that still brings us back to what you were saying before—how you can't talk to me about the case. What about that?"

"I don't know."

"Listen, Cody, you said it yourself—this is not what you'd call a typical day at the office for me. I want to catch this bastard as much as you do. Right now it's a hell of a lot more important to me than filing some damn story. So what do you say we decide we're on the same side for once?"

"How do you mean?"

"You know this case. I know this town. Maybe we can help each other."

"And when you go into the paper every day, you conveniently forget everything you know? That seems like a lot to ask."

"I'm a big girl. I can handle it. The question is, do you trust me?"

"Honestly? I'm not sure. But it looks like I'm willing to gamble my career on it."

"Well . . . thanks. I think."

"And what happens when we catch this guy?"

"When we catch this guy," I said, "I get an exclusive."

16

I'M WILLING TO BET THAT THE NEXT FIVE GUYS I SLEEP with will be built like a middle-aged Marlon Brando, because I've been on something of a hunk streak, and my luck is bound to run out. Let me make it clear that although my mom thinks I'm cute as a june bug, I'm not what you'd call a supermodel. I'm only five-three, I have these stumpy, muscular little legs, and my kind of enormous bosom went out of fashion when Rubens hung up his paintbrush. So it was always a matter of some confusion why a guy like Adam—who, as I'm fond of saying, looked like Michelangelo's David with a Frisbee instead of a slingshot—ever gave me the time of day. And there I was, a year after he died, in the sack with the most muscle-bound guy I'd ever seen outside a Schwarzenegger movie. It was something of an embarrassment of riches.

Now, as I've mentioned before, Cody was not exactly my type. Actually, he was not at *all* my type. I usually go for the lanky intellectual sort, guys who wear glasses and carry copies of *Siddhartha* and know how to use the word "ontological" in a sentence, which I do not. Most (but not all) of these guys have been journalists, and in those cases you can add to the previous description one of the following: (a) alcoholism; (b) a fanatical desire to work at the *New York Times*; (c) deep-seated fear of monogamy; or (d) all of the above. Usually "d."

Cody was different. First off, he was in no way lanky. He was rock-solid, with huge biceps and the kind of stomach muscles you see on those infomercials for The Abdominizer. Just looking at him made me want to skulk off and do sit-ups. He claimed that his physique was the genetic result of coming from "a long line of big Irish lugs" and that he didn't do much to maintain it. As it turned out, however, he meant "not much" relative to what the SEALs put you through, which involves sitting in cold water all day, eating half a hot dog, and then running a marathon. His version of the soft life included jogging five miles a day, lifting large stacks of free weights, and (this one really got me) swimming laps across the lake, which is a mile wide and rarely gets above sixty-five degrees *in the summer*.

I probably would have been annoyed by this regimen, were I not reaping its benefits. Cody's body was quite a treat to behold and even more fun to play with. He was an extremely good lover—let's just call him "athletic"—and at six feet tall and two hundred pounds, he made me feel positively dainty. (Girls like that.) Plus, he satisfied the First Manly Rule of Bernier: in the snugly lulls between the hot and heavy stuff, he let Zeke up on the bed with us. I was in danger of falling hard.

"Weird thing happened to me today," I said into the

crook of his arm, which was draped over my neck in a very sexy half nelson.

"Oh, yeah?" It was after midnight, but he didn't sound sleepy. I could feel his breath against my hair as he spoke, and it felt so good I wanted to ask him an essay question.

"I went out on the Green to interview those psychics who were protesting, about, you know . . ."

". . . that we're a lot of pig idiots."

"Right. And there was this one woman—she said her name was Guenevere. I was on my way back to the newsroom, and she read my palm . . ."

"I'm surprised you go in for that crap."

"I don't. But she kind of, I don't know, ambushed me—like she wanted to prove a point. And she wanted to read my future, but I wouldn't let her, and then she said she'd read my past. And you know what she said?"

"Recently seduced by pig idiot?"

"No. She just stared at my hand for like five minutes and the next thing I knew she was crying."

"You're kidding me."

"No, and I don't think she was faking it either. She just kept saying 'so much death, so much death.' It was really creepy."

"Sounds like it."

"But it gets worse. She said there was death in my future too."

"There's death in everyone's future."

"Yeah, but that's not what she meant."

He rolled me over to face him. "Are you really letting this get to you?"

"Well, no, but . . ."

"She was probably just trying to shake you up."

"Why?"

"Who knows? Why do these head-cases do anything?"

"But she seemed so sincere. And she was right, you know. I *have* seen a lot of death—Adam, and C.A., that girl I found in the woods . . ."

"And this Guenevere person could have read all about it in the *Monitor*."

"That's true, I guess . . ."

"Come on, Alex. You can't let yourself get upset over something this silly. I promise, nothing's going to happen to you."

"It's not myself I'm worried about. Believe me, Cody, I don't believe in this psychic stuff any more than you do. But it . . . I don't know, got me thinking. I mean, I'm only twenty-six, and I've already lost way too many people I care about. What if it's always going to be like this?"

"You mean you think you're . . . cursed or something?"

"Nothing that dramatic. I just don't know how much more of it I could take."

He looked grim all of a sudden. "And you're thinking that the last thing you needed was to get involved with a guy who gets shot at for a living."

I smiled and leaned across the two-inch gap between us to plant a kiss on his lips. "You know the last time a Gabriel cop died in the line of duty?"

"I don't know. Ten years?"

"Try never."

"Never? Really?"

"Never. It's not that kind of town. But I could start worrying about you if it'll make you feel good."

"No thanks," he said. "You make me feel pretty damn good already."

That was the end of the talking for a while, and I must say he did an excellent job of taking my mind off my troubles. I could go on and on about how the earth moved and time stood still and we were transported to another universe, but the truth is that we just had some very fine sex. I wondered whether his, well, *repetitive* ability was a natural talent or merely evidence that he was coming off a dry spell of his own. I had my fingers crossed for the former.

"You tired?" he said later, when Zeke was back up on the bed.

"Nah. I should be, but I'm not."

"Me neither. It's odd. I'm usually asleep by eleven."

"That's frighteningly wholesome."

"But I'm awake now."

"Chalk it up to excessive stimulation."

"Then I blame it on you."

"If I'm keeping you up, I could go . . ."

"Do you want to?"

"Um . . ." *Shit. Now I remember why celibacy was such a rip-roaring good time. No messy latex, no weirdo negotiations about who sleeps where . . .*

"Because, you know," he was saying, "you don't have to stay if you don't want to."

I sat up and started to get out of bed. "Oh, yeah, well, maybe I should be getting back . . ." I started hunting for my clothes, and realized that my bra was twirling from the ceiling fan.

"Alex?"

"Yeah?"

"Come here."

"But I have to find my . . ."

"If you don't get back into this bed willingly, I'm going for my handcuffs."

"But you said you . . ."

"I was trying to be liberated. I'm not very good at it." I got back under the covers. "Damn. I don't know what I'm doing. Do you have any idea how long it's been since I was . . ."

"On the market?"

"Not since college. My social skills are fifteen years behind the times."

"You mean you've only slept with your wife since college? Even when she was cheating on you like that?"

"Yeah."

"Man, you *are* a Boy Scout."

"Yeah, or a total schnook."

"I vote for Boy Scout."

"Come on, let's try to get some sleep." He reached over me and turned out the light.

"Tell me a bedtime story."

"Are you serious?"

"Yep. You had your way with me, now pony up a bedtime story."

"Alexandra Bernier, you are one strange lady."

"Given. Now deliver."

"I can't. You're the writer, not me."

"Then tell me something about you."

"That'll definitely put you to sleep."

"Try me."

I felt him take a deep breath. I wasn't going to prod him anymore. He was quiet for a long time. "I've never seen anything like this," he said slowly. It took me a second to realize he was talking about the case, which was the last thing I'd expected. I just lay there and waited for him to go on. "I've seen a lot," he said after a while. "Things you can't imagine. I once busted a guy who beat his two kids to death because they tried to change the channel during the Superbowl. Then there was this hooker in the Combat Zone whose pimp killed her when she tried to stiff him, and as a warning to his other girls he cut her face off. I'll never forget that, being dragged out of bed at two o'clock in the morning and going down there, and the coroner lifting up the plastic so we could see and these snowflakes falling on where her face used to be, mixing with the blood and just disappearing.

"I remember during SEAL training, we were on a long night swim, and the guy I was buddied with doubled up in pain all of a sudden and started to drown. It was his appendix. He was a really strong swimmer, stronger than I was, but he was in so much pain he couldn't keep himself afloat, and I tried to help him but he was just dragging me down. I tried to talk to him, get him to calm down, but he was terrified. And it was me or him, and I finally had to wrench myself away. I'll never forget the look he gave me, like I was the one who was killing him. But I didn't know what else to do. If I tried to get him back to shore, we were both going to drown. But if I just stayed there, he was going to die anyway. So I swam like hell to try to get help, but I knew what we were going to find when we got back." He paused, and I got the feeling he was living the whole thing over again in his head.

"That was the first time I ever saw a dead body, except for my father's funeral. If I'd known there were going to be so many since then, I'm not sure what I would have done—maybe gone to work on Wall Street or some damn thing. It seems like a long time ago, and since then I think I've seen every possible version of death. You were talking about death before, and I guess my first reaction was that despite everything you went through last year, you have no idea of the depth and the breadth of it—how, when you do the sort of work I've done, you get to feel more at home with the dead than you do with the living.

"Both my dad and my stepfather died of cancer, so I've watched people die of natural causes, and honestly it's no easier than by accident or by violence. Any way you think about it, it seems so goddamn *senseless*. I've seen people who died because they worked in a convenience store, or because they welshed on a bet, or because they cheated on their wife, or because they were on the wrong road at the wrong time, or because they were wearing the wrong color shirt in the wrong neighborhood, or because somebody wanted their car, or because their dad got drunk and threw them against the wall a little too hard.

"Those are the reasons people die in my world, Alex. They're all clichés because they keep being true. Most people kill for the same predictable reasons they always have. You've got your seven deadly sins and that's pretty much it. People kill for money, or lust, or anger, or passion, or maybe just revenge.

"But this is different. I've read about cases like this, where some psycho is killing just for the pure pleasure of it. And it's the hardest thing in the world to solve because all the things you'd normally look for, all the connections that bind the killer and the victim together and led to the murder in the first place, none of that applies. The rules you've always followed go out the window. So here I am, this hotshot from a big-city PD, and everybody's looking at me like I should know what I'm doing. But you know what? I have no goddamn idea. I keep studying cases like this, about the Jeffrey Dahmers and Ted Bundys and Son of Sams of this world, and you know what's the only common denominator? The bodies. Before those bastards got caught, dozens of people got killed. It was almost by definition—that in order for you to catch them, they'd have to kill so many times that it got old. They got sloppy, and they slipped up, and they finally got themselves caught. They overlooked a witness or one of their victims got away, and it was the beginning of the end.

"And that's what I'm afraid is going to happen here, Alex. I'm afraid that this goddamn thing has barely started. I'm afraid that this guy has ambition, that between the letters and the murders he's showing us that he's bound and determined to make a name for himself. And the thing I'm afraid of most is that I'm not good enough to stop him, and neither is the FBI, and there's going to be a whole morgue's worth of bodies before this is over."

I could tell from Cody's voice that he wasn't looking for an answer, didn't expect me to buck him up with some crap about how he was big and strong and could fight the bad guy with one hand tied behind his back. The truth was that he was probably right, and we both knew it. His voice had gotten raspy at the end, so I handed him the water glass from the table on my side of the bed. Then we lay in the dark together, the only sounds coming from the ceiling fan and Zeke's snoring.

"Alex," he said a while later. "Are you scared?"

"Do you think I should be?"

He put his arm around me to pull me next to him, and I realized we hadn't touched the entire time he'd been talking. "No. I told you before I'd protect you. That goes double now."

"My hero." I kissed him, but he didn't kiss me back. "Are you okay?"

"I'm just thinking."

"About what?"

"About what happened to C.A. And when it might happen again, and whose parents I'm going to have to tell next."

"Don't think about it. You'll drive yourself crazy."

"Good advice. Unfortunately, I don't feel capable of taking it right now."

There was something new in his voice, and it sounded so odd it took me a while to place it. "Brian . . ." I said finally. His first name felt strange on my lips. "Are *you* scared?"

"Yeah," he said. "I don't think I've ever been so scared in my whole life."

"Scared of what?"

He pulled me on top of him then, and when he answered he spoke so softly I wasn't sure he wanted me to hear. "I'm terrified," he said, "of letting somebody else drown."

17

AFTER C.A.'S DEATH, THE POWERS THAT BE AT BENSON finally started acting like they gave a damn. Now, the reason for this wasn't quite what you'd think. Sure, they were upset that they'd lost one of their own; C.A., unlike Patricia Marx or Jane Doe, was a bona fide, matriculated Benson student, and that made her death more than a matter of institutional hand-wringing. It meant that the university was going to have to deal with the inevitable parental hysteria, and a certain number of students were bound to do what Marci did—flee.

But as far as Benson was concerned, it could get a lot worse: If another student got offed, the school might get a reputation as Murder U. When people think of the University of Florida at Gainesville they still think of dead coeds, and that sort of thing isn't good for the endowment. And what was worse, it was happening during what was traditionally Benson's finest hour—that lyrical interlude between graduation and reunions, when the campus is at its prettiest (thanks to all the square yardage of bluegrass they truck in from Kentucky) and there are very few students around to ruin it all. The rabble-rousing seniors—including most of the Benson Animal Anarchists—were safely graduated, and it would be months before the new crop got sufficiently organized to cause trouble.

In two short days, five thousand alumni would descend on campus, decked out in Benson togs from stem to stern, and the university would wine and dine them for seventy-two hours straight. They'd row on the lake and sing songs and play rugby against undergrads paid to let them win, and when it was all over they'd be so overcome with emotion they'd whip out their checkbooks and say *here, take it all*.

It was a sacred process with a long and illustrious history. The university had no intention of letting some serial murderer mess everything up, particularly since it was highly unlikely that he was an alumnus.

So it was no surprise when Benson's president, an ill-tempered old Brit who stands five-five in his Bruno Maglis, called Chief Hill up to his office for a royal audience. I only heard about it third-hand, of course—from a very amused Detective Cody, who was new to the vicissitudes of town-gown sniping—but apparently the president fed the chief lots of Walker's shortbread before informing him that if anybody died before the last teary-eyed alum blew out of town, Hill's son Wilfred Jr. (who was enrolling next fall on a baseball scholarship) was going to fail every course he took.

The politics of town and gown are complex, but as far as most of Gabriel is concerned, Benson is only truly benign three weeks a year: between Christmas and New

Year's, when the entire university shuts down for vacation; between graduation and reunion, when the students are gone and everyone on campus is madly cleaning up for the alums; and between the end of summer session and the start of fall semester, when the maintenance men spend the week hiding all the nice flowers before the students come back. The latter is the most bittersweet of all, because although there's a lot of good parking and the restaurants have no lines, we all know that within a matter of days we'll be descended upon by hordes of clueless newcomers, asking directions in Long Island accents and then driving the wrong way down one-way streets anyway.

Townies like me usually treasure every one of those glorious days of peace and tranquillity. But this time, I would've just as soon been crowded elbow to elbow with topless sorority girls. There was something eerie about the quiet, like the town had curled itself up into a ball and rolled into the lake. Or maybe it felt like everybody was holding their breath, girding themselves for another girl to die, and although nobody wanted it to happen the waiting was pretty awful in and of itself. There had been no more letters to the newspaper, and no phone calls other than the one I got the day C.A.'s body was found. I couldn't understand why the letters had dried up, but I hoped to hell it wasn't because we'd had our chance to placate the killer by printing his crap, and we'd blown it.

It didn't help that the outside media was finally starting to sniff around our little burg. Call me a hypocrite, but as far as I was concerned this sucked any way you looked at it. People were used to locals like me chasing them around with a notebook, but camera crews from the network affiliates made everybody feel like they were living in the middle of a war zone. Plus—and I swear this isn't just the usual print-versus-TV griping—half the coverage was just downright *wrong*. One station somehow calculated the body count at five. Another one mixed up the victims and said Patricia Marx was the vet student and C.A. worked at the Gap (which, considering her notorious lack of fashion sense, made Emma laugh and cry at the same time). The CBS guys from Binghamton managed to snag "an exclusive interview with one of Cathy Ann Keillor's roommates." This was quite a mystery to us since we were fairly sure that whoever this person was, she didn't live with us.

As if that weren't bad enough, one of the tabloid crews put two and two together and, recalling my own personal brush with eternity, chased me around for three days trying to do a piece entitled "Gabriel: City of Death." I thought about snipping our cable wire as an act of civil disobedience, but Emma pointed out that we wouldn't be able to watch *Two Fat Ladies* on the Food Network, and that was the end of that.

Back at the *Monitor*, the mood was pretty grim. Bill had gone apoplectic when he found out Gordon was in town covering the story for the *Times*, to the point that he finally lost control of his beloved tennis ball and broke a window. The sudden preponderance of reporters made the pickings slimmer for everybody, and before long all the usual sources dried up, even for the locals. People were just sick to death of answering questions, and I can't say I blamed them.

Fortunately for Wilfred Jr.'s academic future, reunion weekend came and went without another corpse. It did, however, offer me the pleasure of writing the usual alumni drivel, cranked out in yet another effort to convince the Benson community to buy more than twenty lousy papers a day. The university flacks were just as happy to have something other than a dead vet student on our front page, and they went out of their way to come up with cutesy little stories for me. Thus, I spent part of one Saturday listening to old white guys reminisce about their glory days (for a piece on an oral history project the Benson archive was running) and the rest of it watching slightly younger white guys sing Judy Garland songs in drag (for a story about the annual alumni comedy show, which you apparently have to be very, very drunk to appreciate).

By the time the weekend was over I needed a drink myself, so Monday night after work I went down to the Citizen hoping to find someone to complain to. Imagine my joy to discover Mad in the window seat, hefting Molsons with none other than Gordon Band.

"What is *he* doing here?" I said by way of greeting.

Mad looked nonplussed. "Buying me pitchers."

"How nice of him. Hope you've got one hand on your notebooks."

"Come on, Alex," Gordon said. "Sit down and have a drink."

"You're lucky I don't punch you in the nose."

Mad leaned back in his chair and looked from me to Gordon and back again. He was clearly amused. "There is just not enough love in this room."

"Come on, Alex, sit down, will ya? I'll buy y'a drink." Gordon was slurring his words a little. It was the closest to drunk I'd ever seen him.

"On the *Times* expense account?"

"O' course."

"Then I want a very large gin and tonic, with two limes, and it better be made with Tanqueray, not that bar-pour crap."

"Ya got it."

He stood up, tottered a little, then went off toward the bar. I took the chair farthest from his. "How'd you have the lousy luck to run into him?"

"He walked in here an hour ago."

"The *snake*."

"What the hell is up with you two? Lovers' quarrel?"

"Hush your mouth."

"This sure is a night to remember. You're bitchy, he's crocked . . . Who needs pro wrestling? I'm plenty enter-tained."

"Mad, I *told* you what he did to me. That man is a pro-fessional weasel."

"Who among us isn't?"

"Yeah, but he's better at it than we are."

Gordon returned from the bar with my drink and a white business envelope. He put them both on the table in front of me.

"What's that?"

"Bartender said he found it under the door when he opened."

I held the envelope up to the nearest light source, which was the Rolling Rock sign in the window. Under the greenish glow I saw my name typed across the front. I opened it.

I know where you live.
I know where you work.

I know where you sleep.
I know who your friends are.
I can find you anywhere.

I didn't say anything. I just picked up my drink and tossed back as much as I could in one swallow.

"Shit, Bernier, what's up?" Mad said. "What the hell are you reading?"

I hoovered the rest. "Nothing."

"Nothing my ass. Man, even I don't drink like that. Not unless it's tequila."

Across the table, Gordon seemed to be making an effort not to grab the paper out of my hand. He also seemed to have sobered up remarkably. "What was in the envelope?" he said, with the faux nonchalance I'd heard him use on many a hapless interview. "Anything interesting?"

"None of your goddamn business."

"It's from him, isn't it?"

"No."

"Come on, Alex, you're a really bad liar. I can tell you're upset. It's all over your face." I folded the note back up and put it in the envelope. "If it's another threat, you gotta report it to the cops."

"I can take care of myself."

"Where's your police escort, anyhow?" Mad interjected. "I thought they were supposed to be on your back twenty-four seven."

I cocked my head toward the window and the two of them peered out at the uniform standing on the other side of the Green. Val is one of those jolly, overweight cops who always seems about six months short of retirement. It's his job to keep the Green safe from bums and hackeysackers, which he accomplishes with aplomb by boring them all silly with stories about Korea. On his days off, he visits elementary schools dressed as McGruff the Crime Dog.

Mad saluted the cop through the window. "You've got Val guarding your life? I hope you brought your Mace."

"It's just while I'm in here. The other guy handed me off to him. I guess they figure I'm safe in a crowd."

"I hope they're right." Mad plucked the envelope from my hand and read the note before I could grab it back. The muscles in his jaw tightened. "When they find this son of a bitch, I am personally going to beat the shit out of him."

"That's very chivalrous of you, but take a number. You can have him after I rip his balls off with my fingernails."

"Would you *please* let me see that?" Gordon looked like he was going to spontaneously combust. I'd forgotten he was there.

"No can do," I said, and tucked the letter into my purse. "You're playing for the other team now. You wanted it, you got it." Gordon didn't say anything. He just stood up, stuck out his tongue at me, and left. Through the green glow of the plate-glass window, I watched him shove his hands into his pockets and hustle down the street. "Damn, those New Yorkers are rude."

Mad reached for the pitcher and refilled his mug. "You didn't exactly roll out the welcome wagon."

"He's a fink."

"You ever gonna get over it?"

"Yeah, after I make him squirm for a while."

"You dames scare me. Men just throw a couple of punches, bleed a little, no hard feelings."

"You're much more evolved."

He leaned back and stretched his feet out on the chair Gordon had vacated. "Alex, what the fuck is going on?"

"I told you, Gordon . . ."

"Screw Gordon. I'm talking about *you*. You're getting death threats and you don't even seem to care."

"What do you want me to do, start blubbering right here in the bar? Of course I care. It scares the shit out of me. I'm just trying to figure out what to do."

"Easy. Give it to the cops."

"I'm planning on it."

"You mean the next time you bang Brian Cody?"

I stared at him. "How did you know?"

"Lucky guess."

"Seriously, Mad. How the fuck did you know?"

"I know you. I know what you're like when you're getting laid—and, more to the point, what you're like when you're *not*. Let's just say you have a certain rosy glow. He must be pretty good."

"Shut up."

"I'm happy for you, Bernier. Nobody deserves a good clock-cleaning more than you, except maybe me."

"Shit, Mad. Do you think anybody else knows? Marilyn'll kill me if she finds out."

"Yep."

" 'Yep, Marilyn'll kill me,' or 'Yep, somebody else knows'?"

"Yep, she'd kick your cute French-Canadian ass seven ways from Sunday. But I think you're okay. I'm probably the only one who can tell the well-shagged Bernier from the regular kind."

"Lucky you."

"So you'll show Cody the note?"

"Of course."

"You've got your own personal bodyguard."

"What about you? You still saluting the Union Jack?"

"From time to time."

"Jesus, Mad, you've been banging Emma for like, what, over a month? For you, that's like three consecutive lifetimes." I started humming "God Save the Queen," and he threw a cocktail peanut at me. "Come on, what's her secret?"

"I don't know. She's wild."

"Wild how?"

"No comment."

"Come on . . ."

"Give it up, Bernier. That's all you're getting. Now stop trying to change the subject. Be a good girl and show me the fucking note again."

I pulled it out and smoothed it on the table between us. "Okay. So what do you make of it?"

He shrugged. "More of the same, I guess."

"Yeah, but it seems so . . . mean."

"You were expecting nice?"

"No, but what I'm saying is that it's nothing *but* mean. It doesn't try to talk us into publishing his letters. There's none of that 'I'm the devil's disciple' bullshit. It's just like, all he wants to do is scare me."

"That would seem to be his stock in trade."

"No, *killing* seems like his stock in trade. I mean, as far as we know, he never sent any letters to Patricia Marx. C.A. sure didn't get any, or I would have heard about it. So why me?"

"Maybe you're his mouthpiece."

"So you think he doesn't actually want to kill me, he's just using me to get people's attention?"

"Well, you *are* kind of a local celebrity around here."

"Because of my stupid movie column?"

"That, plus your byline in the paper every day, and all the media shit that came down last year. Face it. Everybody in this town knows who you are."

"So maybe I'm supposed to be his greatest conquest."

"Or maybe he's supposed to be yours."

"You think he *wants* me to catch him?"

"Could be. Besides the crime-scene evidence, those letters are the only clues the cops have, right?"

"I guess."

"So there you go."

"That's nuts. There's nothing in those letters that gives us the least hint who he is. I mean, he doesn't give us riddles to solve. He just sort of raves and tries to scare people, specifically me."

"What about the dates on them? Could they be, you know, some kind of hint?"

"There aren't any dates."

"Oh. Well, when did you get them?"

"Let me think . . . The first one came in mid-May, the second one around two weeks later, and this new one two weeks after that."

"So there's a pattern."

"Kind of. But the first one just came addressed to "Police Reporter," the second one was mailed to me at the paper, and the third was dropped off here. And the phone call came to my house."

"Like he's zeroing in on you."

"That's one way of looking at it, thank you very much."

"Well, look on the bright side. At least he didn't nail one of the Benson alums over reunions. Then your pal Cody would really have had a mess on his hands."

"Yeah, and Wilfred Jr. could kiss his scholarship good-bye."

Mad shook the empty pitcher. "The well is dry. You want another G and T?"

"A little one."

"Coming right up," he said, and took off for the bar. I stared at the note for a while, wrestling with the desire to rip the goddamn thing up into little pieces. Cody probably wouldn't approve. "Deep thoughts?" Mad said when he got back. He handed me the drink. "Here, have some anesthetic. Works like a charm."

"I was just thinking . . ."

"No shit."

". . . about what you said a second ago. About how nobody got killed during reunions."

"So what?"

"Well, I was just thinking about these letters I got—three, spaced two weeks apart."

"And?"

"And you got me wondering about Benson—not just reunions, I mean the whole end of the semester."

"What about it?"

"Maybe it's just a coincidence. But you know, the first letter came just as classes were ending. And then there was nothing during the two weeks of reading period and exams, and then another letter. And then nothing during the next two weeks, when most of the students are gone, and then I get this one right as summer session is starting."

"What about the phone call you got?"

"It was a couple of days before graduation."

"So how does that fit in?"

"I'm not sure, but I think by then you can only stay on campus if you're a senior."

"So you think this guy is a senior in college? Seems like a stretch."

"Bundy was a law student. Smart and crazy aren't mutually exclusive."

"You should know." I stood up, and Mad grabbed my arm. "Where are you going? Come on, Bernier, you don't have to get pissed at me."

"I'm not. I'm just calling Cody."

Mad smirked. "Business or pleasure?"

"Oh, shut up, Mad. You know damn well it's both."

18

NOBODY'D BETTER THREATEN BRIAN CODY'S MOTHER. I say this because, judging by his reaction to my latest note, he'd probably shoot first and ask questions later. As it was, he just about put his fist through a wall—and I was just some girl he'd been dating on the sly for a couple of weeks. Clearly, the guy had a slightly overdeveloped protective streak.

I'd called him on his cell, and not five minutes later he'd come barging into the Citizen to pick me up. He and Mad exchanged manly glances, sizing each other up, and I guess neither one of them came up wanting because in the end they shook hands so hard their fingers turned white. Cody relieved Val of responsibility for my wellbeing and took me home, where Shakespeare and Tipsy vied for his attention and gave up when they realized he was in no mood to pet anybody, me included.

"Okay, tell me again," he was saying. I opened my mouth to protest and he cut me off. "I know we've been over it twice already, but humor me."

I was lying on the couch with all forty-something pounds of Shakespeare stretched out on my middle. Tipsy was curled up on the floor, and Cody was pacing. "Like I said before, I spent most of the weekend up on campus covering reunions. I stopped here around five to let the dogs out and then I went to the Citizen to look for Mad. He was already there with Gordon, so . . ."

"And who's Gordon again?"

"Like I told you, he's a reporter for the *New York Times*. He worked for the *Monitor* for a while, but now he's back in the city. He's just up here covering the case."

"And he found the note? Are those bastards planning on printing it?"

"I wouldn't let him see it," I said, trying not to ponder the trouble I'd be in if Cody found out how much I'd already spilled to Gordon. "He just went to get me a drink, and the bartender said he'd found it under the door when he opened at four. The envelope was sealed."

"You know him? The bartender, I mean?"

"Mack? Sure. He owns the place. Used to be a radio reporter once upon a time. The Citizen is kind of a journalists' hangout—most of the *Monitor* newsroom, people from the weekly paper, a lot of radio guys, the local TV crew."

"You go there a lot?"

"More than is probably good for me."

"Do you have any idea how whoever wrote the note would know you'd be there tonight?"

"No. I mean, *I* didn't even know I'd be going there. It was just a spur of the moment thing. But I'm probably there four nights a week, so the odds were pretty good."

"Okay, let's assume that the note was written by someone who'd seen you there before, who knows you spend a lot of time there. Can you think of anybody who's bothered you? Maybe someone you caught staring at you once too often?"

"No, I . . . Well, there was a couple of drunk guys one night who came into the bar to admire, my um . . . my chest."

"Did you get their names?"

"Hell no."

"Did they threaten you?"

"Nah, they were harmless. Drunk and harmless. I really don't think it's connected."

Cody looked as though he'd like to give them a harmless beating. "Okay," he said with a sigh. "Anything else?"

"Not that I can think of. I mean, the Citizen's been kind of a zoo lately. It used to be almost all townies—happy-hour drinkers who came for the free hot wings, and after they cleared out the media crowd showed up and closed the place. But lately there've been a lot more college students, mostly lug-nuts from Bessler, but some Benson kids too. You wouldn't think they could find their way downtown, but they've pretty much taken over the place. Sucks for the rest of us."

"Underage drinkers?"

"Jesus, Cody, don't go calling the vice squad."

"I don't give a damn about that. I just want to know if the bar is lax about proofing, or if we can limit ourselves to suspects over the age of twenty-one."

"I'd say anything goes. In this town, a halfway-decent fake ID goes a long way. The cops usually look the other way unless the D.A.'s running for reelection."

"So what you're saying is that the people who see you at the bar regularly are essentially the happy-hour crowd, students, and other journalists?"

"Well, them and just about anyone who walks by the place. I usually sit in the window seat." Cody gave a strangled groan. "Not very helpful, huh?"

"Is there anything else you can think of? Anything else out of the ordinary that happened in the bar?"

"Nothing. I haven't got a clue."

"Anytime you might have brought attention to yourself?"

"Not beyond just being my usual loudmouth self."

"Great."

"But there's something else, something I was saying to Mad earlier. It's about the timing of the three notes." I told him about how they coincided to the end of the Benson semester. "What do you think? Could it be related?"

"It could." He finally sat down next to me. "You know, Alex, that was really good thinking. You wouldn't make a bad detective."

"Yeah, I'm a regular Nancy Drew."

"Think about it. The cell phone that the call came from was cloned from a phone that was used on campus. The bar is becoming a student hangout. And from what you just told me, you never got a note or a phone call at a time when most of the students were gone."

"But what college student nowadays knows how to use a typewriter?"

"The notes weren't actually typed."

"Sure they were."

"Not on an old-fashioned typewriter. It's a computer font called Courier. It looks a lot like an electric typewriter, but if you look closely you can tell it's done on a laser printer."

"So this guy could have these files sitting on his hard drive somewhere?"

"Only if he's stupid. But he's not."

"What about the phone? Can't you try and track down who cloned it?"

"We tried. There are only a couple of skells in town that deal in that sort of thing—cloned phones, stolen credit cards, bogus passports . . ."

"There's a market for fake passports in *Gabriel*? You're joking."

"A huge market. There are an awful lot of foreign students who'd love to bring their families over here, and a certain number of them don't mind breaking the law to do it."

"Can you blame them?"

"Hey, you're not going to get an INS lecture from me. My grandma used to tell me about signs in stores that said 'No dogs or Irish.' Anyhow, we leaned on the dealers we knew of, but no dice."

"No one would admit to selling that particular phone?"

"They said they hadn't even been able to crack the technology."

"Do you believe them?"

"Yeah. I offered each of them a pass on some other stuff. They would have taken it in a heartbeat if they could've given me a name. One of them tried to bluff but we figured out he was full of it pretty quick."

"So it's a dead end?"

"Hopefully not for good. We're still working on it.

NYPD's helping, trying to track down the dealers in the city who'd be on the cutting edge, technology-wise."

"Yeah, but isn't it kind of a big coincidence that this visiting prof comes to Gabriel, and a few months later her cloned phone is used here? Or did she go through New York?"

"No. She changed planes in Pittsburgh and flew straight here."

I thought about it for a minute. "What you said about cutting-edge technology . . . you know, Gabriel is pretty much ground zero for cutting-edge technology. Up at the nanofabrication lab, they're inventing new computer chips as we speak."

"So?"

"So what if this guy cloned the phone *himself*?" Cody stared at me. "It would explain why you can't find who sold it to him, right? Wouldn't it?" He stared at me more. "What is it? What did I say?"

"Alex, I could kiss you."

"Oh. Well, what's stopping you?"

"I'm too busy kicking myself for not thinking of it first."

"Get over it."

He put an arm around me and planted a quick kiss on my cheek. "Okay, where do I look?"

"Huh?"

"Where do I find some psycho kid who knows how to clone a cell phone? What department?"

"Damned if I can tell you. Science gives me a headache. But I know who to ask." I picked up the phone and dialed the Citizen Kane—whose number, by the way, is listed along with all of our home phones on the official

Monitor call list. Luckily, Mad wasn't too far in the bag yet. "Electrical engineering," I told Cody after I hung up. "Mad says that's his best guess."

"Sounds like a good place to start."

"So what do you do now? Go up to the Engineering Quad and see if anybody looks like a serial killer?"

"We like to be a little more subtle. I'll start with the professors, see if they can give us any leads."

"What do you want me to do?"

"Nothing."

"What do you mean nothing?"

"Alex, this is a police investigation. You have to let us deal with it."

"But I can help. I know way more people on campus than you do . . ."

He put his hand on my shoulder. "You don't know what you're dealing with. Please, Alex, don't argue with me. I promised I wouldn't let anything happen to you, but you have to listen to me. Just trust me, and I promise I'll tell you everything after we catch this guy."

I opened my mouth to say something, then realized I had no idea what it was going to be. There was no way I could talk him into letting me tag along. Besides, he was right—he was the cop, and I was the reporter. It was his job to catch the bad guys, and my job to write about it afterward. And as much as I wanted to do something rather than nothing, I could still see C.A.'s body whenever I closed my eyes. Bravado aside, I was fairly sure I never wanted to meet the man who did it to her. "Wait a second, Cody. What about Nanki-Poo?"

"What?"

"C.A.'s dog."

"Right, of course." He patted Shakespeare. "Do you think she misses her friend?"

"We're all kind of depressed around here. Do you think you'll find him?"

He shrugged. "We haven't seen head nor tail of him. Oh, God, no pun intended."

"Do you think he's dead?"

"I wouldn't want to bet on it either way."

"But the odds aren't good, are they?"

"Alex, there's no use in . . ."

"Come on, Cody. Don't give me a whitewash."

He shrugged again. He looked as helpless as I'd ever seen him. "Okay, I'll give it to you straight. The way we figure it, C.A. must have been snatched when she was out walking Nanki-Poo. The dog probably tried to defend her . . ."

"He would have. He was really protective."

"Right, and the killer had to put him down."

"So where's the body?"

"He must have gotten rid of it."

"But he, you know . . . *displayed* his victims so meticulously. Why would he just get rid of the dog?"

"Who knows? Maybe he has different rules for humans and animals. Maybe as far as he's concerned, an animal just isn't worth bothering with. You probably already know this, but there's plenty of psychological evidence that serial killers graduate to people after years of killing or torturing animals. The dog probably wouldn't even interest him anymore."

"I'd like to sic a goddamn pit bull on him."

"Me too. You want to hear something ironic? Patricia Marx had actually been talking about getting a guard dog—her roommate said she was looking at Dobermans. She even got permission from her landlord. But she never had a chance to do it."

"I wonder if it would have saved her life."

"I don't know. C.A.'s German shepherd didn't seem to make a difference."

"That's true."

"Listen, Alex, I have to start following this up. Something tells me we may finally be on the right track here. But I want you to promise me that you're going to be extra careful. I suppose there's no use in trying to talk you into going to your parents' place for a while . . ."

"No use whatsoever."

"Then I at least want you to promise that you'll follow all the security precautions exactly. Keep checking all the doors and windows. Don't even think about going anywhere at night without a police escort, even if you're with one of your girlfriends. And stay the hell out of that bar."

"You gotta be kidding . . ."

"Alex, I mean it. I've got enough to worry about without thinking that this guy is sitting on the next bar stool over from you."

"Is that all, Detective? Or do you want to put me on house arrest?"

"Christ, Alex, don't whine. Can't you get it through your thick head that I'm just trying to look out for you?"

"I know you are. Sorry."

"Listen, I know this isn't easy . . ."

"It's okay. I'll be good. Seriously, and all whining aside, is there anything else you want me to do? Or not do?"

"Don't talk to strangers." He leaned over and kissed

me. "And definitely don't let any crazy men into your house."

"Too late."

He pulled away and reached into his jacket pocket. "Here, I almost forgot. I brought you a present." He handed me a bright yellow box a little bigger than a pack of cigarettes. It had a belt clip and a loop of string just wide enough to fit your wrist.

"Please tell me there's chocolate in here." I started fiddling with the string, and he grabbed it back.

"Don't pull that out or we'll both be sorry. It's a rape alarm. Haven't you ever seen one of these?" I shook my head. "Lots of women used to carry them in the city, not so much since the crime rate went down. The handle connects to a pin. Yank it out and it makes one hell of a noise. You're supposed to be able to hear it from two hundred yards."

"How do I turn it off?"

"You can't. The only way you can stop it is to unscrew the back and take out the batteries."

"What's the point of that?"

"So the bad guy can't just turn it off himself."

"Oh."

"So take it, and carry it so it's handy. Don't just throw it in your purse where it won't do you any good."

"Okay."

"Do you promise?"

"Jesus, yes, I promise. Now go catch this guy so I don't have to carry this ridiculous thing around any more than I have to."

"Why does it bother you so much?"

"Gee, I don't know, Cody. How'd you like to carry around a symbol of your own physical weakness?"

"I already do. It's called a gun."

"Oh. Right."

"Now give me a kiss and wish me luck. Hopefully I can call you tomorrow with some good news for once."

I kissed him, and I was still kissing him when his cell phone rang. He answered it, and I could tell from the look on his face that it was the farthest thing from good news that it could get. "Son of a bitch," he said into the phone. "Where the hell is she?" Other than when he found me staring at C.A.'s corpse, it was the first time I'd seen him lose his cool on the job. When he hung up, he looked like he wanted to throw the phone through the living-room window.

"There's another missing girl, isn't there?"

He didn't answer. It was a long time before he stopped staring out the window and looked at me.

"Worse."

"They found another body?" He nodded so slightly I almost missed it. "Already? But how could . . ."

"He's really into it now. He's gaining momentum. He's having *fun*."

"Are you okay? You look kind of . . ."

He stood up. "I'll be fine. But I have to go."

"Where is she?"

"You wouldn't believe me if I told you."

"Tell me anyway."

He didn't want to, that much was obvious. When he finally spoke, the words came out very slowly. "They found her," he said, "at the campus baseball field. In one of the dugouts."

"What? But that's right in the middle of . . ."

"It gets worse. The body was found by the groundskeeper's nine-year-old son."

"Jesus."

He flipped open his phone again and called for a radio car to be sent to guard my house. He waited with me until the cop arrived, not saying anything, just standing there holding one of my hands between his big beefy ones.

"What is it, Cody? There's something you're not telling me. I know there is." He didn't look at me, just shifted his gaze from his shoes to the door and back again. "Come on. You know I'm going to find out soon enough. Don't make me stay here imagining something even worse."

"There . . ." He cleared his throat. "There was another . . . mutilation. The eyes. The coroner hadn't made it to the scene yet, but this time it looks like it was pre-mortem."

It took a second for his words to sink in. The image made me want to scream, but I figured it wouldn't put him in a better mood. I just put my arms around him and hugged him hard. "Be careful out there, Cody."

"I will," he said, and he was gone.

I picked up the phone to tell Bill about the latest body so he could squeeze something onto page one before deadline, only to realize that I wasn't supposed to know about it in the first place. *Rats.* I curled up on the couch with Shakespeare on one side of me and Tipsy on the other, and thought about how this relationship stuff was more complicated than I'd bargained for. Then I thought about the girl in the dugout, and my problems didn't seem particularly huge. It did occur to me, however, that if there were ever a time for smoking it was now, and I was about to hunt for Emma's Dunhills when the phone rang. I stared at it for a while, thinking about the call I'd gotten the day the last body was found. Then I remembered to check the caller ID, and saw Mad's number.

"Hey, Bernier, what took you so damn long?"

"I'll tell you later."

"Listen, come on over here. We're gonna run down a couple of leads."

"What leads?"

"I got to thinking after you called me, so I tracked down the head of double-e. He gave me some names of kids he thinks might be up to jacking cell phones."

"You called the chairman of the electrical engineering department at this hour? I'm surprised he didn't hang up on you."

"Nah, he's a big alchie since his wife dumped him. When he's not in the lab, he lives in a booth at Sammy's. I just went around the corner and rousted him. Only cost me a couple of boilermakers."

"He really gave you names?"

"He owed me one. Besides, I just told him it was for a science story."

"And you want to go up to campus now?"

"It's not even eleven. The natives are still plenty restless. So get your ass in gear."

Not half an hour ago I'd had no desire to go prowling for clues. Now I could barely stand the idea of staying home alone, kept awake by visions of an eyeless girl lying in a baseball dugout. I was sure of something else too: Cody wasn't going to like it one bit. I was already starting to draft my tirade about how I didn't try to stop him from doing his job, and he damn well wasn't going to stop me from doing mine.

It was a pretty speech, filled with brilliant insights about lingering patriarchy in the post-feminist age. However, the truth is I was hoping he'd never find out.

"Okay," I told Mad, "but you have to come and get me. I promised Cody I wouldn't go out by myself. Besides, if I do the cop'll follow me."

"I'll be there in . . ."

"Hold on a second. My call waiting just beeped."

I clicked over to the other line, but no one was there. I was about to click back over to Mad when I caught the faint sound of someone singing. I said "hello" a couple of times, and the sound got louder. Finally, I heard it well enough to make out the song.

It was a man's voice, one I recognized from his last call.

He was singing "Take Me Out to the Ball Game."

19

By "a couple of leads," Mad meant eleven. He picked me up in his Volvo (which had logged more miles in the past two months than in the previous two years), tossed me a copy of the Benson student directory he'd swiped from the newsroom, and told me to start looking up names. "Listen, Bernier," he said as we drove up the hill toward campus. "I'm still up for this, but don't you think you ought to tell Cody about that phone call?"

"I'll tell him."

"What are you waiting for?"

"He's got his hands full at the moment. They found another dead girl." I told him the gory details I'd gotten from Cody. "He just about lost it when he saw that note from the Citizen. He doesn't need to hear about my phone stalker right now."

"Aren't *you* the gutsy one."

"Hardly. At this point, I don't even have the cojones to stay in my own house, even with a cop out front. I mean, the guy clearly knows where I live."

"What about Emma?"

There was a catch in his voice I couldn't remember hearing before, at least when he was sober. "Jeepers, Mad, are you getting all soft on her?"

"Shut the fuck up."

"Sensitive. . . ."

"Look, do you know where she is or don't you?"

"I tried calling her at the clinic but she wasn't up there."

"Don't you think you ought to warn her not to hang around your house by herself?"

"I left her a note."

"Where the hell is Steve, anyway?"

"Haven't seen him in days. He's been kind of crazed since the whole mess up at Blue Heron. Plus I'm starting to think there might be another birdman in the picture."

"That was more than I needed to know."

"Hey, I bet she's playing darts someplace. After we're done nosing around campus, what say we check a couple of the bars up there?" He grunted. I took it as a yes. "Listen, do you really think it could be some engineer who's been doing all this shit?"

"How do I know? You just asked me to find somebody who could clone a cell phone."

"Well, Cody seems to like the idea that this guy's some evil genius."

"No offense, but I think he's full of it. Right now, we're hunting down a bunch of geeks in their dorm rooms. Best case scenario, we find whoever sold the phone to your gentleman caller."

"You think?"

"I deal with these gearheads on a regular basis. Most of

them are pretty brilliant, but they're not what you'd call threatening. Wussy is more like it."

"Yeah, but who knows if wussy equals harmless? Maybe they're filled with nerdy rage."

He pulled into the last space in a vast campus lot and shifted in his seat to look at me. "You know," he said thoughtfully, "that may be the single stupidest thing you've ever said."

"Really?"

"Yeah."

"Wow. Maybe I ought to write it down."

I flipped through the campus directory, where Mad had highlighted the names he'd gotten from the department chair. There were four grad students and seven under-grads, with addresses all across campus and its environs.

"Man, couldn't he have narrowed it down a little?"

"He picked eleven people out of a department of four hundred."

"What did you tell him, anyway?"

"That I was doing a story on companies who hire students to try to crack their security."

"And he fell for it?"

"He was pretty drunk."

"Yeah, and he's gonna be pretty pissed when he finds out you rooked him."

"Lucky for me he won't remember it in the morning."

We set off toward a particularly hideous sixties-era dorm, which (were its roof only painted orange) could easily be taken for the HoJo's motor lodge. The building housed two of our suspects, but those first two tries didn't bode well for the rest of the night; neither one was home. We moved on to another dorm fifty yards away but a hundred years different in style, a classic brick-and-ivy job with heavy square-paned windows fit for a Victorian heroine. There, our third target opened the door wearing pajamas with big blue teddy bears on them. When he found out Mad wanted to talk to him about cell phone technology, he invited us in and fed us double-stuffed Oreos with chocolate milk.

"Better warn your friend Cody about that one," Mad said as we hoofed down four flights to the first floor. "That boy is Public Enemy Number One."

"Hey, it was your source who gave us the name."

"Maybe he was drunker than I thought."

"And maybe we're just wasting our time."

"Since when are you such a quitter?"

"I'm not. I just don't have a whole lot of confidence in your loopy friend back at Sammy's."

"Believe me, he's one smart son of a bitch. He just happens to be a stinking drunk. It's nothing to be ashamed of." We got to the next dorm. "Okay, who are we looking for here?"

I consulted the book. "Dong-Hyuk Kim."

"You gotta be kidding me."

"Says here his nickname's Freddy."

We climbed to the second floor and found Kim's room. We knocked, and after a minute a very pretty blond girl answered the door wearing a sheet. "Fuck, *you're* not the pizza," she said, and slammed it again.

Mad and I stared at the closed door. He raised his fist to knock again, then changed his mind and walked away. "I must be losing my touch," he said.

"How so?"

"First time a cute college chick ever accused me of not being a pizza."

"Cheer up. There's always Viagra." He gave me a wounded look. "Where to next?"

"You tell me."

I scanned the list.

"You want to get the hell away from the dorms, maybe try some apartments?"

"Can't get any worse."

We walked across campus to the adjacent student ghetto. Even on a Monday night, the place was hopping. Music blared out of the bars, which made up just about every other storefront in a three-block radius of the university. The sidewalks were sticky and the smell of sour beer wafted out of the doorways, constituting whatever is the opposite of aromatherapy.

"Christ, this place makes me feel old."

"Come on, Bernier. Didn't you ladies cut loose at Vassar?"

"No."

Mad breathed in deeply, like he was savoring the fresh mountain air. I was in danger of puking. "You know, maybe I should think about moving up here . . ."

"It would be the end of you."

I dragged him away from the center of Collegetown toward what passes for the residential area—a strip of ramshackle buildings, each with at least one disintegrating couch on the front porch. Two of the grad students we were looking for roomed together in one of them. We found the apartment, only to be told by their neighbors that the two guys were back on campus working in the nanofabrication lab. We were batting zero.

"Remind me why we're doing this again?" Mad said as we passed another row of bars. "Because, you know, I could really use a drink . . ."

"So could I. This is humiliating. How's about we try a couple more and say fuck it?"

"For real?"

"We can always try again tomorrow."

We went to the next address, which was only a half block away. It was the newest building in the neighborhood, opened just the previous fall, and by student standards it was a luxury high-rise. It had six floors (the very limit of the local building code), and every apartment had its own high-speed Internet connection and laundry to boot. The place was called the Hilltop Arms, and the name was fairly accurate. It had the highest security—or more accurately, the *only* security—of any building in Collegetown. This meant that on weekdays, a so-called doorman sat at the front desk, actually some kid doing his math homework. At night and on weekends, visitors had to be buzzed in by one of the residents. The whole arrangement wouldn't faze someone from the big city, but for Gabriel it was Fort Knox.

"Christ, Bernier," Mad growled. "Why didn't we come here first?"

"I didn't recognize the address."

"Didn't you do a story on this place?"

"Yeah, back when it first opened."

The Hilltop Arms had been the object of much mockery when it was being built. But the developer was laughing all the way to bank, because all the apartments were rented within a month—even at more than twice the going rate. The place turned out to be hugely appealing to faraway parents who heard "New York" and thought "Harlem." The vast majority of residents came from OPEC nations, and parked their BMWs and Range Rovers in the underground garage.

Mad took in the arched glass entryway and brass-potted plants with disgust. "What a dump."

"How do you figure?"

"Why would you want to live up here if you're going to lock out all the local color?"

"You'd rather be in one of those places with the broken bottles out front?"

"Wouldn't you?"

"How are we going to get in? Just buzz the guy?"

"Doesn't seem too smart."

"So what now?"

He winked at me and started pushing buttons at random. Eventually, someone answered and Mad leaned into the intercom. "Somebody order a pizza?" They hung up. Mad tried a few more times, and finally someone buzzed us in. We took the elevator to the sixth floor.

"What's this guy's name?" Mad whispered as we walked down the hall.

"Jeffrey Vandebrandt."

"What kind of a name is that?"

"I don't know, German?"

We were looking for apartment 6-N, which turned out to be at the far end of the hall. We stopped outside the door, and Mad's face reflected the same creepy anticipation I was having myself. Above the knob were four separate locks, each of them a Medeco just like the one Cody had made me buy for my front door. Even in Manhattan, it would have been overkill. Here in Gabriel, it was downright strange. And in this particular building, it was ridiculous.

Mad shrugged and raised his arm to knock, but I grabbed it in midair and dragged him back down the hall.

"Hold on," I whispered. "Let's think about this for a minute. Maybe this isn't our guy at all, or maybe you're right that all he did was clone the phone and sell it to someone else. But if you're wrong, I'm the last person who should show up at his doorstep."

"Right. He knows what you look like."

"No shit. If he sees me he's going to know we made him. And God only knows what he might be packing in there."

"Alex, look around this place. If this is your murderer, there's no way he brought those girls up here kicking and screaming. The whole place has got to be crawling with security cameras."

"So maybe he took them somewhere else."

"Well, there's only one way we're going to find anything out. You hide, I knock."

"What are you going to tell him?"

"I don't know. I guess the same thing I told his prof."

"Yeah, but what if he isn't drunk?"

"I'll make it sound good."

He strode down the hall and I watched from the corner as he rapped on the door once, twice, three times. There was no answer. Mad tried the knob, but since it had been locked four times over, it was no surprise that it didn't budge.

"Okay, what now?" he said when he came back to my hiding place.

"Well, what do we usually do?"

"We nose around."

"You up for it?"

"You bet your ass I am."

"Where's the ambition coming from all of a sudden?"

He glanced down the silver-carpeted hallway and back to the four locks. "I don't like this guy."

We pulled out our press passes and knocked at Vandebrandt's next-door neighbor. The door was answered by two girls who, between the two of them, seemed the apotheosis of the phrase "Jewish American Princess." They were dressed nearly identically, in Armani painter's pants and little cropped Calvin Klein T-shirts (one black, one gray) that didn't come anywhere near the waistbands of their jeans. The faint smell of pot smoke drifted into the hall as they checked out first Mad, then his press pass, then me.

"Hey, what can we do for you?" Black T-shirt said to Mad.

He answered directly to her perky little B-cup bosom. "You think we might ask you ladies a few questions?"

"About what?" said her gray-shirted friend.

"About the guy who lives next door."

Their faces twisted into identical pouts.

"Oh, that *freak*," they said almost in unison.

Gray T-shirt stepped into the doorway to give Mad the full view. "Like, what do you want with that loser?"

"Can we come in for a sec?"

The girls looked at each other, hesitated but a millisecond, and opened the door wide—this in a town that had seen four murdered women in as many months. Were they nuts? Or did they think Mad was just too cute to be a killer?

"Like, have a seat," one of them said as they both disappeared into the kitchen. The entire apartment was carpeted in white shag. In the living room, two black leather couches hulked around a chrome coffee table on which lay a thirty-dollar bottle of wine and a very large bong. The former I knew not because I'm any kind of connoisseur, but because the price tag was still on it.

They came back in carrying two more glasses, plus a plate with grapes, a big slice of Brie, and box of wheat thins. This either meant that they were trying to be hospitable, or they were getting a bad case of the munchies.

"So, like, who do you work for again?" Black T-shirt asked.

"The *Gabriel Monitor*," Mad said, charm oozing from his invisible Nordic pores. "I should introduce myself. My name is Jake Madison. My friends call me Mad. This is my colleague, Alex Bernier."

"Well, hi *Mad*," Gray T-shirt said, putting down the food to shake his hand. "I'm Jennifer, and this is my sister Joanie."

"*Joan*," the other corrected as she sidled up to Mad on the couch. She looked like a Joanie to me. Come to think of it, the other one looked very much like a Jenny.

"You ladies are sisters?"

"Twins!" they said.

Get me out of here, I thought, realizing we'd just stumbled into one of Mad's favorite sexual fantasies. If one of them pulled out a big tub of tapioca pudding, I'd be spending the rest of the night in the hallway.

"And you know what I think?" he said, smiling that

wolf smile of his. "I think you just might be California girls."

"Beverly Hills, 90210!" they chanted. "How'd you know?" I felt more nauseous than I had outside Budweiser Row.

"So, ladies, I was wondering if you might be able to help us an eensy little bit." It was the first time I'd ever heard Mad use the word "eensy." I hoped it would be the last. "It's about that fellow who lives next door."

The pouty looks took up residence again. "Ooh," Joanie said, putting a slab of Brie on a cracker. "What do you want with that *troll*?"

"It's for a story I'm doing."

"On what?" Jenny asked, nearly lying across Mad's lap to get to the grapes.

Mad looked from her to her sister. I could practically see his synapses firing as he calculated how fast he could get rid of me, get back here, and nail them both. He cleared his throat. "On . . . um . . . the biggest losers on campus."

"No *way*," they said in simultaneous glee.

"So can you help me out?"

"Well," Joanie said, "he, like, looks at us funny."

"Yeah," Jenny echoed. "He's so *icky*. He's always giving us the eye, you know, like we'd have anything to do with that little shrimp."

"Have you ever spoken to him?"

They screwed up their faces, as though Mad had asked if they wanted to bear the guy's mutant offspring. "Like, no way."

"Do you see him coming and going a lot?"

"Well, not like we'd care," Joanie said with an expert hair flip. "But mostly he just skulks around."

"Yeah," Jenny said. "He's always bringing big boxes in there, and he looks at you like you'd want to steal his stupid stuff. As *if*."

"Yeah," her sister said. "As *if*."

"Is he out a lot?"

"Nah, he hardly ever goes anywhere," Jenny said. "He just goes to class and comes back at like six and stays in there doing whatever he does. He's such a *creep*."

"And he doesn't go out at night?" They stared at him like he was nuts. "Okay, well, do you ever hear weird noises coming from his apartment?"

Jenny did a mirror image of her sister's hair-flipping trick. "Just, like, *beeping* sometimes."

"Oh, yeah," Joanie said, "and one time we had to bang on his door to get him to turn down his cop shows."

"Cop shows?"

"Yeah," Jenny said. "He, like, loves them. Watches them all night long."

"And what did he say when you asked him to be quiet?"

Joanie rolled her eyes. "Like, nothing. He wouldn't even come to the door. He turned it down, though."

"Why wouldn't he come to the door?"

This time, it was Jenny's turn for an eye roll. "He, like, *never* does. Like, the building had a Halloween party, and he wouldn't even open up for the trick-or-treaters."

"Yeah," her sister interjected. "He probably wouldn't even come out if the building burned down. He holes up in there like a *weirdo*."

Mad shot me a glance. It was nice to know that he

hadn't actually forgotten I was there, considering that I hadn't had the chance to say one damn word.

"Well, ladies, thank you so much for all your help. We need to go talk to a few of your neighbors." He cocked his head toward the exit, and I got the message. I stood up, gave a lame little wave, and walked to the door. "I'd really like to thank you for all the information," I heard him murmur. "Do you suppose I might have the pleasure of taking you out for a drink some . . ."

I left, figuring I'd rather run into their creepy neighbor than listen to Mad scam a couple of sophomores. He came out a minute later.

"Jesus Christ, Mad," I whispered. "Do those girls realize the eighties are over? With all the white wine and Brie and designer jeans, I was expecting them to snort some coke any second." I followed him to the end of the hall and down a stairwell. "Where are we going?"

He kept walking until he found what he was looking for. "You up for an adventure?"

"Huh?"

"The wonder twins said this guy wouldn't leave his apartment even if the building was burning down," he said. "Let's see if they're right."

20

"ARE YOU OUT OF YOUR MIND?" I WAS STANDING BETWEEN
Mad and the fire alarm. He'd reached for it once, and I'd
managed to fend him off. "Come on, you maniac. Don't
make me mace you."

"But I've got a really brilliant . . ."

"Do you have brain damage? You're the one who said
this place is crawling with security cameras."

"You're right. It's a crazy idea. I can't imagine what I
could have been thinking of."

In retrospect, *I* can't imagine that I fell for that smarmy
tone in his voice. But the minute I turned my back, he
yanked the fire box.

"Mad, you fucking juvenile delinqu . . ."

I was drowned out by the shrieking alarm. Red warning lights started blinking on the stairs to help guide people out of the building in case of a real fire. Mad jogged
back up to the sixth floor, and I couldn't think of anything
to do but follow him. We crouched at the end of the hall,
watching the various occupants flee their apartments car-

rying whatever valuables they'd had time to snatch up. (In Jenny and Joanie's case it was the wine, the bong, and six pairs of shoes.)

We kept our eyes on apartment 6-N. Nothing.

"Maybe he's really not in here," I said. "Come on, Mad, let's get the hell out of . . ."

"You got any cigarettes?" I stared at him. "Give it up, Bernier, I know you're carrying."

I dug a pack of Emma's Dunhills out of my purse and threw them at him. "Take the butts out," he said. Then he reached into his jacket pocket, pulled out a miniature flask, and took a swig. "Bacardi 151. Shame to waste it. But whatcha gonna do?"

"What the hell are you up to?"

"Give me a notebook. Come on, hurry." He ripped some pages out, stuffed them in the empty cigarette pack, and doused the whole thing with booze. Then he lit one cigarette off the other until four were burning, set the pack of matches on fire, and shoved the whole pile as far under the apartment door as he could.

"My God, you're having *fun*," I said when he got back to our corner. "What are you, McGyver?"

"Don't worry. I have a plan," he said, and poured the last of the rum over his head. I was starting to think he'd been nipping the 151 on the sly all night.

"That's what I'm afraid of."

"Just watch." Sure enough, not half a minute later the apartment door opened a crack. "Stay here," he whispered.

From down the hall, I saw a figure emerge from the doorway. I got a glimpse of black hair and a bright red Benson sweatshirt, but before I could get a good look at him—and, more importantly, before he could figure out that the only thing burning was a pack of Dunhills—Mad went barreling into him at full speed.

"Hurry up, man!" he shouted in his best pseudo-drunk voice, honed to perfection by many nights of the real thing. "The building's on fire, man. Come on!"

They ran toward the nearest fire door, Mad practically carrying the guy under his arm. I heard their footsteps slamming down the stairs until the door shut behind them and everything was quiet except the fire alarm—which, unlike the blaring in the stairwell, was more of a high-pitched tweet than something that would actually roust you out of bed in the middle of the night.

It seemed like everybody was gone, so I ventured into the hallway. The door to number 6-N was just slightly ajar; Mad had done a good job of not letting the guy close it. I held my breath and pushed it open a bit, then froze; there were voices coming from inside. I was about to flee when I realized the sounds were vaguely familiar.

Emergency control to Gabriel monitors. Repeat, report of an automatic fire alarm at 249 University Place. Two engines and an EMT requested to respond.

Copy that. Units one and three responding.

EMT unit A that is Adam en route.

It was a police scanner. I should have recognized it right away, considering I've spent the past few years sitting on top of one. I called myself a nasty name and opened the door.

My first impression of the place was that I'd walked into CIA headquarters, or maybe the bridge of the starship *Enterprise*. Every surface was covered with electronic gadgets whose indicator lights were blinking red and white and green. The apartment was dark, lit only by a pair of halogen lamps turned halfway down, and the contrast made the blinking lights seem unnaturally bright. It gave the room an aura that was equal parts calming and creepy.

I wasn't sure if I should shut the door or not, so I compromised by leaving it the way I found it, just slightly ajar. That erased most of the light from the hallway, plunging the apartment into slightly deeper gloom. Its occupant obviously wanted it this way, and the mood of the place was starting to make me agree with Mad. I didn't like this guy either.

I ventured farther into the room, although I sure as hell didn't want to. There was something suffocating about it, but I couldn't quite put my finger on what. Maybe it was the sense that the whole elaborate setup was geared toward feeding someone's even more elaborate obsession. Or maybe it was just that the place was so dark, a whole cadre of knife-wielding maniacs could have been hiding in the corner and I wouldn't have seen them.

One by one, I checked out the various devices and gadgets. Most of them left me clueless, but I'm one of those people who needs to assemble a team of experts to plug in my stereo. And, come to think of it, there was nothing like a stereo in the place. There was no television, either, and no CD player or VCR. Whatever all these high-tech gizmos were, they clearly weren't a home entertainment system.

But then again, maybe they were.

I counted a total of three computers, all of them way fancier than mine. One was connected to a flatbed image scanner, another to a laser printer, and another to an eyeball-shaped camera that, as far as I knew, was recording my every move. Although the police scanner looked nothing like the one in the newsroom, I recognized it because it was still spewing details about the nonexistent blaze. I wondered how long it would be before somebody figured out that the only fire in the building was a few smoldering embers outside apartment 6-N, and hoped that the fact it was on the top floor meant I wouldn't be caught anytime soon.

As I made my way to the other side of the room, I heard what sounded like another scanner coming from the opposite corner. The volume was much lower, probably because it was near the wall that abutted the twins' apartment.

Base to unit nine.

Yo, Chrissy, how you doin', sweetness?

Save it, Stimpson. I got a message from your wife.

Finally wants to go for a three-way, huh?

Yeah, right. She says don't forget to pick up diapers on the way home.

Stimpson, you are so ball-busted, man. You gonna pick up some baby powder while you're at it?

I stared at the black box. This was no ordinary scanner. It wasn't just picking up the normal dispatcher calls that we get at the *Monitor*. It was somehow tapping into the car-to-car chatter that's broadcast on a separate police frequency, and is most definitely not for public ears. The box had a series of buttons on the front, and I pressed one at random. Brian Cody's voice came out so clearly he could have been standing there.

. . . back at the station. Tell him I want the autopsy results yesterday. You got it?

Yes, sir.

I'm leaving the scene now to do the notification. If you need me try my cell. Cody out.

Poor Cody. He was on his way to do just exactly what he'd been dreading—drag another family out of bed to tell them that their daughter or wife or sister was dead. I wondered whether he'd want me to comfort him after such a thing, or if he'd just as soon be by himself. I really didn't know him, not down deep, and it occurred to me that maybe that was why I enjoyed his company so much in the first place. There's a lot to be said for simplicity.

Okay, so it wasn't the greatest time for romantic introspection. I snapped myself out of it and kept looking around the room. In a closet, I found a collection of photography equipment, including a tripod and a number of what appeared to be very expensive cameras. On one bookshelf, I found a dozen cell phones nestled in their chargers, and I wondered whether the phone-cloning business was how Vandebrandt financed his high-tech hobbies.

When I figured I'd seen all there was to see in the living room, I opened the door to what appeared to be the only bedroom. It was completely dark, so I groped for a light switch and flicked it on.

What I saw next was the most fundamentally disturbing thing I'd ever had the bad luck to run into, short of an actual corpse. No, there was nobody waiting to pounce on me. There was also nobody tied to the bed, nor a taxidermy collection, or even a copy of the Satan-worshiper's handbook.

But along one whole wall, the one you first saw when you walked in the bedroom door, was something that might be generously described as a shrine. And the subject, quite simply, was me.

There were dozens of my bylined articles, pasted one on top of the other in a creepy college. Every one of my movie columns from the past few months was up there, the little head shot of me and the logo ALEX ON THE AISLE repeated over and over. I counted four copies of the *Monitor* piece on me finding Patricia Marx's body, plus several other versions of the wire story that ran in other papers across the state.

That wasn't even the scariest part. No, any psycho with a pair of scissors and a newspaper subscription could have accomplished that much. But there were photographs too—pictures of me in the window seat at the Citizen Kane, opening the front door of the *Monitor* office, covering the psychics' protest on the Green, walking Shakespeare, getting into my car in front of my house.

He'd been watching me. He'd been following me, recording my comings and goings for what looked to be months. I couldn't believe that I hadn't sensed it somehow, hadn't once caught him in the act, but I'd never even suspected. It made me feel incredibly vulnerable, like he'd not only stalked me but stolen something important—call it the illusion of privacy.

It's strange to see your life laid bare like that, frozen in perfectly focused black-and-white. I hardly recognized myself, and it took me a minute to figure out why. People rarely have their pictures taken without knowing about it, and in nearly every image I'd ever seen of myself I was smiling or at least poised. Here, I was just going about my business, and I realized with a start that this was what I must look like to the rest of the world—short, messy-haired, and serious. Thank God he hadn't resorted to videotape. At least as far as I knew.

The whole thing made me want to scream, but it was also absurdly fascinating. There up on the wall was every word I'd written since April, not just the big stories but also the little stuff on potholes and blood drives. Jeffrey Vandebrandt was either a dangerous nutcase or the one and only member of the Alex Bernier Fan Club; more likely, he was both.

There was nothing particularly threatening about the shrine, beyond its very existence. None of the photos of me were cut in half or had the eyes gouged out. He hadn't written KILL KILL KILL in his own blood, but maybe he was saving that sort of fun for next semester. There were no pictures of any of the murder victims, which was curious; then I thought with a start that maybe there had been, and once he was done with them he ripped the photos down and started over with the next victim.

I considered searching the place for evidence linking him to those four girls, but one look at my watch told me I had to get moving. I walked out of the bedroom, and I'd made it halfway across the living room when the door opened.

There, gaping at me like I was the last person on the planet he expected to see, was Jeffrey Vandebrandt.

He was under five feet tall, and he couldn't have weighed more than a hundred pounds. He had blue eyes, and short, spiky black hair, and the worst acne I'd seen since junior high. The picture didn't add up to very much of a threat, but after what I'd seen in the apartment I was a lot more worried about the guy's brain than his brawn.

He didn't say anything, just stood in the doorway with

his mouth open. I didn't move either, mostly because I was scared stiff, and as the seconds ticked by I had the absurd image of the two of us as duelists at the OK Corral. Unfortunately, I wasn't nearly that well armed; I had the rape alarm in one pocket and my Mace in the other. I was more than willing to use them both.

The silence stretched on for what seemed like an hour until finally I couldn't stand it anymore. *"Who are you?"* He didn't answer. I probably should have kept my mouth shut, but at the time it didn't even occur to me. I mean, it was obvious that there was no way I was going to talk my way out of the apartment, and the direct approach was the only thing I could think of.

"Why have you been following me?" I said. "And why the fuck do you have all those pictures of me in your bedroom? Am I supposed to be next?"

He still didn't answer, just kept staring at me with those beady blue eyes. He closed his mouth and opened it again, but no sound came out.

"Come on, answer me. Why are you stalking me?"

Again with the mouth closing and opening. Finally, his voice came out, slow and high-pitched. "I . . ." He stammered as though the words just wouldn't come. "I . . ."

"You what?"

"I l-l-l . . ."

I watched as he tried to get the words out. If he had a stutter, it was the worst one I'd ever heard.

"I l . . . I l-l-l . . ."

He seemed furious at himself all of a sudden. His face was turning red, and he was smashing one balled-up fist into his leg hard enough for it to really hurt.

"I l . . . I l-l-l . . . I l-l-l . . . love y-y-you."

Now it was my turn to stare at him with my mouth open. "You love me?"

He nodded. It made me so angry I forgot to be scared. "You *love* me?" He nodded again. "You crazy *jerk*."

And then, for no good reason that I can think of, and with a calm I still can't explain, I walked across the room and punched him in the nose.

Mad has told me more than once that in a world of weird chicks I am the weirdest of all. What he found when he came running into the apartment ten seconds later did nothing to change his mind. There I was, standing over Vandebrandt in the closest I ever get to a fury. Our suspected serial killer was on the floor, clutching his bleeding nose and blubbering like a baby.

Mad looked from me to Vandebrandt and back again. Then he pulled out his flask, tipped his head back, and shook the few lingering drops of Bacardi into his mouth. "Seems like you've got everything under control."

"Where the hell have you been?"

"Our boy here gave me the slip. I came back up to save you."

"Oh."

"Do I need to save *him*?"

"Call the cops."

"Where's the phone?"

"Take your pick. They're all over the place. No wait, I'll do it myself."

Mad kept an eye on Vandebrandt while I called Cody on his cell phone. It was something like one in the morning by then, but from the background noise I could tell he was in his car, either on his way to notify the latest victim's family or on his way back from the dirty deed. He was in the midst of telling me that he didn't have time to talk when I finally got it through to him that it wasn't a social call. I explained what was happening, and the anger I could hear in his voice even over the scratchy connection made me think that maybe Mad was going to have to save me after all.

Cody got there about fifteen minutes later, just as the firemen were nosing around the ashes in the hallway. We'd spent the last quarter of an hour getting our stories straight—Vandebrandt huddled in the corner while Mad coached me on how we'd seen some drunken student waving a pack of flaming Dunhills—but by the time Cody showed up it was obvious he'd squared things for us somehow. He shook hands with the fire lieutenant, who mumbled something about getting one of his men to clean up the mess, and I gathered they were going to chalk the whole thing up to the usual student hijinks. Personally, I doubted Cody was going to let me off the hook that easily.

But at the moment, yelling at me was hardly the first thing on his mind. His expression segued from irate to downright bewildered as he took in the sniveling suspect and his collection of electronic toys. Without elaborating, I cocked my head toward the bedroom door. Cody went in, and when he emerged he looked at Vandebrandt with a new flavor of rage. "Do you like to stalk women, Jeffrey?" he growled from six feet above the cringing kid. "Do you like to hurt them? Do you want to hurt women you can't have?"

If there was a right way to approach Vandebrandt, this wasn't it. He just went farther into the fetal position, pulling his legs tighter into his chest and rocking back and forth.

"Why did you do it, Jeffrey? Was it just for the thrill? Or did they make you angry because they wouldn't give you the time of day?"

Vandebrandt's mouth opened and closed like it had before. He looked pathetic, and it made me want to throttle him. "L-l-l . . ." he started. If he said he loved me again, I was going to punch him even harder. "L-l-l-l . . ."

"What? Come on, spit it out, you little freak," Cody shouted at him. I doubted they endorsed this sort of thing in the department's sensitivity training manual. "What the hell is it?"

"L . . . L-l-l-l . . ." He seemed determined to answer, probably because Cody seemed equally determined to kick him if he didn't. L-l-l . . . Lawyer."

"You want a lawyer?" Vandebrandt nodded with an oddly puppyish kind of eagerness. Cody looked down at him in disgust. "Of course you do."

Just as Cody was turning away, Vandebrandt reached under his sweatshirt. Cody must have caught the motion out of the corner of his eye, because in under two seconds he had both the guy's wrists pinned behind his back with one hand and was holding a small gray box in the other. It turned out to be an electronic address book. Cody let him go with a grunt and tossed the gadget at him. Vandebrandt pushed a few buttons and then handed it back.

Cody eyed the device, which looked absurdly small in his big mitts. "Mr. and Mrs. Wallace Vandebrandt, Grosse Pointe, Michigan." He looked back to the suspect. "What do you want me to do with this?" He tried to give the address book back to Vandebrandt, but the kid wouldn't take it.

"C-c-c-c . . ."

"You want me to call your parents?" Vandebrandt nodded his puppy nod again. Cody shook his head. "Call them yourself."

"C-c-c-c . . ."

"I said you'll have to call them yourself, jerk-off."

"P-p-pl-pl . . ."

"Oh, for Chrissake . . ." Cody pulled out his cell phone and dialed. It took a long time for the person to answer, no surprise since it was after midnight in Michigan. "Yeah, is this Mr. Wallace Vandebrandt? Mr. Vandebrandt, this is Detective Brian Cody of the Gabriel Police Department. No, don't worry, your son is all right. Well, physically he's fine but he's in a lot of trouble. He wants you to get him a lawyer. What are we charging him with? Well, stalking, for starters. And he's under suspicion for . . . What's that? Hello?" He put the phone away and stared down at Vandebrandt.

"What happened?" I asked.

"He hung up."

"Why?"

"I have a feeling that our friend Jeffrey here is a very bad little boy."

"No shit. But what did his father say?"

"Well, when I told him he was being arrested for stalking, he said exactly two words."

"What?"

" 'Not again.' "

21

Vandebrandt's father must have calmed down and made some phone calls, because by the next morning an extremely high-priced lawyer was downtown demanding a bail hearing and screaming that the whole case against his client was based on an illegal search. That much was going to be up to a judge. After all, the cops had entered the apartment without a warrant—but in response to a complaint by a civilian, namely me. From what Cody told me, the case was going to hinge on the issue of victim's rights. New York's stalker law is one of the toughest in the country, and the D.A. was gambling that me tracking down my harasser landed on the legal side of vigilante, if just barely.

It didn't hurt that Vandebrandt had a record, and a pretty goddamn twisted one. Whatever he did as a child was sealed by the state of California, but it must have been enough to prompt a judge there to try him as an adult for another offense at the tender age of fifteen. California also takes its stalkers seriously, and apparently the presiding judge in Orange County was no pussycat. Vandebrandt had been convicted of harassing four teenage girls, for which he'd served six months in jail. Then the family must have moved to Ohio, because the other item on his record was one thousand hours of community service for a misdemeanor harassment charge in Cincinnati.

The way Cody explained it, Vandebrandt's M.O. was depressingly consistent: he was obsessed with women connected to high-profile crimes. In California, it was the survivors of a drunk-driving crash that killed a bunch of kids on a school bus; in Ohio, it was two tellers who'd been on duty when their bank was robbed and a guard was shot. And in Gabriel, of course, it was yours truly—the lucky girl who found a corpse.

Between a copy of his probation report from California and a pleading phone call Cody got from the kid's mother, the details of Vandebrandt's little hobby were floating to the top of the cesspool. Apparently (at least according to his shrink), he had elaborated fantasies about rescuing the women. But—and this is the part I think is a bunch of crap—he also felt powerless, and envied the men who'd had the guts to hurt them in the first place. So at the same time that he adored his targets, he also felt compelled to scare them half to death, to keep them in a state of perpetual hysteria so they'd need him even more.

Or something like that. It gave me a headache just thinking about it.

His mother swore he'd never hurt anyone, but it was hard to rationalize that with the way he'd hounded us. He'd only been a high school sophomore when he'd sent four of his classmates elaborate drawings of their friends' dead bodies and called them as much as fifty times a *day*.

In Ohio he had, among other things, sent the pretty young bank tellers wads of Monopoly money dipped in his own blood. I was starting to think I'd gotten off easy.

"Jesus," I said to Cody, "why did these people ever let their psycho kid go off to college?"

"His mom said they thought he was all better."

"Fat chance."

We were lying in my bed, naked and exhausted. Unfortunately, we weren't tired from anything more entertaining than a very long day of dealing with the fallout from Jeffrey Vandebrandt, and naked only as a result of having thrown our clothes on the floor. On top of working on the murder investigation, Cody and his cops had been gathering evidence on Vandebrandt for the D.A., who was just salivating to indict the kid.

Vandebrandt's past explained why he'd gone after me, and the police inventory of his apartment went a long way toward figuring out how. Cody told me that they'd found not only the gizmo he'd rigged to clone cell phones, but a whole high-tech studio for forging documents, from passports to driver's licenses to social security cards. He said it was one of the most sophisticated operations he'd ever seen—he seemed rather amused that I couldn't believe such a thing could exist in little old Gabriel—and that Vandebrandt's only hope for shaving a few minutes off his sentence was to cop to all the sales he'd made and ID the buyers. The police also found the device he'd used to alter his voice, and the techies were in the midst of deconstructing the souped-up scanner he'd used to listen to the cop-to-cop chatter—and which allowed him to follow my comings and goings via the officers who were guarding me. There was even some tacky theatrical makeup; on top of everything else, apparently little Jeffrey considered himself a master of disguise. And yes, he'd even been thoughtful enough to keep copies of the letters he sent me on his hard drive.

"His mom was awful upset," Cody said into his pillow. "She seemed like a nice lady too."

"So what did she have to say about what he did to me?"

"That he couldn't resist."

"What?"

Cody rolled over onto his back and spoke to the ceiling. The movement disturbed Shakespeare and Zeke, who were curled up together at the foot of the bed. It was a new stage of intimacy, having Cody's dog over here, and although I liked Zeke it was all rather terrifying. "She seemed to think it was incredibly rotten luck," Cody was saying. "Of all the places her son could go to school, he had to end up on a campus where a bunch of women were killed. She said it was way too good for him to resist."

"Too *good*?"

"Her words."

"So what's going to happen to him?"

"He's going to jail."

"For how long?"

"Not long enough."

"At least he's kicked off campus for good."

For obvious reasons, Vandebrandt had neglected to mention his past foibles to the Benson admissions office, and the university was already taking steps to expel him for falsifying his application. Justice is rarely that swift on a college campus, but the administrators knew better than to drag their feet or they'd have to answer to the

Benson Feminist Alliance, which was already sharpening its knives and spoiling for some civil disobedience.

While Cody had been busy over at the cop shop, I'd had the pleasure of ghostwriting a page-one story on Vandebrandt's arrest for Wednesday's paper, and then watching Mad slap his own byline on it in the name of journalistic detachment. But of course, that piece had only run below the fold; the main story was about the latest murder victim. The police had released her name Tuesday morning and we'd both run around like crazy all day trying to cover it.

She was called Lynn Smith. It was a plain name for a plain girl who had an equally plain job serving meals in a university dining hall. She lived with her fiancé, a Benson janitor, in one of the outlying trailer parks that serve as affordable housing around here. Mad had tracked him down to get quotes for the story, and Melissa had somehow talked him into posing for a picture outside their trailer. It ran with the piece, along with a copy of their formal engagement photo from the mall portrait studio, and you only had to take one look at the guy in front of the trailer decorated with plastic flowers and butterflies to know his heart was broken.

Sometimes I understand why people hate the media.

"Alex?" Cody said softly, propping himself up on one elbow. "Vandebrandt's not our guy."

"I know. I knew the minute I saw him. He's no killer. He's more like a parasite."

"Good word for it."

"I still want to beat the crap out of him."

"Take a number. Besides, you already did a pretty good job of it. You broke his nose, you know."

"Good. Let me know when it heals and I'll break it again."

"You're sexy when you're trying to sound tough." He kissed me, then ran his hand up my side. I pulled his head down and kissed him back for a while.

"You know," I said a couple of minutes later, "you were right all along."

"About what?"

"When we first got those crazy letters, and you thought they weren't really from the killer, you were right. And that means that our not running them had nothing to do with C.A.'s death."

"That's true. Does it help?"

"Yeah. But where did Vandebrandt get off making threats about killing people? I mean, how did he know that there'd be another murder to prove his point?"

Cody sighed and draped his arm around my waist. "He didn't. He was probably just raving. He knew there'd be another murder sooner or later, and whenever it happened he'd just factor that into his next threat."

"What a whacko."

"Alex, I'd deny this in a court of law, but I think he's a genuine lunatic."

"He's not the only one in town."

Cody's arm tightened. "You know, just because Vandebrandt's not our guy doesn't mean you should go taking any stupid chances. There's still some nut out there killing women. I don't want you going out alone at night—not to walk the dog, not for anything. Got it?"

"Yeah, I got it."

"Promise me."

"Jesus, Cody, I feel like I promise you the same thing

every fifteen minutes. But okay, I promise I won't go out alone at night. You don't have to convince me. I've seen this guy's work myself, you know."

"I know. We've both seen enough to choke on."

There was a catch in his voice that made me think the past forty-eight hours had gotten to him more than he was letting on. I rolled on my side to face him nose to nose. "Did you have to break it to Lynn Smith's boyfriend?"

"Her father and stepmother out in Groton. They were the next of kin."

"Was it awful?"

"Very."

"Do you want to talk about it?"

"No."

"You don't feel like talking about the case at all, do you?"

"Not one damn bit."

"Fair enough."

"You know, Alex, there's something I've been meaning to ask you," he said after a minute. "That painting's not real, is it? It's a copy, right?"

He gazed up at the oil painting that takes up an entire wall of my bedroom. It depicts a woman in the fragile light of an empty apartment, and it's just about the loneliest thing you can imagine. It's also the first thing I see when I wake up every morning, which is probably not healthy.

"No, it's real."

He stared at me, then back at the painting. "It's a Hopper, isn't it?"

"Yeah."

He gave a low whistle. "It must be worth a fortune."

"Probably. It was a gift."

"From who?"

"I got it after Adam died. Call it a consolation prize. Or maybe the spoils of war."

"Shouldn't it be in a museum or something?"

"Probably."

"You don't feel like talking about it, do you?"

"Not one damn bit."

"Well, fair enough then."

"Do you want a back rub?"

"What?"

"A back rub? You've heard of it?"

"Yeah, but it's been a while since one's been offered."

"Roll over."

"You know, you don't have to give me a back rub just to get me to shut up about the painting."

"I know. I just sort of feel like it."

"Then I'd be a fool to resist."

He turned over on his stomach and I produced my various massage aids. I'm not much of a hippie, but I still live in a town where you can't swing a dead cat around your head without hitting an aromatherapist, so I've collected my fair share of oils and unguents. Cody snickered as I lit my lavender relaxation candle, but he shut up once he realized the thing smelled pretty good. I poured some orange-scented massage oil on his back and dug in. His muscles were tight, but considering the pleasant state of his torso, it wasn't what you'd call work.

"Strong hands."

"All that typing."

"Feels good."

"Just relax."

"Where'd you learn this?"

"There's a massage school in Gabriel. I did a feature story on it once. Picked up a few pointers."

"I'll say."

"Be quiet."

I worked on his back for twenty minutes until the muscles finally felt pliant and his breathing slowed to what I thought was sleep. But when I went to pull the sheet over him he gave a little protesting groan and muttered something that sounded like "Don't stop."

"You want me to keep going?"

"Uh-huh."

"Then roll over on your back." He opened one eye. "Don't worry. I'm not going to try and take advantage of you when you're all sleepy."

"Baby," he mumbled as he turned over, "you can do any damn thing you want."

He lay there with his eyes closed, his breathing mixing with the dogs' gentle wheezing from the other end of the bed. And as I rubbed his chest and stomach in the candlelight, it hit me that this was one of those quintessentially intimate moments—the kind you remember later, when the relationship is over and you've gone your separate ways and you're looking back at the things you miss most.

Call me a cynic, but I've never had what you'd call a long-term romance, and regardless of where Cody's dog was sleeping, I had no illusion that our little cop-reporter interlude was going to be any different. I knew it was just a matter of time until it ended, and that in the long run the whole thing was probably going to be counted in weeks rather than months, and although I should have been used to the law of the jungle by now the thought of sleeping alone again made me want to cry.

So to avoid thinking about it, I let my hands wander lower. Cody had said I could do anything I wanted to him, and it seemed a shame to let such an offer go to waste.

22

As Gordon has pointed out more than once, home delivery of the *Times* is not available in Gabriel. You can, in fact, get the *Times* delivered in far-flung metro areas like Chicago and San Francisco, but in a little city five hours north of Manhattan you are expected to brave the elements and get your own damn paper. For the rest of us, it's business as usual. For Gordon, it was a daily reminder that his life had no meaning.

On Wednesday morning, however, the *Times* showed up on my doorstep in the hands of one very tall and very, very annoyed reporter. "Read this now," Mad growled as he came in the front door, "and kill me later." Then he went into the kitchen to make coffee.

I unfolded the paper and scanned the front page. Nothing seemed particularly relevant, so I jumped to the Metro section. There I found Gordon's byline, under the headline FEAR IN A COLLEGE TOWN and the subhead AS FOURTH BODY IS FOUND, SEARCH FOR GABRIEL KILLER IN-

TENSIFIES. "Man, why are their headlines always so lame?"

Mad stuck his head out of the kitchen. "It's their style."

"Huh?"

"It's their style to have no style."

"Oh." He disappeared again. "'Some people are calling him the Canine Killer,'" I read aloud. "What the hell is this?"

"Just read it," Mad yelled from the other room.

"'Some people are calling him the Canine Killer. For four months, residents and students in this upstate college town, home to prestigious Benson University, have retreated behind locked doors as a serial killer preys on young women.' Hey, Mad?"

"What?"

"When did Gordon have a lobotomy?"

"Just read the damn thing, will you?"

"Do I have to?"

"Bernier . . ."

"Oh, all *right*. Where was I? Serial killer, yadda yadda . . . Okay. 'Two days ago, as the fourth body was found in the dugout of a campus baseball diamond, a pattern began to emerge that may provide what police sources call their first break in the case: at least two, and possibly more, of the victims were apparently walking their dogs at night when the abductions occurred.' Man, that sentence *sucks*. 'Although the bodies of both women were meticulously displayed in public places, their dogs have not been found.' So Lynn Smith had a dog?"

Mad came in from the kitchen and flopped into an armchair. "Name's Harley. As in the motorcycle."

"How do you know that?"

"It's in Band's goddamn fucking story."

"So why isn't it in ours?"

"Because I'm an idiot."

"Elaborate."

"I need some coffee first."

"Speak now."

"Argh . . . Okay, here's the thing. I went out there and got my quotes from the grieving boyfriend, and he even mentioned the goddamn dog was gone, but I never put two and two together."

"Mad . . ."

"Come on, Bernier, you know I'm no good at this touchy-feelie-girlie shit. That's why I write science stories—no people in 'em. What was Bill thinking sending me out to get color in the first place? He knows I suck at it. You're the sob sister."

"Yeah, well, that's why he sent me up to interview the girls at the dining hall. He probably never thought the fiancé would talk in the first place, so it didn't matter who went."

"And now Gordon 'The Weasel' Band breaks this dog thing in the fucking *Times*. Makes me want to snap his neck."

"Is your manhood hurting?"

"You bet."

"So what's his scoop? And don't tell me to read the story. I can't bear it."

"Pretty much what you got out of the lead. Smith and C.A. were both walking their dogs when they disappeared. The cops think there's a connection."

"They say that on the record?" I fumbled for the paper.

"You kidding? Unnamed sources only."

"Gordon must still have some contacts in the department."

"Looks like it. Didn't Cody say something to you about the dog thing?"

"No. Wait. Come to think of it, he did make me promise not to go walking the dog alone at night."

"So what the hell do you make of all this?"

"I'm not sure. I mean, now that Vandebrandt's out of it, all that's left is the physical evidence. And it's all pointing in one very fucked-up direction."

"Meaning?"

"Meaning at least two of the women were abducted while they were walking their dogs. The dogs are nowhere to be found. The women were all strangled with a goddamn dog collar, for Chrissake. Maybe they were even dragged around on their hands and knees . . ."

"Like a dog."

"That's what I was thinking before. Then Vandebrandt's little reign of terror kind of got me off track."

"What does your boyfriend think?"

"He's *not* my . . . Oh, screw it. He doesn't seem to want to say a whole lot. Well, sometimes he does, sometimes he doesn't. There's kind of a weird vibe about it, and I'm still not sure what the rules are. Anyway, we didn't spend a lot of time last night talking about the case."

"Bernier, you hot mama . . ."

"Shut up."

"Only if you give me coffee."

We went into the kitchen, and Mad did his patented cup-shuffling trick under the still-dripping coffeemaker. We were out of milk, so I got some of Emma's beloved heavy cream out of the fridge. After informing me how many grams of fat were lurking within, Mad poured an inch of it into his mug.

"You ever go back and bang those twins?" I asked as we sat side by side on the kitchen counter.

"A gentleman doesn't tell tales."

"Oh. You ever go back and bang those twins?"

"Not as such."

"Just a social call, eh? How was it?"

"Trippy."

"Literally?"

"Yeah. The chicks had some decent shit. Turned out to be kind of uptight, though."

"You mean they wouldn't give you a tumble? How refreshing."

"Whatever."

"You going back for another try?"

"Nah."

"How come?" He didn't answer, but his quick glance toward Emma's room told me plenty. "You in danger of becoming a one-woman man?"

"Come on, Bernier, you know me better than that."

"Maybe Emma has you enslaved with her wild English ways."

"This conversation is *so* over."

"You want some breakfast?"

"No time. We have to get out of here."

"Where are we going besides work?"

"To do something to stave off the shit storm we're getting when Bill sees the *Times*."

"You mean you want to get your manhood back?"

"You are so much less clever than you think you are."

"So where are we going?"

"Where do you think we're going?"

"Syracuse?"

"Syracuse."

"Do we get to go to the mall to interview Patricia Marx's buddies at the Gap?"

"I guess so."

"Oh, goody."

"What are you so happy about?"

"It's not every day I get to shop in the line of duty."

We drove up to Syracuse in my Encore, stopping only for bagel-and-coffee provisions on the road. The drive takes about an hour, but it always seems longer with Mad reminding me every few miles that my car is designed for "wimpy little frogs," not a full-grown man such as himself, and it seems even longer than that when Mad does this with a mouth full of whole-wheat bagel.

The Carousel Mall is on the other side of downtown Syracuse, just off Route 81. It rises like a glass fairyland on the outskirts of the city, three stories of conspicuous consumption with (yes) an actual vintage carousel in the middle. The merry-go-round sits and spins at the end of the food court, so you can hear the oompah-oompah music while you're eating your fries, and the arrangement would seem quite wholesome if only the carousel weren't located outside the front door to Hooters.

We got to the mall just as it was opening. Mad—in an ignorance born of not enough estrogen—suggested that we refer to one of the kiosks, whereupon I explained that just as Sir Richard Francis Burton needed no map to explore the Nile, no self-respecting woman needs anything more than instinct to find her way around a mall. He looked at the map anyway.

The store was on the second floor. When we got there, a girl was just raising the front gate, as though to bust a storeful of T-shirts and jeans out of prison. She checked us both out as we walked in, sizing up our spending habits and probably realizing with a glance that (a) there was no hope I was ever going to learn to accessorize and (b) Mad's khakis were older than she was.

"Hi," I said when she approached. "I wonder if maybe you could help us."

"Sure," she said. "What are you looking for? You know, we've got a really good sale on sweater sets . . ."

"We're not shopping . . ." Mad started.

"Yes we are," I interjected, giving Mad a look that meant *back off, you're on my turf*. "We're *absolutely* shopping. And I could totally use another sweater set."

We perused tables of tops folded so neatly you could get a paper cut off the corners. I pawed through various shades of moss and eggplant and ecru and indigo, chose a few likely candidates, and repaired to the dressing room while Mad stayed behind to pray for his own death. After a half hour of careful reflection, I bought a little deep-blue cotton knit tank top with straps thick enough to cover my bra (if just barely), plus a matching hooded warm-up jacket that was supposed to be that season's answer to a sweater for the under-sixteen set. I was admiring myself in the mirror, wondering if I was going to have to stop wearing pigtails when I turned forty, when Mad came storming back.

"You're going to pay for this, Bernier."

"I'm giving you valuable experience at being a harried husband. You ought to thank me."

"Can we start asking questions? Or are you going to buy some pants now?"

"No, *you* are."

"I am not."

"Come on, Mad. We're greasing the wheels."

"Do you have any idea how much men hate this shit?"

"Think of it as research. Besides, it would do my heart good to see those pants of yours go to the Salvation Army."

I dragged him over to the racks of khakis, and the salesgirl looked on with the contentment of someone who was having her job done for her, and well. Five minutes later, I had Mad sequestered in a dressing room with the fourteen pairs of pants he'd picked out, the clerk having volunteered to overlook the six-item limit.

"He must really like shopping," she said as we loitered by the sales racks at the back of the store.

"Nah, I think he's just going into sensory overload. He didn't know there were so many shades of tan."

"Is he your boyfriend?" she asked. I had a feeling I knew what answer she was hoping for.

"Mad? Oh, God, no, we just work together."

"Oh, yeah, where?"

"We're reporters down at the *Gabriel Monitor*."

"Hey, didn't one of you guys call up here after Patsy . . ."

"That's right. Did you know her?"

"Know her? She was my roommate."

Bingo. "Oh, I'm really sorry. It must be awful for you."

"You can't imagine."

"Yes, I can." She stared at me with big open eyes, and I decided to tell her the whole truth. "The same person who killed Patsy . . . He killed one of my roommates too. Her name was C.A."

"Oh, God. That's such a weird coincidence, that we should run into each other in the stupid Gap." There was a chair just outside the hall of dressing rooms, and she sank into it as though it were all too much to think about standing up. "But maybe it isn't a coincidence, is it? That you're here, I mean."

The girl was no dummy. She was smart, and she was friendly, and I couldn't think of a reason to dodge her. "No. We came up here hoping to talk to some of Patsy's friends."

Her delicate brow furrowed in confusion. "And go shopping?"

"Always."

She smiled a little. "Yeah, me too. Shopping makes me feel good."

"What's your name?"

"Kim.'"

"Kim Williams?" She nodded. "I'm the one who talked to you on the phone. My name's Alex Bernier."

She chewed on my name for a minute. "I read about you in the paper. You found Patsy's body, didn't you?"

"Yeah."

"That must have been pretty awful too."

I got a flash of a girl lying dead in the woods, naked, angry red marks across her neck. The memory was worse now that I knew her name. "It was the most horrible thing I ever saw." *Until I saw C.A. with her guts cut open,* I added to myself, and decided to spare her.

"Alex," she said, leaning over in the chair and staring down at her pink high-tops, "can you tell me what's going on?"

"I wish I could, but I just don't know."

"All these girls are dying, and the police don't even seem to have a clue."

"They thought they had something to go on, but it turned out to be the wrong guy. Now I think they're just trying to . . . regroup, I guess."

"How?"

"I'm not sure. I heard they might have another lead, though. That's kind of why we wanted to talk to you."

"About what?"

"Well, this might sound kind of random, but do you think there's any way Patsy might have had a dog?"

"Jeeze, you're like the third person who's asked me that."

"Oh, yeah?"

"First the cops asked about it, and I told them about how Patsy wanted a dog, how she'd even gotten permission from our landlady. She was just starting to save up for the pet deposit. Two hundred bucks."

"And somebody else asked about it too?"

"Some reporter from the *New York Times* came in yesterday asking all these questions."

"What did you tell him?"

"Nothing. He was a total jerk. Like, when he first walked in and I asked if I could help him, he said he wouldn't shop at a mall if his life depended on it."

"You're kidding."

"Nope. And you should have seen how he was dressed, like some college professor. *Ugh.*"

She had to be talking about Gordon, but it hardly sounded like him. I mean, Gordon hates malls with a passion, but I couldn't believe he'd blow an interview like that. Maybe the desperation was making him sloppy. Odd.

"Kim, do you know what kind of dog Patsy wanted to get?"

"One of those Dobermans. She promised me it wouldn't be mean or anything, though. I'm not real great with dogs, but I thought a puppy would be okay—maybe that way I could get to know it before it got all big and scary."

"Why did she want a Doberman? For protection?"

"No, I don't think she really cared what kind she got, she just wanted a dog. The Doberman was supposed to be a surprise for her boyfriend. He's crazy for them."

"I don't get it. If it was for him, why was she okaying it with your landlady?"

"Oh. It's 'cause he lives in the dorms at S.U., and there's no pets. They were talking about maybe moving in together next year, though."

"Where was she going to find it? A shelter?"

"Oh, no, I think she was going to buy it from a breeder somewhere."

"Do you know which one?"

"What difference does it make?"

"Probably none. I was just wondering."

"Well, I don't know. I wasn't real interested. Patsy asked me if I wanted to go help her pick out a puppy sometime but I didn't think I could tell them apart."

You poor ignorant twit. I was on the verge of informing her that people who don't like dogs have no right to take up oxygen when Mad finally emerged from the dressing room.

"What do you think, Bernier? Do these make me look like I have an ass?"

"Mad, you know damn well you have the flattest butt known to man. You could cook pancakes on it."

Kim watched as he peered at himself in the three-way mirror at the end of the hall. "Wow, you're right," she said. "I've never seen those pants hang that way before. It looks kinda weird."

"It's his only physical flaw. Drives him insane."

"I'll tell him to try the ones with the pleats."

She consulted with Mad over the dressing-room door, and a minute later he came out wearing a new pair that, remarkably enough, made it seem like he had something happening in the posterior region.

"They look pretty good, huh?" he said as he surveyed his backside from various angles.

"And guys think *we're* vain," I said to Kim. "Go figure."

"What color is this?" Mad called from down the hall.

"Honey mustard," she said.

"What else do they come in?"

"Chocolate, olive, and, um . . . stone."

"Does this place take credit cards?"

Kim stared at Mad like he'd just emerged from his flying saucer. "Uh, of course. All the majors."

"Tasty," he said. "I'll take one in every color."

23

WE HAULED OUR PURCHASES OVER TO THE MALL COFFEE shop, the kind of place where they sell beans scented like raspberries and caramel side by side with a dizzying variety of mugs depicting Impressionist paintings. We snagged a white metallic table outside the entrance, and I left Mad there while I went in to find some coffee he wouldn't throw back in my face. I settled on something Sumatran, which the clerk swore was the strongest they had, plus a copy of the Syracuse newspaper and a hazelnut biscotti big enough to choke a pig.

When I got back, Mad was perusing his loot with a beatific expression. "Do you realize that I won't have to buy another pair of pants again for . . ." He did some calculations in his head. "For the rest of my life?"

"Yeah, as long as you're still a thirty-four waist." He shot me a dirty look. "What am I thinking? You'll be buried in them."

"What you got there?"

"Hazelnut cookie. Twice-baked and crunchy-licious."

"Junk food."

"Hazelnuts have protein."

"Right," he said, and broke off half. Then, with no attempt at concealment, he produced his flask and topped off his coffee.

"What the hell is that?"

"Whiskey. Want some?"

"No, I'm good."

"What do you want with the Syracuse rag, anyway?"

"Classifieds."

"What for?"

"A hunch."

I found the section and looked for the heading PETS (FOR SALE). What I found was nauseating to a mutt-lover like myself: a long column of ads for purebred dogs, with prices ranging from two hundred dollars to over a thousand. There were five ads hawking AKC registered Doberman pinschers, and I circled them.

"Four hundred dollars for a *dog*?" Mad said when I handed him the page. "Is that nuts or what?"

"It's canine eugenics. Don't get me started. Some people live for it, though."

"Why do we care?"

"Patricia Marx wanted to buy a Doberman."

"But I thought she never got it."

"That's what everybody says. I just want to do a little checking."

"Why?"

"On the off chance we may come up with a decent story for tomorrow."

"About what? 'Third girl had a dog too'? Isn't that kind of lame?"

"Think about it, Mad. It might be the key to everything. I mean, two women nabbed while they're walking their dogs could be a coincidence. Three is, well . . . it's a pathology. And it's a hell of a better story than 'Cops still stumped,' which is our other option."

"Don't you think Band tried this already?"

"Maybe. He seems a little whacked, though, kind of scrambling around. He might not've thought of it."

"Okay, but you have to promise that if we do scoop the little bastard, I'm the one who gets to rub his nose in it."

"The pleasure's all yours."

We moved over to a circular bank of pay phones and divided up the list. I'd called two of the breeders with no luck when I heard Mad give a war whoop from his side of the kiosk. He emerged a minute later, holding up a napkin covered in his scrawl.

"Jackpot," he said.

"What'd you find out?"

"I just talked to a guy in Cortland. He said he and his wife sold Patricia Marx a male Doberman puppy on . . ." He looked at his notes. "The date works out to less than a week before she died."

I stared at him. "That was way too easy."

"Easy? Are you kidding me? Alex, we just got our first break on this story in *three months*."

"Good point. So let's go talk to them."

"They're on their way out. Said we could drop by at three. So since it only takes half an hour to get there, that gives us"—he checked his watch—"two hours to kill."

"We should probably call Bill and tell him what we're up to. What do you want to do after that?"

"I was wondering," he said, "do you think they sell shirts here too?"

We got back to Gabriel around five, after an hour-long stop at a Cortland farmhouse with a row of chain-link kennels out back and a big wooden Doberman out front. There, we'd learned that in the waning days of her life, Patricia Marx had bought a twelve-week-old puppy she'd named Cocoa. The dog had been the runt of his litter, too small and with too many brown markings to ever be shown, and the breeders had despaired over unloading him. They'd offered him for the bargain price of a hundred dollars, and Patricia had jumped at it—particularly when they said they'd keep him until she could square things with her landlady.

So, we'd asked them, what had become of the dog? The last time the breeders saw him was when Marx had picked him up to take him to the vet. When she didn't bring him back, they figured she'd just taken him home to Syracuse. And when she'd died, they'd clucked at the tragedy of it all and never even thought to contact the cops.

"Explain this to me again," Bill was saying. "Why did the mutt have to go to the vet?" With everybody crowded into his office trying to hear—O'Shaunessey, Marshall, Wendell, Melissa, Lillian, et al—it was turning into an impromptu staff meeting.

"The good news is he was going for a checkup," I said. "The bad news is he was also getting cropped."

"Cropped?"

"Yeah, it's a goddamn purebred vanity thing. They lop off the poor dog's tail a couple of days after it's born.

Then, when it's about three months old, they box his ears so they stand up. Some people think it's cute, some think it's downright inhumane. It's actually illegal in some places."

"Like New York?"

"Like Australia."

"Okay, so where did the dog go for this ear-chopping?"

"Well, the girl didn't have a whole lot of money, so the breeder sent her to the cheapest place around."

"Which is?"

"She took him," Mad said, with a pause for dramatic effect, "to the Benson veterinary clinic." It was something that finally tied Patricia Marx to Gabriel, and Mad seemed gratified by the gasp he got from the assembled masses.

Bill scratched his head with a chopstick. "If this cropping is so controversial, how come they do it over there?"

"It's not *so* controversial," I said. "I mean, not like cloning body parts or anything. Most people don't give a damn. You don't actually do the dog any serious harm. It's just unnecessary surgery, that's all. Besides, Benson is a teaching hospital. The cropping is pretty much an accepted thing, so I guess they have to train the vet students to do it. The ones who don't want to can probably opt out."

"So did the dog have the surgery or didn't it?"

"We don't know. I have a call in to a friend of mine at the clinic. Hopefully we can find out what happened."

"Your deadline's in less than five hours."

"You don't say."

"Don't be a smart-ass. Just get me the story."

"Do we have enough to run with as is?"

He grunted. "Be nice to get more. But go write up what you've got and let me take a look."

"Under whose byline?" The onlookers, who could smell an argument coming, took this as their cue to exit.

Bill leaned back in his chair and put his feet on a pile of press releases he keeps at the perfect height for maximum comfort. "Madison's. Whaddaya think?"

"Isn't this getting a bit ridiculous?"

"Works for me," Mad interjected.

"Yeah, no shit," I said. "But isn't it a little crazy to have me running around interviewing people, and then when the sources read the story there's somebody's name on top they've never even met?"

"Think of it," Bill said, "as a return to the olden days of reporters and rewrite men."

"But I'm reporting it *and* writing it."

"You're also in it up to your hips, Miss I-Had-to-Go-Find-a-Body."

"So why do you have me covering it?"

"Because my cop reporter flew the coop and I have no choice, unless you'd like me to drag poor old Lillian in here."

"Well, if it's so bad I'm covering it, shouldn't we, you know, disclose our bias?"

"Nah."

"Bill . . ."

"Why do you want a byline so bad, anyway? Don't you get enough of 'em?"

"Yeah, but it's kind of demeaning to be Mad's ghost-writer."

"Come on, Bernier," Mad said. "Do you know how many chicks would kill to be working under me?"

"Oh, *spare* me."

"What can I say, Bernier? It's not my fault you've got conflicts of interest up the big wazoo. It couldn't be any worse unless . . . Gee, I don't know . . . Unless you were boffing the detective in charge."

Mad—the jerk—made it sound like a big joke. Luckily, that's exactly how Bill took it. "There's a laugh," he said with a lusty snort. "Alex and that big macho man. I'd pay money to see *that* one." The ha-has went on for a while. I wanted to kick Mad right where he lives. "Okay, Alex, I hear you," Bill said when he finally caught his breath. "Give daddy something really juicy, and he'll give you a lollipop and a nice big byline."

"For real?"

"Yeah, what the hell? I can only get fired once."

"You mean," I said with deliberate malice, "like a cute picture of Marx and her puppy? The kind of crap that breaks your heart so bad you just have to buy the paper?"

His eyes turned flinty. "You *don't*."

I pulled a photo out of an envelope and handed it to him. "The breeder lady has a whole wall of these, like baby pictures at a doctor's office. Adopter and new pooch."

He dropped the picture on his desk and stared at it. "This is totally beneath our dignity."

"Like it was beneath our dignity that time those five little kids died in a house fire, and you ran all their pictures under a hundred-point headline that said 'VICTIMS OF A DEADLY DAWN'?"

"I won an AP award for that."

"Yeah, it's on the wall behind you."

"I don't know," he said, still gazing at the picture. "Dead kids are one thing, but this . . ."

"Takes cheesy to a whole new level?"

"Oh, yes."

"And you're not going to run it under a hammer head that says 'COCOA, WHERE ARE YOU?'"

He took the words out for a spin. They seemed to give him a deliciously guilty sort of pleasure. "Marilyn would kill me."

"Yeah," Mad said, "or maybe she'll give you a raise."

"Hard to predict," Bill said. "Be nice if I had a story to run it with."

Having gotten the hint, we repaired to my computer to start banging out the piece. " 'Cocoa, where are you?' " Mad mimicked. "Alex, you *bad* girl. You bucking for a job at the *New York Post*?"

"Scary how fast he went for it, huh?"

"There's a tabloid writer lurking inside us all."

I typed for a while, then turned to him. "Listen, Mad, I was thinking. Should we be telling the cops about this?"

"They'll find out in tomorrow's paper."

"Yeah, but should we tell them now?"

"Why?"

"Why not?"

"Is this because you're banging the detective in charge? Bill sure thought *that* was a hoot."

"I could have killed you, you prick."

"Relax. Now you know you're beyond suspicion. Apparently, the idea of you banging some cop is too nuts even for . . ."

"Will you *cease*?"

"What was your question again?"

"Should we let the cops in on this?"

"Jesus, Alex, Cody isn't doing your job for you. Why should you do his for him?"

"Because his involves catching a killer."

"Oh. Right. Well, tell him whatever you want. I won't rat on you."

"Marilyn might approve, actually. Doesn't cost us anything, and it might earn her some points in the name of official cooperation."

"Whatever."

"Where is she, anyway?"

"Ass-kicking class. She'll be back."

It's long been Marilyn's custom to stop by the newsroom between breaking bricks with her head and having a late dinner with her husband. Sure enough, by the time we'd finished a draft of the story—with both our names on top, might I add—Marilyn was back, wearing her martial-arts pajamas and holding an ice pack on her chin. When I went into her office the first thing she said was that the other guy was in much worse shape than she was. The second thing was that, yes, I should call the cops. "Make sure they know we're not just calling to give them a chance to comment," she said as I was leaving. "Let the bastards know we're doing them a favor."

I called Cody. He wasn't there, but the sergeant at the desk said he'd be back any minute, so I walked over to the station and intercepted him just as he was getting out of one of your garden-variety unmarked cop cars.

"You left before I woke up this morning."

"I bet you say that to all the cops."

"True."

"Sorry about taking off like that. Zeke wanted to go running, and I didn't want to wake you."

"How did it go?"

"Great. We did seven easy. Whatever you did to my back last night, it worked."

"How about what I did to your front?"

He shot a look at the front door of the cop shop. Nobody was in hearing distance. "Um . . . I'd say that worked too."

"Excellent."

"Did you want to try and grab some dinner? I could probably take half an hour."

"Actually, I'm on an official mission. But I guess we could just as well talk about it eating."

We walked the twenty steps to the Green, which abuts the back door of the police station, and went into what's far and away the best sandwich place in town. Schultz's is a German deli owned by a genuine ex-Nazi who, as the legend goes, figured out forty years ago that it was a good idea to decorate his store with a large number of American flags. However, the truth is that (according to local carnivores) the bratwurst is so good, even the PC set would be willing to eat it under a portrait of the Führer. When I'm not in the mood for falafel or tabouli and I want a solid dose of cholesterol (or I'm just feeling sorry for myself), I go to Schultz's and indulge in a mighty Swiss cheese sandwich.

That's what I had when I went there with Cody, and since I pretty much go in there once a week, Herr Schultz's grandson started making it when I walked in the door. The great thing about Schultz's is they pile the cheese an inch thick; I have it on rye with lettuce, tomato, onions, and brown mustard. Cody went for roast beef on rye with lettuce, onions, cheddar, and Russian, which I was beginning to learn was his favorite sandwich in the whole world.

Behold yet another stage of intimacy; I made a mental note not to remember how he likes his coffee.

We sat at one of the heavy butcher-block tables, and the sandwiches came out a few minutes later, served in little baskets with chips and a whole pickle sliced down the middle. Cody took a bite, and a look I can only describe as orgasmic slipped across his face.

"Man, this is *great*."

"Haven't you been here yet?" His mouth was full, so he just shook his head. "I'm surprised. Cops love this place."

He swallowed. "Jesus, I can see why."

"Here, try this." I held up my sandwich for him. He was in mid-bite when I realized it probably wasn't such a great idea to be acting this cozy in public.

"Mmm . . . You want to try mine? Oh, right, sorry. Hey, Alex, does it bother you to have me eat meat in front of you?"

"Nah. To tell you the truth, I always thought vegetarian men were kinda wimpy. See? I'm a mass of contradictions."

"It's awful charming. You know, I don't think I've ever asked you about the vegetarian thing."

"You mean why?" He nodded. "Nothing too interesting. I just never could eat it since I really realized that to get it you had to kill a perfectly nice animal. You gonna eat that pickle?"

"You'd eat a pickle that touched my roast beef?"

"Sure. I'm kind of a hypocrite."

"Also charming."

"You know, since you asked, I'll tell you something else. The thing that bothers me isn't even the killing—okay, it *is* the killing. But it's also that people eat meat without dealing with the morality. Hunting doesn't really bug me that much. But the meat industry hides the ugly part and gives you a nice shrink-wrapped package. It's like putting a contract out on somebody."

"I'll have to bring that up over at the station house. 'Conspiracy to commit hamburger.'"

"Sorry. I didn't mean to go on a tirade."

"Well, since you're on one, what about that business you were covering up at Benson?"

"You mean the animal testing?"

"Right. Where do you stand on that one?"

"I'm not sure. I mean, the thought of a bunch of dogs and cats in cages makes me totally sick. But if it's going to save people in the long run? I don't know. It's a tough question."

"So you're not an extremist?"

"Did you think I was?"

"No. An extremist wouldn't sit here while I eat the best roast beef sandwich of my life."

"To each his own. There's a lot of kids on campus who'd throw blood at me for wearing leather shoes."

"And the protesters thought the issue was black and white."

"Well, most of them have graduated by now, but you're right. They were demanding an awful lot."

"So is it all over?"

"They'll probably regroup in the fall, but it always

takes some time to get going, and the next thing you know it's Christmas break. I think the university will throw them a bone, maybe unload some stock. Anyway, that's how the newsroom pool was leaning when the story dried up."

"You bet on this sort of thing?"

"And cops don't?"

"Well . . . they've been known to."

"So what's the action on your big case?"

"I'm the last guy they'd tell."

"Yeah, but you must have heard something."

He cracked a naughty little smile. "Well, there are two opposing camps. The smart money says the city boy's in over his head, and the chief'll cry uncle and turn the case over to the feds before my guys can crack it."

"And the other?"

"The other's a bit more charitable. They think I'll solve it, but not until there's a few more corpses."

"That's awful."

"They don't mean anything by it."

"Does it bug you?"

"Nah. Comes with the rank."

"Lonely at the top?"

"Something like that." We finished our sandwiches, and I got us a big bowl of Frau Schultz's rice pudding, which is made with so much cream there's no use trying to convince yourself of the nutritional value of the rice. "So what did you want to tell me, anyway?" Cody said, licking cinnamon-coated whipped cream off his spoon. "Didn't you say you were here on official business?"

"I was just about to get to that. Oh, and before I tell

you, I'm supposed to make it clear that we're being a bunch of stand-up guys, and the chief better not forget it."

"So why don't you tell him yourself?"

"Because you're better in bed."

"Ah."

"Did you see today's *Times*?"

"The story about the so-called 'Canine Killer'? Yeah, I saw the goddamn thing. Who is this Gordon Band anyway? How can he just make things up like that?"

"Knowing Gordon, he didn't. Somebody probably said it as a bad joke, and he took it out of context. 'Some people are saying it,' that kind of crap. It's a sloppy way to do business. And believe it or not, it's not his usual modus operandi. When he worked for the *Monitor*, he was rather fanatically ethical."

"I'd expect better from the *Times*."

"You're cute when you're naive."

"So what were you going to say about the story?"

"Well, if you saw it, you know he broke the thing about how Lynn Smith had a dog."

"Yeah, a blind old mutt named Harley. We knew that already."

"Don't you think it's important?"

"If both of them really were abducted while they were walking their dogs? Yeah, probably. It doesn't quite make a pattern, but if the others . . ."

"That's just what I wanted to talk to you about. Mad and I went up to Syracuse today to talk to Patricia Marx's roommate. Kim Williams."

"And?"

"And she did have a dog after all."

"But our guys already looked into that. They interviewed the roommate three times, and she said . . ."

"Yeah, but she didn't really know. I ran down all the Doberman breeders around there, and it turned out Marx had gotten a puppy from a couple in Cortland."

Cody crumpled his soda can. "Son of a bitch . . ."

"Are you mad? Because I was just doing my . . ."

"Jesus, no, Alex, I'm not angry with you. Truth is, I'd like to hire you. You'd do a hell of a lot better than the bunch of Gomer Pyles I've got working for me."

"It's a small-town force. They're not used to this kind of thing."

"Believe me, I tell myself that a hundred times a day just to keep from punching holes in the wall. So what else did you find out?"

"Marx bought a puppy, but she hadn't paid her pet deposit yet, so she couldn't bring it home. The breeder in Cortland let her leave it with them."

"Do they still have it?"

"No, the girl took it to the Benson vet clinic to have its ears cropped. That's the last they saw of either one of them."

"So is it still at the clinic?"

"I don't know. I have a call into my roommate Emma who works there, but I haven't heard back from her yet. You could find out, though."

"Is that why your editor let you tell me? An exchange of information?"

"Not exactly. I think she just wanted to run up some credit with the chief."

"Particularly since it doesn't cost you anything."

"Right. Too late to leak it to the local news. Hopefully none of your guys will go blabbing to Gordon."

"I'll make sure they don't."

"Thanks."

"It was your idea to tell us, wasn't it?"

"Yeah."

"Why?"

"Because I want you to catch this bastard."

"I thought you might be going soft on us brave men in blue."

"Doubtful."

"Or maybe," he said, "you're just crazy about me."

24

WHEN I GOT BACK TO THE PAPER, MAD WAS JOGGING LAPS around the newsroom in his new khakis. Nobody seemed to notice.

"Christ, Bernier, what took you so long?"

"I was talking to Cody."

He leaned against the wall and stretched his hamstrings.

"You were gone for an hour."

"Forty minutes."

"What'd you do, squeeze in a quickie?"

"Give me a break. We just had a sandwich."

"A sandwich?" he said, grabbing his feet to stretch his quads. "I've been waiting for you all night and you're having a fucking sandwich?"

"Jeeze, are *you* all wound up. What gives?"

"Emma called half an hour ago. She's waiting for us."

"Where?"

"Your house."

"What for?"

"She thought she found something up at the clinic, but

she didn't want to tell me over the phone. Said there's not a lot of privacy up there."

"Did she even give you a hint?"

"Nah, but I got the feeling it was something big."

"Because . . . ?"

"Because she wanted to know how fast you could track down your boyfriend the cop."

That was enough to get me to sprint down the back stairs to the parking lot and hightail it over to my house.

But from the minute we got there, it was obvious something was wrong. The front door was wide open, and the living room looked like a war zone. Pillows and couch cushions were scattered all over the place. The TV stand was sitting cockeyed in the middle of the room, its plug pulled out of the wall and the cable wire stretched to the limit. An end table had been knocked over and two of Emma's orchids lay broken on the ground, with dirt and ceramic pot shards everywhere you looked.

Mad and I stared at each other, and I had a bad feeling the expression on my face was just as crazed as his. He started shouting first, calling Emma's name and running from room to room. Since it seemed a fine idea, I followed his example. It took less than two minutes to figure out there was no one in the house.

"He took her," Mad said. "The bastard fucking got to her. Alex, what are we going to do?"

He was more upset than I'd ever seen him. Then something else hit me, and I joined him in the wonderful world of hysteria.

"Mad, where are the dogs? Oh, my God, Shakespeare . . ."

I started calling her name, running around the house

and out into the rapidly darkening yard. It's probably not nice to admit that I was about a hundred times more upset about my missing dog than my missing roommate. I'm not proud of it, but there it is.

I was in the midst of full-scale screaming and sobbing when Mad came barreling out of the house. "Call your boyfriend. Tell him to get his ass over here *now*."

"I can't find Shakespeare," I said, well on my way to hyperventilation. "Oh, Mad, where's my baby . . ."

He shook me, hard. "Calm the fuck down and listen to me. We don't have time to screw around. I'm going to start canvassing the neighborhood. You have to call the cops."

"But I can't find Shakespeare . . ."

Mad kept shouting orders at me, but I just stood there sobbing like a maniac. In retrospect, I realize he was sorely tempted to smack me. But instead, he left me there and went back in the house to call Cody himself. I followed him in a minute later and sank down on the couch, my brain awash with images of my dog—and, yes, Emma—in the clutches of whoever had mutilated C.A.

"Cody's on his way over here," Mad said, stalking around the room like a tiger. "He wants us to stay put."

"Did you tell him about Shakespeare?" I know I was acting like an imbecile, but there are plenty of people on the planet who don't love their mothers as much as I love that dog.

Mad took a deep breath. "No, Alex, I did not tell him about Shakespeare. You can tell him when he gets over here."

"Okay . . ." I said, and settled into the fetal position on the couch for some more sobbing.

Cody found us like that a few minutes later, taking in me and Mad and the trashed room in one long glance.

"What time did you speak to her last?"

"Around six-thirty," Mad said. "We were supposed to meet her here at seven, but Alex didn't get back, so we were half an hour late. When we walked in, the door was wide open and the place was . . . well, you see."

Cody surveyed the wreckage. "What was happening at seven?"

"She was going to tell us something she'd found out at the clinic. Son of a bitch, we should never have dragged her into . . ."

Cody cut him off. "Emma didn't say what it was?"

"She didn't want to talk at the hospital. But I got the feeling it was something more than just what we asked her about the Marx girl's dog."

"Cody," I said in a voice weak from all the crying. "It's not just Emma. Both the dogs are gone too. It's just like what happened to the others . . ."

"Shh . . ." he murmured, stopping on his tour around the room to pat me on the head. "Don't worry, we'll find them. Let me make some calls."

Just as he got up to get the phone, we heard someone struggling at the front door.

I froze. Mad stood up. Cody pulled out his gun.

A second later Emma walked in, dragging Shakespeare and Tipsy behind her. She looked up at her reception—which included two hysterical people and a firearm—and promptly burst out laughing.

"What the bloody hell is going on? Don't shoot. We surrender."

I jumped up and ran for Shakespeare. Mad grabbed

Emma, swung her around, and kissed her on the lips. Cody put his gun away.

"Good God," she said when Mad finally unhanded her. "To what do I owe this greeting?"

By that time, Mad had calmed down enough to get embarrassed about his unmanly display. I was still on the floor showering kisses on Shakespeare's snout. That left it up to Cody to answer.

"Ahem, they . . . Well, they had the impression you'd been abducted."

Emma was utterly confused for a second, then suddenly not. "Oh, Lord, you poor things. You saw the house and you thought I'd been . . . Oh, for heaven's sake, what an absurd notion . . ."

"You don't have to *laugh*," Mad said.

Now it was Cody's turn to look confused. "What happened in here, anyway? It doesn't look like a break-in . . ."

"Break-in? No, it was my sodding *dog*." She indicated the canine in question, now sound asleep on the bare couch frame.

"Tipsy did this?" I said.

"Well, your little angel helped a bit. Quite a lot, actually."

"But what the hell happened?"

She gave a surprisingly ladylike grunt. "Good God, but I could use a drink."

"Coming right up," Mad said, and started mixing martinis at the corner bar—which, mercifully enough, was still standing.

Emma put a cushion back on the couch and collapsed on it. "Our little adventure began when I let Tipsy out back. He ran around the yard like a bloody mental patient,

and then when he finally came in he had some sort of ro-
dent in his mouth. I got him to drop it, but the nasty thing
got away from me and the next thing I knew both dogs
were falling all over themselves chasing it, knocking furniture about. Oh, my *orchids*," she said, noticing that particular mess for the first time. She made as if to get up and
try to salvage them, then changed her mind and flopped
back onto the couch, stretching her legs on the edge of the
up-ended coffee table. "Jake, my pet, is that drink forth-
coming?"

"Dinner is served," he said, and handed her a glass
filled to the brim with liquor and three olives. Mad looked
inquiringly at me and Cody, but we both shook our heads,
so he went to fix his own drink.

"Mmm . . ." Emma said after a long sip. "That'll cure
what ails you. Now where was I? Oh, yes . . . Well, when
Tipsy'd come in bearing gifts, I hadn't closed the door all
the way, so naturally the little beastie went running for it,
and both dogs followed, so I fetched their leashes and
gave chase. I trod a good six blocks before I finally found
them. They'd treed the poor thing in that park by the library. It was a miracle they didn't get their sorry selves
run down in the road." She gave another delicate grunt.
"*Look* at this place. Tipsy, my darling, I could wring your
pretty neck."

"Should've gotten a cat, huh?" Mad said as he perched
on the couch arm beside her.

"Are you joking? Steve's cat *helped* them. It was a
bloody Walt Disney movie in here. I am *so* knackered . . ."

Cody, who'd been making a halfhearted effort to
straighten things up, flipped the coffee table back into po-

sition and sat on it. "I know you're beat, but I really need to know what you found out."

"Pardon?"

"Up at the vet hospital. Alex and Mad said you were going to tell them something."

"Oh, of course. I'd utterly forgot." She drained her drink, put the glass down, and sat up straight. "Alex called and asked me to see if a particular dog had been brought in for ear cropping. Beastly thing. We've done away with it back home, you know. In any event, I looked into it. What was the name again? Ah yes—Cocoa Marx."

"Cocoa marks?" Cody looked to her empty glass as the most likely source of her babbling. "What's a . . ."

"Cocoa was the dog's name. It's how we keep track of patients. The pet's name, then the family name, just like a person. You can't just put 'Fido,' or you might get mixed up. Do you have any idea how many dogs named 'Aristotle' there are in this town?"

"But there's only one Shakespeare," I offered.

Emma looked at me pityingly. "I neutered two last week."

"Oh."

She raised her glass and wiggled it at Mad, who got the message and went to get her a refill. "As I was saying, Alex asked me to look into the matter of Cocoa Marx, and I discovered that the dog had indeed been brought in for an ear bob."

"The surgery was done?" Cody asked.

"It was. And according to our records, the owner paid cash and picked the dog up the next day as scheduled."

"Do you know what time of day?"

"I wrote it down. It's in my handbag. Would you be so

kind . . . ?" Cody handed it to her. "Everything's done by computer, so we can tell the exact time the dog was checked out. It says here that it left at 8:47 P.M. on May 18th."

"You're open that late?"

"We have evening hours until nine on Thursday. Most of the local vets do."

"Patricia Marx worked at the mall in Syracuse until seven-thirty that night. She must have driven straight here to pick up the dog. As far as we know, it's the last time anyone saw her alive."

"How very disturbing," Emma said, and promptly downed half of her second martini.

"No offense," Cody said, "but do you think you could lay off the sauce until you're done telling me everything? I kind of need you sharp right now."

"She's fine," Mad said, looking awfully proud. "Emma can handle her liquor better than I can."

"You see, Detective," Emma said, raising her glass, "I am English."

"I'm very happy for you. Now, would you mind telling me what else you know? It might be important."

"Certainly. As I was saying, Alex asked me to look into whether Patricia Marx's dog had been treated at the hospital. And while I was doing so, I had a thought. I entered Lynn Smith's name, and sure enough, there it was."

"Are you sure it's the right Lynn Smith?" Cody asked. "It's a fairly common name."

"This Lynn Smith had a dog named Harley. Am I right?"

"That's the one."

"Well then, this Harley Smith was in a bad way. He was

a nine-year-old boxer mix, and blind as the proverbial bat."

"Was?"

"I assume they'd have put him down by now."

"He was sick?"

"Not as such. But he had bad cataracts, and it had gotten to the point where he was completely blind. We could have operated on him and restored his sight, at least partially, but the owners couldn't afford it. Quite a shame, really."

"How much would it have cost?"

"Oh, in the area of eight hundred to a thousand dollars, I should expect. And that's a bargain. It would be more at a private clinic."

Cody rubbed his reddish stubble, deep in thought. "So both Patricia Marx and Lynn Smith had dogs that were patients at the Benson vet clinic. I'll be damned."

Emma looked at him as though he were dense even for an American. "Don't forget Cathy Ann. She brought Nanki-Poo to the clinic as well."

"Son of a bitch."

"Just as you say."

"Tell me something. Did all three of these dogs have the same veterinarian?"

Emma shook her head. "The clinic doesn't work that way. Patients don't have a particular vet per se. You might see the same person on two different occasions, but it would just be a coincidence. Different doctors and students rotate through, so who you get is the luck of the draw. That's how a radiologist like me gets the pleasure of snipping testes all the bloody day long."

Both Cody and Mad shifted in their seats. "So it's possible," Cody said, "that they all might have seen the same doctor, at least once?"

"Possibly. I could take a closer look at the records. As could your investigators, I imagine."

"And what about some other connection? An assistant or something?"

Emma gave a long sigh. I could smell the booze on her breath from halfway across the room. "Difficult to know. One doesn't keep track of who assisted with a procedure, did a test, that sort of thing."

"Could you figure it out from whose handwriting is on the charts?"

"I'm afraid not. Doctors write up their own notes, fairly impenetrably I might add."

"Oh, shit," I said. "Mad, it's less than an hour to deadline. We've got to file something or we're dead."

He looked at his watch and stood up. "We'd better call Bill. At least now we've got something to . . ."

"Hold it," Cody said, in as authoritarian a voice as I'd ever heard come out of his mouth. "You know damn well you can't print this." His tone made Mad sit right back down, which was quite a neat trick. "Think about it. It looks like the Benson clinic is the one thing that links these women together. You go breaking the news that the victims took their dogs there, and you blow any chance we have of catching our guy off guard. He knows we've made the connection, he knows we're onto him. He picks up shop and starts killing women someplace else."

"The goddamn *Times* already broke the fact that Smith had a dog," Mad said. "It's just a matter of time until Band figures all this out for himself. Why should we let . . ."

"Gordon Band doesn't have access to the same resources, so he's hardly in a position to dig through patient records. That's confidential information."

"He'll find out," I said. "Believe me, Cody, I know him. Sooner or later, he'll get his hands on all of this."

"And how the hell will he do that?"

"I have no idea. He has his own kind of mojo. But trust me, it works. He may be a little off his game right now, but he'll dig it up eventually."

"And there's probably no use in trying to talk some sense into him?"

"None at all."

"Even if he knows what it will cost the investigation?"

"That'll just make him want to print it sooner."

"Sounds like one cold son of a bitch."

"Sometimes. Let's just say he's the journalistic equivalent of a pit bull."

"Then maybe his editors would listen to reason."

"They might. Frankly, I have no idea where the *Times* draws the line between flackery and good citizenship."

"Well, I'll deal with that particular crisis when it comes. Right now what I'm worried about is you."

"Come on, Cody . . ." Mad started, but I cut him off.

"Look, I'd like to rub Gordon's nose in it as much as you do. But I have to go with Cody on this one. How are we going to feel if this bastard flies the coop because we went off half-cocked?"

"Yeah, and I wonder why you're so eager to agree with . . ."

"I think you better shut your mouth. Because if you're about to say I can't think straight because of who I'm screwing, I'm going to have to kill you right in front of a cop. And then what'll become of me?"

He seemed on the verge of fury, then just decided to drop it. "Oh, fuck. You're right. Band and his Canine Killer are driving me insane."

"Since when do you take this stuff so personally?"

"Christ, I don't know. Band always rubbed me the wrong way, I guess. Didn't get to me so much when we were on the same side, but now . . ."

"Yeah, I know. I kinda miss him, but mostly I want to wring his neck."

"So are we settled on this?" Cody asked.

"The usual terms," I said. "We keep Marilyn and Bill in the loop. That way, they know we're being good citizens, not just incredible dunderheads. If they have a problem with this, they can hash it out with you and the chief. Frankly, I'm just as happy not to be at the top of the food chain."

"And when the story breaks," Mad said, "we get it first."

Cody smirked. "An arrangement Alex and I came to quite a while ago."

"That's just as well," Mad said, picking up the phone and dialing Bill's direct line. "Because if Alex has to start sleeping with the chief, his wife's gonna be really pissed. And I happen to know she has a gun of her own."

25

CODY AND HIS MEN—OR, AS HE'D PUT IT, HIS "BUNCH OF Gomer Pyles"—started trying to dig up info on the Benson vet hospital the next day. It was a delicate operation, he told me, because you couldn't know who to trust; even the most well-intentional source could inadvertently open his big mouth and tip off the wrong person that the police were sniffing around.

And frankly, they had no idea where to begin. All they knew at that point was that the hospital seemed to be the nexus, the one thing that all the women had in common. That sounded like it narrowed things down considerably, but it still left a hell of a lot of possible suspects. The killer could be someone who worked there full-time. It could be a student (either undergrad or vet), or a professor, or a doctor who rotated through. It could be one of the volunteers who came in a few hours a week to groom and play with the sick animals, sort of the vet version of a candy-striper. But then again, it could be somebody who didn't even have a direct connection to the clinic—

one of the hundreds of people who work in the adjacent buildings and see the pets and their owners in the parking lot, on the sidewalk, or just by staring down at them from their office windows.

In other words, Cody had his work cut out for him— off the record, at least. But officially, the investigation was pretty much at a standstill, and that meant Mad and I didn't have a whole lot to write about. Beyond breaking the story about Patricia Marx and Cocoa, we were reduced to rehashing sad tales of the victims, and reminding our readers on a daily basis that it would be a good idea if they locked their doors at night and didn't talk to strangers.

Ironically enough, I also did a story on the fact that so many women had gotten dogs for protection, the Walden County SPCA was out of them for the first time in its history; even ratty little wiener dogs and poodles were being snapped up as soon as they came in. (This seemed rather strange, since everyone knew by now that the victims had dogs themselves, and it hadn't done them a damn bit of good. One woman I interviewed probably summed it up best when she said that regardless of the logistics, she was just too damn scared to live alone anymore.) The piece ran with a sidebar about how the same thing had happened in other cities in similar situations, like Boston during the Strangler case. And as I filed it, I hoped like hell that none of the women decided to bring their new pets to the Benson clinic for a checkup.

Bill also sent me over to the historical society to research the last time Gabriel had a murder spree, which happened just before the Civil War and involved two maiden aunts who decided people's tea would taste better with a little hemlock in it. Even from the fading daguerreotype we ran on page three, you could tell they were total loonies.

Writing these various stories was enough to make me want to chew my own foot off, not so much because they weren't interesting but because they were so far from what was actually going on. It wasn't that I thought we'd made a mistake by cooperating with the cops—at least not in theory—but the reality of it was pretty galling for someone who's as fundamentally nosy as I am.

Not that Mad had it any easier. True, he did a couple of good pieces on the psychology of serial killers and the like, but he also got saddled with one whopper of an apology story. After the barrage of outrage that greeted our lovely photograph of Marx and Cocoa (including a full page of letters to the editor detailing how much we suck), Mad had to trot up the hill to talk to some Benson sociologist about the media's prurient obsession with crime victims, or some such; frankly, the whole thing smacked of a nymphomaniac writing about what a shame it is that people like to screw—and running it in *Hustler*. Anyway, when the story came out I blew it up on the copy machine, wrapped it around a large box of double-chocolate donuts, and left it on Mad's desk with a note that said EAT ME.

I was patting myself on the back for this cleverness when my phone rang.

"Newsroom. Alex here."

No one said anything at first, and I was just about to hang up when I heard a woman's voice, but faintly. "Is this . . . Is this Alex Bernier?" She pronounced my name wrong, so it ended with "yer" instead of "yay." I disliked her already.

"Yeah, this is Alex Bernier. What can I do for you?"

"Well, it's about that story you ran, about the missing girl . . ." She was whispering so efficiently I could barely hear her, but from what I caught she sounded like she wanted to talk about this like she wanted a root canal.

"What missing girl?"

The silence went on so long I thought she'd hung up, but then she spoke again, even more quietly than before. "You're not, uh, recording this are you?"

"No."

"Or . . . tracing this or anything?"

Who did she think we were, the CIA? "No, we don't do things like that."

More silence. "I wanted to tell you . . . Needed to tell you . . . something. About the missing girl. Not really missing . . . I mean, the girl they found in the snow last spring." She paused again, and I decided the best tactic was just to shut up and let her talk. "I know I should have said something back then, but I wasn't really sure. But then you had her picture—I mean, that drawing—in the newspaper again this week, and I really just thought it had to be . . ." Something hugely funny must have happened over at the sports desk just then, because the whole corner exploded into chuckles. I stuffed my finger in my ear and hunched over the phone. ". . . or anything, will you?"

"What was that again? I'm sorry, I didn't hear you."

"You won't tell anybody I called, will you? Can this be, um . . . a secret tip?"

"Sure. Of course."

"So I can tell you anything and you can't tell anybody else?"

I was torn between being honest with her and saying whatever I had to to get her to spill her guts. I opted for the moral high ground. "Well, I can't tell anybody where I got it from, but that's not the same as never repeating it. I mean, you obviously have something important you want people to know, right?" I could hear her breathing on the other end, which seemed a good sign that she'd neither slammed down the phone nor dropped dead.

"I don't know, maybe I'm just imagining . . ."

I summoned up the most gentle motherly tone I've got. "Don't you think you'll feel better if you get this off your chest?"

I caught Mad out of the corner of my eye, ripping open the donut box and preparing to bean me with one, but I made some frantic throat-slashing motions and he got the message. "Yeah, I guess," she was saying. "But I really can't talk about it . . ."

So why the hell did you call me, you loser? "I know it's hard for you . . ."

"Yeah, well, it's my own fault what happened. I mean, why I can't . . . Oh, boy, I'd better start at the beginning. You promised not to tell anybody you talked to me, right?"

"Right."

"Okay, see, I work in an office at Benson. I don't want to say which one. But when I first saw that drawing, I thought . . . It seemed like I recognized that girl, that she was the same one who'd come into our office for something one time."

I waited for her to say something else. She didn't. "That's it?"

"Um . . . yeah."

I was starting to lose my sense of humor. "You know, that's really not very helpful."

"It isn't?"

"Could you be just a tad more specific?"

Click.

"Toss me one of those donuts," I said to Mad as I hung up the phone. "Chocolate takes the pain away."

"What happened?"

"Some squirrelly dame called me trying to tell me who the first murder victim was, and I scared her off."

"Nice work."

He handed me a donut, and I shoved a quarter of it into my mouth. Then the phone rang again, and Mad stood there smirking as I tried to gag the donut down before whoever was calling me gave up.

"Urgh," I said into the phone, hoping it sounded somewhat like a word.

"Hi, listen, I'm sorry I hung up on you a minute ago."

"Oh, uh, no problem."

"Well, I was thinking about what you said, and I do want to help them catch whoever killed that girl . . ." She trailed off again, and this time I really did keep my mouth shut. "I know I already asked you this, but you have to swear you're not going to give anybody any details about me."

"On my honor as a journalist." Luckily, the woman didn't know enough to laugh and hang up again.

"Okay . . . I work as a secretary in the admissions office at the Ag school. Last fall, this girl came in for an interview to get in as a transfer student. We don't get too many of those, so that's mostly why I remember her, but it was also because she seemed really scared. Not just nervous like she wanted to do okay on the interview, but like she was really scared of something or other.

"So anyway, when that picture first ran in the paper, I kind of thought it reminded me of somebody, but I wasn't sure who. But then we got back the final list of no-shows—that's people we admit but who never get back to us to say yes or no—well, there are never very many of those, and this year she was the only one. Usually, it's just for some simple mistake like we mixed up the zip code on her acceptance letter or something. So I went to look up her application file to try to track her down before she lost her spot, and we didn't have one. I mean, it was just *gone*."

"What do you think happened to it?"

"Um, I'm not sure. I guess it could just be lost in the shuffle."

"Or else . . . ?"

"The thing is, we'd had this sort of break-in a couple of months before. Nothing was missing though, so we figured it was just a prank or maybe a fraternity pledge. But I was thinking maybe somebody took some files without messing things up, so nobody noticed right away."

"Have you noticed any other applications missing?"

"Just hers. And I wouldn't have even thought too much about it if I hadn't seen that drawing in the paper again this week. I thought, how much of a coincidence is that— that she wouldn't answer her acceptance letter, and then her file would go missing, and then I'd see this drawing in the paper that looked so much like her . . ."

"How come you haven't gone to the police about this?"

She hesitated again. "Well, that's the thing. I . . . you see, I kind of did something stupid a while back—nothing much, really—just some bad checks I wrote out of state back when I was married. I mean, I use my maiden name now, but I was afraid if I talked to the cops, they'd find out. There's sort of a warrant . . ."

"And you want to keep a low profile."

"Um, right."

"Why didn't you just send them an anonymous letter?"

"Oh. I guess I didn't really think of that. I mean, couldn't they trace it somehow? Like the DNA or something?"

The woman obviously had an elevated opinion of the technical abilities of both Gabriel's journalists *and* its cops. I was about to let her off the phone when I realized I'd forgotten to ask the single most important question. "Wait a second. What was the girl's name?"

"Oh, right. It was Amy Sue Gravink. The address we had for her was 3106 Brazos Street, Sugarland, Texas."

"If the file was gone, how do you know her address?"

"It was on a separate list for the acceptance letters."

"Is there anything else you can remember about her, anything distinctive about the way she looked or talked?"

"I don't think so. I mean, she was sweet, but except for seeming kind of scared, she wasn't all that different from anybody else."

"Well, do you happen to remember what she wanted to major in?"

"No, I . . . Wait. I could be mixing her up with someone else, but come to think of it, I think maybe it was pre-vet."

I hung up the phone a minute later, after promising her five more times that I wouldn't narc on her. Then I spilled it all to Mad.

"Sugarland?" he read off my notes, which were smeared with chocolate frosting. "That's got to be a joke."

"I checked, and it's a real place. Looks like it's part of the Houston suburban sprawl."

"So let me get this straight," he said into his latest donut. "If your Deep Throat is right, then the first victim came from Texas."

"Yeah, but she was in town applying to transfer to Benson."

"So you think he snatched her up here?"

"Sure, why not?"

"If you follow the pattern, wouldn't that mean that she had to have a dog with her? And that she took it to the Benson clinic?"

"Well, what if she did? The lady who just called said she thought the girl wanted to be pre-vet, so she was obviously an animal person."

"Yeah, but would you bring your dog to your college interview? Oh, right, you're crazy. Of course you would."

"Listen, the caller said this Gravink girl was scared about something. Maybe . . . I don't know, maybe her dog got sick and she had to rush it to the hospital. Maybe she was scared about that."

"There's one way to find out." He picked up the phone, and a minute later was murmuring what I'd describe as dangerously close to sweet nothings into the receiver.

Emma definitely had him whipped, and it was very entertaining to witness.

"Ooh, my little table water biscuit," I said when he hung up. "I want to lick up your crumbs too. Can't I, please?"

"You were *eavesdropping*."

"Of course. And I must say I've never considered that particular use for marmalade."

"Bernier, will you stifle yourself?"

"After all the crap you've given me about"—we were in the newsroom, so I just wiggled my eyebrows where Brian Cody's name was supposed to be—"you're lucky I don't take out an ad on the food page."

"Do you want to hear this or don't you?"

"Shoot."

"We're no go. Emma says there's nothing in the computer under the name Amy Sue Gravink, or any other Gravink either."

"Damn. Well, maybe the dog was treated under another name."

"Why?"

"I have no idea. Maybe it belonged to a friend or something."

"And that shoots down your pattern again."

"I guess . . . No, wait. Not necessarily. Remember, we were talking about this a while before. Amy Sue Gravink—well, if the body really is her, but let's call it that for the time being—Amy Sue Gravink was the *first* victim, right? And remember what we were thinking about the first victim?"

"Do you know how many drinks I've had since then?"

"Oh, Christ. We were thinking about how a perfectly

respectable, middle-class girl could go missing and nobody would look for her. And we said maybe it was because the person who would have reported her missing in the first place was the one who offed her."

"Clever idea. Was it mine?"

"No. So what if that's exactly what happened to this girl?"

"Well, like I said two seconds ago, there's only one way to find out."

"Call down there. See if there really is an Amy Sue Gravink who lived in Sugarland."

"Close, but no cigar." He grabbed me by the elbow and dragged me into Marilyn's office. "We gotta go to Texas."

She looked up from her desk. "Okay, what's the punch line?"

"No joke," he said. "We have to go to Texas. Today."

"Mad, I just spent the paper's whole damn travel budget on your gas money to Syracuse and back."

"Send us to Texas, and we'll bring you back the first victim."

"All right, I'm listening."

"We just got a tip. Said the first girl was named Amy Sue Gravink. She's supposed to come from someplace outside Houston."

"You ever heard of the telephone?"

"Come on, boss, you know how much they hate New Yorkers down there. You really think they're going to go out of their way to talk about one of their own to a couple of Yankee reporters?"

"Try."

"Yeah, and what if it just queers it all, so when we finally drag our asses down there, they're all clammed up about her?"

She turned to me. "When did he get this paranoid?"

"Since Band scooped him on that Canine Killer story."

She grabbed her head as though I'd given her an instant migraine. "Do not mention that goddamn thing to me, or Gordon Band either. I swear I'd love to break every bone in his . . . Oh, *fuck*. What do you think, Alex? Is it worth the hassle I'm going to have trying to explain this to Chester?"

"I'll make you a deal," Mad cut in. "If we don't get squat, we'll pay for the trip ourselves."

I punched him in the shoulder, and not gently. "We will *not*."

"I wasn't talking to you," Marilyn said to Mad. "How about it, Alex? It's your call."

"Why is it my call?"

"Because you're the only person who knows this story inside-out and isn't all cranked up on male hormones."

I considered it for a minute, standing there in Marilyn's office with both of them staring at me. I thought about how the truly decent thing to do was probably to turn the information over to the cops, and how not doing it was essentially going against the deal we'd already made. Then I thought about how I was turning into Brian Cody's personal little news bureau and massage parlor, and the idea kind of nauseated me; I was blurring so many boundaries (personal, professional, and God only knows what else) I was starting to wonder who the hell I was.

I pondered how I was going to explain it to him if I went running off to Texas, and exactly how furious he was going to be when he found out the truth. Then it occurred to me that the tipster had wanted to talk to a reporter, not to the cops, and that maybe I should just stop whining and do my fucking job for once.

"Okay, let's do it," I said to Mad. "But if you buy one of those ten-gallon hats, I swear to God I'm leaving you at the airport."

26

It's damn hot in Texas. I mention this because it's just about the only cultural artifact I brought back from my seventy-two hours in the Lone Star State. That, and the fact that what we call Mexican food back home really sucks.

But down there, even the lowliest fast-food places have kick-ass *pico de gallo*—and I probably would have enjoyed it more if I hadn't been in constant danger of either fainting from the heat or catching pneumonia from the air-conditioning. I was raised in New England, where air-conditioning means opening a window. But in Texas, they take their climate control to such an extreme that I was only ever comfortable on my way into (or out of) a building. If I could have, I would've spent the entire trip in somebody's vestibule.

Luckily, the whole visit turned out to be shorter than a typical Jake Madison love affair. We spent exactly three nights in a Motel Six, which, like everything else in Houston, was located just off a highway. We shared a room, because there's no such thing as propriety in the *Gabriel Monitor* travel budget (as you may have guessed, there's usually no such thing as travel, either), and although Emma is sophisticated enough not to care, I had a feeling that if he ever found out, Brian Cody would object on several dozen different grounds.

We got there late Wednesday night, and the next morning Mad dropped me off at Sugarland High and took off in the rental car to "follow his nose." I feared that this might mean following it to the nearest bar to sample the tequila, but I thought it best not to mention it lest I give him ideas. I walked into the school office in my demure little sundress fully prepared to be bounced out on my Yankee butt, but the response I got was so astonishingly friendly and cooperative there was no way I could confuse these people with New Yorkers, upstate or otherwise.

We'd been hoping like hell that Amy Sue Gravink had actually attended the local high school, since it would save us tracking down all the other options, like private or Catholic education. We knew she'd applied as a transfer student, which meant she would have graduated at least a year before—so we were also hoping there'd still be somebody around who might remember her. And to top it all off, we wanted this person to be around in the middle of the summer, and for the damn school to be open in the first place.

We got the whole enchilada. I walked into the office armed with nothing but a name, an address, and a police sketch, and I'll be damned if I didn't walk out of there with Amy Sue Gravink's life story.

The source of this treasure trove of information was

one Mimi Ochoa, a nice Mexican American lady who fed me iced tea and little cinnamon cookies while she answered my every prayer. She was the school secretary, and she had been for twenty years, and she was pleased as punch to tell me about the nice local girl who'd gotten her life together and made good, even though she was practically alone in the world.

It wasn't until the end of the conversation that it occurred to her to ask me who I was and why I wanted to know. I didn't want to tell her by then, once I'd learned who Amy Sue Gravink was and all she'd gone through only to die in the freezing cold two thousand miles from home. But I hadn't come this far not to be sure, so I put the drawing in Mrs. Ochoa's hands, and sat there patting them while she cried like a little girl.

We worked on a draft of the story on the plane, one of the only times I've written something in longhand since junior high. God only knows what our fellow passengers thought as we filled the miles from Houston to Pittsburgh with murder and suicide and pedophelia, but at least it kept them from trying to make small talk with us.

We'd already gone over the facts during dinner the night before. We went to a restaurant called Chuy's, whose festive atmosphere clashed with our morbid conversation so violently it prompted us to drink even more than usual. The meal therefore involved eight margaritas (five for Mad, three for me), plus great quantities of guacamole, sour cream, and tomatillo salsa. And by the time we got to hashing out the story on the plane, we'd gone through the gory details so much they didn't even bother us—which probably made our seatmates think we were not only crazy but callous to boot.

The gist of it went like this: Amy Sue Gravink came from a middle-class family, with a mother who was a secretary for a petrochemical company and a father who worked for the Houston building department. They'd seemed like decent people who did the usual suburban crap—church, PTA meetings, ski vacations, trips to the beach. They'd even gone to high school football games every Friday night to watch their son play second-string halfback while their daughter waved pom-poms and yelled rah-rah-rah.

So when it happened, it came as a complete surprise. No one could have predicted that good-natured Bob Gravink—a guy who couldn't pass a stranded driver without stopping to change the tire—would rip his wife in half with a shotgun before blowing his brains out. They would certainly never have suspected that when the local cops went to the house they'd find stacks upon stacks of sadomasochistic pornography. And even when it came out a few weeks later that the feds had been investigating Gravink for buying kiddie porn over the Internet, people still didn't believe it—until they heard just what had been found on the family computer.

Amy Sue Gravink was seventeen when her parents died; her brother Bobby was twenty. The murder-suicide had left them with no other close relatives and very little money. Their mother hadn't had a life insurance policy, and their father had voided his by blowing his own head off. All they had was the house, which would have been hard enough to sell even if Dad hadn't set a fire in a half-hearted attempt to erase the evidence.

So they moved back into it. The whole school pitched in to redecorate (presumably, this included cleaning up several gallons of blood) and help raise money for them to live on. Since Amy was nearly a legal adult, the court declared her an emancipated minor, and they both finished high school. Her brother was never much of a student—he'd been held back twice in elementary school—but Amy Sue graduated near the top of her class. She probably could have gotten into any college she wanted to (just imagine the admissions essay she could have cranked out) but she decided to save money by living at home, working full-time, and taking two years of community college night school. Then she applied as a transfer student at several universities, all of which had big-name vet schools.

Then she disappeared.

People thought it was strange that she'd leave like that, so suddenly and without saying good-bye. It smacked of rudeness—and in Texas, Mrs. Ochoa explained to me patiently, people still care about manners.

They might even have worried about her, if her brother hadn't explained to everyone that she'd decided to take a little vacation before starting school. Then she was going to go straight to campus, he said, to try to find a cheap apartment and a good work-study job. And everybody nodded their heads at that, and said it was just like her to be so responsible.

Then Bobby left too. He said that without his sister around, the house was too big and empty. And since he'd just lost his job, the best thing for him was to start over somewhere else. He'd closed up the house, paid courtesy calls on the neighbors, and driven away in his Chevy pickup with the promise that he and his sister would try to visit at Christmas. That was the last anyone in Sugarland had seen of them. And other than a few letters and postcards, it was the last anyone had heard from them, either.

"That's it?" Bill was saying. "We sent you two down to Texas for a sob story about some Goody Two-shoes and her big lug of a brother?"

The four of us were sequestered in Marilyn's office. The door was closed, which only happens when someone has died, been fired, or announced they're leaving to work for television. Through the narrow window I could see the rest of the newsroom gaping as they walked up the stairs, wondering which of the three applied to us.

"Don't sweat it," Marilyn said with a nasty smile. "Madison here promised if they didn't find anything useful they'd pay us back for the tickets. So how do you want to do it? A lump sum, or ten bucks out of your paycheck for the next couple years?"

Mad returned the smile in kind. "Actually, I think the paper's gonna end up footing the bill."

Marilyn put down the numchucks she'd been fingering for the past half hour. "Okay, let's hear it."

"Well, if you'd rather," Mad said, "I guess we can eat the plane tickets and see if Band can get us in down at the *Times*."

She picked up the numchucks again, this time in not such a playful way. The look on her face said *don't make me use these*.

"Here's the thing," I said. "We still think Amy Sue Gravink's our victim." Bill and Marilyn opened their mouths, but I waved them off. "I know, I know—what about the letters they sent back to Sugarland? The short answer is we think it was a dodge. All the stuff we just told you was what we got from this Ochoa lady. Well, we did a bunch of other interviews, made the rounds of all the neighbors and coworkers and friends we could dig up. We also made a trip to the morgue down at the *Chronicle*. The big picture turned out to be a whole lot less wholesome."

"Less wholesome," Marilyn said, "than a kiddie porn collector who kills his wife and blows his own head off?"

"Christ, I don't even know where to start. We tried to work the story on the plane, but man . . ." I took a deep breath and a swig of diet Snapple lemonade. "Okay, about the letters. Turns out they were typed—which wasn't, quote 'at all like Amy Sue.' I guess she had beautiful penmanship or something, I don't know. But three different people told us they thought it was weird the letters were typed. The postcards too."

"Postcards from where?" Marilyn asked.

"The Philly area. One from the city, one from Gettysburg, another one from Hershey. And that's not all. In the letters, she said how she was so psyched she was going to U Penn. But we checked, and there's no Amy Sue Gravink enrolled, and none coming in the fall either."

"Holy shit." Marilyn leaned back in her ratty leather chair and put her feet up on the desk. "Keep talking."

"That's not the half of it. We did a little checking on her brother Bobby. Seems he was kind of a weird egg. Was on the football team in high school and did a couple of musicals, but still managed to avoid making any friends. Never had a girlfriend—or a boyfriend either, for that matter. We stopped off at the community college

Amy Sue went to, and it turns out he started there two different semesters, but he couldn't hack it. He had a few different jobs, but he didn't hang on to them. And then there was this thing where he got fired."

"Fired from where?"

"He got canned," Mad interjected, "from the Houston SPCA."

"Holy *shit*," she said again, louder this time.

"He was working as some kind of technician's assistant," I said. "I think he took a couple of training courses and worked his way up from janitor or something. Anyway, it was the longest he ever stayed in one job. But get this. He got canned because . . ."

"Lemme guess," she said. "He was torturing the poor little animals."

"Just the opposite. He was liberating them."

"*What?*"

"He was taking the ones who'd been scheduled for euthanasia, pretending he'd done it and sent them to the incinerator. But he really took them out to the country somewhere and set them free. I guess they nabbed him after animal control brought the same old dog in three different times."

"So he was a dog lover. So what? You'd probably do the same damn thing."

"She probably would," Mad offered. "But from what the shelter people told me, this dude was a couple orders of magnitude crazier than Bernier even. And when they canned him, he went nuts and tried to trash the place. Ran around letting all the animals out of their cages. Real mess."

"They call the cops?"

"Nah. They didn't want the bad PR. He'd probably confiscated a hundred dogs, and I seriously doubt he let 'em all loose. Trust me, the inside of his house looked like a fucking kennel."

"How would you know?" Bill asked.

"Yeah," I said. "Just how the hell *would* you know?"

"Uh, let's just call it an anonymous source."

"Fine," Marilyn said. "Just so long as we don't call it breaking and entering."

He somehow managed to keep a straight face. "Oh, no. Perish the thought. That would be wrong."

"And this house you didn't go into," I said. "It might have looked like what, precisely?"

"Well, speaking theoretically, it might have had dog food stacked up, muddy paw prints, fur all over the place. That kind of thing."

"I take it this was your idea of following your nose?"

"So let me get this straight," Marilyn interrupted. "The dad goes on his killing spree. Little Amy Sue puts her life back together and soldiers on, but the brother's so traumatized he starts liberating dogs for a living?"

"Well," I said slowly, "actually, the thing may not have been as straightforward as that."

They must have gotten the gist from my tone of voice, because their eyes widened simultaneously. Mad just sat there with a little smirk on his face, enjoying himself way too much.

"I tracked down one of the cops who worked the murder-suicide," he said after a suitably dramatic pause. "Apparently, there was some doubt about how it all went down. The cop was just talking from his gut, off the record, but he told me he thought there was something wrong with sonny boy from the get-go. Said he didn't have any evidence to back it up, and there were plenty of folks who'd swear he was a goddamn choir boy. But he would have bet the farm the kid was involved somehow."

"Are you telling me," Marilyn said, "that this guy killed both his parents and got away with it?"

Mad shrugged. "The cop wouldn't go that far. All I'm telling you is he thought the whole thing didn't smell right."

"But why would he do it? It doesn't sound like there was a lot of money in it for him."

"That's true," I said. "But one thing we found out was that a few weeks before they died, they had the family dog put to sleep. I guess he was getting old and had some heart condition. Neighbors talked about it like it was just another tragic element to throw on the trash heap. But what if it's more than that?"

"What do you mean?"

"Well, we know the son was obsessed with animals. Maybe it made him furious."

"You may not realize this, but it's not a capital offense to put down a dog."

"Maybe to him it is. And then there was this weird thing about the yearbooks."

Marilyn looked from me to Mad like she didn't know which one of us to strangle first. "Yearbooks? What yearbooks?"

"After I talked to Mrs. Ochoa, I figured we'd want to get pictures of these guys, right? So she took me to the school library and showed me the yearbooks, so I could snap some black-and-whites. And when I looked through them, I found every single one of their pictures had been cut out. Really neatly, like with a knife."

Mad threw a manila envelope on the desk. "I got these pictures from the *Chronicle*. It's not much. One of them's from around the time the parents died, human interest shit. The other was shot at a football game, but Gravink wasn't a great player, so they just got him in the background. They're both profile shots, and pretty damn grainy. Can't say as it'd help you recognize him on the street."

Marilyn glanced at them, then handed them to Bill. He stared at them for a full minute before speaking. "Are you jokers trying to tell me that you think I'm looking at a picture of our serial killer?"

"Yep," Mad said.

I shot him a dirty look. "We have no idea. All we know is what we told you. Amy Sue Gravink is gone. She's not home, she's not at Penn, and she looks a hell of a lot like a girl in the Gabriel city morgue. Her brother is missing too—and he lied about her going off to college. He may or may not have had something to do with killing his own parents. He sure as hell has a history of weird behavior—specifically, being obsessed with dogs." I paused to see if Bill and Marilyn were following. They seemed to be. "The woman I got the tip from in the first place said Amy Sue seemed scared of something. What if she came up here to get away from her brother? And what if he found her?"

Marilyn's a tough cookie, but even she looked horrified. "Why would he want to kill his own sister?"

"Who knows? Maybe she figured out what really happened to their parents."

"That only applies if it really wasn't just a murder-suicide like everybody thinks. And even if he killed his sister—good Lord, tortured and strangled her like that—why would he go killing those other women too?"

"That one's easy," Mad said in a voice that sounded cold even for him. "He must really be enjoying himself."

The words were unpleasantly familiar. "That's just how Cody put it," I said. "From one victim to another, as the violence was escalating, that's just what he said. That the killer was having a goddamn good time. Too good to stop now."

Bill looked positively sick. If he weren't black, he would have turned gray. "Son of a bitch," he said, then tried to shake it off with a joke. "Aw, come on. It can't be this Gravink guy. Everybody knows serial killers and assassins all have to have three names. You know, John Wayne Gacy, Mark David Chapman. It's a rule, right?"

"If he hadn't been southern-fried, Ted Bundy would probably argue with you," I said. "But just for the record, Gravink's real name is Bobby Ray."

27

THE ARGUMENT OVER WHAT TO DO WITH ALL THIS INFOR-
mation lasted quite some time. It largely happened
around me, because very frankly I had no idea of what to
say. Nobody else did either—not really—but that didn't
stop them from shouting at each other for over an hour.
The truth was that when we went down to Texas, the most
we were hoping for was confirmation that the first victim
really was Amy Sue Gravink. We sure as hell never expected to track down some dog-loving crazy man who
might very well be responsible for the deaths of four
women. And counting.

So what were we going to do with everything we'd
found out? Should we at least run what we had on the victim, since it was based on a dozen solid interviews in her
hometown—including four people who said they'd bet
their life the police sketch was indeed Amy Sue? Should
we run *everything*, including the stuff on her missing
brother and how he'd been trounced out of a job for excessive dognapping? Or should we turn it all over to the

police, smile nicely, and let them tell us how far to bend over?

And if we didn't hightail it over to the cop shop and spill our guts—if another girl died while we played ethical parlor games—were any of us going to be able to live with ourselves?

Maybe at a bigger paper, it would have been an easy call—although to this day I'm not quite sure what that call should have been. I mean, it gives me a stomachache just to think about the breast-beating that must have gone on at the *Times* and the *Post* over whether to publish the Unabomber manifesto. And at the jolly *Gabriel Monitor*, we may have been used to wrangling with the cops (and the mayor, and the Benson administration, and every other local entity) over kibbles and bits of information, but we were most definitely *not* used to having somebody's life riding on the outcome.

The trouble was, none of the options were particularly appealing. We'd done the legwork, and it didn't sit right to hand everything over to the cops—particularly since we'd done that very thing so damn much lately. But we prided ourselves on being at least marginally decent human beings, so we knew we couldn't ignore the fact that we'd stumbled into something that might be vital to the case. Sure, the cops would track it down eventually. I had faith in Cody, and not just because I was (quite literally) in bed with him. But his investigation could still take weeks. How many bodies would there be by then?

". . . to do right by us? Alex?" I looked up to find the three of them staring at me. "Wake the hell up," Marilyn was saying. "I asked you a question."

"Uh, sorry. What?"

"Cody. I said can you trust him to give us the exclusive or can't you?"

"Oh. Gee, I don't know . . ."

"The hell you don't. Mad says you've had closer dealings with him than anyone."

I gave him the evil eye. Just exactly how much had I missed? "Well, sure. I mean, I've been covering the story and all . . ."

Marilyn slammed her fist on the desk so hard her Munson baseball jumped out of its holder and rolled onto the floor. "Spare me the waffling. Come on, Alex, make the call."

"Why do I always have to make the call on this? Can't somebody else make the call? Like somebody whose roommate didn't get killed?"

She had the good grace to look a tad sheepish. But just a tad. "Point taken. It's my goddamn decision anyway. I suppose I'm just looking for absolution."

"Absolution?"

"Permission to roll over and get fucked."

"Don't take it so hard," I said, picking up the ball and tossing it to her. "After all, this isn't exactly a normal situation."

"Somebody let me know if we ever have one of those," Bill snorted from his corner, "so I can drop dead from the shock."

"All I meant was, maybe we're no more prepared to cover some serial killer than the Gabriel cops are to catch him."

"Bullshit," Mad said. "Who the hell tracked down this Bobby Ray Gravink? Us, that's who. And I'll be damned if . . ."

There was a knock on the door then, and Lillian stuck her head in. "There's a young woman on the phone for Alex," she said. "I offered to take a message, but she was quite insistent. And, I might add, somewhat less than cordial."

When I picked up the phone, I realized that Lillian had once again defended her crown as the queen of understatement.

"How *could* you?" my tipster from the Ag school admissions office was shrieking into my ear. "You gave me your word, and then you went right ahead and told the cops, you goddamn lying *bitch*."

"Hey, hold on a second . . ."

"How could I have been stupid enough to trust you people? Christ, I knew better. If I go to jail because of this, I swear to God I'm going to . . ."

"Look, I know you're upset. But I have no idea what you're talking about."

"Oh, *sure* you don't."

"No, I really don't. Can you please just calm down and tell me what's going on?"

"Why the hell should I ever tell you anything else *ever*?"

"Well, don't I even get a chance to defend myself?"

There was a long pause, and I was afraid she'd hung up on me yet again. But then I heard her give an exasperated groan and say something nasty about my mother. "As if you didn't *know*," she said, "the cops were all over our office this morning."

"Doing what?"

"Trying to find Amy Sue Gravink's file, interviewing

everybody about what they remembered about her. Now how do you suppose they found out about that, huh?"

"Well, I . . ."

"You ratted on me, didn't you?"

"No, as a matter of fact I didn't."

"So how come the cops were all over my office? And how come there's a goddamn *New York Times* reporter asking us all kinds of questions?"

Oh, shit. "Look, I know you're not going to believe me, but I didn't tell a single person outside this newspaper."

"Yeah, right . . ."

"And what's more, I've been down in Texas for the past three days, so I've hardly . . ."

"Texas?" The word seemed to pull her up short. When she spoke again, she sounded a lot less angry. "You went down there looking for Amy Sue?"

"That's right."

"Well . . . what did you find out?"

"Nothing for sure. But it's probably her."

"Oh."

"Listen, just for the record, I really didn't tell the cops about your phone call. They must have gotten her name on their own somehow. Like, could somebody else from your office have recognized the picture too?"

She thought about it for a minute. "I don't know. Maybe one of the other secretaries."

"Or it could have been somebody else on campus who met her when she visited. I mean, over twenty thousand people would have seen that sketch last week."

She contemplated the magnitude of this fact for a while, and when I finally got off the phone with her I went back to Marilyn's office. The boss was still playing with her numchucks, and I hoped she wouldn't be inclined to strangle the messenger. "Remember our high-level intellectual discussion about what to tell the cops? Well, fuck it. They already know. And what's worse, so does Gordon."

These tidings put the newsroom into something of a tizzy. Gordon knew about Amy Sue Gravink, either through his own digging or a tip from one of his police sources, and it was just a matter of time until he found out everything that had happened in Texas. He could file his story on the ID tonight (if he hadn't already), and although Cody might try his manly magic on the *Times* editors, I didn't think for a minute that it would work. Cops riffling through a Benson admissions office—not to mention the *Monitor* nosing around, which whatever stringer the *Times* got to do the Sugarland interviews was bound to hear about—hardly made for a hush-hush situation. I was willing to bet that Amy Sue Gravink's face was going to be staring out from the front page of the next day's Metro section, damn it all.

That meant we had to run with it, or look like complete morons by breakfast. So Mad and I hunkered down to finish the story. It turned out to be forty inches long, covering the whole sordid tale of what happened to Amy Sue's parents, how she'd persevered (cue the violins) and gone to night school and applied to college—complete with quotes from her teachers and neighbors about what a plucky little thing she was. It talked about her brother's trouble in school, and how his teachers always said he wasn't really dumb but just wasn't any good at, quote, "book learnin'."

What the story didn't suggest, of course, was that he might have killed his sister, and his parents to boot. That was just speculation, based on nothing more solid than circumstantial evidence and the off-the-record hunch of a single policeman. Even if Mad and I had wanted to put our bylines on something that flimsy, the paper had no desire to wind up in libel court. We just hoped Gordon didn't come up with something better in time to make his deadline.

Eventually, and no matter how I tried to procrastinate, the moment came when one of us had to call up the police for comment. Now, if this had been a relatively normal situation, the call might have gone one of several ways. The cops could have just said "no comment"; they could have gone postal and tried to talk us into holding the story, *New York Times* be damned; they could have confirmed they were looking into the possibility that Amy Sue was the first victim (for my money, the most likely scenario); or they could have positively identified her, assuming they'd had the time to find her dental records and notify whoever passed as her next of kin, sans her brother.

None of these possibilities would have made me break a sweat. But in the present situation there existed a whole galaxy of much uglier options, which included having Detective Brian Cody hate me for the rest of my life or (what's worse) never sleep with me again.

So it didn't take much for Mad to convince me that since he was supposed to be the primary on the story anyway, he should be the one to call Cody for comment. I guess he thought he was going to have a fight on his hands, though I can't imagine why; if he hadn't offered, I would not only have begged, but bribed him with enormous quantities of alcohol.

I couldn't stand to sit around while he made the call— listening to his half of the conversation and trying to guess what the hell Cody was saying on the other end— so I went out on a rat run for Mad's and my dinner. I was standing at the counter in Schultz's, waiting for Mad's turkey on rye and my Swiss cheese delight (which I had proscribed for myself as a tranquilizer for mounting hysteria), and of course I flashed back to the time I'd eaten there with Cody just a week earlier. I wondered for the hundredth time how pissed he was going to be when he found out about our nosing around down in Texas, and then I thought for the hundredth time how he had no right to be mad because I was just doing my job, and I didn't go telling him he couldn't do his, and what was with his sexist attitude anyway?

And then, having worked myself into a frenzy, I realized (also for the hundredth time) that I was upset with him for something he hadn't actually said. This did not seem the definition of sanity.

I kept thinking about Cody as I was walking back to the paper, about how what we were up to was probably obvious to everyone even though we thought we were being so sly. I remembered that time in Schultz's when I started feeding him—which is a pretty intimate thing to do, and definitely not standard practice between cops and reporters—and our little debate over vegetarianism and the Benson animal-rights thing, and how he'd been lots more open-minded than I would have thought.

Something struck me then—call it dog-lover's intuition. I'm not sure how long I stood there on the Green, gaping like an idiot, holding two sandwiches and some fat-free chips and two cans of Diet Pepsi. First it all seemed to make sense, then it seemed ridiculous—as though someone who killed women for fun would make himself that conspicuous. But I couldn't shake the suspicion that it might be irresistible to him, that he couldn't find himself among so many like-minded people and just sit on his hands. He was, after all, a man of action.

I ran back to the paper, found Melissa in the darkroom, and got some contact sheets from her. Then I went in search of Mad, who was just getting off the phone. He grabbed the food the minute he saw me and cracked open one of the sodas, which promptly exploded all over him.

"Christ, Bernier, what'd you do, shake this thing up?"

"I ran all the way back. Listen, I thought of something."

"And that Kraut bastard better not've put mayonnaise on this . . ."

"Will you shut up and listen to me for a second? I had a brainstorm."

He put his feet up on the desk and proceeded to unwrap his turkey on rye. "Heaven help us."

"Okay, it's like this. What's the one thing we know about Bobby Ray?"

"He likes to kill chicks."

"Come on, we don't know that for sure. But what's the one thing we do know about him?"

He shoved a quarter of the sandwich into his mouth, chewed a little, then gave me a lovely view of the contents. "I dunno. You tell me."

"Come on, play nice."

He shoved another quarter. "Loser who can't hold down a job at the dog pound?"

"Argh . . . You are *such* a jerk. The correct answer is, he's nuts about animals. Dogs, anyway."

"So?"

"So if he's really in this town, he's not alone."

"Do you have to be so goddamn oblique on deadline?" I shoved the contact sheets under his nose. "What are those?"

"The shots from the animal-rights protesters. Four rolls' worth."

He squinted at them, then at me. "Don't tell me you think he's in there. *That*'s your brainstorm? Give me a break, Bernier. You don't really think he could be that stupid, do you?"

"Well, I thought maybe . . ."

"No way does a guy go out and kill chicks and then show up at some asinine rally where he might get himself arrested. It makes no fucking sense."

"I thought about that, and you're probably right. But if he's really such an animal fanatic, maybe he couldn't resist."

"Wouldn't he be more likely to just break into a lab and liberate the beasts?"

"So why hasn't he done it?"

"Because he's not even *in* this stinking town, how about?"

"Well, if he's not in this stinking town, then he's not our problem, and we're looking for the wrong guy. But so far he's our only lead, so we might as well follow it. Right?"

"If you insist."

"What's your problem? Wait, I get it. You're just pissed because you didn't think of it first."

"Am I that transparent?"

"Yes."

He waved the contact sheets. "So what do we do with these?"

"We scour them for anybody who might be Gravink. Then we get Melissa or Wendell to blow them up for us."

"Scour them? They're so small, I can't make out a damn thing." I handed him one of the loupes I'd lifted from the darkroom.

"Bernier, has it escaped your little brain that we have a story to finish?"

"Oh, right. I sort of spaced."

He threw the loupe and prints on the desk. "Not a good time for it."

"You finish the interviews?"

"I was just getting off the phone with your boyfriend when you came running in with your titties in a twist."

"He is *not* my . . . Oh, hell, what did he say?"

Mad screwed his face up into something resembling pity. "He wants you to call him."

"So he can wring my neck?"

"Probably."

"Oh, fuck. I knew this was going to happen. How the hell did I manage to get myself into this crazy goddamn mess? I swear, I'm never dating another cop as long as I . . ." I stopped ranting long enough to notice that Mad was trying not to laugh, and failing. "Are you messing with me?"

"Totally. Truth is, I got the impression he was rather proud of his little sweetie."

"Now I *know* you're setting me up."

"No shit."

"I can't believe it."

"What did you expect, that he'd go all macho on you?"

"Of course."

"Well he didn't. Can we finish the story now?"

"Hmm . . ."

"You still got something up your skirt?"

"You men are very vexing."

"We like to keep you guessing, cutie pie."

"And at that," I said, "you are damnably adept."

28

It was Amy Sue Gravink. There was no denying it, and the cops had no desire to try. They'd gotten a tip from a student intern in the Ag school admissions office—someone considerably less paranoid than the woman who'd called me—and went barreling up to campus. There, they'd proceeded to mess up a year's worth of files, without managing to unearth Amy Sue's application. (And one of their number had, presumably, found the time to leak the whole story to Gordon, thank you very much.) Within hours they'd faxed Sugarland for her dental records, made the match, and notified a great-aunt in Minneapolis whose main concern was whether she was going to get stuck paying for the funeral.

Mad and I filed our story, whereupon he declared that he wasn't doing a damn thing until he got himself a beer, and not one out of a bottle either. So we moved over to the Citizen Kane (arguably the worst place in Gabriel to do something you don't want every other reporter in town to know about), huddled in a back booth, and tried for the first time in our lives to be inconspicuous. But our favorite watering hole isn't known for quiet contemplation; we would have blended in better with a drunken shouting match. Mack came over twice to ask us what the hell we were doing—which, frankly, was a good question.

"Tell me again what we're looking for?" Mad said after Mack was safely back behind the bar.

"You know. White guy in his early twenties."

"Yeah, he'll stand right out on a college campus."

"Okay, a white guy in his early twenties who looks criminally insane."

"Maybe I ought to switch to tequila."

"Look, I'll bet my boots this guy's no joiner. I seriously doubt he'd get in the cops' faces with that civil disobedience crap. All I'm saying is, let's look through the crowd shots and see if we can find somebody who looks like a loner."

"Somebody in the *crowd* who looks like a loner?"

"Oh, hell, you know what I mean. Hanging back. Watching but not participating. Strangely fascinated, but not quite . . ."

"Okay, okay, I get the idea."

But after twenty more minutes of squinting through a haze of secondhand smoke, all I was getting was a headache. I didn't need Mad to tell me this might very well be the most pointless tangent I'd ever sent us on.

"Oh, crap," I said finally. "You win. I give up."

"Are you saying uncle?"

"Uncle, aunt, and all your goddamn cousins."

"At last."

He poured out the rest of the Labatt's, stretched his enormous wingspan toward the ceiling, and managed to elbow the girl behind him right in the head. She turned around with a very bitchy look on her face, which promptly melted into a toothy smile.

"Sorry about that," he said.

"Oh, wow, *no* problem." She slithered into her seat and turned back to her girlfriends. They all giggled, and one of them said, "What a hottie."

My mood was deteriorating rapidly.

"You want me to leave you alone with your new friends?"

"Hey, I was just being nice." He held the empty pitcher over his mug in case he'd missed a few molecules. "Time to fill the trough. You want another soda?"

"I'm thinking something stronger."

"G and T?"

"Tanqueray, two limes, not too boozy."

"But of course."

He went to the bar, leaving me to choose between staring at the Bessler cheerleading squad or the headache-inducing photos. I opted for the photos.

Even with the loupe it was hard to distinguish one person from another, or just tell the men from the women. (Come to think of it, they look pretty much the same around here even when they're life-sized.) And since all I'd ever seen of Gravink was a couple of lousy profile shots, I had no prayer of picking him out. I decided to suck it up and mark every frame that someone of his description might possibly be in—which meant just about all of them.

"You find something?" Mad said when he sat back down to find me circling frames in red grease pencil.

"Nah. I'm just marking these so Meliss can blow them up."

"All those? It'll take her four hours."

"I know. It's gonna cost us."

"Us?"

"Jeeze, your enthusiasm for this story goes up and down like the Assyrian Empire. One minute you're dragging me to Texas, the next you don't give a damn."

He shrugged and looked at the contact sheets again, then tossed them away. "Christ, these guys make me want to heave."

"Because?"

"Because to them it's all so fucking facile."

"Yeah, well, they're not much into ambiguity. They think animal testing is just evil, no matter what."

"Never mind that some actual good might come out of it."

"I guess they don't think the ends justify the means."

"And how about this joker?" He jabbed his finger on a close-up of a screaming protester. "Didn't you tell me he won't even talk to his own parents because they own a goddamn Burger King?"

I glanced down at the picture. Even in miniature and in black and white, you could tell the guy was apoplectic. "David Loew? Actually, he's just about the most reasonable of the lot. Most of the time, anyway."

"Yeah, I'd still like to—"

"Wait a minute. That's it. I can't believe I didn't think of it before."

"What?"

"David Loew."

"You think this big-mouth hippie is your serial killer?"

"Oh, Christ, of course not. But he's the ringleader. If Gravink . . ."

"Hey, what are you guys up to back here?"

We looked up from our confab to find Gordon Band standing over us, and taking what I would definitely call an unhealthy interest in our contact sheets. Before he could lay his paws on them I scooped them up and shoved them into my backpack.

"Just got a new pitcher," Mad said, suddenly every inch the jolly pub-crawler. "Get yourself a mug."

"Already got one," Gordon said, pulling the frosty object from behind his back. Mad raised the pitcher, and Gordon extended his mug. Then he sat down next to me, forcing me to scoot over or have him half on my lap. "Hey, Alex, what's news?"

"Not much. You file yet?"

"Just did. Ten-incher. How about you?"

I reached across him to relocate my drink. "Hour ago."

"How about that Amy Sue Gravink shit? What a rush, huh? Poor little country girl comes up here to the mean streets of New York and gets herself dead. My editor totally gobbled it."

"Gordon, the girl came from *Houston*, and she got whacked in the middle of the woods. I think you're mixing your metaphors."

"Yeah, whatever. Guess where they're running it."

"Gee, I don't know. Page one?"

His face fell, and even farther than usual. "Uh, no. Guess again."

"They're holding it for Sunday Styles."

"No, it's on the front page of the Metro section. Stripped across the bottom."

"Jeepers."

"That's twice in a row. I'm doing a follow-up for tomorrow too."

"With your real name on it and everything? You must be *so* proud."

"Hey, Band," Mad said when he tired of the spectacle, "I gotta know. Where did you come up with the Canine Killer crap? Brilliant."

"Source."

"Oh, twaddle," I said. "Nobody's calling him the Canine Killer, and you know it."

He wiggled his eyebrows at me. "They are now."

"You know, I remember when you were Mr. Ethics. And now you're chumming the waters like you're reporting for the *Post*, and I don't mean the one in Washington."

"You're just jealous."

"Of what?"

"That I broke the Canine Killer thing. And that you didn't get the scoop on Amy Sue."

"Poor little white boy. Wait until you read tomorrow's *Monitor*."

That got him. *"What?"* He gave me a pleading look, then tried it out on Mad. "Come on, please tell me. What've you got?"

"Paper costs thirty-five cents, Gordon. Enjoy it with your morning coffee."

Mad made a meowing sound. "Ouch, Bernier, pull in those claws. No reason to torture the man." He said this, but made no move to relieve Gordon's agony.

"So?" he said in a voice that came perilously close to a whine. "Come on already. I'm groveling here."

"Band," Mad began slowly. "Do we look tanned to you?"

"Huh?"

"Well, do we?"

"Yeah, I suppose so. What's your point?"

"Doesn't it make you think maybe we might have spent some time in a very *sunny* place recently? Hmm?"

When he wanted to, Mad could be plenty bitchy himself. Even I couldn't stand to watch the poor guy squirm much longer. "Gordon," I said, "who the fuck do you think dug up Amy Sue Gravink in the first place?"

He gaped at us. It was very satisfying. "No. Oh, *God*, no. You're not serious. *Are* you serious?"

"Yep."

"I'm sure that ten-incher of yours is dynamite," Mad said with a nasty smirk. "But it just so happens that we have a whole package on the little lady running tomorrow. Quotes, color, the whole shebang."

Gordon made a strangling sound. It wasn't pretty. "Oh, crap," he said once he'd gotten a hold of himself. "And me kvelling about my lousy ten inches."

"In your *dreams* you've got ten inches," I said. They both ignored me.

"Don't sweat it, Band." Mad topped off Gordon's mug, his version of offering the olive branch. "You scoop us, we scoop you, you scoop us back. Keeps life interesting."

"I feel like such a schmuck."

"Don't worry about it. Let it go. Have a beer nut." He pushed the bowl across the table, and Gordon nibbled a few.

"Can I tell you guys something?" he said after a while.

"Sure," Mad said. "Shoot."

"It's not exactly easy for me. I don't talk about my, you know, *feelings* very much."

Mad looked queasy all of a sudden. I recognized the expression as one I'd often seen on his face upon exiting the men's john. Uh-oh. "Oh, man, Band," he said. "Don't tell me you're queer."

"*Mad!* Don't be such a jerk. If Gordon wants to come out to us, we should . . ."

"Stop," Gordon shrieked. "Oh, *God*, just stop. If my mother heard you, she would've had a coronary by now. And no, I am not gay." His eyes darted from me to Mad and back again. "Did you really think I was gay?"

"Don't worry about it," I said. "Mad just thinks any guy who shares his feelings is a member of the man-boy love club. Go on."

"I can't even remember what I was going to say." He watched as Mad tried to top off his glass again. It was full, so all he could do was go through the motions. Gordon ate another conciliatory beer nut. "Oh, right. What I was going to say was that, well, last year was the best year of my life."

It was my turn to stare at him. I couldn't have been any more surprised if he *had* come out to us. "Are you out of your mind? For the record, last year was the *worst* year of my life. And since when do you have such romantic memories of this place, anyway? Need I remind you that you spent last year living in a town you hated, working at a paper you said was hardly good enough to wrap a fish in, and stuck two hundred miles away from any decent corned beef? Or have you had some sort of seizure?"

"I know, I know. All those things are true. But I'm not

kidding. I really . . . I mean, last year was the first time I ever really worked with anybody else, like on a team."

"I'm gonna cry here," Mad offered. "Jeeze, man, I love you too."

Gordon turned an even rosier shade of pink. "Mock me all you want. But what I'm trying to say is that you know damn well my work is my life. And last year I did the best work I've ever done. The three of us . . . well, we complemented each other."

I patted his hand on my way to the beer nuts. "And being on opposite sides isn't so much fun, huh?"

"I was really looking forward to it at first. I suppose I wanted to prove I'd been the one carrying everything last year, and I could do the same thing all over again on my own. It's made me kind of insane to realize I can't."

"Lucky for you," I said, "there happens to be a cop reporter job open at the *Monitor* as we speak."

"Whoa. I'm not that crazy."

"Then what's your point?"

"I don't know. I'm just trying to apologize for being such a . . ."

"Manipulative wanker?"

"Um, yeah."

"And this isn't some lame effort to worm your way back into my good graces so you can rip off my story again?"

He looked wounded. "Of course not. How could you even think I'd . . ."

"Then consider yourself forgiven." I kissed him on the cheek, and he wiped at the spot like a little boy in fear of cooties. "I'll even let you buy me a drink."

I followed him to the bar, then started out the front door.

"Where are you going?"

"Phone call. I'll be right back."

"Isn't there a phone behind the bar?"

"This is business," I said. "And I wouldn't want to tempt you."

I left before he could say anything else and went to the bank of pay phones on the Green. There, my slobbish tendencies paid off when I found the right notebook among the legions at the bottom of my backpack. I flipped through it until I found David Loew's phone number, then got an answering machine that played "Meat Is Murder." I figured it was the right guy.

After I left a message, I crossed my fingers and called Cody at the station house only to strike out again. I didn't know the cop at the switchboard, so all he'd say was that Cody was "out"—and when I asked him to elaborate, he informed me that this meant Cody was "not in." I tried calling his house, and again no dice. That left the only other number I had for him, which I'd never used. I checked my watch, hoped that 9:25 wasn't too late to call an old Irish lady, and dialed his mom.

Luckily, she sounded awake when she answered. She seemed to recognize my name instantly, which made me wonder what the hell Cody had told her. It turned out that he was actually on his way over there for dinner, and the next thing I knew she was giving me directions to her place. I promptly went back into the bar, drained the gin and tonic from Gordon in the name of liquid courage, and sallied forth to let Cody's mother scope me out from top to bottom.

29

To find someone more momlike than Mary Cody, you'd have to order her out of a goddamn catalogue. Okay, I know that sounds bitchy, and I don't really mean it that way. Mrs. Cody is a nice lady, and she sure makes great oatmeal. But it's kind of hard to compete with such a paragon of womanly virtue. Mary Cody keeps a spotless house; suffice it to say her kitchen floor is cleaner than my dining-room table. But that's just the beginning of it. She volunteers. She plays bingo. She knits things, feeds the squirrels, and cooks wholesome meals that include applesauce.

She even owns a red checkered apron. I saw it with my own two eyes.

Now, Brian's mother was very sweet to me, and very accepting of the vegetarian thing. (She had, after all, spent ten years of her life in Gabriel.) But I would have been considerably less intimidated by her if she'd been, say, a federal judge. That kind of lady, I know how to relate to.

But what do I say to a woman who knows how to iron? And what must she think of the fact that I'm fairly unfamiliar with the word "hairbrush"?

As you may have gathered, I did not grow up with this sort of mother. My mom wears bright red lipstick, has an excellent manicure, and wears Chanel suits to court, where she makes sure rich people don't go to jail; to her, "home cooking" means takeout. My dad is a fairly high-powered history scholar at Williams who's always on the prowl for some expensive gizmo that'll make his golf balls go farther. Frankly, both of them wonder when I got switched in the bassinet, and which Woodstock alumni are raising their real kid. It's a miracle we get along so well; it may have something to do with their great relief that I haven't followed all their friends' kids into rehab.

I'm not sure what Mary Cody and my mom would make of each other, since they seem like products of such different times; imagine June Cleaver having lunch with Ally McBeal. Anyway, I'm still not sure what Mrs. Cody made of *me*.

Cody's car was in the driveway when I got there, and as I knocked on the door I hoped to hell she'd actually told him I was showing up. She had, of course (I don't think Mrs. Cody has a devious bone in her entire body), and for the next hour I watched her dote on him while I ate the aforementioned oatmeal, plus a huge chunk of cabbage doused in real butter. It was not an unpleasant way to spend an evening.

We were digging into the homemade strawberry short-cake when Mrs. Cody said good night, kissed the top of her son's very large head, and told us to leave the dishes in the sink.

"Wow," I said when she was gone.

"Great food, huh?"

"I was talking about your mom."

"What about her?"

"She's a force of nature."

He smiled and shrugged. "She's my mom."

"Cody, she's a domestic goddess."

"That better be a compliment."

"Of course it is. She's amazing."

"Well, thanks."

"Are your sisters like her?"

"A little. Not really, though. I'd have to say Maggie is more than Dierdre, since she's got kids. But she still works, which my mom isn't too much in favor of."

"She must have been pretty upset when you got divorced."

"You'd think so, wouldn't you? But the truth is, she had a party."

"No way."

"Yes indeed. She invited her whole Bible study group and cooked a big ham."

"What? Why?"

"I probably shouldn't say this, but my mom *hated* Lucy."

"Are you kidding? I can't imagine that sweet middle-aged lady hating anybody."

"Yeah, well, she couldn't stand her. Always said she was trouble."

"Do you think that was part of the reason that . . ."

"That my marriage went bust? Not really. I just think my mom was right. She *was* trouble."

"How so?"

"Well, the way my mom put it after we split was more or less that even if Lucy was with me, she always played to every other guy in the room. And, great detective though I am, I never even noticed."

"But if she's such a churchgoer, didn't she, you know, worry you were going to hell? Breaking the vows and all?"

"Well, first off, Lucy and I never got married in the church. She wasn't even Catholic, and I pretty much dropped out of it after high school anyway. I just go with my mom some Sundays to make her happy. But there's also the fact that I was the one who got dumped, which goes a long way toward expiating my sin."

I picked up the dessert plates and started washing them, which seemed the least I could do in this temple to the domestic arts. "Wouldn't she disapprove of you and me?" I said over my shoulder. "I mean, nice girls don't let good Catholic boys have their way with them, do they?" The next thing I knew Cody was grabbing me from behind, and with my hands covered with dish soap there wasn't a lot I could do about it. "Cody, your mom . . ."

"Is sound asleep."

I turned around and kissed him back. "Are you planning to nail me in your childhood bedroom?"

"I'd love to. But unfortunately, I didn't grow up here."

"I forgot. Too bad."

"And besides, we should talk."

"About what?"

"You tell me. I didn't think you came all the way over here for my mother's strawberry shortcake."

"True."

"So you want to tell me about Texas?"

I dried off my hands and sat back down at the kitchen table, narrowly stopping myself from putting my dirty sneakers on one of Mrs. Cody's chair cushions. "You already know a lot of it. Amy Sue Gravink, I mean."

"How did you find out about her?"

"Anonymous source. Gave us her name and home address, so down we went."

"Poor kid."

"Yeah. You heard about what happened with her parents?"

"Two seconds after we called the local PD. The case is still fairly infamous down there."

"Mad went to the house. Said it was really creepy."

"That kind of crime changes a place. Takes a lot of good karma to change it back."

"Karma?"

"Did I just say that?" He shook his head and sat down next to me. "This town must be getting to me."

"Happens to the best of them."

"Did you two find out anything else I should know about? Just between you and me?"

It was decision time, the very call Marilyn had told me to make in her office—and which I had dearly wanted to avoid. But sitting there with him in his mother's kitchen, it didn't seem all that complicated. "What do you know," I said slowly, "about Amy Sue Gravink's older brother?" As soon as the words were out of my mouth, Cody leaned over and kissed me hard. "What was that for?"

"I was hoping you'd tell me."

"So you already know?"

"We found out about Bobby Ray's run-in with the

Houston SPCA when we started looking for Amy's next of kin. Tracked it down as his last-known job, and one of my less incompetent guys got the director to talk. It definitely got us thinking."

"Did you hear about the house?"

"What about it?"

"Well, off the record, someone who will remain nameless may have taken a look inside. Apparently the place looks like a kennel—dog food everywhere, and worse."

"Interesting."

"Interesting? Aren't you thinking what I'm thinking?"

"I'd say so."

"But, Cody, wouldn't that . . . I mean, if you follow the logic, are we saying Bobby Ray Gravink murdered his own sister?"

"I suppose we are."

"That's . . . unthinkable."

"I wish it were, Alex. But trust me. It isn't."

"But *why*? And why all those other girls? Why C.A.?"

"I can't imagine. Even after all these years, I honestly can't."

"How are you going to find him?"

"The usual ways. We've got people on campus right this minute. Tomorrow morning we do a full-scale canvass. If he's here, we'll find him."

"Do you even know what he looks like?"

"State of Texas sent us his driver's license photo, but it's not great." He pulled a paper out of his back pocket. It was a photocopy of a fax, which made the image even murkier. What you could make out, though, was a very intense pair of eyes, a meaty nose, and a head shaped like a potato. "Taken when he was sixteen. May not look much like it anymore."

"Christ, somebody must have a picture of this guy. Did you get your hands on the Sugarland high school yearbook?"

"One of our guys tried the school, but it turns out his picture was cut out."

"I know. I saw it."

"Doesn't go a long way toward making him look innocent, does it? Anyway, we're trying to run down another copy."

"Can I use the phone for a second? I need to check my machine." I dialed home, but there was no message from David Loew. I hung up the phone and picked up the photocopy. "What are you guys going to do with this?"

"Well, since the vet clinic seems to be the center of it all, we're asking around to see if anybody recognizes him. But as I told you before, we have to be careful. The last thing we want to do is tip this guy off so he bolts and takes his show on the road."

"You know, I was thinking, have you considered looking into the animal-rights angle?"

"That Gravink might be one of those . . . what do you call them?"

"Benson Animal Anarchists. BAA."

"Yeah, it crossed my mind. But the brains down at Quantico think it's unlikely. Apparently that kind of conspicuous behavior doesn't fit the profile at all. Which brings me to something else I haven't told you. It looks like the feds are taking over the case."

"Now? Why?"

"Because they're saying if it really is Bobby Ray

Gravink, then he took his sister across state lines. And that makes it a federal offense."

"But she was already in New York for her Benson interview. I don't get it."

"Neither do I. But the truth is they've been trying to grab the case for weeks. Now they at least have a reason to claim jurisdiction, even if it's a bunch of bullsh . . ."—he seemed to realize he was about to say a bad word in his mother's kitchen—"even if it's a load of garbage."

"What does the chief have to say about it?"

"He's putting up a fight. I'm just not sure it'll do any good."

"But, Cody, what happens if we're all on the totally wrong trail? What if Bobby Ray has nothing to do with this?"

"Well, we're looking into some other possibilities too. We have to keep all the bases covered. But Bobby Ray is the closest thing we've had to a suspect since . . ."

"Since my dear friend Jeffrey Vandebrandt?"

"Right."

"What's up with him, anyway?"

"He's the court system's problem now. I'm sure the D.A. will cut a deal, so you're not going to have to testify at a trial or anything."

"Is he going to do time?"

"Definitely."

"How can you be so sure?"

"Because I told the D.A. that if that little creep's butt didn't end up behind bars, I was going to kill him."

"Really?"

"No. I asked him to do it in the spirit of interdepartmental cooperation. But I also mentioned that if he didn't, the evidence for his big drug trial might go bye-bye, and the headlines along with it."

"Wow. Whatever happened to my big Boy Scout?"

"Yeah, well, I wouldn't really have done it. But that kid deserves to go away for a while."

"Listen, Cody, I gotta ask you something else. Are you pissed about Texas?"

"That you went down there working on the story? Of course not. But I'm a little pissed that my girlfriend left town for four days and I only heard about it from one lousy answering machine message."

I stared at him for a second, wondering if he'd used the G-word accidentally or on purpose. I decided now wasn't the best time to bring it up. "I'm sorry about that," I said. "It just happened so fast. One minute I was answering the phone in the newsroom, and the next thing I knew I was packing my suitcase. It was kind of crazy."

"The last I heard, they had phones down in Texas."

I thought about making some stupid excuse, then opted for the plain vanilla truth. "I was afraid if I told you what I was up to, you'd be furious."

"Why?"

"I . . . Well, I . . ." I couldn't put my finger on it. "I don't know, I just didn't think you'd appreciate a couple of reporters digging around behind your back."

He laughed then, a big raucous guffaw. "Alex, I'm fairly sure I don't have to tell you this, but that's what reporters do. You don't honestly think the *Boston Globe* used to call the precinct house and ask permission to go nosing around my cases, do you?"

"Well, no, but you weren't dating the *Globe* at the time."

"Alex, since we've been together, have I ever once asked you not to do your job?"

"Well, no, but . . ."

"Have I?"

"No."

"So what makes you think I would? Just because you've got me pegged as some Neanderthal?"

"Come on, Cody. From the day we met, we've been butting heads about what the paper was or wasn't going to publish."

"Right. Because it's part of my job to try and control what the public knows about the case. It's not my favorite part, believe me."

"And you really think we can both just go about our business and not have it bug us at the end of the day?"

"Alex, haven't we already had this conversation? More than once?"

"Yep. I guess I just need some massaging."

"Then come home with me."

So we drove the three miles to his apartment in separate cars, and spent the next couple of hours not talking about the case. The sex was as athletic as ever, but there was also a kind of Zen about it too. I'm not sure how to describe it, except to say that for the first time I got the feeling that maybe there might be a future in it after all. The phone rang just as we were falling asleep, and when Cody answered it I could feel the muscles in his back tense up next to me. He talked for a long time, then jumped out of bed and pulled on his boxers. I listened to the rest of the story as he was getting dressed, although I'd pretty much figured out what was going on from his half of the conversation. He told me he'd probably be gone all night, asked me to stay long enough to let his dog back in, and said he'd call when things got less crazy.

Then he kissed me good-bye. And the next time I saw him, he was dying.

30

ZEKE CAME HOME TWENTY MINUTES AFTER CODY LEFT, and he seemed so happy to see me I didn't have the heart to leave him in the empty apartment. So I scribbled a note that I'd taken the dog to my place to play with Shakespeare, drove home, and called Mad. Then I crawled into bed, and when I woke up the two dogs were curled next to each other in a yin-yang pattern, which was just about the cutest thing I'd ever seen.

When I got to the paper, Bill was already at one of the layout computers mocking up the next day's page one— a good ten hours earlier than usual. They'd obviously already heard. Unless the killer turned himself in before deadline, there was no doubt about what the lead story was going to be.

"Nice of you to show up," Bill said.

"It's nine-thirty. The last thing I heard, this was still an A.M. paper."

"Madison's been here since seven."

"Bully for him. Who do you think tipped him off last night?"

Bill stopped messing with the mouse. "How'd you find out so soon?"

"Reliable source."

"Who?"

"Anonymous reliable source. Don't worry about it. It was legitimate, am I right?"

"Yeah. Mad just got back from the house. Family's going crazy."

The family in question was the Kingman-Finkelsteins, some of Gabriel's most celebrated loudmouths. I'd been covering them for years, chronicling their crusades for social justice at home and abroad. The father, Joe Kingman, was a Benson law professor who'd helped convince the university to found one of the nation's first Peace Studies programs during the early seventies—or, more accurately, helped drive the administration batty with protests and takeovers until it finally gave in. Mom was Shayna Finkelstein, an antihunger activist who'd chucked a career as a nutrition researcher to start soup kitchens and food banks around the country. They were always good for a quote on topics ranging from welfare cuts to CIA recruiting to the skyrocketing price of quinoa.

I'd done a profile of Joe Kingman last summer when he'd been named to a vacant seat on the Gabriel city council, and I'd spoken to his wife as recently as the week before. But the first time I'd ever met the family was shortly after I got on the city beat, when the council was debating whether or not to revive Gabriel's moribund curfew law. It'd been discovered during a routine review of the city ordinances, and the cops (who'd had no idea such a thing existed) started licking their chops at how handy it would be in making the streets safe from slackers.

It sounded sensible enough. No one under the age of sixteen could be out after eleven o'clock without an adult, except for a list of special circumstances about a mile long. There were exceptions for going to and from arts events, sports games, errands for their parents—just about everything but drug deals and drive-bys.

Still, a few people promptly went nuts. What everyone on the council (even the serious lefties) thought was going to be a routine thing turned into a month-long debate. Protests were duly conducted, petitions circulated, open meetings held. By the time it came to a vote, fifty kids and their parents stormed the council hall to exercise their fundamental right to shout in public. And the most eloquent of them all—the one who gave a speech on the beauty of walking the city streets at two A.M. to commune with the wholesome quietude of Gabriel—was Justice Kingman-Finkelstein.

She was fifteen years old at the time, a sophomore at Gabriel High who'd been agitating for change (energy-saving lightbulbs in the gym, vegan food in the cafeteria) since she was in the third grade. She was tall and pretty, with long legs and light brown hair that flowed down her back. She was more poised than most people twice her age, and when the votes were counted the anti-curfew people won 8–2.

And now, two years later, she was gone.

She was about to start her freshman year at Benson, where she planned to major in labor relations. Justice (yes, the name on her birth certificate) was staying with her parents during a break from a summer program in grassroots union organizing when she disappeared. She'd been out running with the family dog at dusk, and she didn't come home. Her parents might not have been concerned at first—might have figured she was chasing her inner child around campus and lost track of time—if her dog hadn't wandered home alone three hours later.

The Kingman-Finkelsteins immediately called the cops, the very folks who'd hauled them away in plastic handcuffs so many times before. The next morning, with still no sign of Justice, their house had been turned into a command center. From what Mad said, it sounded like every liberal activist in Gabriel had shown up to help print posters, work the phones, or just pray. I made some lame crack about a candlelight vigil, whereupon Mad informed me there was already one set for that night.

The press releases started hitting the fax machine at ten-thirty. Justice's parents had always been masters at working the media, and getting their daughter back was the most important campaign they'd ever been on. They were clearly determined to get her name and face out there, maybe in the hope that whoever took her might think of her as a human being rather than a piece of meat. They issued statements about Justice, about the family, even about the damn dog. Although they'd already given Mad an interview at their house, they came right to the phone when I called to ask a few more questions. They even got Chief Hill himself to give a speech on their front steps; it was covered not only by local TV but affiliates from the three networks, Fox, and CNN. The Kingman-Finkelsteins had been cultivating their media contacts for two decades, and now they were calling them in.

Mad was writing the mainbar about the apparent abduction—that's what the cops were calling it—and I was working on a sidebar profile of Justice. I chronicled her various bouts of activism over the years, got a few quotes from her teachers and friends, did a break-out box on all the awards she'd won. The whole thing would have been enough of a tearjerker even without the coup de grace: her dog was terminally ill.

His name was Karl (as in the father of modern socialism), and he was a racing greyhound she'd adopted through a group based in Gabriel that saves them from the track. He'd been with the family since he was three, but after he turned six last spring he'd been diagnosed with cancer. He had a tumor in his left front leg, and when the vet wanted to amputate, Justice said no; it wouldn't have saved the dog's life anyway, just bought him a little more time. So she did her homework and started treating him herself. She cut all the preservatives out of his diet, bought homeopathic remedies at one of the co-ops, even found an acupuncturist in town who was willing to work on him.

The vets were amazed at how well he did. They'd given him two months to live, and four months later he was still running around—apparently fast enough to get away from whoever had abducted his owner. The tumor was still growing, though, and sooner or later the cancer would spread to his internal organs and he'd have to be put down.

But the doctors had to admit that this time, alternative medicine had done a hell of a lot more for him than they could have. And yes, those doctors worked at the Benson vet clinic.

I put all of this at the end of my profile of Justice, but I wasn't sure that even Bill would have the stomach for something that shameless. (Stupid question; of course he did.) But what happened with Karl seemed important for another reason: it broke the pattern. As far as we knew, this was the first time one of the dogs had gotten away.

No one had any way of knowing how that might affect what happened to Justice. Would it somehow make her captor less willing to kill her? Or—and as far as I was concerned, this was by far the more likely—would it piss him off so much, he'd strangle her even sooner?

Was she already dead?

We debated these options across the newsroom with a surprising lack of sarcasm. Journalists can joke about anything—and I mean *anything*—but for some reason getting our rocks off over the imminent demise of some poor hyphenated teenager was beneath even us. Go figure.

I was putting the finishing touches on my story, waiting for the phone to ring with one last quote, when in walked David Loew. He was dressed the same as always, in a PETA sweatshirt, jeans, and canvas sneakers, all of which had holes in them; I was starting to wonder if he owned any other clothes. But his hair was pulled back in a neat ponytail and his beard was trimmed, and that much (plus the conspicuous lack of what we townies call "the crazy eyes") put him in the top one percent of his social group, appearance-wise.

"How are you, Alexandra?" he said in that weirdly formal way of his. David Loew is a very polite guy—so polite, you almost don't notice he's talking about blowing up labs and throwing pig's blood on people. "I received your message," he was saying. "Do you still need to speak to me?"

"Yeah," I said. "Why don't we go someplace quiet?" I took him back to the library, a closet-sized room where we archive old articles. It has a phone and exactly one chair, but it's the only place in the newsroom (besides the darkroom) where you can lock the door. Legends abound about staffers who have supposedly gotten lucky in the library, and whether such action took place during actual working hours. And no, I haven't.

I gave Loew the chair and sat on the librarian's desk. Then I handed him the picture of Bobby Ray Gravink that Cody had left in his apartment, and which I'd taken.

"Do you recognize this guy?"

He studied the picture for a long time, then raised his head. "No," he said. "I do not."

"Are you sure?"

"Who is this person?"

"His name is Bobby Ray Gravink. Does the name ring a bell?"

"No. Should it do so?"

"Probably not. It's a crazy idea anyway."

"How so?"

"Did you hear about what happened to Justice Kingman-Finkelstein?" His face was blank. "You know her, don't you?"

"Of course. She is a fellow traveler."

"Right. Great. Well, she was abducted last night. Probably by the same person who killed those other four girls."

That seemed to get to him. "And you believe this Mr. . . ."

"Gravink."

"This Mr. Gravink had something to do with this?"

"He may have a whole hell of a lot to do with it. Anyway, the cops want to talk to him."

"And you now work for the police?"

"Oh, come on, you know I don't work for the cops any more than I eat at Sizzler. I just wanted to know if you recognized him. I said it was a long shot."

"Isn't that convenient?"

"What?"

"Isn't it convenient that when the police look for someone to blame, they invariably choose a person whose ideals are different than their own? Someone who is out of the so-called mainstream?"

I was tempted to remind him that anybody who killed four women was plenty out of the mainstream to begin with, but I decided it wasn't the right approach. "David, I really don't think this guy's a patsy. Trust me on this."

"Just as you say."

"And you really don't recognize him? I know the picture's pretty grainy . . ."

"I do not. May I go now?"

"Sure."

He opened the door, then stopped. "Will you be attending our action next week?"

"Um, which one would that be?"

"Our two days of hunger to honor the millions of animals slaughtered each day to satisfy the blood lust of the human minority."

"Oh. That one. Sure."

He walked out, leaving me to ponder how much fun it was going to be to hang out on the Green for a couple of hours to watch people *not eating*. Whoopie.

Our package on the disappearance of Justice Kingman-Finkelstein ran the next morning, and the papers sold out downtown within two hours. Since the *Monitor* is way too cheap to do another press run, the circulation director sent his office staff around to the outlying areas to liberate extra copies from the vending boxes, and those sold out too.

The entire city was on edge, waiting for the word that her body had been found. Her parents said on TV that they refused to believe their daughter wouldn't come back safe and sound, but volunteers were combing the woods anyway. No one could remember a worse time, not even when cops were cracking heads open during the Vietnam War. Four women were dead, and the stress of it had settled on the skinny shoulders of one seventeen-year-old girl. No one said it out loud, but there was this feeling in the air that if she didn't survive, part of Gabriel was going to die along with her.

I hadn't seen Cody for a day and a half, only gotten a quick phone call from him late the previous night. I could tell from his voice that the stress was starting to get to him, and I thought of the night he'd told me about the SEALs and how he was afraid of letting someone else drown. But that was what was happening now—the clock running on Justice's life, and no way for him to save her.

It was all I could think about—all anyone could think about—and as I sat at my computer typing in background for one of the follow-up stories, I started having these awful daydreams about how the next day's headline would read. LOCAL GIRL STILL MISSING. FIFTH VICTIM FOUND IN WOODS. FBI TAKES OVER CASE; HUNKY COP LEAVES TOWN. There was no newsroom betting pool for this one, but even if there were, COPS CATCH CANINE KILLER would have been a hundred-to-one long shot.

I got sick of thinking about it, and I was on my way out of the newsroom for a bagel when the secretary yelled that I had a phone call. I went back upstairs, and found David Loew on the line. The first thing he did was apologize for waiting so long to call.

"I've had time to consider it," he said, "and I think that perhaps I was mistaken."

"About?"

"I think perhaps I do recognize the man in your photograph."

"You do? What's his name?"

"I cannot tell you over the phone. You are well aware of my feelings on government surveillance."

"Right. Well, I'll meet you on the Green in ten minutes."

Then he told me he couldn't get into town because his bike was busted, and asked me to come out to his place. He gave me directions to a house five miles out of town, and I drove out there for the interview.

It was, of course, one of the stupidest things I've ever done. Anybody who's ever seen a horror movie knows that when somebody says "I can't talk about it over the phone; come meet me at an abandoned warehouse," you should make haste in the opposite direction. All I can say in my own defense is that I'd been dealing with David Loew for months, and I'd never had a reason to suspect him of anything worse than zealotry and excessive diction. I certainly had no reason to mistrust him. But then again, if I'd known I was trusting him with my life, I would have given it more thought than I did—which was none at all.

So that's how I ended up in front of a house in the country on a sunny afternoon in July. That's how I knocked on the door, and found myself face-to-face with Bobby Ray Gravink. And that, in short, is how I very nearly got myself killed.

31

I WOKE UP IN A CAGE. I MEAN AN ACTUAL *CAGE*, AS IN A BOX made out of chain link with a lock on the front. I had no clear memory of how I'd ended up out cold, except that it had something to do with Bobby Ray Gravink and a big smelly rag. But this much I do know: when I woke up, I felt like hell.

To begin with, I had a headache. And I was hungry, having skipped breakfast and been on my way out for a snack when I was lured to my doom. Also, it wasn't a particularly large cage, not the kind you could stand up in and yell to the guard that you'd been framed. No, this was a cage designed for four-legged creatures. It was a dog kennel.

I looked around the room, and wished I hadn't. There was a stainless-steel table in the middle, and along the walls were jars and instruments and some smaller cages. The place was a goddamn surgical suite, and it didn't take long for me to remember what had happened to the other patients. C.A., with her reproductive organs laid on her stomach like lunch meat. Lynn Smith, dumped in a base-ball dugout minus her eyes.

I had a very bad feeling those eyes were around here somewhere, floating in a jar of formaldehyde. This was probably not going to end well.

But then I saw something else, something everyone in Gabriel was looking for. It was Justice Kingman-Finkelstein, and she was across the room, naked and locked in a cage of her own.

I whispered her name, and when she didn't hear me I said it a bit louder. Her head snapped around, and I saw that her mouth was taped shut. Even from twenty feet away I could read the terror in her eyes. I called her name again, tried to say some idiotic crap about how we were going to be okay, but she started shaking her head from side to side with a desperate kind of violence.

"Where the hell is he?" I said, then remembered she couldn't talk. "Which direction? Come on, point or something. He could be back any minute. Where is he?" She shook her head again even harder than before, and made these high-pitched whimpering sounds. Then I realized her hands were tied behind her back, and she couldn't point if she wanted to.

I'm not sure how long we stayed there like that, but it didn't seem like long enough. Because, you see, it's plenty scary being locked in a cage by some psycho serial killer. But even that is nothing compared to looking him in the eye.

He walked in wearing a white lab coat with a tie on underneath, and a stethoscope around his neck like Marcus-fucking-Welby. My initial thought was that he didn't have the crazy eyes either. He just seemed cold, businesslike, totally indifferent. He walked over to Justice, and as he approached the cage she threw herself back against the wall and got as far away from him as he could.

"Bad dog." That's what I heard him say. I'm not kidding. "Bad dog." He even said it again. "Bad, bad dog." And then: "You'll have to be punished." He went over to the counter and reached for what turned out to be a hose connected to the utility sink. He turned the water on high and sprayed her, and she jammed herself so far into the corner I could see her flesh pressing through the chain link. I had a feeling I might actually faint sometime soon.

I'm not particularly proud to admit it, but the truth is that I wasn't thinking much about poor Justice and what she was going through—what she might already have gone through in the past thirty-six hours. I was across the room cowering in my own little prison, trying to figure out how the hell I had gotten myself into this mess. And, more to the point, how was I going to get myself out of it?

I wondered if anybody at the paper had missed me yet, and the awful truth was that they probably hadn't. No one would really start worrying until deadline that night, which was hours and hours away. No telling what might happen in the meantime. Actually, there was plenty of telling. I just didn't want to think about it.

After spraying Justice for a good five minutes, he turned off the water, coiled the hose neatly, and came over to me. He looked me up and down with that same oddly detached expression, which for some reason made me furious; it seemed as though someone who goes to all the trouble of abducting women and locking them in cages should actually give a damn.

But there he was, looking at me like I was a moth on a pin. He did it for quite a while before he spoke to me, and that interlude gave me plenty of time to go quietly nuts as I crouched there in the metal box, trying to figure out what I could possibly say or do to get out of this. I thought about everything I knew about this case, this *man* (although, frankly, it was hard to include him in the human race), and I couldn't come up with a single thing that wouldn't leave both myself and Justice as dead as the others.

"Are you a good dog, or a bad dog?"

Hearing his voice up close and personal scared the bejeezus out of me. It was low and quiet, with an underlying Texas twang that only made it more menacing. I stared at him, at a loss about what to say, when he repeated himself.

"Are you a good dog, or a bad dog?"

I opened my mouth to say something, although to this day I'm not quite sure what it was going to be. I like to imagine that it would have been something brave—big lies about how the cops were right behind me, and if he didn't let us go he was going to wind up with a needle in his arm. Truth is, though, I was probably going to engage in some serious begging. But just as I was about to speak, I caught sight of Justice out of the corner of my eye. She was shaking her head madly, as she'd done every time I'd spoken to her. And all of a sudden I got the message: *don't talk.*

I'm not saying I'm any smarter than his other victims. But I'd been thinking about the case for weeks, and I had another girl there to warn me. But I'm convinced—dead certain—that the only reason I'm alive today is that I never said a single word.

He treats people like dogs. He treats dogs like people. He tortures people and rescues dogs. People are bad dogs. Real dogs are good dogs. Or something. What the hell?

It was a long shot, but it was the only chance I had. So I put my head down, raised my eyes in as pleading a look as I could muster, and barked at him.

Yes, barked. As in woof-woof, ruff-ruff, yip-yip. I also panted, and gave him my goddamn paw. And I was so fucking scared, I didn't even have the good sense to feel stupid.

But it worked.

"You're a *good* dog," he said, and stuck his fingers through the cage to scratch me on the head. "Good dog gets a cookie." He went over to a jar on the counter, pulled out a gigantic Milk Bone, and stuck it through the chain link. I stared at it for a minute, then took it out of his hand with my teeth and dropped it on the floor. This didn't seem to piss him off too much (it was, after all, extremely doglike), but it didn't take long for me to realize that he was waiting for me to eat it.

When you're a vegetarian, people ask you lots of stupid questions. Chief among them is this: "If you were stranded on a desert island and the only thing you had was a case of Jimmy Dean sausage, would you eat it?" And the answer is: "Of course I'd eat it, you numbskull. If I were in a plane crash in the Andes with a bunch of dead soccer players, I'd eat them too."

I'd never actually had an opportunity to test this theory. But there I was in a cage, staring at cookie made out of dehydrated pig snouts and God only knows what else. I almost made the (possibly fatal) mistake of picking it up with my hands. But I remembered in time and picked it up with my teeth. Then I gagged that sucker down with all deliberate speed.

The biscuit was crunchy, gross-tasting, and very, very dry. It made me incredibly thirsty, and when Gravink shoved a bowl of water through the slot at the bottom of the cage I didn't have to pretend to lap it up.

This seemed to satisfy him. He scratched me behind the ears again, told me to be good while he was gone, and walked out. I heard the door lock behind him. Then I gave him the finger.

Okay, think, Bernier. The guy is insane. It's only a matter of time before he notices you don't actually have a tail. You have to get out of here, and you have to take Justice with you.

I tried the cage, which was depressingly solid. I checked all the hinges, and thought that maybe I could unscrew them if I had enough time. But when I reached for my trusty Spyderco penknife, I realized it was on my key chain in my purse, which Gravink had not been kind enough to incarcerate with me. I tried to figure out if I had anything useful, and the only thing I could come up with was the zipper on my new Gap warm-up jacket. I was too scared to take the jacket off, in case Gravink walked in and caught me using an opposable thumb. So I stretched the zipper tab to the corner of the cage, stuck it into the screw head, and started turning. At first it wouldn't budge. But then it gave, and after a whole lot of sweating and chipped fingernails I got the first screw out. One down, seven to go.

I was only on the second one when I heard a key in the door, and in walked Gravink. He was holding a leash in one hand and a collar in the other, and what he said gave me equal parts terror and hope: "Do you want to go out and play?"

He opened the cage door, and for a second I considered making a break for it. But then I realized that at least one of the other girls must have tried to get away, and failed. And if I didn't outrun him, there was no way I could fight him off. He was around six feet tall with wide shoulders, big arms, and a thickish neck. Given his proportions, it was odd how much he looked like his petite sister. He had a surprisingly delicate nose on that big spud of a head, and his cupid's-bow mouth might have been lifted straight from the police sketch of Amy Sue.

Truth is, he didn't look much like a killer to me. Just goes to show you what I know.

He put the collar on me. For a second I was terrified that this was it—that I'd just let him put the instrument of my demise around my neck without even fighting back— but he didn't seem interested in killing me at the moment. He even put two fingers under the collar to make sure it wasn't too tight, then snapped the leash on and pulled it gently. I followed him across the floor on all fours, which wasn't too bad; the linoleum was smooth, and for whatever reason he hadn't decided to strip me. Yet.

We went through another room that had sofas and chairs and orange wall-to-wall carpet, but from my floor-level vantage point it was impossible to get my bearings. I had no idea where the front door was, and how long it might take to get to it. The next thing I knew he was opening a different door, and I was being blinded by sun-light. I had to stop myself from covering my eyes—way too human—and a second later he'd unsnapped my leash, pushed me outside, and closed the door behind me. When my eyes finally adjusted to the brightness and I got a chance to look around, what I saw can only be described as a dog utopia.

The yard was huge, a field of grass and wildflowers surrounded by an eight-foot privacy fence. Off to one side, by the house, was a water trough fed by a garden hose. Where I was crouched the ground was hard-packed dirt, an infield that held the kind of dog entertainment de-vices you see in agility trials. There were sawhorses to jump over and tunnels to go through, platforms of differ-ent levels for lounging and a kiddie pool to splash in. All in all, it was the canine equivalent of Romper Room.

My first instinct was to stand up and run for it, but on second thought it seemed like a bad idea. I couldn't see any break in the fence where a gate might be—it would be locked anyway—and I was pretty sure that wherever Gravink was, he was watching me. So I stayed down on all fours, and before too long some of the dogs who'd been off playing in the high grass came over to check me out. Most of them were wary, but one came running right up to me and licked my face.

Nanki-Poo.

The name was out of my mouth before I could stop myself, and I hoped to hell our host hadn't heard me. The dog seemed incredibly happy to see me, and I had a sink-ing feeling that he thought it meant C.A. would be com-ing to get him any minute. He did a happy little dog dance. And when he turned his tail to me, I saw that he'd been neutered.

Oh, my God.

I guess that's when I started to figure it out, crouched there in the dirt on all fours. And what I saw next did nothing to shake my suspicion that I'd stumbled onto what was driving Bobby Ray Gravink's mania. It was an elderly boxer-mix who wandered over to sniff me. I whispered the name *Harley*, and he started barking and wagging his tail. But here's the really creepy thing: *he could see*. Someone had performed cataract surgery on Lynn Smith's dog. And I had a strong suspicion just who that someone was—the same person who mutilated his owner in some weirdly symmetrical act of revenge.

I stayed out there for a while, looking around and trying to get the lay of the land. Then I realized with a start that Justice was still in there with him, and God only knew what he was doing to her. So I crawled back to the house and did the most doglike thing I could think of. I scratched at the door.

He opened it immediately, looking down at me and the rest of the pack with what I could swear was genuine adoration.

This was fucking *nuts*.

"Do you want to come in?" I looked up at him and panted some more. I hoped this meant yes. "Don't you want to sit outside with Dr. Daddy?"

If you really want to know, the truth is I'd like to rip Dr. Daddy's throat open and get the hell out of here.

I kept this fact to myself and did some more looking and panting. Finally, he went outside and sat on a big wooden bench. The other dogs followed him, so I did too.

We all settled on the ground around him. It looked like goddamn story time at doggie day camp. Humiliating.

"What *gooooood* dogs you are." He spoke in that awful singsong voice people use on animals and little babies. I promised myself then and there I'd never use that tone again—assuming, of course, that I got out of this alive. "You know, we'll have to go far away soon," he was saying. "The bad people are looking for me. But I promise, I'll take you all with me."

Oh, goodie.

"The bad people don't understand," he went on. "They think Dr. Daddy does *mean* things. They don't care what happens to you. All they care about is themselves. They were going to let you suffer and suffer . . ." He was starting to get teary, as though the idea of their (our?) suffering was just too much for him to bear. I thought for the fiftieth time how much I'd like to kill him. But I had to admit that it wasn't quite as much as it would have been if he'd been murdering the women *and* the dogs.

"Amy Sue didn't understand," he was saying. "She didn't care when Mom and Dad killed you . . ." I wondered if he was talking about the family dog that had been euthanized, and decided it was best not to ask. "She didn't try to stop them. She didn't understand what I had to do. She didn't want to help. All she wanted was to get away. She was as bad as they were. She was a killer just like they were. She had to be punished. It was for her own good. She was a *very bad dog*."

He'd worked himself into quite a lather by now. I was worried his head was going to explode, then decided it was fine with me if it did. But he calmed down eventually, and started throwing a tennis ball around the backyard. It was retrieved by a frisky young Doberman I assumed to be Cocoa. Its ears were still cropped, but there probably wasn't much Gravink could have done about that. I stared at those two perky little points of flesh, and realized they had probably cost Patricia Marx her life.

After Cocoa came back with the ball for the umpteenth time, Gravink told him "no more," and started back into the house. I followed him, because I didn't want to leave him alone with Justice, but he seemed to take it as a compliment. "You want to come inside with Dr. Daddy?" he said, and I tried to look all loyal and happy. I never realized being a dog was so much work.

We went indoors, and Nanki-Poo followed as though he didn't want to let me out of his sight. We passed through what I guessed was the living room, and since I wasn't on the leash this time I could go more slowly and look around. The room was cheaply furnished, and there was grime on the windows that made everything look even dingier. I tried to remember what the house had looked like from the outside, and all I could think was that it had been pretty ramshackle. But that hadn't warned me off at all; there are PhDs around Gabriel who spend the best years of their lives in an Airstream jacked up on cinder blocks.

Gravink held open the door to his ersatz laboratory, and Nanki-Poo and I went in. He told us both to sit, then went to the cabinet and pulled out a drug vial. He reached into a drawer and pulled out a hypodermic and proceeded to fill it with blue liquid, measuring the dose carefully. When he was finished he put the vial back on the counter, and it was close enough so I could read the label.

It was pentobarbital. Nasty nickname: "Blue Juice."

If I hadn't lived with three veterinarians, I might have

been in blissful ignorance about just what that was. But as it was, I knew that although pentobarbital is sometimes used as an anesthetic, when it's colored blue that means the concentration is only meant for one thing. Euthanasia.

He approached Justice's cage with the needle and said that nasty mantra of his one more time. *Bad dogs have to be punished.* I started looking around frantically for something to whack him with, something that could knock him out before he had the chance to turn the needle on me.

Then everything happened at once. Out of the corner of my eye I saw Nanki-Poo's ears prick up, and he gave one sharp bark. Then the door to the lab was kicked open, and through it came Detective Brian Cody, scanning the room with his gun in classic cop fashion.

It would probably have worked out fine if only I hadn't been there. But seeing me on the floor was the last thing he must have expected. It took him by surprise, and he hesitated just for a second, so he didn't see Gravink in the corner behind him until it was too late. His gun dropped a few inches, and it gave Gravink the chance to grab him. He got Cody in a half nelson with his left arm, then reached around with his right and jammed the needle into his heart.

Cody stood there for what I will call one of the longest and worst moments of my life. Then his knees started to buckle, and his eyes fluttered shut. And as he toppled to the floor I'm pretty sure the last thing he saw was me.

What I did next owed more to self-preservation and excessive viewing of cop shows than to any sort of bravery. When Cody fell his gun fell with him. It slid halfway across the floor and I grabbed it, faster than I would have thought possible. I have a fleeting memory of hoping the safety was off, and realizing I had no idea where to find it if it wasn't. Then I stood up, aimed it at the middle of Bobby Ray Gravink's chest, and fired.

It was the first and only time I've held a gun in my life. But it seemed to have the desired effect. Gravink was rushing toward me, and then he wasn't. He stared down at the hole in his chest and back at me. The look on his face said he couldn't have been more surprised if an actual dog had stood up on its hind legs and cold-cocked him. He took another step forward, and I shot him again.

I've always had very little patience for people in movies who think they've put the bad guy down, then turn their backs and get themselves killed. It always seemed to me the height of stupidity and bad taste. If you've got the gun in your hand, you use it. So even as Bobby Ray Gravink lay there bleeding on the ground, I stood over him and emptied the rest of the bullets into his midsection. And it was something of a disappointment to me that when I raised it to his head for the coup de grace, all it did was go *click.*

I dropped the gun and felt Cody's neck for a pulse, but couldn't find one—not that I really knew where to look. I thought he was still breathing, maybe just faintly, so in what was probably not the best medical treatment, I shook him. Then I shook him harder, yelled at him, tried to bully him into waking up. I called his name over and over as I sat there crying on the ugly linoleum. I told him that he was going to be all right, that he'd saved my life, and that tough as I am, I couldn't stand having two men I loved die in a single year.

32

THAT'S HOW THE COPS FOUND ME. CODY MUST HAVE called for backup before he came blazing in there, because within two minutes guys in bulletproof vests were swarming all over the place. I heard one of them yell *officer down*, and the next thing I knew people were pushing me aside to get to him. There were ambulances, and guys shouting into walkie-talkies, and at some point Chief Hill showed up and took me outside. He handed me my purse, and told me they'd found my car in the barn behind the house, where Gravink must have moved it after he locked me up, and that he was going to have one of his men drive it into town for me.

Then I saw a body bag being wheeled out through the front door, and I nearly keeled over. "Cody . . ."

"It's not Cody," he said, grabbing me before I could hit the ground. "That's Gravink. Alex, did you hear me? That's *Gravink*."

"Where's Cody?"

"On his way to the E.R."

"He saved my life. The girl's too."

"I know. Try to calm down. Here, let the EMTs take a look at you."

"I'm fine."

"The hell you are, young lady."

"Look, all I have is dirty hands." I showed him my palms, filthy from crawling around in the backyard. It really was all I had to show for my brief stint in captivity. Unbelievable.

But Chief Hill made me sit for an exam with the paramedics anyway, and when they were done he put me in the front seat of his official car and drove me back to town.

"Alex, for the love of Mike, what were you doing out there?"

"I thought I was going out for an interview. He tricked me."

"Gravink?"

"No, it was David Loew. You know, the head of the Benson Animal Anarchists."

"That long-haired hippie creep? He was in on this?"

"I can't believe it. But he's involved somehow. He's got to be."

I explained how I'd gotten suckered out to the house, and when I was finished the chief pulled the microphone from the dashboard and barked orders into it. Since Bobby Ray Gravink was way too dead to be prosecuted, I had a feeling the ax was going to fall hard on David Loew. And although there was no way Bill would let me, I was unhinged enough to have a few fantasies about covering the trial myself. The execution too.

"You want to tell me what happened in that house?"

the chief was saying. "Or would you rather let it sit awhile?"

"Aren't I going to have to, you know, make a formal statement anyway?"

"Yeah."

"Then I guess I'd rather do it all at once."

"However you want to play it. You're one tough little girl, you know that?"

I let that sink in for a while, then thought about something else. "Chief, am I going to be in trouble?"

"For killing Gravink? Mayor's gonna pin a medal on you."

"No, I mean . . . I really shouldn't be telling you this. But I think I shot him, like, eight times."

"Six. Cody still carries a revolver. Thirty-eight special. Six shots max."

"That's comforting."

"You telling me you think you used excessive force?"

"He was down. I kept shooting."

"I really shouldn't be telling you this either, Alex. But good for you."

"Chief, I tried to shoot him in the *head*. The only reason I didn't was I was out of bullets."

He laughed out loud. After all that had happened, the sound seemed completely foreign. "Like I said, you're one tough little girl."

We were getting into town, and when I expected him to go in one direction, he went in another. "Where are we going?"

"Hospital."

"Thanks."

"I gotta warn you, Alex. Cody didn't look so hot when

they took him out of there. Had to jump-start his heart. Wasn't breathing on his own."

"But he's still alive?"

"They would have radioed me if he wasn't. I just don't want you to get your hopes up. It might be an ugly wait."

"Then why aren't you trying to talk me out of it?"

"I had a feeling you might have a little bit of an interest in how our Cody makes out."

So we'd been fooling exactly no one. Big surprise. "But how did he get out there? How did he find me?"

"I can't say, 'cause I don't know," the chief said. "But with any luck, you can ask him yourself."

It's rather ironic, and the subject of no little teasing on my part, that Cody is alive today for no better reason than that he's a big Irish lug. That, and the fact that whatever else Bobby Ray Gravink was, he was a meticulous dispenser of lethal drugs. The dose in that hypodermic had been precisely calibrated to dispatch a young girl of 108 pounds. Cody weighs in at more than twice that—but minus the medical intervention, it still would have killed him. He owes his life to the paramedics in the Walden County Sheriff's Department, and I guess I owe my life to him.

The atmosphere at the hospital was a cross between a throne room and a madhouse. It's not every day that a Gabriel cop nearly gets killed in the line of duty, and it seemed like everyone in the whole county who wore a uniform (including the postmen and the meter maids) showed up to pay their respects. I was pretty much a fixture at the proverbial bedside, and I was kind of astounded at the deference I got from everybody—not because I was the hero cop's best girl, but because I'd been the one to pull the trigger on the son of a bitch. It had never occurred to me that killing somebody could win you so much respect. Perhaps that's why it's such a popular activity.

As for the newspaper, the general consensus was *not again*. There I was, smack-dab in the middle of another mess, and it was up to Bill and Marilyn to figure out how to play it. Mad won some big AP award for all the stories he wrote; he had five bylines the next day, a *Monitor* record. Plenty of other reporters kept calling, appealing to my sense of collegial goodwill to cut them some slack. But in the end I only gave one outside interview, and it was to an old friend of mine named Gordon Band.

"You know," Cody was saying to me on his last afternoon in the hospital, when we'd finally gotten rid of everybody. "My recall of what happened after I walked into that room is pretty hazy. But I have this strange feeling that maybe there was a pretty girl there telling me not to die."

I sat down on the edge of the bed and kissed the top of his head. "There might have been."

"And this same girl was saying all this stuff about how much she loved me."

"You were hallucinating."

"I was?"

"Must've been the drugs."

"Ah." He pulled me down across him and kissed me. "Well, I'll have to hope for another near-death experience one of these days."

"You know, Cody, if you're well enough to talk about

these daydreams of yours, maybe you wouldn't mind telling me how the hell it was you found me out there."

"I've been avoiding it."

"I noticed. How come?"

"Because I feel like an idiot. I let that amateur bastard get the better of me."

"From what the doctors said, it was a pretty goddamn lucky shot on his part. If he hadn't jabbed you right in the heart with that thing, you might not have even felt it for a while. You sure as hell wouldn't have conked out on me like that."

"Yeah, but the way things played out, I'd be dead right now if it weren't for you."

"Cody, if it weren't for me, you never would have been caught off guard in the first place. And if you hadn't come barging in there, I'd be dead right now."

"So you think we should call it even?"

"Let's shake on it." We did. "Okay, now spill it."

He leaned back against the pillows. He was in good shape for a guy who'd been on a ventilator four days ago, but he still looked like hell.

"After that girl Justice disappeared, the pressure on the department was unbelievable. I never saw anything like it before, not even in the navy. We had people camped out, senators calling us—the mayor pretty much pitched a tent in the goddamn squad room. We were running interviews up at the vet clinic, still trying to pretend it was some investigation about stolen medical equipment so Gravink wouldn't get tipped off. Finally, we thought we had him. Five different people ID'ed the picture as a lab tech named Peter Anderson."

"And that's how you found me?"

He shook his head. "It was a dead end. We had them pull Anderson's documentation, and it was all fake. The address he put on his application was a post office box, and that's where he had his paycheck sent. We searched high and low for a Peter Anderson, and we turned up four of them, none of whom were our guy. So we figured he had to be living under yet another name."

"Couldn't you just grab him when he came into work?"

"We would've loved to. But the day Justice disappeared, he called in and said he had to leave town because of a death in the family. Pretty bad joke, huh? But I got to thinking. Granted, we only had the photocopies of his ID from his file at the clinic, but the stuff looked top-notch. From what I hear the human resources people up on campus are no dummies. They've got a big labor relations school up there, and last thing the university wants is to get caught hiring illegal aliens."

"Right. So?"

"So like I said, I got to thinking. If you planned to get into mischief in this town, and you needed fake papers so good there wasn't much chance your cover would get blown, where would you go?"

I gaped at him. *"No way."*

"You got it. I went out to the county lockup and had a little chat with Jeffrey Vandebrandt."

"And he talked?"

"Not at first. But when I informed him that if he'd helped Bobby Ray Gravink escape justice it would make him an accessory to murder, it got his attention."

"Isn't that stretching it a little?"

"Lucky for us, Vandebrandt's no lawyer. Within five

minutes he was singing like Rosemary Clooney. Told us the same guy who'd hired him to make fake papers in the name of Peter Anderson also bought another set for an Alan Johnson."

"How did he afford it? Vandebrandt's fakes must have cost a bundle."

"Same way he afforded everything else."

"Which is?"

"Easy. After he killed his sister, he took all the money she saved for college."

"Son of a bitch."

"You said it. So once we had Johnson's name, we put every guy we had on it, checking utility bills and rental agencies, that type of thing. But my instincts were telling me that wherever this guy was, it had to be out in the country somewhere. He'd need privacy, and if he really was keeping all those dogs he stole he'd have to have someplace to put them. So I went out to this little office in Etna that posts places for rent out in the sticks. Johnson's name was in their records. That's when I called for backup, then broke about fifty regs by going in there before it showed up."

"It's a damn good thing you did. Gravink was about to stick that needle in Justice."

"You would have stopped him."

"How?"

"I don't know. But I just know you would have."

"I think you're giving me a lot more credit than I deserve. I'm a big chicken."

He gave me a look that said *yeah, right.* "You might not even want to hear this," he said a while later, "but since we're coming clean on everything, Jeffrey Vandebrandt told me something else when he was spilling his guts. He's been in your house."

"*Excuse* me?"

"Do you remember I told you that along with all the high-tech crap we found in his apartment, there was also some makeup?"

"I guess."

"Well apparently, part of the thrill of his little hobby was seeing his targets up close and personal. So one night, right after your name was in the paper for finding Patricia Marx's body, he dressed up as some senior citizen and knocked on your front door."

"You're kidding me. I don't even remember."

"He said there was a big party going on. Anyway, he never even saw you. One of your roommates answered the door, and with all the people around he lost his nerve. Said he pretended to be looking for the previous owners."

"Jesus Christ. How long did you say they're locking him up for?"

"Not sure yet."

"Let me ask you something else, Cody. Do you think Vandebrandt knew what Gravink was up to?"

He gave me a long, assessing look. "You smart chicks are *so* sexy."

That made me laugh. "You sound like Mad."

"Where is he, anyway?"

"He wanted to come by, but he figured you had enough to handle with the admiring hordes. He sends his regards. Wants to buy you a Guinness when you're up to drinking it."

"Sounds damn good. I've just about had it with ice water and Jell-O."

"So what do you think?"

"About Vandebrandt and Gravink? Good question. I never asked the kid straight out, but my gut tells me he knew, even if he didn't *know* he knew."

"It takes one to know one?"

"Exactly. Maybe that's why he had such a compulsion to stalk you, even though his parents thought he was cured. He'd actually met the guy in the flesh, so he felt like he owned a part of it. Or maybe I'm just full of it."

I stood up and went to the window. The hospital has a great view of Gabriel, with the lake snaking up to the city's edge and Benson looming above. I know it was all in my head, but even from this distance the city seemed different from the Gabriel of a week before—the one that was starting to feel more in tune with the dead than the living.

"Cody," I said, still looking out at the landscape, "why do you think he did it?"

"I don't know. But from the way you just asked, I have a feeling maybe you do."

"I'm not sure. I only spent a couple of hours with him, and definitely not of my own free will. But maybe I got a better look inside his head than anyone who's still alive—except Justice, and she's way too traumatized to think about it. But while I was out there, it all seemed to make sense. At least from his point of view."

"What did?"

"Look, I have no idea how he got the way he got—whether some priest diddled him when he was six or what. I don't know if Jack the Ripper was pissed because some hooker gave him the clap, and in the long run it doesn't make a damn bit of difference. It seems pretty clear that all that S and M shit in his parents' house was really his, so he obviously had some sick ideas about women. But I do think I know why he picked his victims."

"We already know how he found them. They were all in the Benson vet clinic database."

"But there's more to it than that. The women he killed had something else in common. As far as he was concerned, they didn't deserve their dogs."

"What?"

"I know it sounds crazy, but just listen. Patricia Marx had taken Cocoa in to have its ears cropped, which a lot of people think is inhumane. C.A. hadn't had her dog neutered even though he was suffering from this prostate disease, just because her family wanted to breed him. Lynn Smith's dog was blind, and she didn't scrape together the money to fix it. And Justice shucked off modern medicine completely and treated her dog herself."

"And you think he was hunting the women down to punish them?"

"That too. Once he got going, he obviously messed with them in ways that related to what was wrong with their dogs. Look what he did to C.A., and to Lynn Smith's eyes. But mostly I think it was to liberate the dogs."

"That's ridiculous."

"Maybe. But it doesn't seem a whole lot more ridiculous than strangling women who were stupid enough to let you in the front door. Or shooting couples in parked cars. Or picking up some guy in a gay bar and eating his . . ."

"Point taken."

"All I'm saying is, in his criminally insane little universe, he thought he had the moral high ground."

"But what about killing his parents? And his sister?"

"His parents had the family dog put down against his wishes. Maybe as far as he was concerned, it was a capital offense. And as for his sister, he said something about being furious that she hadn't stopped them from doing it. But the bottom line is probably that after what went down at the Houston SPCA, she couldn't ignore her suspicions about what really happened with their parents. We know for a fact it was around that time that she started applying to schools far away from Texas. But beyond that, who knows?"

"Are you telling me some nut job with a high school education performed surgery on these dogs? And he didn't kill them?"

"I guess. I mean, it was his obsession since he was a kid, but he knew he'd never have the grades to get into vet school. I don't know, maybe the frustration helped drive him nuts. Anyway, that house you found me in was chock-full of vet textbooks. What if he was self-taught, spent hours and hours studying his stuff on his own . . ."

"Alex, will you do me a favor?"

"Sure."

"Stop talking about Gravink. Then come over here and kiss me."

We were in mid-grapple when he heard someone clear his throat, and looked up to find a mildly amused Chief Wilfred Hill. Cody blushed, but in his condition it only made him look slightly less undead.

"Didn't mean to interrupt," the chief said. "But there was something I wanted you to know before it gets around. David Loew's dead."

A few days ago I'd been planning what I'd wear to his

lethal injection, but for some reason the news still didn't make me want to jump up and down. "What happened?"

"We'd been hunting for him ever since you told us what he did, but he managed to keep a low profile. Then we got a report of a gorge jumper a couple hours ago, and guess who it was? Did it in front of plenty of witnesses, so don't go thinking conspiracy theories. Anyway, there was a letter addressed to you in a Ziploc bag in his back pocket. I don't have a copy for you yet, but I can tell you what it said. You want to know?"

"Yeah."

"Said he couldn't live with the guilt."

"What guilt?"

"What he said was that when you asked him to ID Gravink at the paper, he lied. He really did recognize him as this guy named Anderson from his bunch of animal freaks. Then he went to the guy and warned him the mean old cops were about to frame him and he better blow town. Said he never even imagined Gravink might actually have *done* it. As far as Loew was concerned, Anderson was one of their own. And when he told him, I guess Gravink convinced him all he needed was a chance to talk to you and prove he was innocent. So he asked his buddy Loew to get you out there on a sham interview and . . . well, you know the rest."

"But why would he kill himself? I mean, if he didn't know what Gravink was really up to . . ."

"Look, as far as I can tell Loew was as high-strung as they come. What he said in his note was that he'd spent all this time trying to save lives and here he was aiding and abetting a killer. Said if you and Justice had gotten dead it would have been his fault."

"But we didn't."

"Yeah, well, seems like that was a minor detail. Guy was a fruitcake." He turned to Cody. "And by the way, Detective, you're on disability for a month. If I so much as smell you back at the house before then, you're out on your ass. Get well soon." Then he kissed me on the cheek and left.

"You heard him," I said. "You're on the shelf for a while. What are you going to do with yourself?"

"Good question. Any ideas?"

"You want to get the hell out of here for a couple days? Go lie in the sun someplace?"

"I burn."

"How about the Adirondacks? Hiking and stuff?"

"Sounds pretty damn good."

"I gotta warn you, Cody. Homegirl doesn't do tents. I want four walls and a bathroom."

"Deal. On one condition."

"Name it."

"The dogs are coming too."